W9-CHP-828

Britannia's Wolf
The Dawlish Chronicles
September 1877 – February 1878

Britannia's Reach
The Dawlish Chronicles
November 1879 – April 1880

Britannia's Shark
The Dawlish Chronicles
April – September 1881

Britannia's Spartan
The Dawlish Chronicles
June 1859 and April – August 1882

Being accounts of episodes in the life of
Nicholas Dawlish R.N.

Born Shrewsbury 16.12.1845

Died: Zeebrugge 23.04.1918

Britannia's Wolf

The Dawlish Chronicles
September 1877 – February 1878

Antoine Vanner

Library of Congress Cataloging-in-Publication Data:
Antoine Vanner 1945 -
Britannia's Wolf / Antoine Vanner.
(The Dawlish Chronicles Volume I)
ISBN 978-1480275270 (pbk.) — ISBN 1480275271 (Kindle)

Published by Old Salt Press

Old Salt Press, LLC is based in Jersey City, New Jersey with an affiliate in New Zealand

For more information about our titles go to www.oldsaltpress.com

A Note on Ottoman Naval and Military Ranks
and their equivalents in Western Armies and Navies
can be found at the end of this book.

Introduction

In 1876 Bulgarian Christians, oppressed beyond endurance by their Ottoman Turkish overlords, rose in revolt. They underestimated the ferocity of the response. Indiscriminate massacres followed when irregulars known as Bashi Bazooks were unleashed in savage reprisal, evoking condemnation across Europe. The Ottoman Empire itself was already in turmoil as reformers and traditionalists intrigued and manoeuvred for control of the half-modern, half-traditional, but wholly corrupt government which ruled vast territories that stretched from Albania to Mecca, from the Adriatic to the Persian Gulf, from the Caucuses to Libya, and populations which included Muslims, Christians and Jews.

The reigning sultan died under mysterious circumstances shortly after the Bulgarian revolt erupted. The nephew who succeeded him was deposed in a palace-coup three months later and replaced by his half-brother, Abdul-Hamid. Perceiving this new sultan to be weak, reformers gained approval of a new liberal constitution, the Mesrutiyet, which guaranteed elective representation for the first time. Hated by conservatives, this constitution rapidly became a focus of internal conflict rather than of unity.

Russia, traditional protector of Orthodox Christianity, seized on the Bulgarian atrocities and the weakness of the Ottoman government as an opportunity for cloaking a thrust southwards towards her centuries-old goal of an outlet on the Mediterranean with the mantle of a humanitarian crusade. In April 1877 Russian forces crossed the Danube, with the Ottoman capital of Istanbul as their objective, and drove deep into Bulgaria, while across the Black Sea other armies pushed south-westwards into Anatolia from Georgia.

By late 1877 dogged Turkish defence, though weakening, was still blocking Russian advances. After repeated failed assaults the Russians had settled down to starving out an Ottoman army entrenched round the Bulgarian town of Plevna while in Eastern Anatolia Turkish forces withstood successive Russian attacks.

But movement of hardened Russian troops from the Bulgarian front eastwards, around the great northern curve of the Black Sea, shifted the balance in Anatolia – and so too the appointment of a competent new commander, Archduke Michael. A ferocious Russian pincer attack at Aladja Dagh in October 1877 cost Ottoman forces over sixteen thousand casualties and threw them back on the fortresses of Kars and Erzurum.

The spectre of Ottoman defeat brought with it the prospect of a major European war for it would realise Moscow's centuries-long ambition of taking Constantinople – called Istanbul by the Ottomans – and the Straits. A Russian presence in the Eastern Mediterranean would menace the Suez Canal and threaten

6

British communications with India. Russia's recent conquests in Central Asia and advances towards Afghanistan had already raised the spectre of a descent on the sub-continent. Were Britain to allow Turkey to be defeated then it could spell the end of British power in Asia. Already the Royal Navy was being mobilised for possible intervention and troops were being shipped from India to the Mediterranean –but open conflict with Russia, and general European war, might yet be averted if Turkish forces could fight the Russians to a standstill.

Hard pressed on both the Bulgarian and Anatolian fronts, the Ottoman Empire's hour of crisis was at hand...

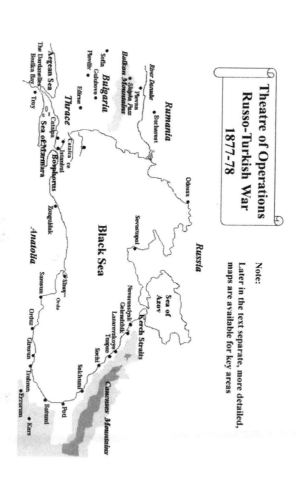

Theatre of Operations
Russo-Turkish War
1877-78

Note:
Later in the text separate, more detailed,
maps are available for key areas

8

1

Dawlish raised his head above the lip of the hollow that sheltered his small group of freezing, famished, exhausted men and saw the frozen clods of mud flying from the hooves of the horses thundering towards him, steaming breath pulsing from dilated nostrils, wicked lance points reaching before each wild right eye. There were eighteen of them to his nine, all warmly clad, well-armed, their blood up, Cossacks intent on slaughter.

Kaptan Nicholas Dawlish of the Ottoman Navy, once and so recently a commander in the navy of Her Majesty Queen Victoria, glanced towards his crouching men, each with his carbine ready, its magazine fully charged, each waiting for the signal to rise from cover. "Hold fire until I order it!" he had instructed, and he knew that their obedience would be absolute even though he was not just ordering them to fight, but to die. They had already given him loyalty and lion-like courage, and yet he had brought them to this end.

Now the line of riders was splitting, obedient to the shouted commands of an officer in the centre, who alone carried an upraised sabre. The main body, ten men, still came pounding on directly but eight riders were peeling away to the right, down the slope, to cut off retreat seawards. Salvation had been so close …

"Heads down still, lads," Dawlish shouted, and the young officer by his side translated into Turkish. "Wait for my word, then up and select your target. Rapid fire then! The horses, mind! The horses!"

He forced himself to ignore the fear washing through him. His life was going to end on this barren hillside – quickly he hoped, with no shame of cowardice at the last extremity –and he felt infinite regret. For his hand had moved to touch the oilcloth package in his inside pocket and within was a transcribed poem. Florence Morton would never know that her handwriting had been with him to the end or that he had acknowledged to himself that he loved her.

As he had, so silently, so painfully, so hopelessly, ever since that October morning off Troy only few weeks before …

…the weak October sun, a glowing red ball in the morning haze, was rising over Asia Minor that morning when Dawlish, well muffled against the chill, came on deck. He made his way to the bridge to check the position. The captain of the small Turkish mail packet-steamer greeted him effusively. He had been flattered yesterday, as the ship had steamed north-eastwards through a calm Aegean, by the interest

9

Dawlish had shown in the vessel's management. Lady Agatha too had been interested and he had shown her how to use a sextant and to calculate the midday fix. He was surprised now not to see her on deck already.

"Besika Bay, Sir." The captain pointed eastwards towards the arid coast. "We'll pass into the Dardanelles in an hour."

It was what Dawlish had come on deck to see. A full British naval squadron had penetrated this narrow, treacherous, strongly defended strait once before – in 1807 – and might have to again.

He glanced astern. A single tall figure stood by the rail at the poop, looking eastwards, identifiable immediately by her thick blond hair as the young woman Lady Agatha had introduced as her companion, a word that indicated a paid position, more than a maid, but no less a servant. He had seen little of her the previous morning when the two women had boarded at The Piraeus, Athens' port, just enough to remember the easy mutual-regard that seemed to prevail between her and her mistress. She was consulting a book frequently as she scanned the Asian shore. Mildly interested, Dawlish made his way aft.

"A pleasant morning, Miss Morton," he said as he approached.

She turned, grasping the book towards her, as if to conceal it. "Good morning, Commander." Her tones were cultured, up to a point, but still with hint enough of regional flatness to betray her origins.

"And Lady Agatha?" He noticed that the book was old, its leather cover scuffed.

"Indisposed, Commander. Last night's meal did not agree with her."

Dawlish sympathised. "And yourself, Miss Morton, you are well?"

"Well or not, Commander," she said, "I would not have missed this for anything. Those must be the Plains of Troy." She gestured shoreward with a gloved hand.

Her face was bony, the mouth too large, but it was transformed into a thing of beauty as it flushed with enthusiasm and a smile spread across it. A man might be entranced by it were he not to know she was a servant.

He reached out and said: "May I, Miss Morton?"

She hesitated, then handed him the book. The words on the spine were illegible. He flicked it open. A pencil mark on the flyleaf told that it had cost her sixpence at some second-hand stall. It was a copy of Chapman's translation of the Iliad. His face must have registered

10

surprise for she said quickly "It's not only ladies who try to educate themselves, Sir."

"It's not unusual…" He was embarrassed by her directness.

"Not unusual for a coachman's daughter to appreciate such things?" There was a note of reproach in her voice, but she was forcing herself to smile.

Dawlish realised that this clever girl had long-since accepted the necessity of being agreeable to her betters. Now she was including him too in that superior class.

"Keats' father was a coachman too. You've heard of Keats? Yet he became a great poet." He immediately regretted that his words were patronising. He rushed on, eager to cover his embarrassment. "Keats valued this book also, wrote a poem about it."

"And now I'm seeing it," she said. "That wide expanse that deep-browed Homer ruled as his demesne. I never thought I'd see such things." Tears were welling in her large brown eyes.

"Then we are fellow enthusiasts, Miss Morton, both seeing Troy for the first time." Dawlish was eager to redeem his gaffe. "Look astern now. That must be Tenedos, to where the Greeks withdrew when they left the Wooden Horse behind."

The atmosphere relaxed. The open plain, broken only by the mounds that hid the remnants of Priam's city, slipped past.

"Have you been to Constantinople before, Miss Morton?" The destination was a strange one in wartime.

She shook her head. "Agatha's – Lady Agatha's brother is First Secretary at the embassy there. She wants to see some old Turkish maps in the archives – a man called Piri Reis made them – and to write about them. A monograph, she called it." She hesitated, then said "Lady Agatha's very clever. Most people don't give her credit for that. They don't take her studies seriously."

They wouldn't, Dawlish thought. He had encountered her once before, for minutes only, at a reception in her family's London mansion. For all that her father, Lord Kegworth, owned half of Northamptonshire most would only see a stout woman of thirty, with the face of a friendly sheep, who had long accepted that few men might want her for a wife and that she had nothing to gain by pretence to allures she did not possess. But the eyes behind her thick-lensed spectacles sparkled with intelligence. The meeting at Athens had been unexpected.

"The war doesn't worry Lady Agatha?" Dawlish said.

11

Miss Morton looked surprised. "Her brother told her there's no danger so far from the fighting. But she would have come anyway."

Dawlish was leafing through her Chapman. Three thousand years had passed since Achilles and Hector had fought here, and still there was no end of war. And it was war that had drawn him here too – war and the prospect of advancement.

"You know Greek, Commander? You studied Homer as a boy?" There was a hint of longing in her voice, not he suspected, for the language alone but for the broader culture it represented.

He laughed. "Little Latin and less Greek – and little means just that and less means nothing." It was a secret shame, a deficiency he felt but never showed when he encountered men whose means and circumstances had permitted them to attend university. He realised that he had never confided it before to anybody but he found it easy to speak of it to this – he had to admit it – attractive young woman. "Virgil and Livy take second place to mathematics where naval schoolmasters are concerned," he said. Such instructors, usually clergymen who doubled as chaplains on board ship, had provided his formal education since he was twelve.

"But you still know about Homer, Commander, and Keats," she said.

"Like yourself, Miss Morton. I suspect we're much alike. Outside my profession I'm self-educated too." It pleased him to see her smile again.

"You must have seen so much, Commander, so many wonderful places. Though I've seen some too. We passed through Venice coming here, and Paris, and Lyon. France was so beautiful. Have you been there, Commander?"

"As a boy," he said, "to learn French. My uncle lived at Pau, near the Pyrenees. He thought it would be good for his lungs there but … he died young anyway. He'd been in the Navy too. I spent a summer with him when I was eleven." Twenty years ago, but the memory still fresh.

"I'm sorry." Her tone conveyed sincerity, not just some empty formula. "But he would have been proud of you, an officer also. He must have been an inspiration."

She had caught the sadness in his voice and misinterpreted it. For it was not memory of that kindly, ineffectual man whose dull, necessary career as a naval paymaster had ended in ill-health and early retirement, and whose inspirational stories almost certainly related to other men's

12

exploits, that had prompted Dawlish's regret. It was the memory of the daughter of the dignified Frenchwoman his uncle always referred to as his housekeeper, a girl like a sister to Dawlish then, but who had obsessed him as a woman a decade later. He carried her exploitation and rejection of him like an invisible wound.

He was suddenly embarrassed by his too-easy admissions to a chance acquaintance – for Miss Morton could be nothing else, for all that he found her attractive, very attractive. To cover his unease he quickly pointed out another mound on the shore.

"Perhaps one of the topless towers of Ilium, Miss Morton, now sadly fallen?"

She smiled – and was beautiful. "So you know Marlowe too, Commander?" she said. "Her Majesty must be proud of her officers' erudition!"

"I hope His Majesty the Sultan will be equally proud," Dawlish said, smiling, "It's his service I'm now entering."

"Perhaps so you can have half a dozen wives, Commander?" She too was smiling now.

"I fear even one is too much, Miss Morton," he said. "The Navy's wife enough for me."

A Turkish patrol vessel guarded the strait's entrance and after an exchange of signals the packet moved ahead into the Dardanelles. Dawlish produced the pocket reference guide to navigation in Turkish waters with which Topcliffe had provided him back in London and began to identify features.

"The Greeks called this the Hellespont, Commander." Miss Morton's voice might have been lyrical but for the occasional flat vowels. "Are you thinking of Xerxes' bridge of boats, or of Lord Byron swimming across successfully where Leander failed?"

"Who could not, Miss Morton?" he replied, but nothing was further from his mind. His gaze was fixed on the Turks' flanking fortifications. From Sedd el Bahr to the west and Kum Kale to the east, they extended up the narrowing waterway at irregular intervals, their stubby black gun-muzzles half hidden behind massive masonry bastions. This would be a terrifying gauntlet for warships to run against opposition. It was no wonder that the prospect of these straits falling into the Czar's hands had so haunted Britain's rulers. With a base secured by these defences a Russian fleet could dominate the Levant and strangle the British lifeline to India, already threatened as it was by Russian expansion southwards from Central Asia.

13

The passage continued through the morning up the ever-narrowing channel, scarcely a mile wide at Chanak Kale, where it turned north and then widened again. Miss Morton had been silent, but Dawlish sensed her glancing towards him more than once while he studied the defences, then looking away suddenly as he turned to her. He found himself wanting to look at her too, drawn equally by those great brown eyes and by her lack of pretence.

Beyond Abydos Point the broad expanse of the Sea of Marmara opened before them, its tranquillity broken only by the white sails of a handful of fishing craft.

"Lady Agatha will regret she missed this," Miss Morton said. "I must go now and see if she needs anything."

He did not want her to leave. "Have you known Lady Agatha for long?" He asked to make this moment last.

"Most of my life." She flushed slightly then paused, clearly deciding her next words. "My whole family serve Lord Kegworth and his family. And so I became a maid in their house." She looked away, obviously not finding the words easy. "But Lady Agatha found I liked to read. She lent me books. Then she took me up, even though some of her family didn't like it. She made me her companion. Raised me, you might say."

He sensed her embarrassment, was unsure how to answer. At last he said "I doubt that she needed to do that. I think she recognised you for what you are, Miss Morton. As her equal, and as a lady." Yet even as he said the words he knew that he could not forget what she had been, still was. A servant.

She turned away, eyes brimming. "I really must go now, Commander," she said.

When she was gone he felt not a little foolish that her absence could leave him feeling somehow empty. He was a man, an officer, mature and responsible, not a callow boy to be entranced by a chance acquaintance, however attractive. It was her intelligence and her determination not to be limited by her birth that had impressed him. It had been nothing more.

Then, remembering why he was now in Turkish waters, he focussed his thoughts on what might await him at Constantinople. It could be his making – or his undoing. He had advanced far in the Royal Navy already – only Jacky Fisher, with whom as a boy he'd once cowered in a muddy ditch in China, had risen as fast – and he'd achieved it, like Fisher, without family influence, through willingness to

14

accept tasks, deadly ones, others had found plausible reasons to decline. The Navy had formed his ambition and furnished his models – unflinching, fear-conquering, professionals, men whose willingness to sacrifice themselves when necessary cast shame on men as complacent and self-indulgent as his own father. He had applied himself to his profession, had studied when others had relaxed, had mastered the complexities of steam machinery while others bewailed the decline of sail, had hardened his body with mast and cutlass drill when rank might have spared him, had held himself celibate when brother officers has consoled themselves with women. He had faltered only once – best not think of that, or visualise the face that led to it, or even recall her name – and had but one focus since then, advancement to the highest ranks. Topcliffe, that old Lucifer, had recognised his hunger, had exploited it without conscience, had rewarded ruthless action and discreet silence with accelerated promotion. But Topcliffe's continued support was conditional on success –

and what might constitute success in the Sultan's service was as yet unclear. Dawlish only knew with certainty that failure, if he survived, would mean a career of worthy obscurity. And that would kill him, more slowly and more painfully than any armed enemy.

*

The packet-steamer reached the city in the last hours of darkness. Thousands of pinpoints of light identified the three major districts. To the west was the city proper, the capital of Constantine and Justinian and a long line of Byzantine emperors until the Ottomans had wrested it from them just four centuries before. Its hills were dominated by the dark humps of its huge mosques and the sharp pinnacles of their minarets. The Pera quarter was to its north, separated from it by the Golden Horn inlet, and to the east, on the Asiatic shore of the narrow Bosporus strait, which entered the Marmara here, lay the sprawling, hilly expanse of Scutari.

Dawlish was on deck with the ladies, their baggage stacked by the entry port. The vessel's engine panted softly, its revolutions just high enough to hold it stationary against the Bosporus current. A pilot boat came alongside, dropped its passenger, took off mailbags and moved away. The lights of another craft neared and Dawlish recognised the trim lines of a steam pinnace. It pulled alongside the packet. An instant later a slim, handsome, clean-shaven young officer came bounding up

15

the ladder. Capped with a fez, his uniform was exquisitely tailored, his linen immaculate, his brass buttons gleaming. There was a slight whiff of eau-de-cologne. The rings on his sleeves identified him as a senior lieutenant of the Ottoman Navy.

"Commander Dawlish? Hobart Pasha sends his compliments. He asks me to welcome you to Istanbul." His English was barely accented.

Istanbul, Dawlish thought, not Constantinople. That was how he himself, now also a servant of the Sultan, would now have to refer to it.

The officer bowed. "Jerzy Zyndram Birinci Yüzbashi at your service." Then he noticed the ladies and he swept their hands to his lips in succession, bowing even deeper now, charming both.

"A Pole by birth, Ladies, and faithful to my oppressed country, but also the loyal servant of His Majesty Abdul-Hamid," he informed them, "and your devoted servant while you honour us with your presence." Dawlish saw that he had taken Miss Morton as the more distinguished of the two and had greeted her first.

"From Warsaw, perhaps?" She asked, clearly impressed. Far from looking bleary-eyed at this hour, Zyndram might have been on his way to a ball.

"Alas, No!" His smile instantly gone. "I've never seen Poland. I was born in Polonezkoy, close to here – but we count it as soil of our motherland."

"Zyndram! Zyndram!" A querulous voice came from the ladder, its owner still invisible. "Zyndram, can't you offer a fellow a hand up?"

Dawlish joined the Pole at the side and looked down to see a portly figure toiling upwards. Zyndram reached down and took his hand. Lord Kegworth's eldest son reached the deck, red-faced and puffing.

"Oswald! Dearest Oswald!" Lady Agatha was embracing him and he, embarrassed by her affection but obviously glad to see her, was pushing her away. Then he caught sight of Miss Morton. He flashed her a glance of obvious dislike and ignored her pointedly.

A few minutes' polite small-talk followed. Oswald would stay with the ladies until the vessel docked in the Golden Horn and conduct them to his villa thereafter.

"Thank you, Commander Dawlish." Lady Agatha gave him her hand. "I trust we'll meet again. Perhaps I can show you some old charts of Piri Reis!"

Dawlish bowed and turned to Miss Morton. She reached out her hand. Suddenly, insanely, he wanted to kiss it, not formally, but to

16

crush it to his lips, though he restrained himself. "Good bye, Commander," she said. In her seriousness her face was bony again and her mouth too large, and yet he still somehow found her lovely. He sensed that she regretted, as he did, that their brief familiarity was at an end.

"I'm most obliged to you for helping my sister... Dawes, isn't it? No? Dawlish then – much the same. Most obliged." Oswald was already turning away.

"A moment, Sir." Dawlish drew him aside. "Plevna? Kars? Erzurum? Is there news? Are their garrisons still holding out?"

"Oh, still resisting to the best of our knowledge," Oswald sounded irritated. "Tough fellows, these Turks, you know, damned tough. So if you'll excuse us now, Dawes..." He turned away. "Morton!" he called as he did. "Morton! See to my sister's baggage, can't you! And don't dawdle, woman!"

Dawlish retreated, unwilling to see the girl who loved Keats and Homer once more relegated to her true position, unwilling too that she should have him see it. Her ambiguous position must expose her to constant humiliations of this sort. He was glad that he was to go ashore immediately with Zyndram. He swung himself down to the pinnace. His trunk followed.

The small craft chugged shoreward, carrying Dawlish to his meeting with Charles Augustus Hobart-Hampden – younger son of the Earl of Buckinghamshire, ex-officer of the Royal Navy, hero of slavery-suppression off Brazil, ex-blockade runner to the Southern Confederacy under the alias of Roberts, and who now, as Hobart Pasha, Head of the Ottoman Navy, had made the Black Sea virtually a Turkish lake.

Dawlish's hand slipped inside his coat to feel the oilcloth packet that contained his resignation from the Royal Navy. He must be, like Hobart, the Sultan's man now.

2

Dawlish had expected to be in Portsmouth by now, the newly appointed Deputy to the Senior Instructor at H.M.S. *Vernon*, a position that had more to do with development of the Navy's newest weapon, the torpedo, than with training. It was an appointment that most officers of his age could only dream of, one bought so recently, almost at the cost of his life, in clandestine service in an African swamp.

17

Topcliffe's rewards were dearly earned. But instead of *Vernon* Dawlish found himself sitting in Hobart's office overlooking the rain-swept Golden Horn.

"It looks convincing enough," Hobart said, glancing at the resignation letter. He was in his mid-fifties, heavily built, florid and bearded. Leaning back in his chair, gold-embroidered Ottoman tunic thrown open, boots on the desk, teeth clamped on a cheroot, he radiated the sort of cheerful determination that inspired men to follow leaders like him in forlorn hopes. "I'll keep this copy and you'd better keep the other on you at all times." He tossed the letter into the desk drawer and reached the duplicate to Dawlish. "I trust Topcliffe has the other copy?"

Dawlish nodded. Formal secondment to the Ottoman Navy in wartime would have had unacceptable diplomatic implications. Resignation was essential.

"A legal fiction" Topcliffe had called it. "Should you be captured you could prove that your association with the Royal Navy was at an end. And in the event of your ... of a more permanent termination of your services then both Hobart and I would have evidence enough to ensure no embarrassment for Her Majesty's Government." His copy wouldn't leave his desk until Dawlish returned, he said. The *Vernon* position would be kept open in the meantime.

"You'll have your Ottoman commission this afternoon," Hobart said. "Captain's rank, until the war ends. You're happy with that?"

"Very happy, Sir," Dawlish said. As the son of a Shrewsbury solicitor, with no naval connections other than a long-dead and undistinguished uncle, he knew that neither industry nor merit would assure advancement if he had refused this offer of Topcliffe's – or indeed any he might make.

"I asked for a man I could rely on," Hobart said, "and Topcliffe said you were hungry. Hungry and damned effective. Able to keep your mouth shut too, so I won't ask what you've done for him, just guess that it was damned hazardous."

Nobody ever seemed to know much about what Admiral Sir Richard Topcliffe got others to do for him. Dawlish suspected that Topcliffe's own superiors, who seemed to be politicians rather than service chiefs, didn't want to know either, just as long as the outcome suited them. And Topcliffe had never alluded to what Dawlish had undertaken for him, not even the last service... What had played out in an African swamp, and afterwards on the Victoria Embankment, must

18

not be remembered, must never be alluded to, had never happened. Reward, in the form of promotion, had been sufficient.

"Topcliffe's an old friend," Hobart said, "An old taskmaster too, and a hard one. I served under him in my youth. It's in his interest to send you, of course. It's in Britain's interest."

Topcliffe had been insistent on that. "If the Czar's forces reach Constantinople we'll have no option but to send the Mediterranean Fleet there to stop them," he had told Dawlish in the Pall Mall club where they had met, both in mufti, for Topcliffe was seldom seen at the Admiralty. "It won't be popular with everybody here, even in the cabinet. Those outrages in Bulgaria last year make any idea of alliance with the Sultan unpalatable. But if we must..." he raised his hands in an eloquent gesture, "...our friend in Downing Street won't hesitate." Benjamin Disraeli's climb to power had been marked by impudence, daring and calculation. Now, as Lord Beaconsfield, he would not shrink from war – but before doing so he would rely to the limit on bluff, threat and cunning. "The plans are well in hand," Topcliffe said. "We'll fight the Czar if we have to but it's so much more preferable if the Turks do the job for us."

Now Dawlish saw rain drifting in grey columns across the Golden Horn, obscuring the domes and minarets beyond and drenching the men loading stores from a barge moored alongside an ironclad. She was British-built, like most of her sisters in the Sultan's navy, the best that money sweated from twenty million peasants could buy. Hobart followed Dawlish's gaze.

"The *Orhaniye*," he said. "She'll be back on station off Odessa before the week's out. We've got the Czar's ships bottled up everywhere except where it really matters. Not too difficult either – the Russians have minimal naval forces in the Black Sea. They were forbidden any by treaty after the Crimean affair. It's only in the past few years they've been free to build them up again, and they've been damn slow about it, put too much effort into circular freaks – you've heard of them? The Popovkas? Damn stupid things, barely seaworthy. They don't give us any trouble. But the rascals are strong on land, too damn strong." He suddenly looked grave. He swung his feet off the table and moved to the map that covered one wall.

"Plevna is still holding," Hobart's finger stabbed at the small Northern Bulgarian town that Turkish fortitude and spadework had turned into an improvised fortress, "though God knows for how much longer. It's been under siege since July and now it's starving. Once it

19

falls there's little but Turkish courage to stop the Russians driving down over the Balkan Mountains and on into Thrace, perhaps even here to Istanbul." He turned to Dawlish, his smile grim but genuine, that of a man inspired rather than cowed by danger. "But it's worse over there," he said, his hand sweeping along the eastern coast of the Black Sea, "much worse. Russians are bad enough but treachery is worse."

"Admiral Topcliffe said there was something of the sort, Sir," Dawlish said, "and that you needed me as an outsider for that reason, somebody whose loyalties aren't in question. But no details."

"Istanbul's a pit of serpents," Hobart's voice was bitter with contempt. "The Sultan, Abdul-Hamid, God bless him, is weak, damned-weak, and he's had only a year on the throne. The only man close to him who's worth a tuppenny damn is a half-brother, Nusret Pasha. He's clever, open to new ideas, spent several years in Britain. You'll meet him today. He'll be the *eminence gris* of the new reign, mark my words, and he'll control Abdul-Hamid. But there's another half-brother – there's a dozen of them in fact, but only one counts. His name's Haluk."

"A rival for the throne, Sir?" It sounded inevitable.

"Precisely, Dawlish. Haluk's a fox, ruthless and cunning enough to have cultivated the softas in the Istanbul medresses for years back."

"Softas? Medresses?" Dawlish was mystified.

"Students, from the theological schools. They're a power here in Istanbul, and they've opposed every reform of recent years. They've got links to medresses across the empire. They fear last year's Constitution and all it implies – European ways, modernisation, equality and representation for Christians and Jews as well as Muslims. They hate Nusret for standing for all that. They distrust Abdul-Hamid, because they think he's weak, and Nusret's puppet. For them Nusret's an apostate and they'd tear him limb from limb if they could get their hands on him."

"And Haluk?"

"They'd acclaim him tomorrow as the new Sultan. He damned nearly was, twice over – Sultan Abdul Aziz had a little assistance in slashing his wrists after he was deposed last year and Haluk played the concerned brother to perfection in getting Murad, who succeeded, declared mentally incompetent within weeks. Haluk thought he had the sultanate in the bag then, but our friend Nusret was one step ahead of him. Nusret had their half-brother Abdul-Hamid, whom everybody knows is not too bright, sitting on the throne before Haluk knew it."

"And now Nusret's the power behind that throne?"

Hobart laughed. "Nusret's been whispering in Abdul-Hamid's ear from the start and running affairs and even having himself proclaimed pasha, though I'm damned if I know if it's for military or naval command – he knows equally little of both. But it might have been plain sailing from then on – the Constitution has a lot more support than you'd credit – if that Christian rising hadn't erupted in Bulgaria and hadn't been suppressed so brutally and stupidly and if the Russians hadn't seized their chance to play themselves up as the saviours of Christendom."

"So what did Haluk do?"

"He laid low until three months ago. Then, out of the blue, just as the Russians were smashing their way out from the Caucuses and into Eastern Anatolia, Haluk gained control of Trabzon – its garrison, the naval forces there and the brand-new ironclad *Mesrutiyet*, which means "Constitution", by the way. She'd just arrived from Britain. Haluk had the softas and the mullahs with him and he'd prepared the ground well. He's been lurking there in Trabzon ever since, with half his supporters paid in gold and the other half convinced that he's a prophet who'll purge the empire of infidels and restore the faith. He's been deliberately inactive in order to allow Archduke Michael's forces to advance into Anatolia. When Kars and Erzurum finally collapse, which can't be long now if the Russian supply lines aren't cut, Haluk will put up a show of force – but nothing too dangerous for him. Then he'll proclaim that the disaster is due to the incompetence of his half-brothers and divine retribution for their lack of piety and he'll head back here to Istanbul with the *Mesrutiyet* to depose Abdul-Hamid and murder Nusret. He'll have supporters enough here for it too – the softas will see to that."

Hobart's bearded face broke into a smile. "You're impressed, Dawlish? It's clever, damn clever! They call it Istanbul, but it's Byzantium still with all its intrigues and treacheries! Haluk's willing to let the Russians dismember the Ottoman Empire as long as he can rule as Sultan over what's left of it. But we'll put a spoke in Master Haluk's wheel, damned if we won't, Dawlish, eh?"

And Dawlish understood now. "You intend me to recapture the *Mesrutiyet*, Sir?" Topcliffe had implied as much when he had brought

21

him to see her uncompleted sisters in a Thames-side shipyard in Poplar on the day this surprise assignment had been sprung upon him.

Hobart laughed. "I'm sure you'll find a way, Dawlish," he said, "because you won't have a deck under your feet if you don't. And that'll just be the start of it. If you get her you'll have the most powerful warship in the Black Sea, and a few more vessels besides that Haluk has detained at Trabzon, and you'll have carte blanche to attack Archduke Michael's supply lines in any way you can to halt his offensive. A pleasant prospect for an enterprising young officer, eh?"

"Yes, Sir," Dawlish hoped that his growing fear that he had taken on more than he could handle did not show. Ships needed manning and that meant that seamen must be trained and drilled and, above all, inspired and led. The quality of the officers was crucial and so far the only Ottoman officers he had met were this buccaneering English aristocrat and a displaced Pole. And then the language... An elementary phrasebook had shown him that acquiring anything but a smattering would be impossible in the time available, for Turkish had no similarity to any language he had previously encountered.

But his choice had been made in London. "I'll give you my best, Sir," he said.

Hobart looked him straight in the face, laid down his cigar. "Not me, Dawlish," he said, suddenly grave. "You'll give your best to the Sultan, even if he is a half-wit, and even more, you'll give it to the Turks, and, by God, they're worth it, the best friends and the worst enemies a man could have. Their backs are against the wall now, and that's when they fight best. God knows how this business is going to end for them, but well or badly I'll be with them – and I expect you to be with them too." He stopped suddenly, as if embarrassed by his emotion, and when he smiled it seemed forced. "And by the way, Dawlish, you'll need uniforms. Zyndram's the man to recommend a tailor. The fellow always looks like he's stepped from a bandbox but he's a damn good officer. He did well with his gunboat off the Danube mouths last summer. It helped that he hates the Russians so damned much. With him it's personal. But now ..." he consulted his watch and started to button his tunic, "You and I have a meeting with Nusret Pasha in an hour. We're going to the Yildiz Palace."

The rain had died before Hobart's carriage pushed through the streets. Dawlish saw – no, felt – for the first time the jumble of East and West, of traditional and modern, of telegraph offices and trams and banks and railway stations and men in European business suits, of

22

grandiose French architecture, all inextricably mixed with mosques and bazaars and spice-laden stalls and pack donkeys and occasional camels and crowds clad as if they had stepped from the Arabian Nights. Orthodox priests pushed past raucous tea-sellers with felt-insulated tanks on their backs and brass trays around their waists. Beggars cowered on corners, hungrily eying skewers of lamb roasting over charcoal at open cafés, and black flies feasted on hanging sides of sheep outside butchers. A column of infantry tramped past, probably en-route for Bulgaria. Their blue Prussian-style uniforms might be faded and their boots scuffed, but the American Martini-Peabody rifles on their shoulders were brand-new. Black enshrouded women drew their veils higher across their faces at the sight of the carriage while others, unveiled, Greek or Armenian or Jewish, smiled boldly when Dawlish's glance met theirs. Everywhere was the smell of sewage, at times just a hint, at others overpowering.

As Hobart's escort cleared a passage through the throng on the Galata Bridge the view afforded of the Golden Horn showed steamers from a dozen countries moored next to sailing craft whose design had not changed in centuries. Beyond them lay the brutal might of the *Orhaniye* ironclad and the more subtle menace of several smaller ships worthy of the Royal Navy itself. High on the hill beyond, within the walls of the gardens of the Yildiz Palace, eunuchs guarded women gathered from across the empire for the pleasure of a man who might never even see them through the years in which they would grow old there, yet from there decisions were being taken – or being avoided – on which the lives of millions and the future of Europe depended.

It was this ramshackle empire, struggling painfully towards modernity yet constantly dragged back into medieval ignorance and chaos, that guarded British interests against Russian ambitions as surely as did the ships of the Royal Navy and the regiments of the British Army. It was to preserve this empire that Britain had fought in the Crimea two decades before. For it the Light Brigade had charged and the Thin Red Line had stood firm. And now, Dawlish knew, it must have his loyalty as long as he wore its uniform.

Hobart's carriage slowed as it ascended the hill towards the Yildiz, where Nusret Pasha waited to meet the man who would recover the *Mesrutiyet* for him – or die in the attempt.

*

23

Dawlish left Istanbul under cover of darkness two nights later, on a steamer that also carried Zyndram and eighty selected Imperial Ottoman marines, all proven in action previously in shore raids on Russian positions around the Danube mouths. All had boarded in secrecy. A plan had been agreed and now intensive training was needed before it could be implemented. The transport crept northwards up the narrow strait, emerged into the Black Sea, and headed eastwards. Dawlish paced the deck and tried to put aside his troubling memory of Miss Morton.

They had met again the previous evening, at a soirée in Hobart's villa by the Bosporus. All the invitees had been British residents. He had seen her sitting alone, pretending to enjoy the music, aloof, proud, yet obviously conscious that she was being shunned by the other ladies. Lady Agatha might introduce her as her companion but they saw her as a servant nonetheless. Across the room Lady Agatha was discussing the economics of the raisin trade with some merchant and was oblivious of her companion's plight. Dawlish felt admiration as well as sympathy as he approached.

She tried to look composed but was clearly glad to see him. "I'd ask you to dance, Miss Morton," he said, bowing, "but I can't. I'd only tread on your toes." He tried to smile, to seem humorous, but realised that he just sounded awkward.

"It must be a general deficiency in naval officers, Commander," she said. "Hobart Pasha danced with me just now and I fear that my toes did suffer somewhat." She forced a laugh. "And hero though he is, I doubt his veracity too! He said I danced like a Southern Belle from Charleston, and that I should take that as high praise."

Hobart was on the other side of the room, clapping a guest on the back and laughing heartily at some witticism. It was no surprise to Dawlish that he had been attentive and complimentary to one whom others might look down upon. Whether on a deck or in a drawing room, Hobart's unaffected manner evoked loyalty and respect.

"May I sit with you, Miss Morton?" Dawlish said. She had no objection. There was a pause. "Does Istanbul agree with you?" he said at last.

Her smile entranced him. "More than I ever could have dreamed," she said, and then, seeing that he was genuinely interested, her eyes lit up as she began to tell him of the Blue Mosque, and the Mosque of Suleiman and the Great Bazaar.

"I've seen none of it," Dawlish said. "I've been too busy." But he realised that it would be a delight to explore this city with her, to share her pleasure in discovery, to be infected by her unpretentious joy, to feel her arm linked in his.

"But perhaps you'll have a chance when you are settled in, Commander?"

He shook his head. "I'm leaving Istanbul tomorrow. God knows when I'll be back."

"Oh," she said. "I didn't know." He sensed regret – and maybe hoped for it. Then she began to speak quickly of the beauty of the Dolmabahçe and the Topkapi palaces. The Sultan lived in neither and under Lady Agatha's prodding her brother Oswald had already arranged private visits.

"Treated like the Queen we was," Miss Morton said. Then, realising her slip, and colouring with embarrassment, she said "I meant to say that we were treated like the Queen." She emphasised *were*, then looked away, and was silent. Her lower lip was trembling.

Dawlish was embarrassed. It was worse than her odd flat vowel. He wanted to tell her it did not matter to him but knew that doing so would wound her further. Her fierce pride, her determination to educate herself moved him. He sensed strength and courage and honesty. For all his confusion in her presence he wanted to be with her, if only for ten minutes. It felt... his brain raced, trying to identify the word... so satisfying. "Shall we take the air on the terrace, Miss Morton?" he said. "You wouldn't object if I lit a cigar? A small one?"

She didn't object. They stood stiffly by the balustrade, two feet apart, watching in silence the lights of the vessels gliding downstream with the Bosporus current or straining upstream against it. She had clasped her shawl close against the chill and Dawlish had little pleasure from his cheroot. He did not know what to say, yet wanted to hear her voice.

"What is your name, Miss Morton?" He had wondered ever since they had met. "Your Christian name, I mean ... if I am not too bold in asking."

"Florence," she said. "After Miss Nightingale."

"A fine namesake," he said. "She did great work in this city. You've perhaps seen where she had her hospital? Near here, in Scutari?"

She hadn't, not yet, though Lady Agatha had asked Oswald to arrange a visit. She must be twenty-one or two, he thought as she

25

spoke. Half the girls born in England in the Crimean War years must have been called Florence. That made her ten years younger than him, the same age as he had been when, when... His mind shied away from the memory of the hurt he had endured at that time. But this young woman could never bring him such misery because there could never be anything between them. Her background precluded it. And then he sensed that she was trembling slightly as she stared silently out over the dark waters.

"You're going away to fight, aren't you, Commander," she said at last, turning to him.

"Probably," he said. "Yes. Probably. It's likely." He saw that her gaze was fixed on the livid coin-sized scar on his left cheek, just above the line of his beard. She looked away.

"You might be ..." she paused, unwilling to say the word.

"Be killed, Miss Morton?" He tried to smile. "Better not think about that." And indeed he had trained himself not to, though death had been close when his cutter had raced to intercept slavers in the Zanzibar Channel, and when the sun had flashed on a thousand spearheads on an Abyssinian hillside, and in the dark claustrophobia of the Ashanti bush, and a few months ago among the African mangrove Topcliffe had sent him to, and on countless occasions at sea.

"But why, Commander? You're not a Turk. You owe them nothing. And after what they did last year in Bulgaria ... those massacres. I read the newspapers. About those poor women there, those little children..."

"It's because..." He stopped. There was no denying Turkish guilt for the atrocities she spoke of, the killings that had initiated the present war. Though it might be in Britain's interest, he was now serving a regime that had countenanced horrors, had the previous day taken an oath of loyalty to Sultan Abdul-Hamid. He had accepted the Sultan's commission and had donned his uniform. He was silent for a long moment. "It's because it's my profession" he said at last. He realised immediately how inadequate it sounded. He had never spoken like this to anybody before but he wanted her to understand what he was. "I want to rise in my profession," he said. "I want ..." Words failed. He lapsed into frustrated silence, thoughts racing through his mind, thoughts that defined who and what he was, thoughts that he suddenly, unaccountably, wanted to share with her.

He had known no other life since childhood. He had found joy in mastering skills few possessed and had served under men whom he

26

respected and had led men he recognised as his superiors in all but education. He had survived storms and had gloried in calm dawns, had seen the grandeur of ice-fields and the splendour of the tropics. He had faced death a dozen times and more, had been sickened by atrocity and cruelty and moved by heroism and sacrifice. And though fear had always lurked somewhere close, and had often come close to dominating him, he had still prevailed over it. He wanted to excel in that life, that profession, to reach its pinnacles, because in the code that governed it he had discovered qualities that both satisfied and challenged him – honour, and service, and loyalty.

Words he seldom spoke aloud, yet words to live by. Words he could not articulate, not even to this woman whose respect he so unaccountably wanted.

It's all I've got, he wanted to say but could not, though he sensed that she had already recognised it. She was looking at him intently, her face perhaps all the lovelier for its frown of concern. For him. But she turned away to avoid his gaze.

"The price seems very high, Commander," she said.

And suddenly it did. A decade before, an infatuation – no, better acknowledge it for what it was, a deep love such as he believed he could never experience again – had culminated in such rejection, such humiliation, had left such a wound so painful as to drive away all thoughts of marriage, of any goal but professional advancement, of any motive but ambition. That hard path of excellence he had resigned himself to tread alone. But for an instant he saw that with a woman like Miss Morton by his side, fearless, intelligent, comforting and honest, he might…

"I will be … I mean Lady Agatha and I will be thinking of you, Commander" she said. "You'll be in our prayers. This awful war, it's…" Her voice trailed away.

Then he did what he knew he should not have done, had no right to do, yet he could not restrain himself. He reached out, took her hand, held it to his cheek for a moment, then pressed it to his lips. She made no effort to withdraw it until, overcome by the enormity of what he had done, he turned away, stammered an excuse, and left.

He had one last glimpse of her, back turned, looking out into the darkness. He knew instinctively that she was moved as much as he was, as attracted to him as he to her, and, worse still, that she too recognised what he saw so clearly. That nothing could come of it, that nothing must come of it.

27

As the transport's bows rose and fell with the Black Sea's swell, and as he paced the windswept bridge, he wondered how she would react were he not to survive whatever lay ahead. The memory of his so-few minutes with her, he knew, might haunt him to his end.

3

October was almost gone. There was a chill in the breeze off the Black Sea, enough to warn in the clear afternoon sunshine of the bitter cold the winter would bring. It was a fortnight since Dawlish had left Istanbul, a time of days and nights of relentless training and rehearsal for the marines in a secluded bay near Zonguldak, the naval base near Turkey's only coal mines. The men could have done with longer training but every day counted now.

Dawlish reined in. "How much longer?" he asked, closing his fur-lined jerkin over his uniform.

"Ten minutes, Nicholas Kaptan." Nusret Pasha's English was only slightly accented. He gestured towards the ridge ahead. "The hut should be in the valley beyond."

Which meant that Giresun, the small port that Nusret had sent a squadron of Circassian cavalry to occupy earlier in the day, would be somewhere to the left, hidden by the hills. Ostensibly reinforcements en route by the coastal road for the collapsing Turkish front east of Trabzon, but their true objective had been to occupy the Giresun telegraph office and prevent transmissions eastwards. Line breakages were sufficiently frequent at the best of times that a twenty-four hour blockage would raise no great alarm in Trabzon – though it would deny Haluk information on the action now getting underway. Nusret's informants in Trabzon still assured him that Haluk was unaware that he had left Istanbul.

"And what if Vifiades won't co-operate, Nusret Pasha?" Zyndram, the third rider, had taken advantage of the pause to light a cigar.

"He'll want to co-operate. Men with families always have reasons to co-operate." Nusret stated it as obvious.

Zyndram nodded, in acceptance rather than agreement. Poles were used to suffering – and enduring – he had told Dawlish quite cheerfully during the sea-passage from Zonguldak. That had been before they had been landed at the port of Ordu, where they joined Nusret and his cavalry escort. The transport that brought them had stood out to sea again with the marines and even now should be loitering unseen over

28

the horizon outside Giresun. Dawlish and Zyndram had ridded with Nusret for twenty miles to the east, the first step in a plan that involved complex timing and coordination. And so far everything had gone according to schedule.

They moved on at a comfortable trot towards the ridge, from where two troopers were beckoning that it was safe to proceed. The remainder of the escort followed behind, lean men in faded blue uniforms riding leaner horses and armed with ten-shot Winchester repeater carbines. They had seen action in Bulgaria and had lost a third of their number there. After the respite at Giresun they could expect to be flung into defence of the fortresses of Kars and Erzurum. And if those fell, Anatolia would lie open to the Russians.

Unless…

Unless, Dawlish told himself, unless we cut out the *Mesrutiyet* from under the guns of the Trabzon batteries tomorrow.

The shepherd's hut nestled in a cleft below the ridge, half hidden by bushes. The advance party had taken up picket positions at a distance and had left their horses tethered. Two saddled white donkeys stood incongruously between them. It showed that the Greeks must have arrived already. The only Christians permitted to ride horses were those in the Sultan's military service. Christian civilians, however rich, must be content with donkeys.

The two men in the hut were frightened, very frightened. The rough robes thrown over European suits did not disguise what they were – businessmen, more accustomed to managing a small shipping empire from behind a desk and fussing over accounts and bills of lading than plotting with one half-brother of the Sultan against another. They looked fearfully from one to the other of the three newcomers, all of whom were of approximately the same age, obviously uncertain as to which they should most defer.

Zyndram sensed their discomfort and, gesturing, said gently: "This is Nusret Pasha."

They dropped to one knee. The elder, a heavy man, white haired and moustachioed, drew Nusret's hand to his lips.

"Your Excellency. This is an honour and…"

Zyndram was translating rapidly into English for Dawlish. Facility in languages was a Polish quality, he had assured him.

Nusret drew the old man to his feet and kissed him on both cheeks. "I greet you as a brother, Demetrios Efendi," he said. "The Mesrutiyet, the Constitution, makes us all brothers, Turk or Greek,

Armenian or Kurd, Muslim or Christian or Jew. We are all brothers under the Mesrutiyet."

The Greek – Demetrios Vifiades, ship-owner of Trabzon – was overcome by Nusret Pasha's condescension. "The Sultan has no more devoted subjects than his Orthodox community," he said, weeping. "And none more than myself, and my whole family, and my son Phaidon."

Phaidon stepped forward. He was in his twenties, waist already thickening, eyes clever. If he was embarrassed by his father's effusiveness he disguised it well. He too kissed Nusret's hand, but he shook Zyndram's and Dawlish's. His own was soft and moist.

"You may speak English for Nicholas Kaptan," Nusret said. "I understand you speak some?"

"Assuredly, Your Excellency." The older man's voice was silky, ingratiating. "We do much trade with British companies..."

"You left Trabzon yesterday?" Nusret cut him off.

"By our own coaster, the *Irene*, our smallest," the older man was still dabbing his tears.

"You have other ships there?"

"None, Your Excellency. The largest have been impressed by the Ottoman Navy and the remainder are in the Marmara, in the Aegean. With trade with Russia suspended..." A sigh and a shrug told the rest. Trabzon's Greeks, stranded in the Ottoman Empire since Byzantium had collapsed four centuries before, were somehow still surviving, even prospering, against all odds. That prosperity was resented by many of their Muslim neighbours.

"Where's the *Irene* now?" Nusret said.

"By the quayside in Giresun, Your Excellency. Next to my brother-in-law's warehouses."

"How large?" Dawlish asked.

"A hundred and fifty tons." The son, Phaidon, spoke. "A schooner. Ninety-five feet, two masts, a single hold. We use her for trading with small harbours along this coast."

"She can carry eighty men?"

"If she must. They won't be comfortable – but, yes, she'll carry eighty."

"When you left Trabzon – you saw the large warship there?"

"The ironclad? The *Mesrutiyet*? Still at anchor in the harbour. She hasn't moved for six weeks."

30

Discipline would be slack then, Dawlish thought, lookout-keeping lax. A small advantage to us, better than nothing.

"Your schooner, the *Irene*, she's ready for sea?" Dawlish said.

"Tonight if you wish it. You could be in Trabzon a day from now." Phaidon paused, then said carefully "And the payment, Efendi?"

"The Sultan's gratitude!" Zyndram cut in, his voice impatient. "You know that if Haluk Pasha prevails there will be an end of the Constitution and that it will go bad with all Christians."

"We know it, Efendi," the older Greek said. "Haluk Pasha comes ashore each day for midday prayers at the Charshi mosque and always afterwards the talk against us Greeks and against the Armenians grows. Haluk speaks of us as being secret friends of the Russians."

Which you probably are, Dawlish thought, not that I'd blame you. Knowledge of what happened to the Christians in Bulgaria last year must haunt you.

"We must be at the quayside at... at when, Nicholas Kaptan?" Nusret asked.

"Midnight, Your Excellency."

That would give time for rest and food at the Giresun barracks now occupied by Nusret's Circassians and for the two Greeks to return separately to the town on their donkeys, as surreptitiously as they had come. Secrecy had been preserved so far but it would be better to board the *Irene* and slip away under cover of darkness.

When they stepped outside the hut again the wind was colder still. Dawlish was grateful for the black cavalry-issue sheepskin kalpak on his head. He was determined to keep it and damned if he was going to look ridiculous in a fez, regardless of the uniform regulations of the Ottoman Navy.

*

Four hours later Dawlish and Nusret were resting in the commanding officer's quarters in the Giresun barracks, two miles outside the town, cheered by the telegram from Istanbul confirming that Plevna was still holding out. There was still hope ...

A cavalry yüzbashi entered and spoke briefly to Nusret. Dawlish looked up quizzically.

"He reported several troops of Bashi Bazooks," Nusret said. "Kurds, irregulars, camping on the eastern side of the town. They're being sent to Bulgaria"

31

"Isn't there any nearer enemy for them to fight?" Dawlish asked, surprised. The Russians were three-day's ride to the east. Bulgaria was hundreds of miles westwards.

"There is, but they're not keen to fight them and the army wants to be rid of them. They're undisciplined, useless for anything but looting and raping. They're a liability."

"Could they be a problem for us tonight?" Dawlish asked.

Nusret shook his head. "They'll drink and sleep and we'll be gone before they're awake tomorrow."

The room was shabbily comfortable, heavily strewn with kelims and suffused by an aroma of coffee, cigarette smoke and sweet, sticky honey and nut cakes.

"Bearable here, but not up to the standard of the bar of the Lyceum, is it Nicholas Kaptan?" Nusret said.

He was sprawled on a divan and alternately drawing on a cigarette and sipping from a half-tumbler of brandy. He seemed as little troubled by Muslim strictures on alcohol as most other Turks Dawlish had met. Not all Nusret's four years in Britain has been spent learning about efficient taxation at the Treasury, efficient local government in Birmingham or efficient sanitation in Manchester. Wistful reminiscences about London nightlife occupied much of his conversation. Alone of his plethora of half-brothers he had managed to talk his uncle, the then-Sultan Abdul-Aziz, into freeing him from the confines of the Kafes – the gilded cage in which all junior male members of the Sultan's family were confined, sometimes until madness or senility claimed them – and allowing him to study modern administration in Western Europe.

Dawlish found himself liking him since they had met in Istanbul. They were of similar age, though Nusret's fondness for brandy and his constant air of wariness were beginning to take their toll. His ambition was obvious but his belief in progress seemed genuine. The daring of the plan now in motion confirmed his willingness to accept personal danger to attain his goals.

Zyndram entered. He had viewed the *Irene*. "It'll be a tight fit," he said, "but we'll get them all below deck."

Suddenly there was a commotion, a cavalry yüzbashi opening the door respectfully and a dishevelled figure pushing past him and throwing himself on his knees before Nusret.

"Save us, Your Excellency!" The words were a sob. Phaidon Vifiades was no longer the astute young businessman of that afternoon

32

but a terrified, bruised and tattered fugitive. Tears had scoured channels in his soot-blotched face and one sleeve of his shirt – he wore no coat – had been torn away. His left eye was black and closed. Blood oozed from a gash above it.

Nusret drew back. "Sit him down," he said to Zyndram. "Bring him brandy."

"They burst in when we were eating, Sir!" Phaidon's voice was a croak. "Fifteen, more, Bashi Bazooks. All armed. They wanted money and drink. So we gave it. And then, and, and..." He stopped, overcome with horror.

"Go on." Zyndram forced him to sip the brandy.

"They wanted women. My cousins, even my aunt..."

"And then?"

"We had no weapons, Efendi. But my aunt's husband, Spyridon, a strong man, he attacked their leader. He only had his hands, and..." He sobbed. Nusret looked away.

"They killed him?" Dawlish's voice was gentle.

"They cut his throat. Like a sheep. Then..."

"Don't say it. I can guess." Dawlish felt revolted. It must have been like this in Bulgaria – the accounts in the London *Daily News* had horrified him no less than most of the civilised world. Now a reality no less terrible confronted him. Worse still, he was now allied to these brutes, however remotely.

Phaidon was weeping quietly now. Nusret was silent, still looking away. Dawlish sensed his impatience.

"But you got away?" Zyndram asked.

"They were, they were... occupied... my cousins... my aunt..." Phaidon retched before he continued. "They'd beaten me, knocked me down. I lay still. When nobody noticed I got out through a window."

"Was your uncle's the only house attacked?"

"No, Efendi. The whole Greek quarter by the harbour. And the Armenians also. Houses were burning. There were bodies in the street and, and..."

Nusret turned to him. "I regret this, Phaidon Efendi," he said. "Believe me, I regret this deeply. But we can do little about it tonight. Especially not tonight. But afterwards, when there's time..."

The Greek was weeping again, trying to catch Nusret's hand and kiss it. Nusret half turned away and Dawlish caught his glance towards Zyndram, his implied command to get rid of this man.

In that instant Dawlish knew he could not remain silent.

"We must stop this, Nusret Pasha," he said. It might be in Britain's interest that he serve the Sultan, but if he did he was damned if it would include standing by as a passive witness to massacre.

"Such things have been going on for centuries, Nicholas Kaptan." Nusret spoke patiently. "They're regrettable, but the Kurds almost believe that the Sultan owes them the right to slaughter Christians every now and then in return for their loyalty."

"Even though their loyalty stops short of fighting in the line like disciplined soldiers?"

"We can't change this country overnight, Nicholas Kaptan. But with time the Constitution will bring harmony. Under the Constitution our different peoples will ..."

"So men will die and women will be raped while the Constitution works its mysterious ways!" Dawlish felt his temper rising, was striving to suppress it.

"There's a guard of Circassian cavalry on the quayside," Nusret said. "The *Irene* isn't in danger. We can board as planned at midnight."

"We might as well not bother," Dawlish spoke deliberately quietly. The germ of a stratagem was stirring in his brain. "Our mission is as good as useless if this riot continues."

"What do you mean?" Nusret's composure was shaken.

"Because success at Trabzon – and afterwards – will be worthless if you forfeit the sympathy of Her Majesty's Government."

Nusret paled. Turkey was virtually friendless among the Great Powers, and he knew it. Only Britain was providing her the modicum of support consistent with formal neutrality. Only Britain would stand by her should outright defeat be imminent.

"The British Government?" Nusret said, "Surely not? Lord Beaconsfield understands..."

"The Prime Minister is having difficulty enough to secure the assent of his own cabinet to support the Ottoman Empire. His government could fall." Dawlish was guessing now but he doubted if Nusret was any better informed. "The opposition is baying for repudiation of all the Sultan stands for," he said. "Gladstone could be in Downing Street within a month."

It was close to the truth. Reports of the Bulgarian atrocities had stung the sanctimonious old Liberal to leave retirement and denounce the unspeakable Turk furiously in an unprecedented campaign of

34

pamphlets and speeches. Tens of thousands had turned out to hear him thunder.

"But this riot has no official sanction!" Nusret stammered.

"No, Nusret Pasha! But it's taking place within pistol shot of yourself, an Imperial Prince, a half-brother of the Sultan! A half-brother whom many in Britain see as the leader of reform and toleration in the Ottoman Empire!"

"The town governor will restore order in the morning and..."

"Nusret Pasha, please hear me," Dawlish's tone was firm but respectful. "Do you know who the Princess of Wales is?"

"Princess Alexandra!" Nusret was surprised by the question. "Of course I know – I've dined often enough at Marlborough House."

"Do you know who her brother is?"

A look of horror spread over his face. "The King of Greece," he said. "King George."

"Exactly, Nusret Pasha! Her favourite brother! And if she learns of this riot – and of your unwillingness to intervene to save Christians, Greek Christians, even if they're not his subjects, then not all Lord Beaconsfield's pleadings for understanding can help you! Princess Alexandra has the ear of Her Majesty herself!" Dawlish had no idea of the warmth of relations between the two ladies, but he suspected that Nusret had even less.

"And if I restore order?"

"Turkey's critics would be confounded, Nusret Pasha. You would be recognised as the man who made the Constitution live. You would..."

But Nusret was already moving to the door and shouting for the escort commander. "I'll take command myself," he said, "and you, Nicholas Kaptan, you'll take a troop. Jerzy Yüzbashi will support you."

The cavalry miralay entered and received rapid instructions. He was nodding. *Evet, evet,* yes, yes, his men were ready to move.

"Can we trust them?" Dawlish asked Zyndram. The question would have been unthinkable in British service.

"They're Circassians, we can trust them." Zyndram said. Then he added "The Bashi Bazooks are Kurds," as if that in itself was obvious reassurance. Over the previous forty years a series of Russian campaigns had driven the Muslim Circassians from their homes along the Eastern Black Sea coast. The Ottoman Empire had welcomed these tough warriors and settled them across Anatolia. But other ethnic groups in the Empire, the Kurds most of all, had resented the newcomers and the favours they enjoyed.

In the square outside the troopers were mounting. Dawlish joined them, dragging a shock-numbed Phaidon with him. He put him on a horse and thrust its reins into Zyndram's hands.

"We'll need him to guide us," he said, "but you'll have to steady him."

He swung himself into the saddle and beckoned the troop's yüzbashi to approach him. After a few simple instructions, translated by Zyndram, two score horsemen went clattering through the gates in the wake of Nusret's force, sabres drawn. Before them lay a town in torment.

*

They reined in on the crest of the hill to the southwest of Giresun. Below them acrid black smoke, flame-shot, billowed above blazing houses of the Greek quarter. Isolated shots and distant screams were audible even from here. Through his field-glasses Dawlish could see maddened human shapes outlined against the flames. In one street a small knot of people was surging towards the protective darkness at its end, burdened with children or possessions. Horsemen, Bashi Bazooks, suddenly emerged from an alley ahead of them and drove them back towards the inferno with a ragged fusillade. Beyond them a roof collapsed and a geyser of flame erupted skywards as fire took hold in an olive-oil store.

Cavalry would be useless in these narrow streets, Dawlish told himself. There was nothing for it but to go in on foot, to clear them one by one. He glanced towards Phaidon. He sat hunched on his mount, his pallid face void of expression, his eyes dead. Dawlish needed him. Only Phaidon knew this town well enough to guide the troop through its warren of streets.

"Time to move," Dawlish said to Zyndram. "Nusret Pasha's troop should be in position now." It must be somewhere in the darkness over there, on the far side of the town, ready to move in.

The Pole relayed his commands in rapid Turkish. Thirty troopers and their lean yüzbashi were to dismount and follow Dawlish and Zyndram into the inferno. Phaidon, dazed or not, was to guide them. Four men were to guard the horses. The remainder, ten troopers, were to remain on horseback and under control of a scar-faced chavush,

36

who seemed as if he could look after himself. They would patrol the outskirts, send Greek fugitives towards the refuge of the barracks outside town, detain fleeing Bashi Bazooks and shoot those who would not stop.

Before swinging himself from his saddle Dawlish glanced towards the harbour and the *Irene*, bathed crimson by a burning warehouse nearby. She looked trim and seaworthy and her safety was assured by the dozen troopers already sent to the quayside. Beyond her several smaller craft were pulling out of the harbour, laden with terror-stricken adults and wailing children.

The troopers formed in two single files, one to either side of the street, sabres pushed into the broad red sashes that concealed their ammunition pouches. Their Winchesters were better suited for the task ahead than edged weapons. Dawlish grabbed a carbine and stuffed a dozen extra rounds in his pockets. His holstered Tranter revolver would provide a reserve. He took his place at the head of one file, nodded to Zyndram at the head of the other, then moved forward in silence.

Phaidon led them through a succession of alleys, all dark and deserted, windows shuttered, the occupants, Turks in this quarter, huddled fearfully within. The smell of burning was all-pervasive and a wall at an intersection ahead reflected scarlet flickering. This was the edge of the Greek neighbourhood. Against the sound of intermittent shots and the roar of flames growing louder they pushed onwards, keeping to the shadows.

Now came the first sign of devastation, no fire, but a smashed door and a lifeless figure draped across its threshold, darkness inside. Beyond it two houses were untouched, both heavily barred and with iron-studded doors, but past them smoke billowed darkly from a gutted shop, its roof already collapsed. Three bodies lay on the cobbles outside, one an old woman, her head almost severed from her shoulders. A younger man was crumpled dead beside her, a child clasped in his arms, sightless eyes staring from a bloodied face. The stench of burning flesh told that others had not gained even the illusory safety of the street.

There was a corner ahead and caution was needed in approaching it. A dozen bodies littered the street beyond, children among them. The troopers crept forward through the shadows on either side. Four houses were well ablaze and the fire was spreading to others, crackling and roaring. Several of the remaining dwellings had been looted, doors torn from their hinges, windows gaping shutterless, interiors dark.

A piercing scream, suddenly cut off, rose from a house to the front and left, its door beaten in. Dawlish gestured for a halt and the files behind him shrunk into doorways and shadows. Zyndram translated Dawlish's whispered instructions and the yüzbashi flitted forward with five troopers. He stopped by the door with three of them, carbines at the ready. One of the others climbed on to his companion's back and, half-throwing himself over the sill of the open window to the right, blasted five shots in quick succession into the interior. As he fired the yüzbashi and his men disappeared through the doorway. Four more shots, then silence.

Three men, Kurds by their dress, were dragged out. One collapsed, his front a crimson mess. He vomited blood as he was jerked again to his feet and the yüzbashi, angered, raised his carbine and fired into his chest. He fell and lay still while his companions were forced to their knees before Dawlish. They might have been any age from twenty to fifty, hard-eyed, sunburned men, Bashi Bazook irregulars, engrained with dirt and smelling of months of stale sweat. They wore huge baggy pantaloons with the crotch between the knees, untanned leather boots, short fur-trimmed jackets and green turbans. One's hands were bloodstained.

"There's nobody alive in the house," Zyndram translated. "Three adults, five children."

"Stavros Papagos and his family," Phaidon said numbly. "A baker. A kind man."

The prisoners were terrified and were attempting to grovel. Dawlish, disgusted, kicked the nearer. "This one," he said. "Ask him who his leader is."

A long, cringing reply. Dawlish picked up a name familiar since childhood.

"Saladin?" he asked.

"Selahattin," Zyndram corrected. "From near Diyarbakir. He's famous among the Kurds. He hates Christians."

"Where is he now?"

"They don't know. They've been busy themselves."

"Busy," Dawlish felt cold anger. "They've been busy." He'd served since he was thirteen, nineteen hard years, had killed when he had to and had seldom regretted it. But nothing had ever hardened him to the slaughter of innocents. "Take them back inside," he said quietly. He looked both men in the eye, could find no compassion in himself. "Shoot them both."

They moved on down the street, two shots behind confirming justice done. Phaidon gestured to the left. They found two houses burning and others ransacked. Distraught women in torn clothing wailed in the street over the butchered bodies of their menfolk and scuttled into their wrecked homes as Dawlish's force appeared. Three drunken Kurds sprawled on the steps of a looted wine shop, one asleep, the others too far gone to sense danger until they were pinioned and trussed up. A little further on, two more Bashi Bazooks lurched from a house, a chest held between them. One tried to run and was shot, the other was taken prisoner.

Another intersection lay ahead. "To the left, my uncle's house," Phaidon's voice was quavering with fear of what they must find. The smoke was thick, ash-laden and choking. Flames roared to either side. A woman's body lay in the centre of the street, her skirts bundled about her head, her naked body bloody and eviscerated. Her infant lay smashed against the wall a few feet distant. The troopers moved on, eyes smarting and red-rimmed from the smoke, hearts thumping in the knowledge that the majority of the Kurdish irregulars must still be somewhere ahead.

The reality was even worse than any might have feared. Phaidon sunk to his knees as they entered the courtyard of his uncle's house, a wail of misery rising from his throat that Dawlish would never forget. The storage buildings to either side were already gutted, but the walls of the main house still stood. It had been large, perhaps the largest and richest in the town, three stories, all stone. The roof and floors had collapsed and an inferno roared from the windows and doorway so that the walls themselves glowed red. An iron balcony ran along the second floor and from it, suspended by the heels, hung the naked, blackened body of the ship-owner Demetrios Vifiades, the crotch a scarlet gash. Dawlish looked away. He had spoken to this ... this thing, in the shepherd's hut, only hours earlier.

"Cut it down," Dawlish choked back nausea and anger. "Cover it, but don't leave Phaidon with it. Take him with us."

A marine climbed on another's shoulders and hacked at the rope. The pitiful remains fell to the ground and Phaidon, sobbing, threw his hands over his eyes. Dawlish pulled him away. He knew that yet worse might lie ahead.

39

4

They moved forward again. Just before the end of the street four horsemen blundered around the corner at a canter, one dragging a screaming, half-naked girl, her feet trailing and bloodied. They were among Dawlish's force before they realised it. Without waiting for an order the troopers were on them, dragging two from their saddles and butchering them on the ground, and blasting the third from his seat. His beast, panicked, eyes straining, nostrils flared, burst through its ring of attackers and stampeded down the street, dragging the body with it by one stirrup.

The fourth horseman released the shrieking girl and reined in, drawing a sabre, slashing wildly about him. He was plunging his mount, and circling, and its flailing fore-hooves were keeping the nearer Circassians at bay. Dawlish swept up his Winchester and the rider's jerking torso lay momentarily in his sights. He fired, realised he had missed, but even as he ejected with a flick of the wrist the horse was on all fours for an instant. The rider rose in his stirrups and leaned low across its neck, and almost too late Dawlish saw the sabre arcing towards him and, behind it, the rider's face contorted with rage, his teeth bared like a jackal's. Dawlish swung up his carbine instinctively and the blade bit into its stock just above his hand, knocking it from his grasp. He ducked, reached to free his revolver from its holster but already the horseman was urging his mount forward, knocking him over, and drawing his arm back for another swing. Then somebody was pushing himself between Dawlish and the stamping beast and firing his Winchester. The horse screamed, its left eye and ear torn away and fountaining blood, but somehow the rider still had control. He pulled its head around and kicked into its flanks. Horse and rider careered down the street, somehow escaping the fusillade that crashed out after them, skidded into a turn at the corner, and then were lost to view.

Dawlish saw that it was Zyndram who had saved him. He stammered thanks and gained his feet. "The girl," he said, "look to her."

She was scuttling, white with terror, towards a plundered house, clutching her rent clothes around her. Her misery deepened Dawlish's cold fury. He'd had a mother, still had a sister, and an image of Miss Morton flashed unbidden across his mind. This outraged girl too was somebody's daughter, somebody's pride, somebody's love. "Leave a

40

trooper with her." He told Zyndram. "Tell him that if he molests her I'll kill him."

There was one more street, deserted, a short one, but no less wasted and corpse-scattered. Beyond was a smoke-hazed and flame-lit space, a market square. Shouting and occasional shots and the insistent tolling of a bell rose above the roar and crackle of the burning houses. The Circassians were pulled back silently to the shadows, the yüzbashi regrouping them, as Dawlish and the Pole moved forward from cover to cover. At the end of the street they crouched in the shadow of an exterior stair.

The worst atrocity of all now confronted them, scarce fifty yards distant.

A mob of Bashi Bazooks, eighty or a hundred, was milling before an Orthodox church at the side of the square. Some were throwing broken furniture on the pile that blazed at its door, others were shooting wildly towards the windows each time a terrified face appeared, more were staggering about drunk or shouting insults at the wretches trapped inside. The roof was burning, flames licking up from the rafters beneath through the glowing tiles and it could only be minutes before the collapse commenced. Screaming from dozens of voices, but as from a single throat, told of the greater part of a whole community trapped within and knowing that it was going to die terribly.

Anger can wait, Dawlish told himself. First must come deliverance.

His orders were clear and Zyndram sprinted back to relay them. Dawlish pushed more rounds into his Winchester's magazine.

A fear-crazed figure at a church window leaped for the illusory safety of the square, pleading for mercy as he landed hard and struggled to his feet. Bloodied sabres chopped him down before he was cast into the inferno at the door. High above, a bell tolled incessantly and hopelessly.

Dawlish glanced back. Zyndram had formed the dismounted cavalrymen into two ranks and they were advancing down the street, carbines ready. Out in the square the Bashi Bazooks, intent only on murder, were oblivious of the retribution gathering behind them.

A single whispered word of command and the front rank kneeled, carbines to the shoulder, sights lining up on individual targets. The second rank stood behind them. Dawlish locked his own weapon on a horseman who was yelling taunts towards the church.

"Atesh!" - the command to fire.

41

The volley was deafening and smoke engulfed both ranks, some thirty carbines discharging simultaneously, blasting down perhaps a dozen Kurds and causing the remainder to turn, frozen in shock. Two horses were felled and kicking. Thirty wrists flicked down the ejection-loops behind the trigger guards, flicked them up again to feed the next round. As the smoke cleared the troopers were seeking new targets. Several Kurds were rushing stupidly towards their executioners, sabres raised.

And again. "Atesh!"

Screams of rage and agony rose as bodies spun and jerked and fell. Dawlish felt a savage wave of satisfaction wash through him as he reloaded with the rest.

As their smoke cleared, they loosed one more volley that panicked the Bashi Bazook survivors into a rush from the square, down the alleys that led to it on either side. The cobbles were deserted but for the bodies of dead and wounded men and horses and three pillage-laden carts.

The church roof was now an inferno. The screaming from within had reached a new crescendo. Saving the trapped families must now be the first priority. Half a dozen troopers – their repeater carbines made them the equivalent of several times their number – were sent to seal off the exits from the square. Dawlish led the remainder sprinting towards the church. A face appeared at a window, curiosity at the sudden lull in shooting overcoming fear, and Phaidon shouted up that deliverance was at hand. Other figures appeared at the windows, hoisted on shoulders within, and struggled across the sills and were lowered to safety. A child was passed out, then another, dropped and caught in outstretched arms.

Sparks showered down. A glance upwards told Dawlish that the roof could not last much longer. The window sills were too high - only a handful could be got out across them, even though the yüzbashi and two others had somehow backed a cart up against one and were plucking shrieking women and children from the interior. Only the door could release in time the mass of humanity imprisoned there.

"Zyndram! We must clear the door! Use planks, beams - anything you can find to push that wreckage from it!"

To bellowed commands the troopers raced to pull lengths of wood from damaged houses. Burning debris had been piled six feet high against the iron-studded timbers of the door and now they too were charred and glowing. Dawlish toiled like a madman among the others, levering and shoving, his face and hands scorched, pushing the blazing embers to one side. Zyndram was beside him, and a dozen troopers, all frenzied now as they neared the door. A rasping, grating sound came from beyond it, of something being pulled back against resistance and then, relief suffusing him, Dawlish realised it was the bolts being withdrawn.

The doors swung outwards, propelled by scores of hands. A human torrent rushed through them, hesitating only for an instant before tumbling through the narrow, blistering pathway extending through the remains of the pyre. Weeping, screaming women carried hysterical children, men dragged the old and infirm, two black-clad priests clutched icons, girls and youths leaped over flaming obstacles, all still disbelieving their deliverance as they stumbled towards the open square. Several, clothes alight, rolled on the ground. Dawlish and his helpers were all but trampled. They retreated, contenting themselves now to assist some fallen wretch or carry some half-cripple. Still they streamed out, two hundred souls or more, and behind them the first blazing timbers began crashing to the floor. Zyndram was inside now, four troopers with him, hunting the last occupants towards the door, a deformed child under his arm as he hustled its mother before him.

A tearing, rending sound came from above, no longer from a single rafter, but from the whole roof as a single entity, beams and columns and masonry and red-hot tiles collapsing inwards. "Hurry!" Dawlish shouted as Zyndram and the others reached the doorway, pulling and urging the fugitives. Then he was joining them in headlong flight as the full mass of flaming debris impacted on the church's floor and a hurricane of smoke, dust and glowing embers blasted out through the gaping portal. Dawlish stumbled, fell, felt the hot breath of the building's dying agony wash over him and almost sobbed with the knowledge that he – and hundreds whom he did not know, but who seemed as valuable to him at this instant as his own life – had somehow survived.

Shouting at the other side of the square now attracted his attention. A mass of men was entering, hands upraised, herded by others with carbines. Dawlish lurched to his feet, aching, scorched but otherwise unharmed, and saw that it was Nusret's force driving its prisoners before it. He pushed towards them through the dazed survivors. He found Zyndram at his side, singed but equally whole.

"Nusret Pasha's troop cleared the Armenian Quarter," Zyndram gasped. "They have Selahattin."

43

Bloodied, tethered and cowed, the prisoners had all the sullen truculence of beaten curs. Circassian troopers moved among them, cuffing and punching mercilessly as they stripped them of anything valuable they carried. The Greeks would be seeing little of their property back, Dawlish guessed.

Nusret Pasha advanced to meet him, face blackened, clothing scorched, pistol in hand, no longer the liberal student of economics and public administration but a worthy descendant of the fierce conquerors who had burst into Anatolia from Central Asia centuries before.

"Will Princess Alexandra be happy now, Nicholas Kaptan?" His grin was wolfish.

"Delighted, Nusret Pasha! And I myself will be happier still if I have Selahattin!"

"You want him dead?"

"I want him living," Dawlish said. "I want him shamed before his men so that the memory follows him home and to his grave." His fury was cold and rational now, fed by memories of defiled women and a blackened suspended body and dozens of throats screaming as one in that burning church.

Nusret barked an order. Four troopers forced a prisoner forward, his shaven head bowed and glistening with sweat. He was struggling and shouting. They halted before Nusret and Dawlish and pushed him to his knees. His face was a mask of malevolence. The eyes that blazed hatred above the heavy black moustache might have been of flint, the skin of leather. Dawlish recognised the horseman from whom he had rescued that terrified, half-naked girl and who had so nearly killed him.

Selahattin had recognised Dawlish also. He screamed something and spat.

"What did he say, Zyndram?'

"He called you a Christian dog. He says bring him your mother and he'll rape her before you."

"Stand him up, show him to his men," Dawlish said quietly, then glanced behind him. A cluster of Greeks was gathering, Phaidon among them.

Dawlish walked to the nearest trooper and pulled the sabre from his sash. He felt the balance. It was close enough for comfort to a cutlass, a weapon he had always handled well. And if he didn't, this time, it hardly mattered. "Bring me a plank, a short one," he said in English to Phaidon. The Greek pushed through the throng, returned a moment later with two feet of splintered timber. At a nod from Dawlish, Zyndram took it.

Selahattin was on his feet now, defiance ebbing as he saw the sabre. He was locked by his arms between two troopers. As Dawlish approached he howled – for mercy probably, since Nusret just shrugged and ignored him.

"Put the plank on his shoulder, his left shoulder," Dawlish said to Zyndram. "That's right – push it against his neck."

He stepped forward, carefully measuring the distance. Selahattin's bloodshot eyes were bulging with terror now and he was pulling his head away from the wood. "Tell him to keep steady, or it will be worse," Dawlish said. "Tell him to look at me."

A hush had fallen on the square, broken only by the crackling of burning timber. Selahattin was weeping now, moaning softly.

"Tell him he's a coward", Dawlish said, looking him straight in the eyes. "Tell him I'll mark him so he'll never forget it." Then, as Zyndram translated and ground the plank further against Selahattin's neck, the sabre came slicing down and sheared the ear away from the head and laid open the cheek beneath. Dawlish skewered the bloody ear from the cobbles on the tip of his blade and flicked it into the embers of a dying fire.

"Tell him he can go now," he said. "Home to tell his village of his heroism." He turned from the shocked and bleeding Bashi Bazook and tossed the sabre back to its owner.

The sea, cool and clean, beckoned.

*

Shortly after midnight the *Irene* stood out from Giresun's harbour, sails filling, rigging creaking. The waters reflected still-burning fires and ash-heavy smoke drifted above and covered them with a filthy sheen. Survivors were creeping back to what remained of their houses and realising the extent of their loss. The Circassian cavalry unit had been left behind and, with the town-governor's garrison, was rounding up the last demoralised remnants of Selahattin's irregulars.

Only Nusret, Zyndram, and Dawlish himself, all treated as saviours by the Greek crew, boarded the vessel, accompanied by Phaidon. Now their eyes searched the northern horizon for the naval transport from which they had landed at Ordu scarcely twenty-four hours since. They knew they would sight it in the next half-hour. Then

45

the transfer of eighty Imperial Ottoman Marines and their equipment to the *Irene* could commence.

Dawlish lit a cheroot, drew on it and scanned the horizon. Success in the hours ahead would give the Ottoman Empire one last chance of halting the Russian thrust from the east. And failure would mean death – his own.

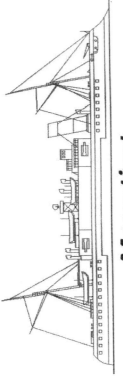

Mesrutiyet

Central Battery Ironclad,
Imperial Ottoman Navy

Builder: Samuda Ltd, Poplar, London
Launched: March 1876
Sisters: *Orion* and *Belleisle* (Royal Navy)
Displacement: 5000 tons
Length: 250 feet
Beam: 52 feet

Machinery: 2-shaft Maudsley Horizontal
4040 Horsepower
Speed: 12 Knots (Maximum)
Armament: 4 X 12" Muzzle-loading rifles
4 X .45" Nordenveldts
Armour: 6-12" Belt, 8" Battery, 3" Deck

5

Giresun lay far behind. The heavily laden *Irene* clawed eastwards across a choppy sea, sails set to take advantage of the cold breeze from the north. Dawn was near, and across the moonlit waters to starboard the Anatolian coast was a dark streak. The marines were packed below in the cramped and foetid hold. Zyndram stood by the helmsman and watched for signs of other shipping, fearful that Haluk's deliberate inactivity might embolden Russian auxiliaries, fast, lightly-armed merchantmen, hastily impressed, to range along this coast.

Dawlish slept uncomfortably on deck, sheltered by a bulwark, close by Nusret, his head pillowed on a coil of rope. Zyndram shook him into wakefulness.

"It will be light soon, Nicholas Kaptan."

The first rosy tinge was visible to the east.

"Any activity?"

"Nothing. The sea's empty."

"Trabzon?"

"Two, three hours more."

"Sleep an hour yourself, Zyndram. I'll take the watch."

Scalding coffee banished some of his stiffness as he paced the deck. For the hundredth time he recreated in his head the port of Trabzon, one he knew only from charts and from two poor photographs, the harbour where Haluk Pasha kept the *Mesrutiyet* swinging uselessly at anchor beneath the guns of the shore batteries. In the first months of war the eastern littoral of the Black Sea, where the Caucuses foothills ran down to the shore, had been dominated by Turkish warships. Since Haluk's seizure of Trabzon, and the inactivity that followed, the Russians had resumed coastal traffic, their unhindered vessels pouring in supplies and men to support Archduke Michael's offensive into north-eastern Anatolia.

It already seemed an age to Dawlish since he had planned this operation with Hobart and Nusret in Istanbul. Only the information feeding back to Nusret's offices in the Yildiz Palace from a thousand confidential sources across Anatolia had made planning possible – information reliable and unreliable, purchased and volunteered, information telegraphed by provincial governors and police chiefs or scribbled on scraps of paper by half-literate informers. And most valuable of all was the information from the Greek traders who dominated the shipping business and who lived in well-justified terror of the consequences for them should Haluk's sway extend westwards from his Trabzon base. Nusret was at the centre of all this flow of information, weighing and calculating, as astute and wise in a labyrinth of lies and half-truths as any of his ancestors, despite his almost childlike trust in the inevitability of the golden age that the Constitution and sound administration on the British model must bring. Yet while he and Hobart and Dawlish had pored over maps and charts the news flowing in from both eastern and western fronts was ever more desperate. The now-starving and disease-ridden defenders shivering in their trenches at Plevna and the garrisons behind the masonry ramparts at Kars and Erzurum were still holding out. But for how much longer?

The plan that had evolved might yet strangle the supply lines that fed the Russian colossus in the east and leave it starving in the coming winter's merciless snows. All would depend on the marines - and in the ten days' rehearsal near Zonguldak, where a moored hulk represented the *Mesrutiyet*, Dawlish's confidence in them had risen steadily.

"They're superb," Hobart had said, "hard as nails and brave as lions. Give them leadership and they'll follow you through Hell."

The *Irene* ploughed on. The sun was up now, the coastal hills distinct to starboard. The first white specks that were Trabzon's buildings were just visible in the far distance.

The plan had seemed practical back in Istanbul. It was time now to prove it by action.

*

Irene had turned south. It was a straight run for the harbour now, the breeze a single point on the port quarter, fore and main-course bellying, backstays bar-tight. The wind and sea conditions could not be better for Dawlish's purpose.

The details of the town were coming clear. Phaidon, his emotions dulled with brandy so that all that remained was his sullen fixation on revenge, was identifying the main features for Dawlish. Crenellated walls ran parallel to the harbour and a tower-protected gate gave entrance from the quays. A mole ran out perpendicular to the walls and curved around, giving shelter against gales from the north. Behind it were only a handful of vessels, their yards and rigging black against the walls behind.

And there was the *Mesrutiyet*, anchored to a buoy in the centre of the harbour, two hundred yards from the mole and quays. She was all but bow-on to the *Irene*, and the foreshortening made her seem squatter than Dawlish had expected. He raised his telescope and braced himself to hold the narrow disc of vision stationary on the ironclad.

Before he had left London Topcliffe had taken him to Samuda's shipyard in Poplar to see this ship's two uncompleted sisters. Like her they had both been ordered by the Ottoman Government but when war had erupted they had been first impounded by Britain to avoid embarrassment with the Russians, then purchased for the Royal Navy and renamed Belleisle and Orion. But there they had been ships in embryo only when Dawlish had seen them and the visit to the yard had not prepared him for the emotion the reality before him now roused in him. The lines and proportions were the same, but in Poplar two empty hulls had lain inert and forlorn so that an effort was necessary to imagine them ever taking on lives and identities of their own. But here, framed in the telescope's small circle, the rust-streaked black hull, and the white upperworks and battery, and the raked buff funnel and masts, and the clutter of ventilators and the figures moving on the fo'castle all spoke of a ship that had come to life. A wisp of smoke, yellowish black, drifted from the stack – "Damned poor quality that Zonguldak coal," Hobart had said, "but it's the best we've got" – and indicated that the furnaces and boilers were being kept warm, if not necessarily ready for sea.

A living ship.

Dawlish suddenly wanted her with a desire that was almost painful. He wanted to pace above that battery and feel the engines throb deep below his feet, to see and smell smoke billowing astern as the ship rushed forward with the bow-wave foaming over that long, wicked ram. He wanted to hear the rumble of her twelve-inch cannon running out to gape through those thick-walled ports and to wait, in an agony of expectation, for that moment of terrible fulfilment, of blasting flame and hurtling iron. He wanted it as another man might want a woman, or office, or wealth. And he was going to fight to get it.

"Batteries, Nicholas Kaptan," Zyndram said, "there and there, and over there." He knew this harbour from peacetime visits, knew it better still from the endless study of charts that had led to this desperate stratagem.

Dawlish scanned the row of guns gaping from embrasures above the walls, the majority ancient muzzle-loaders. He swept his glass along the line, stopped, then returned. Something more massive, and more

50

modern, was there - and there, and there, and there, four in all. He knew what they were, and feared them, even before Zyndram spoke.

"Nine-inch Armstrongs. And over there, Nicholas Kaptan – below that ruined castle to the east – yes, that's it, on the high ground – two more."

They were among the most efficient ship-killers British gunmakers could deliver, mounted behind solid masonry bastions scarcely two years before. There were eight in all, not to mention the dozens of lighter or older weapons that dominated the harbour approaches. One shell would be enough to dismember the *Irene*, protected as she was only by speed and bluff.

"Are we in their range yet?" Nusret's pallor was not due to sea-sickness alone.

"Near enough," Dawlish said, and then, as much to reassure himself as Nusret, he added: "But what do the lookouts see? Only a Trabzon vessel they've seen dozens of times, running for home after trading along the coast."

It was time for Zyndram to take the helm. He bore slightly to port, another point, so the mole could be rounded with room to spare. Now the *Mesrutiyet's* hull was lost to sight beyond the pier and the ships moored on its far side, only its upperworks and masts and funnel visible. Above the mole Dawlish spotted the single mast and twin funnels of what must be the *Burak Reis* – a partially armoured gunboat. No smoke rose from her – there was no immediate danger there. The curving mole ended in another battery, with three embrasures and light weapons, sixteen-pounders, yet all the more deadly for their low trajectory and the range at which they must be passed.

Dawlish pulled the oilskin cape closer across his uniform. He, like Nusret and Zyndram, had borrowed protective gear from the crew. The feel of the hilt of the cavalry sabre he had retained comforted him. He loosened his holster flap and tugged the lanyard on the Tranter revolver's butt to check it was secure.

The hatch covers had been stripped away and only a tarpaulin lay spread across the hold, ropes secured at the corners so the deckhands could sweep it off quickly on command. Beneath it the marines were standing to, only a third carrying firearms – for there must be minimal bloodshed if loyalty was to be easily bought – and the remainder armed solely with cutlasses. Their other, more important, equipment lay inside the port bulwark. They waited in the semi-darkness, only poorly informed of their location by muffled shouts from the deck, certain

51

only that the moment of maximum danger was close and that they were at present powerless to defend themselves.

"I see gunners on the harbour battery," Nusret said. "Is that usual?"

"Usual at this time," Phaidon roused himself. "Morning drill."

"Ins' Allah," Nusret said quietly, and Dawlish saw that he was frightened, for he was the one Turk he knew who normally avoided that fatalistic rejoinder.

Nusret's watch was in his hand and he was forcing it not to shake. "The time is good," he said. "Haluk will still be on board. He never leaves for midday prayers earlier than eleven."

The open harbour lay before them now, the *Mesrutiyet* square in its centre, six cables ahead, and the present course would carry the *Irene* slightly to the east of her. Four points off the starboard bow, the mole battery was two cables distant.

Suddenly somebody at the battery sensed something amiss – the undiminished speed perhaps. Immediately the alarm was being raised and figures that a moment before had been moving leisurely were now scuttling for their stations.

"They're suspicious, by God!" Dawlish said quietly, sickeningly aware, like all around him, that there was no option but to maintain course.

Flame and smoke spat from one of the battery's embrasures. The shot passed fifty yards ahead of the *Irene*'s plunging bow before it dropped to slash a running plume of spray away to port.

"Only a warning shot!" Zyndram said. "They're not sure!"

Seconds passed, long, priceless seconds in which the *Irene* surged ahead towards the battery's blind spot within the harbour, seconds in which the chief gunner must be agonising whether he had been too hasty and whether the familiar trader would heave to.

Then the respite was past and the battery exploded into life again, two weapons simultaneously, their reports deafening. One must have barely missed the main mast but the other found a mark. For one fleeting instant a perfectly round hole appeared in the centre of the fore course before the canvas split and the sail thrashed itself into long, flapping shreds. The *Irene* lurched, shuddered, and then plunged on, its speed perceptibly diminished. Zyndram's bellowed commands called the deckhands standing by the fore-course sheets aft to supplement their mates attending to those for the main boom. On their speed would depend the critical manoeuvre ahead.

52

The battery slipped by, no longer a threat, its weapons' arcs across the harbour mouth safely passed. The *Irene* surged on, driven now by her gaff-topped main course. The *Mesrutiyet* was off the starboard bow and figures were scurrying on her fo'castle and battery – her own marines falling into line along her starboard flank. The ironclad's twelve-inch cannon offered no threat at this close range but her marines' rifles did.

"Should our men be on deck?" Nusret sounded nervous.

Dawlish shook his head. "We need clear decks for the turn". He would have added that the hold provided some minimal protection in the long seconds ahead had the crash of musketry not blasted out from the ironclad at that moment. He resisted the urge to fling himself down – and so did Nusret, to his credit – and he felt something pluck at his oilskin cloak. Phaidon spun and cried out, blood erupting from his chest as he pitched over, and a deckhand was down too, crying in agony.

"Open the hold" Dawlish said. Zyndram translated and the *Irene*'s deckhands swept away the tarpaulin from over the hatch. The marines beneath, eyes suddenly exposed to the sun, threw up arms to shield them against the glare.

The wheel was moving only slightly through Zyndram's hands as he held the course remorselessly, glancing to starboard only to determine his position relative to the massive ironclad. The warship's long black flank was slipping past, and the *Irene* was level now with the central battery's white octagonal box, above which a score of the *Mesrutiyet's* own marines were crouched. Scarcely fifty yards separated the two vessels.

Dawlish flung his cape aside, revealing his double-breasted, brass-buttoned frock coat. Nusret threw off his also and the gold-lace of an Ottoman pasha glinted in the morning sun.

"Stand by to come about, Zyndram!" Dawlish forced a calm into his voice that he did not feel. He braced himself for the rifle fire that must surely soon rain from the ironclad's deck. He pulled a whistle from his pocket and gripped it between his teeth.

The *Irene* was level with the *Mesrutiyet's* stern as the expected hail of fire struck her, bringing down another deckhand, splintering bulwarks and yet, by some miracle, doing no worse.

Zyndram yelled a single command and threw the helm over to wear the vessel. The bow surged across to starboard and the deckhands were releasing the sheets there, and hauling them in on the port side.

Dawlish, crouching already, pulled Nusret down with him as the main boom scythed across, the sail flapping as it passed above them and then filling again as the wind caught it. The hull rolled to port, tilting the deck to perhaps thirty degrees before it heaved level again. And still the bowsprit was sweeping about until it was almost touching the *Mesrutiyet's* stern. On it rotated, and Zyndram bellowed again and the main gaff halliard was released. The gaff dropped suddenly, collapsing the maincourse, and the jib and foresail sheets were also let loose. Free of the wind's urging, only the hull's momentum now carried it forward. The helm was still over, the *Irene* still turning, and now it was almost parallel to the ironclad.

Now! Dawlish's long whistle blast urged the marines from the hold. Another volley from the ironclad struck as they scrambled on to the deck, rushing for the equipment stored along the port side. Two marines went down, killed by deadly, plunging shots from above, but in the excitement they were forgotten as their fellows reached for the grapnel-ended ropes coiled in the port scuppers.

The two hulls ground together with a groaning sound that killed the *Irene*'s momentum. Grapnels were heaved upwards, ropes snaking behind. They bounced and clattered unseen across the *Mesrutiyet's* deck above, seeking a purchase. One caught, then another, and then six or eight more, and then ropes were pulled taut and the first of the marines, chosen for their agility during that endless training on the hulk near Zonguldak, dragged themselves upwards. Dawlish was with the throng that cheered them on, and Nusret and Zyndram too, and he saw with satisfaction that the Pole's placing of the sailing craft had been perfect, its bows beneath the central battery, the stern alongside the ironclad's quarterdeck.

The crash of rifle-fire was deafening, the air thick with gunsmoke as the *Irene*'s marines blazed upwards to give cover to the climbers. Two marines had reached the quarterdeck and one beat down a seaman who ran towards him, and then three more gained it, and then another half-dozen were up and over the rail, clubbing and bludgeoning.

Further forward grapnels had locked on to the much higher objective of the central battery. The cluster of the *Mesrutiyet's* own marines atop it made its roof an impossible goal, but volley-fire upwards from the *Irene* drove them back from its edge. Here too climbers shinned upwards, their goal the two gaping and apparently undefended gun-ports. Several pulled themselves inside and then

54

reached out for the ropes tossed to them to drag up the corners of a net from the sailing craft beneath.

Aft also, a thick-stranded net had been pulled upwards and secured to the *Mesrutiyet's* quarterdeck rail. The marines clawed their way up the mesh from the *Irene*, Dawlish among them, dragging Nusret with him, shouting encouragement and guiding his hand to the next hold above. Boots crushed fingers but the progress was ever upwards. Dawlish's face came suddenly level with the deck. Another three steps brought him over the rail and he pulled Nusret across to flop over behind him.

There were corpses on the deck, fewer than he had dared hope, and the *Irene's* marines had driven a cowering group of the ironclad's crew back against the rear of the battery, hands upraised in surrender. A small knot of men was involved in a savage brawl among the ship's boats stowed further aft. Amidships *Irene's* marines were swarming off the net there, and into the battery's open ports. The first to have done so must have found their way on to the fo'castle, for noise from there indicated that they had drawn away the *Mesrutiyet's* defenders who had been on top of the battery. Surprise was proving itself to be the most potent weapon of all and the ironclad's crew, caught out in their complacent mid-morning routine, must still be bewildered as to who and what had hit them. And sustained pressure, persisting momentum, would exploit that surprise.

"Go forward, Nusret Pasha!" Dawlish yelled, unsheathing his sabre and drawing Nusret with him. Zyndram had somehow appeared on their other side, a weal from a whipping rope livid across his forehead, otherwise unharmed.

As he straightened up and adjusted his red, tasselled fez, tall in his dark and gilded uniform, Nusret was again that implacable and ruthless inheritor of the blood of conquerors that Dawlish had glimpsed in the glare of the burning square at Giresun. He strode forward, hands empty, disdaining to carry a weapon against men whose loyalty he aspired to command.

"Nusret Pasha! Nusret Pasha!" The cry rose from the *Irene's* marines as he thrust his way through them and towards the meleé by the boats. The rising cry of his men, rhythmic now, reached the combatants and gave them pause. The shouts of acclaim were stilled and when he spoke his voice was loud and calm.

"Brothers! Why do you fight? The Sultan himself has sent his faithful brother Nusret to call you back to duty!"

55

Zyndram was translating for Dawlish and his voice told that he himself was moved.

"Brother Turks!" Nusret called. "Lay down your arms! The Russians are more worthy enemies for brave men!"

There was a howl of discord from a single throat, immediately drowned by shouts of approval. Suddenly, as if by some miracle, weapons were being cast on the deck and hands were reaching for Nusret's and drawing them to lips that pledged loyalty. There was cheering, and more men flowing aft from the battery, boarders and crew alike catching the enthusiasm for Nusret's acclamation and joining in.

Zyndram too moved towards the throng but Dawlish drew him back. "Haluk," he said. "We need Haluk."

The Pole, suddenly sobered, barked orders and eight marines joined him, flushed with success, half-incredulous that the gamble had paid off so far.

"Four to follow me," Dawlish said. "No rifles, cutlasses only. You know what to do yourself."

Zyndram moved aft with four men and Dawlish, with his own four, turned to find the companionway close to the starboard side. Half-obscured by two huge ventilator cowls, it was exactly where it had been when a foreman had guided him around the uncompleted Belleisle at Poplar. Then, the cold, dim, unpainted passages and the unfinished compartments had felt more like some long-disused catacomb than the living, pulsating entity they would one day comprise but the experience had been invaluable, offering a feel for the innards of the sister that lay a thousand miles and more to the east. Dawlish's notebook had filled with sketches and diagrams that he had memorised until he felt he could navigate the labyrinth blindfold. Now he steeled himself to enter the reality.

The steps were deserted. He descended, sabre drawn, and turned into a dim and deserted passage. The marines followed. The din on deck above was hushed now, and silence grew as he padded cautiously aft. There were green doors on either side – officers' accommodation – and painted canvas underfoot. Light cut through the gloom from an open door ahead. Dawlish approached with infinite care, blood pumping, pulse racing, but found nothing more menacing than a neatly furnished cabin with an open scuttle.

He deliberately kept his pistol in its holster and fought down the urge to draw it. Ahead was another open door, barely ajar. He gestured

56

a marine forward to swing it inwards, ready to pounce himself should it be occupied, but it too proved empty.

Dawlish knew from the afternoon at Poplar that the wardroom extended across the ship's complete beam. The closed door at the end of the corridor led to it, as did a twin on the vessel's opposite side. He paused at it, listening for movement. The silence was broken only by the thump of boots on the deck overhead. He beckoned the marines forward and they crouched by him as he turned the knob slowly. It was unlocked.

The wardroom was bright from sunshine streaming though the overhead skylight. It held a huge table, disrupted meals at one end, dining chairs in disarray, heavy armchairs to the side, a carved sideboard, exquisite framed calligraphy, Koranic verses. It was deserted.

A face looked down from the skylight – Zyndram, finger to his lips, gesturing further aft.

There lay the captain's accommodation and semi-circular saloon enclosed by the rounded stern. On either side of the wardroom a door led aft. Both were closed. The memory of the Belleisle was like a map in Dawlish's mind. He knew that a short corridor lay beyond each door, with the captain's cabin and bathroom opening off it on the starboard side, mirrored by a steward's pantry on the port. There would be doors at the end of these passageways, opening into the saloon.

Dawlish chose the door on the starboard side, keeping two men with him. He gestured two marines towards the far door, then felt the knob before him. It was locked, but inward opening, as was the other.

The time for silence and subtlety was passed. A gesture from Dawlish told the marines on either side what was expected – two men to each door, one kicking at the lock, the other standing aside. Wood splintered and yet both doors somehow held. Then more kicks, followed by an explosion of gunfire through the far door, three, four shots in quick succession. The marine who had just stamped against the wooden surface slid down it, eyes locked open in death. But the door before Dawlish was yielding, and one more kick tore the lock away from the frame and it swung inwards. The marine stumbled and fell, but Dawlish and the other marine charged over him. The third marine deserted the far door and followed in their wake.

There was one last door beyond the bathroom and it was closed. Dawlish and the leading marine smashed into it. It was of light material, and it collapsed before them. They plunged into the saloon,

57

dazzled by the brightness streaming in from the glazed windows at the stern. The compartment was carpeted and furnished like a comfortable drawing room, but Dawlish had eyes only for the frail and bearded figure, long, cadaverous and sallow, who stood with his back to the light. He wore a robe, and his head was turbaned, and Haluk Pasha looked exactly as he had done in the photographs Hobart had shown. He held a pistol in his hand and he looked as calm as if he had risen from his prayer mat.

Dawlish moved slowly towards him, gesturing to him to lay down the weapon. But Haluk was raising it, slowly and deliberately, and with sick clarity Dawlish remembered Nusret relating boyhood memories of him, of hours spent shooting sparrows off branches at fifty paces with a Colt revolver. Dawlish flung himself down behind an armchair's meagre protection as Haluk fired and heard the marine behind him cry out as the bullet took him down.

Two men – traditionally dressed, Haluk's bodyguards, not seamen or marines – burst into the saloon from the other corridor which they had successfully defended. One was shooting with a revolver, twice, three times, but wildly, without effect, though the noise was terrifying in the enclosed space. The air was filling with gunsmoke, but he was masking the fire of his companion. One of the surviving marines rushed forward, cutlass outstretched. A fourth shot must have shaved past him in the instant before he impaled the bodyguard on his point. He was tugging his blade free as Haluk's shot took him in the side and flung him down.

Dawlish was edging forward, sabre ready, as the remaining marine charged. The second bodyguard's revolver brought him crashing down and another shot finished him as he hit the deck.

Haluk's eyes locked on Dawlish and he smiled as he swung his pistol towards him. For one blood-chilling second Dawlish saw the muzzle pointed directly at his face and realised that the nine feet separating him from it were too immense a distance for him to cover before Haluk fired.

At that moment the glass behind Haluk shattered. A darkly uniformed body came swinging through, feet first, releasing the rope that suspended it as it smashed inwards. Haluk's pistol exploded, its shot wild and missing Dawlish. Another body crashed through, and another followed through the gap, then two more, all swung down by rope from the quarterdeck above. Jerzy Zyndram struggled to his feet and lunged towards Haluk while the marine who followed him rushed towards the remaining bodyguard. The man shot wildly, then flailed with his emptied pistol before falling to the marine's cutlass.

Haluk had evaded Zyndram and rushed towards Dawlish, his revolver rising again, but his composure had left him. Dawlish swung out with his sabre and somehow had the presence of mind to beat down Haluk's arm with the flat rather than the edge. The revolver dropped and Dawlish brought up the sabre's hilt to strike Haluk on the side of the jaw. He fell with a groan, his mouth bloodied. Zyndram grabbed him from behind, doubled his arm against his back and held him fast.

"Get him in a chair." Dawlish picked up the revolver and pointed it towards him. "Tell him that if he moves I'll shoot him."

The fight had gone out of Haluk, though not the venom, and he alternately swore through his bleeding mouth and spat out broken teeth.

"He's calling us dogs, infidel dogs." Zyndram was shaking, amazed that he had somehow managed what had been asked of him.

"He can call us what he likes, damn him!" Dawlish hoped that his own trembling hands were not too obvious. "Send for Nusret Pasha."

There was little evidence of brotherly love at the meeting, though Haluk did his best to maintain his dignity despite his bloody countenance and stained robe.

"He says he's sorry the age of silken bowstrings is past." Zyndram translated Nusret's words in a whisper. "But he tells Haluk he won't hesitate to kill him anyway – and not quickly – if he doesn't co-operate."

Haluk was snarling now, his dignity lost in dribbling blood and swollen lips. Nusret drew his own pistol and whipped Haluk across the face with the barrel, opening a gash.

"Their mothers hated each other," Zyndram whispered, "and they've hated each other since they were children. Haluk knows Nusret won't hesitate to kill him."

Dawlish watched, half-sickened, half-fascinated, conscious that within this smoke-laden, corpse-strewn space there were no limits to enmity or revenge, no code or law to restrain or curb. Haluk knew it too and he yielded, though with eyes still blazing defiance.

Zyndram sat at the writing desk and took Nusret's dictation, rapidly covering two sheets in fluent Arabic script. As Dawlish saw the half-brothers glowering at each other in silent and undisguised loathing he suddenly had a memory, a fleeting one, but no less sad for that, of his own older brother James, dead at twenty-nine when his gelding failed to clear a five-barred gate. Dawlish had been half a world away when he had received the news two months later and the grave was already thickly grassed when he had at last seen it. He would have given anything to bring back the kindly boy who had so protected his younger sister and brother when their mother had died. Dawlish had been four, so very young, and only eight years of childhood had remained to him ...

Nusret scanned the completed documents – orders to the fortress commander and to the town governor to submit to him in the name of Sultan Abdul-Hamid. Nusret smiled and shoved them towards his half-brother, pushing an ink-laden pen into his hand. Haluk's bruised face was contorted with fury but he scrawled his signature.

Haluk was pulled to his feet and brought on deck, encouraged by a revolver jammed against his lower spine. The small group emerged, blinking in the sunlight, to be confronted by the ship's company, drawn up in raged order, disarmed and still watched by the *Irene*'s triumphant marines. There were ragged cries of "Nusret Pasha! Nusret Pasha!"

Nusret stilled them with his upraised arm. "Brother Turks!" he began, his voice loud and confident, "the true enemy lies there!" He pointed eastwards, towards the Caucasian littoral, towards the supply lines that fed the Russian onslaught. "That is where you will be led, Ins'Allah, to victory and revenge!"

In the cheers that drowned Nusret's last words Dawlish knew that the greatest challenge now lay ahead. He had his ship, a command such as he had dreamed of since he was a boy, but he had a crew whose language he did not speak, whose religion he did not share and some of whose members still lay bloody on the deck. He would need their courage and their efficiency but most of all he would need their loyalty.

And that he would have to earn.

6

Trabzon was Nusret's by early afternoon.

The fortress commander had submitted and the loyalty of the gun batteries was guaranteed by detachments of the *Irene*'s marines. Now the sun was setting and Dawlish's first inspection of the *Mesrutiyet* was depressing. The vessel had been his to command for five hours and already it was obvious that three months of inactivity had been as detrimental to the ship's readiness as to the crew's efficiency.

Though built in Britain, the *Mesrutiyet* had been designed by the Turks themselves for the sole purpose of defence of the Straits. It was short for its five-thousand ton displacement –two hundred and fifty feet – but Dawlish remembered from seeing the exposed curves of the Orion, high on the slipway at Poplar, that the underwater form and twin screws would make her handy and allow tight turning, though she would probably roll badly in any significant sea. The long, massive ram lent her a pugnacious aspect but the low bows above it meant that she would be wet, very wet. She was well armoured, with a belt that was twelve inches at its thickest amidships and which protected the entire waterline and much of the flanks above. Unseen within, internal bulkheads up to nine-inches thick provided transverse protection to the magazines, boilers and engines. The decks above were armoured up to three inches.

The single funnel was sited incongruously ahead of the central battery, an armoured octagonal box that rose high amidships. In each of the battery's four corner-faces angled forty-five degrees to ship's axis, two on either side, a deep port was cut. Through each an Armstrong twelve-inch rifled muzzle-loader commanded an arc of one hundred and twenty degrees, from direct ahead or astern to out beyond the beam. A small but massively armoured oval conning tower perched above, at the centre of the box's iron roof, with a wheelhouse and open bridge surmounting it. The vessel's two stumpy masts carried no sailing rig to supplement the limited bunkerage for the twin three-thousand horsepower engines but the mainmast had a massive boom for handling the ship's boats nestling aft.

"We'll see the engine and boiler rooms now," Dawlish said to Zyndram. He expected further disappointment there and hoped his rising sense of unease was not showing. This ship was in no state yet to a face any enemy, not even in a state to take to sea safely, yet his future career, maybe even his life, depended on it.

Zyndram, now the ironclad's First Officer, turned over another leaf of his notebook and wrote the date at the top, Thursday, October 25th. He had already filled a dozen pages with remedial actions that Dawlish dictated with mounting, tight-lipped exasperation and still the tour of the vessel was scarcely half-over.

The brass ladder-rails left their hands soiled with grime, but there was worse below. The engines were in poor condition, with leaking glands unattended, stuffing boxes jetting steam when pressure was admitted, incipient patches of rust on shafts that should have been

61

mirror-bright, bearing lubricating-bowls empty and handfuls of oily cotton-waste tossed carelessly under gratings. The furnaces were clogged with ash and cinders, so that even the meagre fires kept burning to maintain harbour-pressure might have died of their own accord in a few days more. Lumps of coal strewed the deck and a glance into the bunkers told that trimming was a skill that would need to be relearned. Several of the boiler gauges were inoperative, three of the relief valves appeared jammed, one feed-pump was broken down and half the piping joints and couplings would need replacement of their packings.

"You can start by cleaning, Mahmut Mülazim," Dawlish told the commissioned engineer, his tone icy. "Then you'll start the maintenance. I want this ship ready for sea within two days." The engineer spoke tolerable English and had spent five months at Samuda's yard in Poplar as the ship was completed. He had witnessed the *Mesrutiyet's* trials. He had signed off the builder's form that confirmed that the furnaces, boiler and engines met specification. He had returned from Britain with the ship. There was no excuse for him. He knew how the vessel should be run but he had been complicit in allowing its decline.

"In two days. Ready in all respects," Dawlish repeated. "You understand?"

"Ins' Allah," Mahmut looked down, unwilling to meet Dawlish's gaze. "If God wills."

"God wills it – and so do I," Dawlish said. He flipped his watch open and noted the time. "I'll be back in five hours and the cleaning will be complete by then." He left, Zyndram following.

They emerged on deck. The ironclad's previous captain and his most senior lieutenant, recalcitrants who had the courage to proclaim their continued loyalty to Haluk, were being pulled away in the longboat towards the transport now moored close by, the same vessel that had brought Nusret and Dawlish and their force eastwards. Haluk was already in close but respectful detention on board, guarded by marines. The extra weapons, munitions and other supplies the vessel had carried were already safely unloaded and it would depart within the hour, carrying Haluk to the traditional fate of Sultans' half-brothers, incarceration and an uncertain future in Istanbul.

A cutter was approaching from the quayside, marines disposed among the rowers. Nusret sat in the sternsheets, a green cloak thrown across his uniform. As the boat nudged alongside he bounded up the ladder, ignoring the guard falling in to salute him. He kissed Dawlish on the cheek and then stood back, beaming. He had gone all but alone into the city and his demeanour told that he had carried its garrison and its people with him as surely as he had carried the *Mesrutiyet*.

"Behold a man whose devoutness so far outstrips his brother's," he said, grinning, but his tone ironic. "Haluk only prayed at the Charshi mosque, but I have been at the Hatuniye and the Iskender Pasha and the Semerciler mosques as well, draped in the Prophet's sacred colour."

His piety had impressed the crowds, leaving no doubt that his years of absence among the infidel had strengthened rather than corrupted his faith and that his commitment to the Constitution was no impediment to religious devotion. He had pushed through the growing throngs that had gathered to see him with only a handful of marines to protect him. In speeches in mosque courtyards and at street corners he had reminded them that the Russian menace was all but at their gates. Had his beloved brother, Sultan Abdul-Hamid, not sent him to deliver them from Haluk's treachery, then their lives and their wives' and daughters' honours would have been sacrificed within days to the infidel invader.

"A week, two weeks ago, they mightn't have believed me," he said, "but now the town is packed with villagers fleeing before the Russians. They've all got the same story – murder, rape, burning. And they blame Haluk's inactivity for it."

"And the garrison, Nusret Pasha?"

"Secure and loyal." His smile was bitter. "That gold we landed guarantees it."

They passed into the saloon, its shattered windows temporarily covered with tarpaulins. Nusret lit a cigarette, called for brandy, tossed back a glass, then filled another. Dawlish asked the steward for coffee.

"Your news, Nicholas Kaptan?" Nusret had drained his second glass already.

"All ships in the harbour secure and I'll inspect the *Burak Reis* tonight." The two Krupp rifled cannon she carried could make the iron-hulled screw gunboat moored at the mole invaluable. Dawlish paused. The next news would not be welcome. "With luck we can maybe have the *Mesrutiyet* to sea for trials in three days. But we'll need at least another week of exercises before I'd want to risk her in action."

"Three days! Another week!" Nusret looked stunned.

"It's essential, Nusret Pasha. I apologise – but I can't promise more yet."

Nusret's hands were shaking.

"You know the situation," Nusret said. "You know what's at stake. The Russians won't let up."

Dawlish nodded, felt numb. Surprise was still on their side, but could only be a rapidly wasting asset. The earlier success could be scored, however trifling, the sooner the Russians might hesitate to push supplies along the coast to their armies with such impunity and the sooner some respite might be afforded the hard-pressed defenders of Kars and Erzurum. Dawlish knew that at this moment he alone could provide that respite – if only he could get to sea.

"There is a chance of something else, Nusret Pasha," Dawlish said. "Only a chance. I need time to work out the details." For the germ of an idea was forming, though he could not yet to commit himself to it. Everything would depend on the spirit of the crew. His experience so far of the Ottoman Navy had been confined to one elite, well-led unit, the Marines, and he was hesitant to draw inferences about how a normal ship's complement might respond to a rapid escalation of combat training. It was dawning on him that he had always unthinkingly taken for granted the cheerful efficiency and unlimited willingness of the British bluejacket under any circumstances. It might be otherwise here.

Nusret was splashing more brandy into his glass. "I know you're being honest, Nicholas Kaptan," he said. He sat down, tried to look calm, then said "The telegraph is open again. Does that help?"

"It does," Dawlish turned to Zyndram. "The first requirement is coal – at least two thousand tons within a week, as much as possible thereafter. Telegrams if you please to Istanbul and Zonguldak to that effect."

"Have you any contact with Batumi, Nusret Pasha?" Dawlish asked. Telegraphic contact with the most northerly of the Turkish Black Sea bases had been blocked since Haluk had taken control at Trabzon. A single small central-battery ironclad, the *Alemdar*, had remained inactive at Batumi ever since then. Her captain, Hassan, had not risked antagonising the Sultan's rebellious half-brother by venturing to sea until he was sure how the struggle for power would resolve itself.

"The line to Batumi is open," Nusret smiled bitterly. "Hassan Kaptan assures me of his unswerving loyalty. He thirsts to serve the Sultan's interests."

"And his ship?"

"Not ready for sea for at least a fortnight he said."

64

"We'll see about that," Dawlish said grimly. "If it's longer than a week I'll recommend you hang him from his own yardarm."

"An even less merciful suggestion has already been cabled to him. You can assume that he'll be ready when you arrive in Batumi yourself."

The addition of force would be welcome, Dawlish thought, though heaven knew what state the *Alemdar* was in. Though built in the same Poplar yard as the *Mesrutiyet*, she had been laid down six years earlier and had been poorly spoken of to start with. The months of inactivity would not have improved her.

"I've had direct contact with my brother, the Sultan," Nusret said. "He sends his thanks and his congratulations. And Hobart Pasha too – he sent a message for you personally."

Dawlish took the paper on which the telegraph strips had been pasted. Zyndram translated.

"It says *Time to unleash the Grey Wolf*." He sounded puzzled.

"No matter," Dawlish said. "I understand."

In his mind's eye he could visualise Hobart, at their last interview before he'd left Istanbul, the ex-Confederate blockade runner leaning back in his chair, boots on his desk, drawing on a cigar and gazing towards the dome of Aghia Sofia.

"They're corrupt and effete, too damn many of them, these Ottomans," Hobart had said, "but they've still got a memory of what they were when they rode out from the heart of Asia and brought down Byzantium. They're still grey wolves of the steppes at heart. Given a leader, that's what they'll be again. And that's what you must be, Dawlish – a wolf ravening on the Russian flanks, tearing the guts from their supply lines and striking where they least expect you!"

But not just an Ottoman wolf, Dawlish thought. Topcliffe had been clear about that. This was Britain's war also, even if undeclared. He must be Britannia's wolf too.

But first must come the needs of the moment. He left Nusret. The inspection of the galley lay ahead. It promised to be revolting, if the state of the rest of the ironclad was any indication. Then he must see the heads, which would probably be even worse, and then the stores and finally make a return visit to the main battery to view progress on the cleaning of the four massive twelve-inch cannon. There would be an address to the assembled crew on the lamp-lit quarterdeck to follow, leaving them in no doubt of what the change of regime implied for discipline, efficiency and fairness. And above all for action. Then he

65

would be rowed across to the *Burak Reis* and finish by investigating what was available at the small naval repair yard.

The night was still young. Dawlish was exhausted, but his mind still teemed with possibilities. The Russians were three hundred miles away, and pressing closer by the day, their advance sustained by supply by sea along the Caucasian Coast that Haluk's treachery had left unmenaced for three months. News of the coup at Trabzon could not yet have reached Archduke Michael.

The Wolf's first rampage must come before he could learn of it.

*

Even the darkness could not hide the *Burak Reis's* shame. Idleness, a drunken captain, and the absence on private business of his two officers had reduced the one-sixty foot, eight-hundred ton gunboat to a floating slum. Paint flaked and metal rusted, filth encrusted the decks, the passageways and accommodation smelled of sweat and urine, and the furnaces had been cold for a month, maybe longer. The coal bunkers were empty – their contents sold, Dawlish suspected – and several families were in residence in odd corners, their grimy children watching shyly from behind corroded ventilators and sun-cracked boats as the inspection party boarded.

A lurching, puffy-faced stout figure in a stained uniform and a crushed fez saluted as the remnants of his crew – scarcely half of the vessel's forty-man complement and all as dishevelled as himself – mustered behind him. He smelled of alcohol and his eyes were full of guilt and fear.

"Mehmet Birinci Yüzbashi," Zyndram translated, embarrassed for his Navy by the squalor. "Captain of the *Burak Reis.* He welcomes you and places himself and his ship at your service."

"Thank Mehmet Yüzbashi for his best wishes and tell him that as of this instant he's relieved of the command of this vessel," Dawlish said. "Tell him to report immediately to the *Mesrutiyet.* We'll decide his new duties later."

The unkempt officer opened his mouth to protest but then seemed to sense Dawlish's cold fury and thought better of it. He came to attention, saluted and shambled towards the entry port.

Dawlish beckoned to a short, olive-skinned officer who had accompanied him. "Onursal Mülazim – you will take command of His Majesty's gunboat *Burak Reis* forthwith."

66

The *Mesrutiyet's* young fourth lieutenant, a Macedonian, had impressed during the inspection, one of the few officers who had apparently struggled against the tide of sloth that had suffused the ironclad. The English he had picked up at the yard in Poplar when the ship had been delivered made communication easy. His face registered amazement and trepidation at his new command. Appointing him was a gamble, but there was no alternative.

The task of cleansing and restoring this gunboat would be no less daunting than on the larger ship. There was the additional problem of crewing it, for there was little hope of rounding up the deserters. The engines were in a sorry state, the furnaces and boilers no less so. And yet the *Burak Reis* had two outstanding virtues – its shallow draught, some nine feet, and a powerful armament, a six-inch calibre Krupp breech-loading rifle behind an armoured breastwork forward and a similar three-inch weapon aft. The Germania yard at Kiel had delivered a potent vessel three years before, however run-down she might now be.

"Have you experience of these weapons, Zyndram Yüzbashi?" Dawlish asked. Breech loaders, in which the shell and charge was inserted in the rear of the gun barrel, were still a novelty, faster to load than traditional muzzle-loaders. But the stresses on their more complex mechanisms were much higher, the metallurgy more critical. A series of accidents – burst breeches and barrels, and several deaths – had caused the Royal Navy to step back from their wholesale introduction. But Krupp, the German cannon-founders, seemed to have mastered the problems that still dogged British companies. Their products had sold well to other navies on the strength of a reputation for improved design and metallurgy.

"They're excellent weapons, Kumandanim." The form of address was traditional – My Commander – but Zyndram invested it with something personal. "The six-inch Krupp is accurate to well over two thousand yards, more in quiet water. And it's easily served."

"We'll need crews then, from the shore batteries if necessary."

The greatest lack of all would be of skilled engineering staff. The state of the propulsive equipment on both ships worried Dawlish deeply. Had Hobart asked Topcliffe to send a dozen seasoned Royal Navy engine-room artificers he would not have underestimated the need. Dawlish rejoiced inwardly that he did not share the contempt for the technical branch fashionable among so many of his brother officers and that he had even spent leisure hours, much to their merriment,

67

learning to use a lathe. In the coming days he would have to act as his own chief engineer.

They ascended to the bridge, an open platform atop the small deckhouse ahead of the fore-funnel, with minimal weather protection around the steering position. A single mast rose abaft it, for signalling and observation only. If the engine failed there would be no sailing rig to fall back upon.

"We'll mount a single Nordenveldt there, Onursal Mülazim," Dawlish said, pointing to the rectangle of deckhouse roof before the bridge. Six of the multi-barrel machine guns had been landed from the transport, all destined for the *Mesrutiyet*, but the ironclad would manage with one fewer.

He leant on the rail, now feeling his fatigue. Looking forward across the six-inch Krupp bowchaser, knowing that this vessel could risk shallows that would defeat the *Mesrutiyet*, he felt quickening excitement. The idea that had been growing since he had first sighted the *Burak Reis* was looking ever more practical – but only if that dilapidated engine and neglected boiler could be got in working order. Yet he felt slightly more confident now than when he had spoken of a chance to Nusret. That chance seemed slightly stronger now.

And there was one other possibility, a long shot perhaps, one that depended on two small vessels he had heard lay in the repair facility ashore, though in what condition nobody seemed to know.

Exhausted or not, it was time to see them. He lit a cigar, savoured the smoke, and headed for the ladder. Rest must wait.

7

It was four days before the *Mesrutiyet* nudged past the Trabzon mole under her own steam and into the swell built by a brisk breeze from the north. The skies were leaden and rain squalls drifted on the horizon. Even in such moderate conditions, and at half revolutions, she was pitching significantly, and the huge bow wave generated by the ram ran up green over the fo'castle and foamed about the mooring tackle as she plunged under. The patent log reported seven and a half knots. Eight miles out she turned westwards, parallel to the coast, and as she took the waves on the beam she began to roll quickly.

"An uncomfortable ship, Zyndram," Dawlish said, "but we'd better get used to her." It would be unwise to anticipate significantly better sea conditions in the winter months ahead. The wind was icy and he was grateful for the shelter of the open-backed wheel-house. Nusret Pasha had already gone below, almost certainly to vomit privately.

"It was worse in the Bay of Biscay after we took delivery," Zyndram said. "There wasn't a dry corner or a hot meal until we reached Gibraltar."

Dawlish suspected that the same experience had contributed to the vessel's previous senior officers' acquiescence in Haluk's inactivity. He himself had grown up a blue-water sailor and he'd make the same of this crew whether they liked it or not.

"Maintain revolutions and course," he said. "I'm going to the engine room."

He passed down through the battery. Its ports were shuttered closed and the armoured box was like a great gloomy barn that reverberated as the occasional high-cresting wave slammed against it. The four huge twelve-inch calibre cannon were secure on their pivot-mountings, the training tackles taut, but the spaces between were clear, the gun crews' hammocks and mess-tables neatly stacked in racks against the sides. The men were at their stations, polishing and burnishing so that brass gleamed and black iron had a dull sheen. The metal deck underfoot, covered with white paint mixed with sand for better grip, was spotless. As Dawlish entered a shouted order from the gunnery officer, Selim Yüzbashi, brought the men to attention. He was a small, intense, shaven-headed man with a huge moustache, an artillery enthusiast for whom the three months at the Armstrong works, near Newcastle, when these weapons had been tested and accepted, must have been close to paradise. He was a martinet, like so many gunners, and he had obviously welcomed the mandate Dawlish had given him to drill and train his men without respite. The type was common in every navy and Dawlish did not envy the two junior officers, the mülazims, who were responsible to him for the port and starboard weapons, or for the midshipmen, the mehendis, who supported them. He had endured similar tyranny in his own youth.

The four huge, squat guns had rifled barrels a mere fifteen feet long, tapering from a diameter of four and a half feet at the rear. Loaded through the muzzle, as cannon had been for centuries, their massive six-hundred pound shells, and the sixty-pound bags of gunpowder that would propel them, were too heavy for human muscles. Chain hoists were used to lift the munitions through the hatches leading to the magazines far below, and to manoeuvre them into the barrel. Handling such weights in a ship that might be pitching

69

and rolling, yet maintaining a steady rhythm of gunfire, demanded automaton-like precision from every gun-crew member. It could only be achieved by relentless drilling. Selim Yüzbashi seemed like the ideal man to ensure that.

Dawlish inspected three of the weapons cursorily. He could feel the tension – no, rather the fear – of each crewman as he stroked metal surfaces, reached into muzzles and felt the cleanliness of the rifling, shook a block to check the security of a tackle, examined the greasing of sliding surfaces. Stronger still, he could feel Selim's anxiety until he voiced tempered approval. It was too soon to do more, and it would be time enough after firing trials, but this was the first occasion he had given even this much.

He left the fourth cannon, starboard aft, for last. His inspection of it was deliberately meticulous, ending with half-crawling beneath the mounting to view the undersides of the recoil-slides. The crew's dread was almost palpable and he was confident that no Ottoman officer had ever done this. A nervous tic was jerking on the gunnery officer's cheek as he emerged.

"Accept my congratulations, Selim Yüzbashi," he said, meaning it, for the condition of the weapon would have done credit to a British flagship, "and convey them to your men."

Selim barked Dawlish's appreciation at his crews, half-suppressing a smirk of satisfaction. The look of sullen fear that had worried Dawlish earlier seemed to lift from the men's faces and he could see furtive side-glances of relief. The yabanchi – the foreigner – might not be so terrible after all.

Time now to use the oldest trick of all for gaining loyalty.

"Tell me, Selim Yüzbashi," Dawlish said, "is there an Üschavush called Fahrettin present? A gunner who distinguished himself at the Danube mouth in June. I believe he was transferred to this ship afterwards?" He knew very well that there was, for he had checked records and knew of half a dozen such notable men on the ship. Sooner or later he would recognise them all like this.

"Fahrettin?" Selim said, amazed. "Yes, Kumandanim – here is the man, the gun captain."

The petty officer was a heavy, swarthy man in his forties. He looked uncomfortable as he was called forward.

"Tell Fahrettin Üschavush that Hobart Pasha himself told me how Fahrettin lifted a Russian shell with a burning fuse with his own hands and threw it overboard when it penetrated the bulwark of the gunboat *Yozgad*."

The man flushed with pride as Selim translated.

"He is honoured, Nicholas Kaptan."

"No, Selim Yüzbashi. It is I who am honoured by the presence of such a man on my ship. Tell him I am honoured to shake his hand and hope that his example will inspire all my crew to similar heroism."

He took the man's hand, felt his pride as he pressed it, then drew him closer and kissed his cheek in the Turkish fashion. The story would be about the vessel within the hour, bringing a step closer that unity of ship, crew and purpose he must forge.

The engine room was like a steam bath and despite the maintenance of glands and replacement of packing in recent days there were still leaks aplenty. Condensed water gathered and dripped on every surface and the crew's sodden shirts stuck to them in the stifling, humid atmosphere. But the twin Maudsley compound engines, each rated at two thousand horsepower maximum, were operating smoothly, pistons panting resolutely as they drove the cross-heads and connecting rods and the cranks beneath.

"An improvement, Mahmut Mülazim," Dawlish said to the engineer, "but much still to be done. Now show me the furnaces."

The sweat-soaked Mahmut smiled nervously and led the way into the bakehouse that was the boiler-room. As always when he entered such a compartment, Dawlish wondered how flesh and blood could endure such conditions. Even steaming at half power the temperature was almost unbearable and the flames in the open hearths cast a ghastly glow over the glistening bodies of the wretches who fed them. They fought to keep their footing as the ship rolled and pitched, and as they strewed the coal evenly through the open fire-doors, shovelful by shovelful, raking and levelling to ensure uniform combustion. The trimmers lurched from the bunkers with their wheelbarrows, bracing themselves against the ship's motions. Their responsibility was to shift the coal steadily from the remotest recesses of the bunkers and towards the entrances to facilitate the stokers' relentless shovelling. It was a humble skill, but an essential one. Like others that had been neglected and half-forgotten in the months in port it was now reasserting itself.

The best of all was that the boilers were holding pressure and there was no sign of tube leakage. The relief valves had been overhauled and tested, so there was no worry on that score, and the repaired feed-pump was holding its own.

71

"I may be signalling for full power in half an hour," Dawlish said. "Be prepared."

As he was about to return to the bridge the boiler-room supervisor approached Mahmut. He obviously was asking something, respectfully but persistently, and the engineer was denying him, shaking his head. Hayir, Hayir, No, No.

"What does he want?" Dawlish asked, curiosity aroused.

"It is nothing to bother you, Kumandanim. Just a request of the men."

"Tell me."

"It is nothing – it is that they would be honoured if our Kaptan would drink chai with them. But I have told him Kumandanim is busy."

"But your Kaptan has two minutes to drink chai with men who are so important to this ship." Dawlish's heart lifted. He could not have hoped for better. "Tell them. Two minutes now, longer at some later time."

Boiling water tapped from a cock filled the pot – "It must be fresh for our Kaptan," Mahmut said – and then deep red tea half-filled a glass, one of a dozen on a tray in a corner. The stokers were watching shyly, half-smiling, and one took the glass and diluted it with more water from the boiler. Dawlish sipped, scalding his lips and tongue, knowing that he should be back on the bridge and yet that this moment was perhaps more important still.

He paused, glad to let the liquid cool, looking at the men individually, holding their gaze. They were not that different from a British stokehold crew in appearance, but a world apart perhaps in culture and expectations.

"Tell your men that they have done well in the last days," he said, uncertain how his intention would come across in translation, hoping that it would somehow bridge that yawning gap of language, "but tell them that I'll be asking much more of them in the weeks to come. Tell them that this is the heart of the *Mesrutiyet* and that with their support we'll take the battle into the Russians' own waters."

Mahmut translated while Dawlish drained the glass. There were murmurs of "Ins' Allah" as he finished. One man, bolder than the rest, dropped to one knee, took Dawlish's hand and kissed it.

He turned to Mahmut as he left. "Ask them if I'll have full power when I call for it."

72

With the chorus of "Evet, Evet," he knew he had progressed another step. The *Mesrutiyet* was sloughing off her sloth and her deadlier self was emerging. But time was still needed, time that was so scarce.

The wind had risen while he was below and the ship now had a pronounced and uncomfortable screwing motion. It was time now to try evolutions, a succession of turns and circles that exposed the hull to the sea from every direction. As the great ram bow swung across into a head sea, water surged and coursed across the foredeck, washing around the mast and funnel to break against the superstructure. As the vessel circled further, and as it rolled with the waves, taking it on the beam, foam and surging water climbed the sides and battery walls, drenching decks and fanning spray from the sharp corners of the recessed gun-ports.

And yet, Dawlish told himself, she's handy, turning in three cables in these conditions, and probably tighter in quiet water, making the ram a potent weapon. Like many officers, he instinctively distrusted the tactic of deliberate collision as being potentially as dangerous to the attacker as to the enemy target. The guns, those four massive ship-killing twelve-inch cannon, would be his weapons of choice – if they could be worked, and in a sea like this he had his doubts. The firing trials tomorrow would determine the limits that breaking water on the ports would impose on the battery's ability to run out and fire.

"Advise the engine room that I'll require full revolutions in fifteen minutes," he told Zyndram. As the wind knifed icily around the scanty bridge-protection it was difficult to imagine that only three decks separated him from the tropical conditions in which stokers and trimmers must now slave to feed the furnace mouths and load the boilers almost to the point of lifting relief valves.

Dawlish walked out along the bridge wing, raising his oilskin collar, grateful for the kalpak's warmth about his head, yet relishing the feel of cold spindrift against his face, accommodating himself to the roll. So he had stood before, a thousand times and more, yet never before on a bridge that was wholly his own, never with a vessel so potent under his command, never with a challenge so daunting. It was for a moment like this that he had trained and hardened himself since childhood, as he had found himself so inadequate in explaining to Miss Morton that night at Hobart's villa. And yet for all his inarticulacy she had somehow understood, as nobody else had before. He wished for a moment she could see him now, could know that he was facing the

73

uncertainties before him with resolution, if not without fear. It should not concern him whether she would care or not – and yet it did.

A rain squall had blotted out the mountains to the south but somewhere to the east, beyond the tumbling crests of the chill Black Sea, the enemy lay, weak to impotence on water, massively powerful on land, pushing remorselessly towards the Anatolian heartland. Haluk's criminal scheming had encouraged daring Russian commanders to support Archduke Michael's drive with coastal trading craft, protected by little more than a few hastily-armed auxiliaries. Partly fed by the single-track railway sandwiched between the Caucuses and the sea along the north-eastern littoral as far as the port of Sochi, and drawing also on supplies from the larger ports further north, audaciously-managed Russian coastal shipping was the key to the merciless Russian thrusts towards Kars and Erzurum. Conventional Russian naval strength in the Black Sea might be confined to a few freakish circular ironclads built to protect the estuaries in the north – the Popovka monstrosities, which seemed seldom to leave port, and then only to the derision of foreign observers – but that relay of humble coasters represented a far more insidious threat. Without the steady stream of supplies they delivered the Russian offensive would have ground to a halt long since.

Dawlish returned to the wheelhouse. As the engines built to full revolutions. The *Mesrutiyet* burrowed into the waves ahead, rolling and pitching more furiously than before, no deck other than the roof of the battery free from running water. She wallowed deeply in the turns, waves pounding and breaking along the flank. Yet come around she did, and tightly. The log was run – eleven knots, and that with every boiler straining and both engines panting at their limits. There were coal consumption estimates available now, not wholly accurate, but enough to show that the furnaces' appetites were greater than when trials had been run in the Thames Estuary on prime Welsh anthracite. Unless the colliers Dawlish had requested from Zonguldak arrived in the next twenty-four hours further exercises – including the vital testing of the guns – would have to be postponed.

It was time now to turn again for Trabzon. A failed steam-chest packing on the port high-pressure cylinder reduced the speed to six knots. Further work would be needed before the engines could be trusted far from base.

She was not an ideal vessel, Dawlish thought as the mole slipped past two hours later, nor a stable nor dry nor comfortable one either,

74

but she was his, and for what he had in mind she would answer. And the crew would answer. They had spirit enough and victory would feed it. He was satisfied too in Zyndram, who had shown that he had a feel for ship handling that matched his obvious personal courage. Should necessity demand it, he would have little hesitation in entrusting command of the ironclad to him.

His eye caught the *Burak Reis*, now swinging at a buoy. Smoke was drifting from her funnels. His confidence in her new commander, the young Macedonian, Onursal, had not been misplaced. The gunboat was mobile again, perhaps even ready for sea, a living ship once more, and he had a second weapon in his armoury.

*

Mehmet Birinci Yüzbashi, the *Burak Reis's* former captain, was flustered and anxious to please when Dawlish was rowed across to the repair yard in late afternoon.

"They are ready for your inspection, Nicholas Kaptan," he said. His words were translated by Nedim, the eighteen-year old English-speaking mehendis that Dawlish had brought in tow. "They're afloat at the jetty, both of them, and *Number Nine* has steam raised."

Despite his undoubted activity in previous days Mehmet's uniform was neater and cleaner than when Dawlish had first met him, and there was no smell of drink. A middle-aged officer facing dishonourable discharge, as a blunt interview with Dawlish behind closed doors had made abundantly clear, he seemed to have taken the warning to heart. The task that now busied him was his last chance. He had a wife and five children, Dawlish had learned, and no source of income but the navy. He could not afford to be cashiered. He might not like his demotion from command of a gunboat to responsibility for two tiny craft, but he had no option.

"The boats are ready for your inspection, Kumandanim." If his hands were trembling slightly it was because of withdrawal, not indulgence.

"I'm pleased to hear it," Dawlish said. "Show me."

The third and fourth weapons in his armoury, twins, were small and frail by comparison even with the *Burak Reis*. Two forty-five foot steam launches lay against the jetty, craft that had rested half-forgotten in Trabzon's repair yard since they had been dropped off there from a fleet unit more than two years before. Deliberately forgotten, Dawlish

75

surmised, for their weapons might be as dangerous to their own crews as to the enemy.

Number Nine was already crewed. The seamen, as scrubbed and neat as the boat itself, snapped into a salute as Mehmet ushered Dawlish on board officiously. A few paces brought him from stem to stern but were enough to prove that the stubby half-decked craft, with the pot-boiler and twin-cylinder engine amidships, had been utterly changed from the dust-caked relic he had found abandoned four nights since. A glance showed that the other craft, *Number Seven,* had undergone a similar metamorphosis. The beamy and stoutly-built wooden hull had been sanded and varnished, the decks holystoned to a standard worthy of a Channel Fleet flagship, the boiler's insulation renewed and the brass funnel polished to mirror brightness. The engine might have been new. Whether fear or pride had driven the transformation was immaterial – Mehmet was obviously a man to get things done when he had a mind to it.

"Would my Kaptan wish a trial run?" His voice had a quaver, like that of a child expecting a rebuke.

"With great anticipation, Mehmet Birinci Yüzbashi."

Across the calm waters of the harbour the launch made perhaps eight knots maximum. It was a pitifully low speed for the duty she was designed for. Only her handiness could give some meagre degree of protection, that and the darkness in which her work should be done were it ever required.

"You have done well, and so have your men," Dawlish said. "Accept my congratulations."

A smile of relief spread over Mehmet's strained features as he inclined his head in thanks.

"Have you ever used the spar?" Dawlish asked, hesitating to share the crude weapon's full name, spar torpedo, with the graceful and deadly mechanical fish that he understood perhaps better than any officer in the Royal Navy.

"No, Nicholas Kaptan. Alas, no. Nor have I seen it used."

Only a hero – or a madman – would dare use it, would run his own unprotected wooden launch up against an enemy ship, poke an explosive charge at the end of a long pole – the spar – under its hull and explode it there. It might rupture the enemy's bottom but the attacker's chances of survival would be slim. And yet the Russians had proved months earlier that they had both madmen and heroes. Three heavily armoured Turkish gunboats now lay on the Danube's riverbed as evidence of their audacity. Had those gunboats survived the Russians could not have crossed the broad river barrier so easily and have driven so fast into Bulgaria.

"I've never used the spar either, Mehmet Yüzbashi," Dawlish said. "But we'll try it together tomorrow, with reduced charges to start. You know somewhere outside the harbour perhaps? With half-submerged rocks? We could use one as a target."

Mehmet paled but he nodded and then asked "You would indeed come also, Kumandanim?'

Dawlish would, though the idea knotted his stomach with fear. But if he was to command these men he must sound confident.

"We'll need resolute men," he said. "Men that you – and I – can rely upon. You can select me two such crews? For *Number Seven* as well?"

Mehmet nodded, half-flattered, half-fearful – as fearful perhaps as Dawlish himself of the near-suicidal weapon. And yet Mehmet was disguising his terror as best he could, and he was to be admired for it.

"Yes, Kumandanim," he said, "You can rely on me."

Either that, Dawlish thought, or else I'll find you dead-drunk and useless tomorrow morning. It's make or break, Mehmet, and the odds are so close to even that I'd bet on neither outcome.

"Tomorrow, at seven," he said. "We'll prepare the charges together. And now, if you please, carry me to the *Burak Reis*."

Dawlish jumped across to the *Burak Reis* from *Number Nine's* turtle-decked fo'castle. He acknowledged the hasty salute of the watch hurrying aft to meet him and passed the after three-inch calibre Krupp mounting towards the broad deckhouse that took up much of the vessel's length. Given the shallow draught, the greater bulk of the boilers and engine were enclosed by this unarmoured superstructure, the forward section of which enclosed all the cramped accommodation. He met Onursal, the new commander, emerging from the engine room, greasy, filthy and proud in a shapeless overall.

The inspection revealed another transformed vessel. Steam had been raised, the last leaking glands were repaired and the vessel was ready for trials. The multi-barrelled Nordenveldt had been mounted ahead of the bridge and a two-man crew had been found for it from the *Irene's* marines. When he left her Dawlish was satisfied that the *Burak Reis* was showing promise.

At last, in darkness, Dawlish was carried across the harbour's frigid waters towards the *Mesrutiyet*. There was still lamp-lit activity on her

77

decks and sides, men chipping and wire-brushing and dabbing red-lead, while others laboured aft of the battery to reinforce the main-boom and boat-hoisting gear, and to fashion the cradles on which *Number Seven* and *Number Nine* would be carried when the ironclad next went to sea.

The saloon aft smelled of coal-smoke from the stove heating it. The smashed stern-windows had been repaired and the kelims underfoot had been washed clean of the gore that had soaked them so recently. Nusret's writing desk was drawn close to the stove and was covered with papers. He looked up, sweeping off the spectacles he disliked being seen wearing. His expression told enough before he even spoke.

"Bad news?" Dawlish asked.

Nusret pushed a telegram towards him. Then, remembering Dawlish could not read it, he said: "From Mukhtar Pasha. The army commander at Erzurum. The Russians seem unstoppable – more men every day, no shortage of weapons or food or ammunition. Mukhtar fears losing communication with Kars."

"Can he be reinforced?"

Nusret shook his head. "I've nothing to reinforce him with. Only the winter can save us now." He paused, looked imploringly at Dawlish. "Or the *Mesrutiyet?*"

Dawlish confirmed what Nusret already knew. "Not enough coal for that." The colliers from Zonguldak were due imminently but transfer of their cargoes would take another day at least and in the meantime the ironclad would swing uselessly at anchor. Nusret groaned. He had banked on the *Mesrutiyet* to devastate the Russian supply lines along the Eastern Black Sea coast. But naval operations needed more than ships. Above all, in this new age of steam, they needed coal.

At that moment Dawlish knew that he must commit to the plan that had grown and matured in his mind in recent days, one he had not yet dared share with Nusret, one that would serve notice that Turkish naval power would make Russian supply by sea hazardous, maybe impossible, and force reliance on slow, tortuous and limited-capacity land routes. There were so many untried elements in the plan, so much risk ... But he thrust his doubts aside.

"There's still a chance, Nusret Pasha," he said. "Let me show you on the chart."

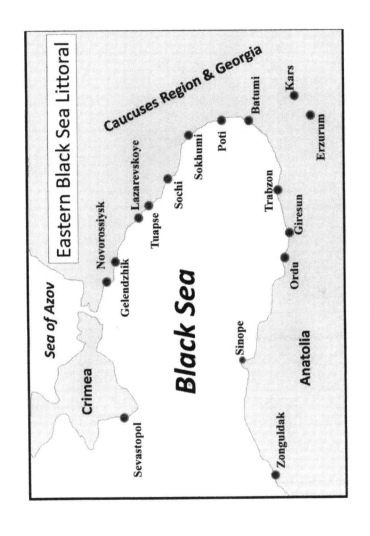

Eastern Black Sea Littoral

Caucuses Region & Georgia

Kars

Batumi

Erzurum

Sochi

Sokhumi

Poti

Lazarevskoye

Novorossiysk

Tuapse

Trabzon

Giresun

Gelendzhik

Ordu

Sea of Azov

Black Sea

Sinope

Anatolia

Crimea

Zonguldak

Sevastopol

8

The night of October 30th was overcast. Darkness and a sullen drizzle had brought visibility down to a few hundred yards when the *Burak Reis* slipped her moorings an hour after sundown and headed for the open sea. A low ceiling of rain-laden cloud blotted out the stars and forced navigation by dead reckoning.

"Does my Kaptan wish to retire?" Onursal asked as the mole slipped astern. Dawlish's presence on his bridge obviously made him nervous.

"A short rest would be welcome, after I've visited the engine room," Dawlish said, then added hastily: "With your agreement of course, Onursal Mülazim. You command this ship. But I'll be happy to stand the next watch to allow you to rest also."

"An honour, Kumandanim, an honour."

The wind had all but died over the last day and conditions were calm, comfortable for the shallow-draught gunboat as she maintained a steady eight knots on half revolutions. Her course would be northerly for two hours before turning northeast. With the reliability of the single engine proven only by one day of albeit successful trials, and with no sailing rig as reserve, Dawlish was eager to stay far offshore during the passage.

No coal had arrived, though telegrams had advised of two colliers underway, carrying twelve hundred tons between them, and a third was loading at Zonguldak. Scouring of the last stocks ashore at Trabzon had yielded enough to take the *Mesrutiyet* to sea for four hours after other needs had been satisfied. A target-raft towed by a paddle-tug had provided practice at five hundred yards for the ironclad's main armament. The gun-drill had been efficient, thanks to the efforts of the martinet gunner Selim, but only time could improve the accuracy of the shooting. Less than one shot in ten had scored a hit. And time was not available, Dawlish had told himself grimly as the vessel returned, its bunkers almost empty – in action there would be no option but to close the range to almost point blank.

But there had been a higher priority than the *Mesrutiyet* for the remaining coal. The *Burak Reis's* bunkers had been filled to capacity after her sea-trial and now, as she headed north through the rain-sodden dark, even her decks were stacked with coal. Two trimmers were staggering below with sacks on their backs as Dawlish passed aft. The deck-stored reserves must be the first consumed in the interests of stability. He stayed some minutes in the engine room – and was there invited to drink chai brewed direct from the boiler. The story of his earlier acceptance must have passed across from the *Burak's* larger sister and a ritual seemed to be establishing itself.

Afterwards Dawlish slept in Onursal's tiny cubby-hole of a cabin, exhausted from a day that had included not only the *Mesrutiyet's* trials but deployment of *Number Nine's* crude weapon as well. He had shared her crew's terror, though he could not show it, as the steam launch had been driven towards a half-submerged rock, its spar extended before it like a lance, the tin-encased explosive charge thrust four feet under the water ahead. He had seen the sweat streaming off Mehmet's face, despite the cold, as the canister had scraped on the rock and as he himself had signalled with a nod that the electric switch should be thrown. But despite his fear, Mehmet's trembling hand had pushed the switch forward, flashing a current down the cable strapped to the spar. The charge had exploded instantaneously, sending a white plume cascading skywards and a hammer blow reverberating through the wooden launch. The craft had rolled and bucked in the expanding circle of foam, and was drenched as the plume collapsed, but *Number Nine* was strongly-built and it survived. From the glances exchanged afterwards among its relieved crew Dawlish knew that the experience could never be so full of dread again. And, best of all, there was a look of triumph on Mehmet's face, of realisation that he had indeed the strength to conquer his weakness and to put his humiliation behind him. That pride, that growing confidence, would ripple out to others in the coming days. A team was being forged.

Dawlish was roused at midnight and relieved Onursal. The young officer was meticulous in his hand-over report, as if painfully aware of the weight of the confidence placed in him. The rain had ceased and broken cloud gave improved visibility across an empty sea. The course was now northeast, towards a point just north of Poti on the Georgian coast. Batumi, the last significant harbour still held by Ottoman forces, lay somewhere off the starboard bow. A determined Russian assault might have taken it weeks before had the focus not been on the more promising axis of advance further inland. Somewhere to its north – the reports of Ottoman cavalry patrols that had reconnoitred the disputed ground there were inconclusive – lay the furthest point of Russian progress along the littoral. And beyond lay Poti, the small port through which coastal shipping was supporting Archduke Michael's thrusts towards Kars and Erzurum.

81

And Michael cannot yet know, Dawlish told himself, cannot yet suspect that the *Mesrutiyet* has changed hands and is revitalised, or that this gunboat is creeping stealthily towards Poti. But if news has filtered through then ... He blocked the thought. Before action it never served to dwell on personal annihilation.

Progress was satisfactory so far – the boiler and engine were holding up. A gap in the clouds allowed a fix. Dawlish welcomed the diversion the calculation offered as he cross-checked the reckonings of the mülazim who shared the watch.

The hours passed, cold, uneventful, and yet uneasy. Here on the bridge, or among the gun-crew stamping against the chill around the forward Krupp mounting, or in the tone of the masthead lookout's regularly shouted assurances of clear horizons, Dawlish could sense the tension, the awareness that action was imminent. He felt it in himself, the suppressed anxiety that somehow he might fail in the hours ahead. He had first known that gnawing unease on the day, scant months after he had first left home, when he had crouched, a terrified thirteen-year old, in a flooded ditch in North China, waiting with Jacky Fisher for the signal that would launch them and a thousand others in a suicidal assault across the mudflats towards the Taku Forts. The aftermath still haunted the occasional nightmare, the heads impaled on stakes, eye sockets empty, remnants of hair and rotting flesh still clinging to them. But he had endured then, and had become stronger for it, though it had been a brutal coming of age. That fear that he might fail was worse than any terror of death, and it had grown, not lessened, with time. Now responsibility, total and absolute, for a ship and for her complement had lent it an even keener edge.

Then, on that gunboat's cheerless bridge, and for the hundredth time since leaving Istanbul, he remembered Miss Morton with a combination of longing and guilt. He should not have taken her hand that night at Hobart's villa, should not have perhaps aroused hopes that could never be satisfied, should not – and this was the hardest to admit – have acted with a freedom he would not have allowed himself with a woman of his own class. Yet even so, her honesty, her courage, her beauty – for he remembered how her face was transformed when she smiled – had given a glimpse of a happiness they might have shared.

What might have been ... He pushed the thought from his mind, for it was dawn at last, red fingers reaching across a grey horizon, slowly lighting a calm, bleak sea.

82

*

There were three hours more to landfall. The entire crew was roused, a full meal provided for all, the last coal-sacks manhandled below and the decks hosed clean. The armoured breastworks were hinged up around the Krupps fore and aft and locked with iron pins. Ready-use ammunition lockers were opened, weapons were loaded and the gun-crews stood to them. The cutter was swung outboard to port, the gig to starboard. A single ripple of fire guaranteed that the Nordenveldt's mechanism was clear. The dozen marines who had come across from the *Mesrutiyet* crouched under oilskins along the line of now-raised metal shields along the top of the accommodation. The clouds were closing and lowering again. Intermittent rain, soaking and dispiriting, blotted out the horizon for long minutes at a time.

It was full daylight when the lookout's call identified a sail to the north, half-obscured by the intervening drizzle.

"A brig," Onursal said, passing a telescope to Dawlish. "Becalmed, laden. She must be heading for Poti."

The black-hulled trader swam into Dawlish's circle of vision, well-weathered, perhaps three hundred tons and a hundred feet, grey sails hanging limp and sodden, four miles distant. There was no sign of either armament or escort.

Dawlish thought quickly. Another hour would see landfall just north of the Georgian port, and surprise was essential, and yet here was a prize for the taking, a source possibly of information, and certainly of profit for each member of the crew. The knowledge that every man, however humble, would share in her value might give an extra impetus in the hours ahead.

"We'll take her, Onursal Mülazim," he said quietly. "Approach her cautiously."

"Yes, Kumandanim." From his expression Dawlish saw that this was the first time Onursal had detained a vessel and that he was nervous.

"She looks harmless," Dawlish said quietly, the remembrance of a dozen boardings of slaver-dhows in the Zanzibar Channel fusing into one. "But don't assume it. Turn your Krupps on her, and the Nordenveldt too – it'll clear her decks quickly if there's resistance. The Krupps are your last resort though – that ship's worth money to you and your men."

83

Onursal nodded, relieved, as Dawlish continued. His advice reflected hard experience.

"Now, Onursal Mülazim," Dawlish finished, "you do it. This is your ship – and that's your prize."

The *Burak Reis* swung towards the becalmed merchantman, her engine now panting at maximum revolutions. She had been seen – there was movement, figures on the poop pointing, one swinging a telescope – but escape was impossible, for there was not enough wind to flap the limp sails. The range closed, under a mile now, and the Krupp bowchaser had the brig squarely in its sights. The boarding party, a marine chavush and half-dozen men, was in the gig and ready to be lowered.

Dawlish focussed his glass on the vessel's sagging white, blue and red mercantile ensign. Onursal called an order to the quartermaster and rang simultaneously for reduced revolutions. The *Burak* slowed to a crawl, pulling over and heaving-to so that she lay parallel to the brig, a cable length distant. As her bow and stern chasers slewed around the Russian ensign dropped. Two figures waved a white sheet on the poop.

The gig dropped and drew across to the brig. An entry port opened and hands reached out to pull the marines on board. A minute later Ottoman colours ran skywards.

As the *Burak* approached the brig deckhands scurried to drape fenders over her side and rapid juggling of engine and helm brought the vessels together. It was well done, Dawlish noted, and Onursal was a competent shipmaster. He had chosen him well.

The trader's crew, cowering under the threat of the marines' rifles, was plainly terrified and her captain, when he was brought across, was the most frightened of all. A portly, bearded weather-beaten man in his fifties, he looked imploringly in turn from Dawlish to Onursal and poured out a torrent of Turkish. It was impossible to think of him as an enemy. But now Dawlish knew that he must harden his heart.

"Tell him to be quiet," he said. "I want to know what ship, and where from."

"He says his name is Butakov," Onursal translated.

The Russian, hearing his name, nodded vigorously and added: "Boris Stepanovich."

"He trades grain regularly with Istanbul and Smyrna in peacetime – that's why he speaks Turkish. He has many Turkish friends."

"That's not what I asked. Tell him not to waste our time." Loathing himself for it, but knowing that this man was a source of priceless information, Dawlish loosened his holster flap – nothing more, but the Russian's eyes were fixed on it in horror.

Another exchange, then Onursal translated again. "His ship's the *Kataska*, from Odessa."

"How? Odessa has been blockaded these last six months."

"He was at sea when hostilities commenced. He's operating out of Gelendzhik now, carrying supplies for the army."

"What supplies on this voyage?"

Another consultation followed, and more fearful glances towards the opened holster.

"Flour – one hundred and twenty tons. Small-arms ammunition. And clothing – overcoats and boots."

A worthwhile haul, Dawlish thought, and likely to be sorely missed with winter drawing on.

"He's begging you to spare his ship. He owns a quarter share. It's all his family have to live on." Onursal was clearly moved. So too was Dawlish, though he knew he must not show it.

"Tell him an Ottoman prize court will decide what becomes of it," Dawlish said. "Tell him he doesn't even own his life unless we let him have it back."

Onursal, clearly troubled, translated. Butakov fell to his knees, trembling, eyes still on the exposed hilt of the revolver. Dawlish looked away, ashamed of what he was doing. Then he asked "Has he been in and out of Poti before?"

He had – five times in recent months.

"Then he'll be pleased to buy his life by piloting us in to Poti," Dawlish said. "Tell him." He wondered what he would do if Butakov refused, for the idea of physical abuse of a helpless man was repugnant to him.

But the Russian agreed, if uncomfortably, and he called on God to bless the gentleman, though he wept uncontrollably when a small prize crew was detailed to possess his ship and compel its crew sail it to Trabzon.

"Pass the word among the crew, Onursal Mülazim, that I'll make it my personal business to ensure that each man receives a fair share of the value of the prize," Dawlish said. And he thought grimly: It's the last prize we'll take today.

The gig was recovered and within minutes the *Burak Reis* was again underway, thrashing at full revolutions on an easterly course. The brig was soon lost astern in the drifting rain, waiting for the wind that would carry her into captivity.

Confronted with a chart, and comforted with a cigarette and chai in the accommodation, Captain Butakov proved informative. Poti had a guard-boat, yes, a converted pilot-boat from Novorossiysk that mounted two cannon – what size he could not say. It was a small harbour, suited only to fishing craft and light coasting schooners. Larger craft, even his own *Kataska*, offloaded into lighters outside, and days could be lost if sea conditions were poor. And yes, there were stores ashore, from which convoys of army wagons and pack-animals carried supplies inland to the Russian armies. Shore batteries? He hadn't noticed, he had been too concerned with offloading quickly in the exposed roads and getting to sea again.

If there are guns there, you're damned if you're telling us, Dawlish thought as he detected the cunning glint beneath the Russian's helpful demeanour. He respected him for it.

The shoreline emerged like a thin, dark streak on the horizon that took on definition as it grew closer. Butakov, now brought to the bridge, confirmed that they had arrived some five miles north of Poti. The *Burak Reis* swung to starboard and crept east of south, parallel to the coast, two miles offshore, once more at half-revolutions. Drifting rain reduced visibility and it was fifteen minutes before the outlines of a small town and a cluster of masts became apparent.

Dawlish's telescope revealed the accuracy of the Russian captain's description. Square buildings, once white, were now sodden grey. A stone jetty curved round from the north to shelter the harbour from winter gales blasting down from the Crimea. Half a dozen schooners and small sailing craft were moored there, and moving figures were active in their unloading. South of the town was a clump of brown and dark grey that resolved itself into scattered tents, large ones, and mounds of crates, some covered with tarpaulins.

But the most immediate quarry lay in the roads outside the harbour. Two steamers were anchored in the drizzle-pocked calm, each single-funnelled and with auxiliary sailing rigs on two masts, thousand or twelve-hundred tonners. Two barges were secured alongside one, a single barge by the other, all heaped with cargo and fed by the ships' own derricks. Another lighter, laden with a truncated pyramid of brown sacks, was being towed slowly towards the harbour by a tiny, straining tug. A sailing brig, a near-twin of the prize just taken, lay at anchor beyond, waiting for her turn to offload.

"There, Kumandanim, the guardship." Onursal's pointing finger identified the first target, a vessel that might have been a diminutive steam yacht with clipper bow and raked buff stack a mile distant, swinging towards them from her station seawards of the roads. A plume of steam and a long blast emanating from her siren signalled that she had detected the intruder and that every eye in the harbour and on the ships outside it would be drawn seawards. A flurry of activity in her bows indicated a weapon being prepared for action.

"Sink her first, Onursal Mülazim," Dawlish said quietly. "Then the transports."

It was time to blood the wolf.

9

The Russian guardship was a thousand yards distant and the range was closing.

Onursal snapped orders and the quartermaster swung the helm. Then he was shouting by hailing trumpet to the Krupp crew forward. His orders also had the Nordenveldt's oilskin covers stripped away. The marine manning it was adjusting his sights and his loader was checking that its vertical feed-tracks were fully charged.

The *Burak Reis* lunged to port in a wide, smooth sweep, speed eight knots, rock steady in the calm waters, broadside-on to the advancing Russian.

A sharp report and a puff of smoke from the guardship told of a three-pounder, a pitiful counter to the wrath bearing down on her. A tiny fountain rose fifty yards off the *Burak's* port bow but the Krupp's muzzle was edging across, the layer's eye glued to his backsight as he spun the brass traverse wheel. Still the Russian came on, driven forward by some desperate hero, ramming now her forlorn hope.

"Atesh!"

The Krupp barked and its foul yellow discharge obscured its target. Already the breech was swinging open for sponging and the loading numbers were standing poised with the next bursting-shell and separate powder charge. As the smoke wreaths drifted clear of the *Burak's* bridge Dawlish heard a dull explosion and saw black billows, shot with flame, rolling upwards from the guardship. She lurched drunkenly to port, her flank exposed, her forward superstructure shattered and burning. Dazed men stumbled on deck. Dawlish knew he could afford no pity.

87

"Nordenveldt!" Onursal called, directing the gunner to rake the deck.

The gunner rocked the crank of the five-barrelled weapon, each forward motion feeding and firing, each return ejecting empty, smoking cartridges. The heavy rounds lashed the Russian, scything bodies and splintering woodwork. And the Krupp was ready to fire again.

"Atesh!"

Another shell slammed into the dying guardship, gouging into the side beneath the funnel before erupting there. An instant later the dull "whumf" of the boiler's rupture tore the hull apart. The vessel rolled over as men flung themselves overboard, and its back broke. The bow disappeared immediately and the upturned stern submerged to the stilled propeller and jutting rudder. A score of men struggled in the water, as the *Burak* steamed past, turning now towards the merchant steamers.

One was getting underway. The barges alongside had been cast adrift and the anchor struck free. The vessel was moving slowly seawards. Smoke vomiting from the stack indicated frantic efforts to build up steam pressure. She was moving at little over two knots as the *Burak* pulled on to a parallel course, revolutions minimised, at a cable's separation.

Both Krupps blasted, their shells tearing jagged holes at the waterline. The steamer began to list. A boat was being lowered amidships, and men were dropping into it, others throwing themselves into the sea as she rolled further. All forward way had been lost and steam blasted from a relief pipe at the funnel.

"Leave her," Dawlish said. "She's finished."

The gunboat headed for the remaining steamer in a wide, slewing turn, again at half-revolutions. The steamer was high in the water – the unloading must have been almost complete – and she was still firmly anchored. Her two boats were heading shorewards, laden with crew and stevedores from the barge still secured alongside.

"One shot should do it, Onursal Mülazim," Dawlish said.

The *Burak Reis* slowed. The range was two hundred yards, close enough for the forward Krupp to place a shell in the hull directly below the funnel. For one instant Dawlish saw the neat circular black hole that was punched in the rust-streaked flank, then orange flame came jetting back through it as the shell exploded within. Hull plating heaved, rivets sheared and fissures opened. A second later the wooden deck above splintered and rose as the boiler burst. Steam and flames

88

gushed from the chasm it tore and the thin funnel whipped and toppled. The gunboat surged ahead, saving itself from the falling debris and from the glowing coals scattering like tiny meteors from the wrecked furnace. A fire was taking hold, blazing brightest in the remains of the midships deckhouse and licking forward and aft.

Onursal circled the gunboat around the burning steamer to bring the laden wooden barge on the other side under fire. One end was stacked with jute sacks, the other with barrels. A shell at the waterline did for it, disintegrating the structure and dumping the cargo in the water in a cloud of flour from splitting sacks.

The *Burak* headed now for the remaining victim in the roads, the anchored brig, from which the last boat was pulling hastily away. A feathery plume of water suddenly rose some hundred yards to port. The boom of the artillery piece ashore that had caused it came reverberating across the intervening water. Then another plume was rising, also short, and astern.

"Field-guns," Dawlish said, "light, but they'll be troublesome as we move inshore. Get another man aloft with the lookout. We need to locate them"

They must be standard Russian weapons, he thought, probably nine-pounders. The rating was deceptive, a convention based on the weight of spherical ball for the weapon's calibre. But those pieces would be throwing elongated, conical-nosed, explosive shells, twenty-four pounds each, well capable of wreaking devastation on the *Burak*.

He scanned the town and the open ground to the south. For an instant he saw the bright stabbing tongue of a muzzle flash from what looked like an earthen redoubt. It was instantly obscured by a puff of greyish smoke as another Russian shell sped on its way. The lookouts saw it also, crying out as the weapon's report reached them. The projectile fell short and then came another report, and another, and a fourth in quick succession, equally harmless for now. Cries from the *Burak's* lookouts confirmed that they had located the other redoubts that sheltered the guns along the shoreline.

But Dawlish's attention was distracted by Butakov, the Russian captain, who was grabbing Onursal by the arm, yelling in near-panic and gesticulating towards the brig, now only a cable distant. A seaman moved to drag him away but Onursal waved him off, snatched up the hailing trumpet and yelled to the Krupp crew forward. The gunners jumped back from their piece, bewildered by the instruction to hold

89

fire. Then Onursal snapped an order to the quartermaster and the helm was flung over into a tight starboard turn seawards.

"What ..." Dawlish began, exasperated by his linguistic incapacity.

"It's loaded with powder and shells." Onursal interrupted, clearly shaken, normal deference forgotten. "Butakov knows the ship. He saw it loading at Novorossiysk."

The Russian captain was nodding violently, guessing the import of words he could not understand, then blurting out a further torrent of Turkish.

"What's he saying?" Dawlish was impatient – Butakov was obviously frightened.

"He thinks it carries about a hundred and fifty tons of powder, and over three hundred crates of shells. If we fire on it, and we're too close, it will take us with it."

"Will it, by God?" Dawlish said. Suddenly, as if from nowhere, an idea dawned – difficult, but potentially devastating. "Then we'll leave her for now, Onursal Mülazim. We've targets enough ashore."

Onursal was looking at him in surprise.

"Stand off the harbour entrance," Dawlish said, his mind racing, "but stay outside the shore batteries' range. And have the cutter manned – put all the marines in – and ready for lowering. But hold your fire for now – I'm going aloft."

He stuffed his telescope into the front of his tunic, then hauled himself up the rungs set into the mast to the tiny platform where the two lookouts perched. They reached for him, shifting to accommodate him, half-awed, half-delighted by his presence.

"Top, Kumandanim, top," one said, pointing, his hand sweeping along the shoreline, "top, top."

Dawlish remembered that *top* in Turkish meant cannon. Then, guided by the seaman, he picked out the four earthworks of the shore battery, a hundred yards separating each from its fellow. The weapons they sheltered had fallen silent, the gunners realising perhaps the improbability of hitting a vessel moving at eight knots across their front, and holding their fire until she should advance closer.

He swung his telescope towards the jetty. There were men there, soldiers in shabby brown greatcoats crouching behind offloaded cargo, and more were doubling forward along it from the town behind, rifles in hand. Six, seven wooden sailing craft were moored against it, and three smaller vessels secured outside them in turn. Drifting slightly to the north were the two barges cast off by the first steamer to be

90

attacked. But Dawlish was seeking the sack-laden barge he had seen under tow by a tiny tug – and there it was, grounded a hundred yards from shore, abandoned by the tug he now searched for. He ran his glass along the waterfront and found the squat tugboat nudging against the harbour wall, close to the intersection with the jetty. Smoke still drifted from its spindly funnel but it seemed deserted.

He needed that tug, and only the marines could get it for him.

Rifle-fire crackled from the jetty – uselessly, at this range of a thousand yards – and the guns of the shore-battery were twice as far distant. The *Burak Reis* was all but invulnerable as she crawled forward on minimum revolutions. Dawlish glanced down to see Onursal's upturned face.

"The jetty and the vessels there, Onursal Mülazim," he called down, pointing. "Ten rounds from each weapon if you please. And I wish to speak to Bülent Chavush."

He was down on the bridge again as the forward Krupp opened, followed immediately by the smaller weapon aft. The shells fell among the crowded sailing vessels, throwing down masts in thrashing tangles of rigging, flinging up sundered timbers. The Krupps lashed out again, and again, and again, the three-inch firing slightly faster, three rounds to her larger sister's two, raining devastation on the helpless craft and on the troops on the jetty behind them.

Choking gunsmoke wreathed the *Burak Reis*. Through it an inferno could be seen erupting along the jetty – flashes of exploding shells, flames leaping from shattered hulls, masts toppling over, troops fleeing in retreat, rolling black clouds shot through with orange.

There was a break in the firing as the gunboat came about so as to cruise slowly on an opposite course. Forward and aft the Krupps trained around to bear again on the stricken vessels. Already the harbour and jetty were like some vision of hell, flames and smoke and destruction beneath a weeping sky, ash and cinders drifting down on the debris strewing the rain-pocked waters. The Russian guns ashore could only spit futile defiance that threw up harmless waterspouts short of the author of this misery.

The marine chavush, Bülent, stood stiffly to attention on the bridge, hard and muscular, one of the first to have swarmed up on to the *Mesrutiyet* from the *Irene*. Onursal translated.

"You see that tugboat?" Dawlish pointed out the small vessel and handed the telescope to Bülent. "I want it. Take your men in the cutter – we'll cover your approach."

The chavush scrutinised the tug intently before snapping to attention again. He had a question.

"He asks if he can have assistance, somebody from the engine room. He says he'll take the tug, Ins'Allah, but he's not sure he can bring it back. He needs somebody who understands engines."

Dawlish turned to Onursal. "You know your men. Who do you recommend?"

"Sinan Chavush – engineer's mate. A good man."

"Send for him."

The Krupps were barking again as the bemused Sinan was hustled to the bridge, a greatcoat flung over his sweat-soaked overalls. After a hurried explanation he was bundled into the cutter with Bülent and his marines. They had cast off their oilskins and the rain soaked their blue uniforms to sodden black as they crouched between the seamen who would pull the boat to shore.

The cutter dropped to the water. Its course would take it past the blazing wrecks strung along the jetty, directly towards the harbour's inner wall. An open strip, littered with piled cargo, separated the quayside from the row of buildings beyond. There would be defenders there, Dawlish realised, men who had fallen back from the shambles on the jetty to take shelter in those solid structures. They could lash the cutter with rifle-fire until it gained the quay's shelter. And further southwards, four-hundred yards from the forlorn tug-boat, and most deadly of all, was the first of the Russian nine-pounders.

"We need to shift fire now," Dawlish told Onursal. "That nearest field-gun – you see it? Engage it with the bowchaser. And there – between those buildings, there and there, you see those men? Five rounds of the three-inch."

The Krupps swung round on their new targets and elevations were raised - none too soon, for a white column of spray rising suddenly off the cutter's starboard bow told of the nearest Russian field-gun changing aim. Still the oars rose and fell with regularity, urging the cutter towards the tug. It was level now with the first of the burning vessels, and half-obscured by drifting smoke.

The forward Krupp fired. Seconds later there was a flash and a rising column of smoke far beyond the first field-gun emplacement. The three-inch Krupp sent her next shell to tear a jagged gap in the wall of a building directly in line with the cutter's dogged advance. As the *Burak's* guncrews sponged and reloaded, small-arms fire crackled from the shore and the Russian field-gun sent a shell close enough to drench the cutter's occupants and urge them to yet more furious rowing. Dawlish had the cutter fixed in his glass and could discern water spurting in tiny fountains as rifle-fire lashed it. A rower suddenly jerked back, his oar dropping. A marine dragged him away and took his place.

The *Burak's* forward six-inch blasted again. Its range was over-corrected for it flung up a muddy geyser in the shallows just ahead of the field-gun's earthwork. Already the Krupp gunner was raising the barrel a fraction.

The forward Krupp's corrected aim might have been perfect – or just lucky. Screaming on its low trajectory, its shell tore through the embrasure behind which the field-gun hid. A flame-shot volcano blasted upwards and outwards, carrying fragments of the gun-mounting and rent bodies in a rolling cloud of smoke and earth. As the debris fell, another explosion, more powerful still, erupted within the redoubt as stored munitions detonated.

All the while the *Burak's* after three-inch was pounding the buildings on the quayside. Round after round breached walls and collapsed the cover from which the Russian defenders still attempted to keep the nearing cutter under fire. A house was ablaze and figures flitted from it, some dragging wounded companions.

Dawlish swept his glance across the harbour. A single raging conflagration was devouring the shipping at the jetty. The quayside shook under the gunboat's bombardment, for her forward weapon had now shifted aim and was adding its fury to that of its sister aft. The cutter was still stroking towards the forsaken tug, safe now from the nine-pounder. The earthwork that had sheltered it was lost beneath a rolling pall of smoke, and the three other field-guns in the positions to the south had not the range to do more than hurl an occasional ineffectual shell in the general direction of the *Burak*.

The rifle-crackle died. The cutter had reached the lee of the quay, sheltered from the few heroic Russians still holding the shattered buildings. As it drew alongside the tug, marines leapt across, pulling the engineer's mate, with them. He disappeared below with two of them, while others made ready to cast free. Two long minutes passed while the gunboat hurled further destruction to deter any sally from the rubble-strewn quayside. Then Bülent was waving his fez on the muzzle of his rifle, signalling success. The Russian crew had bolted ashore without incapacitating the tug. Black smoke vomited from its funnel as

93

fresh coal was piled in her furnace and minutes later she pulled away from the harbour-wall, the cutter in tow, heading seawards. A few last rifle-shots followed her as she emerged again into the sight of the defenders ashore but they quickly fell silent.

"Cease firing for now," Dawlish said. "Recover the cutter – and I believe there's a wounded man to be seen to."

"And the tug, Kumandanim?" Onursal had accepted unquestioningly that Dawlish wanted the craft but was still unaware of why.

Dawlish pointed southwards towards the moored brig. An expression of admiration – and horror – spread over Onursal's face as comprehension dawned.

"Dangerous, Kumandanim, very dangerous," he said. "But wonderful!"

The gunboat hove to and the tug pulled alongside. Bülent snapped Dawlish a smart salute from the tiny steering platform.

"I want to speak to the Russian captain," Dawlish said as the wounded seaman was hauled up from the cutter. He was semi-conscious, his torso blood-soaked, his face the colour of paper. There could be little help for him in the coming hours. Dawlish felt the despair of impotence that always overcame him when confronted with injury but, as so often before, he shut himself off from it by turning brutally to the matter in hand.

Captain Butakov had been on the *Burak's* bridge throughout the action. He looked pale as he was prodded towards Dawlish.

"He knows the harbour and its approach. Ask him how close into it the brig can be manoeuvred."

Onursal translated, then repeated the question more angrily, as the Russian started to argue. Finally he said: "Around level with the end of the jetty. But he isn't sure."

"Will he be sure if he's on the tug? If he pilots it in?"

The Russian was terrified when asked, shaking his head, stamping, shouting and at last pleading.

"He won't do it, Kumandanim. He's afraid for his life."

"He'll be more afraid if he refuses," Dawlish said, putting his hand on his pistol butt. "Tell him Bülent Chavush will have my authority to put a bullet in his skull if the brig grounds one yard short of the centre of the harbour. Now get him across."

Captain Butakov, pale and shaking, was hustled over to the tug. Shouted instructions from Onursal relayed Dawlish's orders to Bülent

94

and to the engineer's mate who had joined him on the tug's steering platform. If they were daunted by the hazard now before them they did not show it –

the elation of snatching the tug successfully still buoyed their spirits. And *Evet*, Yes, Sinan the engineer called back, it was a powerful little vessel, strong enough, Ins'Allah, to pull that brig to Trabzon itself if Kumandanim wished it.

The tug chugged away purposefully across the rain-swept, smoke-shrouded waters towards the munitions-laden brig, skirting the drifting wreckage to which a few survivors of the earlier sinkings still clung miserably. Dawlish directed his glass towards them. Faces numbed with cold, exhaustion and despair swam into focus, some draped inertly across floating timbers, others trying desperately to support a comrade – as he himself had once been supported in waters far from here. His heart went out to them.

"No need to hoist the cutter just yet, Onursal Mülazim," he said, pointing to the flotsam. "It can pick up those men."

"God will bless you for this, Kumandanim," Onursal said. He bellowed orders and the cutter moved away.

There was time aplenty now to wreak havoc on the supply dumps south of the town. There were lines of grey tents and stacks of crates and barrels and mounds of sacks, all awaiting transportation southwards to feed Archduke Michael's insatiable and victory-flushed armies. Panic reigned there – horses and men and wagons frantically manoeuvring among the piles, some already laden and hastening towards the track leading inland, many snarled in hopeless confusion as bottlenecks developed, others furiously loading. The three remaining field-guns were firing again, hopelessly, incapable of doing more than raising futile plumes of spray five hundred yards short of the *Burak*.

"A splendid target, Onursal Mülazim," Dawlish said. "You have the range advantage."

The *Burak* commenced a series of slow sweeps parallel to the coast, raining shells on the supply dumps. The gunners were close to exhaustion but neither that, nor the drizzling rain that chilled them, deprived them of a savage joy that burst into cheers as the fall of round after round was marked by rising columns of flame and smoke. Onursal went aloft on the mast's observation platform, calling new targets and reporting mounting devastation.

Dawlish swung his telescope away from the burning shoreline. The tug had reached the brig and was secured to her bows. Several

95

marines had boarded and were cutting the anchor-cable and readying the tow. Five minutes more and she would be underway. Closer by, the cutter was moving cautiously through the debris that remained of the sunken guardship, hauling survivors from the water, dropping back others who had already lost to the cold.

It was time now for the bombardment to slacken, to rest the exhausted crews, to cool the Krupps' over-heated barrels, to leave the stricken port to suffer under its pall of drifting ash and smoke while its final devastation was readied. The *Burak's* cook moved between the gunners with a bucket of water, and tired men slurped gratefully from tin-cups while deckhands manhandled shells and charges from the magazines to replenish the ready-use lockers.

The brig was crawling forward now at the end of the tugboat's straining cable. The two linked vessels were moving parallel to the shoreline, a terrified Captain Butakov standing by Bülent Chavush at the tug's helm, a Martini-Peabody muzzle jammed under his right ear by a marine private.

The *Burak Reis* lay a thousand yards off the end of the jetty. The blaze there was dying down, most of the craft secured there burned down almost to the waterline. Beyond, the harbour-front's shattered buildings previously raked by the gunboat might shelter defenders who had been emboldened to return there.

"Covering fire if you please, as the tug goes in," Dawlish told Onursal. "Both weapons."

Both tug and brig were now starting to pull over towards the centre of the harbour, slowly, ever so slowly, the tow cable bar-tight as the small vessel's engine panted at maximum power. Butakov was pointing, directing the manoeuvre, despairingly resigned to the role of pilot. A single rifle-shot echoed from the harbour-front, then another and another, presaging a ragged volley focussed on the exposed figures on the tug's steering platform.

The *Burak's* bowchaser hammered a shell into an already shattered facade that might have sheltered Russian infantry, bringing it down in a torrent of masonry. Yet in the brief interval that followed before the *Burak's* after three-inch also fired there still came the staccato crackle of rifles. Dawlish saw a figure on the tug stagger and fall beside the helm. It was Butakov, he was sure of it, though the tug was now partly obscured by the brig's bulk. The vessel was still inching forward, dragged by her straining captor.

Two more shells gouged into the wrecked buildings, silencing the remnants of opposition. The towed brig was close to the harbour's centre, well within the jetty's extremity, when suddenly a shudder ran through her hull and up both masts so that rigging strummed and yards jerked. Her keel had touched bottom, stranding the munitions-packed vessel less than a cable from the quayside, placing a vast unexploded mine directly before the town.

"Cease firing! Stand out to sea, low revolutions!"

The *Burak Reis* crept slowly westwards, trailed by the tug that came bustling in her wake, rapid now that her tow had been slipped. Bülent was still at her helm but marines were lugging down from her steering platform the bodies of the Russian captain and of the marine who had menaced him, prisoner and guard struck down together by the last defiant volley from shore.

When the gunboat hove to at a distance of two and a half thousand yards offshore, still within range for the six-inch Krupp, Dawlish climbed to the observation platform. His telescope confirmed continuing chaos at the burning supply dumps and showed dark columns, women and children as well as men, streaming inland and northwards on foot, with donkeys or on carts. Even at this distance he could sense their panic. The message that a ship loaded with munitions had been grounded in the middle of the harbour must have spread like wildfire. A quarter-hour's grace could be allowed.

The cutter was hoisted aboard and the eight shivering Russian seamen it had lifted from the water were brought, not untenderly, to warm up in the boiler room. Dawlish guessed that there would be hot chai there for them, and rough kindness. The tug drew alongside, the marines transferring, the passage across of the two corpses dampening the welcome. The chavush and the engineer's mate came beaming to the bridge, exhausted but elated. Dawlish felt a surge of respect for them. Tongue and creed and nationality might be different but they were from the same mould as the simple, unappreciated men he had seen so often achieve the impossible in his own Royal Navy. He spoke words of thanks, feeling awkward using the term "Evlatlarim" – My Sons – to men older than himself, though neither of them found it strange. He kissed them on the cheeks as he knew would be valued.

"The marine who died. What was his name?" he asked.

"Mustafa. From Simi. A brave man, Kumandanim. The son of a fisherman," Bülent said. "And the Russian – he was brave in his way and a good man, though a Christian. But God is merciful."

97

But Dawlish himself could afford no mercy.

"The brig, Onursal Mülazim," he said. "The six-inch can hit her from here?'

"Evet, Kumandanim. Bursting shell?"

"Bursting shell. Send all men below who are not essential on deck."

"And the tug?"

"Have Sinan Chavush screw down the boiler's safety valve, stoke the furnace and cast it adrift."

The gunboat edged forward when the engineer's mate returned, leaving the tug abandoned astern. Further inshore, half-obscured by the smoke drifting from the dying and dead vessels along the jetty, the doomed brig lay motionless in the ash-scummed water, like a condemned prisoner numbly awaiting execution. There was no sign of movement among the tumbled buildings and gutted warehouses beyond her. The columns of fugitives seemed to have cleared the outskirts of the town and the burning supply-dumps seemed similarly deserted.

"Steam up?" Dawlish asked. "Ready for maximum revolutions?"

"Ready, Kumandanim."

"Then fire and continue firing until a hit is scored."

Dawlish strolled to the bridge wing, deliberately nonchalant. He lit a cigar, hoping his fear did not show, for he had no idea how the explosive-stuffed brig might behave when hit. But if Onursal as commander, or the helmsman, could not leave the bridge, then neither could he.

The forward Krupp belched flame. Seconds later a plume climbed from the grey waters just short of the brig. The next shell fell just aft of the brig's mainmast, its impact marked by flying timbers in the instant before it exploded. The mast whipped, stays parting and lashing, and began to topple, crashing over the port side.

The six-inch barked again. Its shell buried itself somewhere in the vitals of the vessel before detonating, punching deck planking up from below and hurling it skywards. Smoke wafted among the wreckage, not just the dispersing fumes of the shell's eruption but now also the first wisps of burning wood.

It was time to leave, Dawlish gestured to Onursal. His relief all too plain, he reached for the telegraph and rang for full revolutions. The screw bit and the *Burak Reis* turned westwards, rushing from the hell brewing astern.

The brig was ablaze now, flames washing across the deck and licking up the foremast's standing rigging. Horrified, yet fascinated, Dawlish's gaze was locked on it, knowing the end could be only seconds away. Then the first eruptions came, sharp reports of shells exploding, one by one initially, then rising to a staccato that became a single crash as great rents appeared in the sides and fire jetted from them. Yet still the tortured wooden carcass somehow held, and contained the furnace within, until the inferno reached the main powder stores. Then the hull seemed to lift itself above the surface before bursting asunder to release an expanding sphere of incandescent light.

Dawlish felt its scorching breath though he threw up his arm to shield his face as it lashed past the hastening gunboat, its force dispersing. When he looked again he saw that what had been left of the burning shipping was gone and the jetty itself was scoured clean as a marble table-top. Buildings along the harbour-front that had survived the earlier bombardment were devastated now and fires were raging there, and further into the town. The Russian forward supply depot had been devastated.

The burning shore was lost in the drizzle astern. This, Dawlish told himself with grim satisfaction, was only the start. The wolf would find even fatter prey further north.

10

Captain Butakov's canvas-shrouded body lay at Dawlish's feet on the quarterdeck. The greater part of the crew was drawn to attention before him. The *Burak Reis* was too small to carry an imam, but Sinan, the engineer's mate, who was apparently known for his piety, was crying out verses from the Koran. He was standing over the flag-draped corpses of the marine who had died by the Russian's side and of the seaman who had been shot in the cutter and who had bloodily coughed his last scarcely an hour since.

"They must be buried before sundown," Onursal had explained. "That is our way."

It was bitterly cold and a strong breeze carried odd lashes of sleet from the leaden sky and raised white horses on the growing waves. Some of the men were shivering, from weariness as much as cold, the pitiful remains before them a reminder of their own mortality and of the price of glory.

99

Sinan's prayers ended. Onursal called an order. Amid a chorus of muttered farewells and the smothered weeping of one of the marines, the planks on which the two Turkish bodies rested were raised and the weighted bundles shot overboard and disappeared, humble victims of Great Power rivalry who would soon be forgotten by all but their families.

Now it was the turn of the Russian. Dawlish felt regret, and more, as he remembered how he had used this decent seaman so remorselessly and concentrated on recalling as much he could of the Service for the Dead.

The seamen were rigidly at attention again. Dawlish recognised curiosity as well as sympathy as they watched one Christian prepare to consign another, officially his enemy, to the depths below. Head bared, he began to speak loudly in English, calling on God to take unto himself the soul of his dear brother Boris Stepanovich even as his body was committed to the deep. Doubt had weakened Dawlish's faith years before, yet there was comfort of a sort in fraternal recognition of the dead man. He silently vowed to return somehow the pathetic wallet found in the captain's pocket to the matronly, kindly-looking woman smiling shyly in the creased sepia photograph it contained. With it were a small, garishly coloured, lithograph of an icon, what looked like a house address and a hundred and sixty roubles. She might well need them badly. All too soon she would know that her modest happiness was at an end and perhaps even that she was reduced to penury. Dawlish came to the end of his prayer and nodded to the seamen by the plank. Butakov's remains slid into the foaming rush alongside.

The men were dismissed. "See to it that they have hot coffee," Dawlish told Onursal. "A tot of brandy too for any who won't be offended by it." He had brought several bottles aboard for the purpose, knowing how welcome the grog ration was to seamen he was more familiar with.

"Evet, Kumandanim. They will be thankful."

Dawlish passed through the ship later, offering a word of general appreciation here, of individual thanks there. Tired as they were, he sensed new confidence among men whose self-respect had been rotted by the months of inactivity Haluk had imposed upon them. There was no need now to resort to the trick of identifying for commendation individuals whose previous exploits Hobart had mentioned. His praise was sincere. He felt something else stirring in himself for the first time

– gratitude that he had the chance to wear the same uniform as these men.

The weather deteriorated quickly through the short winter afternoon as the *Burak Reis* pushed southwards. As darkness fell she was pitching and rolling badly in vicious seas driven by a rising northerly gale. The gunboat's shallow draught made her not only lively but wet also, increasing the exhausted crew's discomfort. The night watches, one of which Dawlish insisted on standing, were miserable. A leaking steam gland in the engine-room was a nagging worry, for losing power of the single engine in these conditions could be disastrous. The leak was somehow contained, allowing the gunboat to batter and wallow ahead at half-revolutions. Even so, Batumi, the most northerly harbour still held by Ottoman power, was off the port bow shortly after midnight. The *Burak* turned into the wind to endure an uncomfortable and interminable wait until daylight permitted safe entry.

"She's been in action!" Onursal said as they at last followed the guardship, a wooden gunboat, into the harbour. He gestured towards the buoy-moored ironclad before them.

Scorch and blast marks showed rusty brown around the *Alemdar's* starboard battery. The armour plating surrounding the recessed forward gun port had been half-wrenched from position and the bulwark and decking above it were twisted and humped. The cowls, vents and davits there jutted at crazy angles, and the bridge wing had collapsed, its supports buckled.

"It'll be worse within, depend upon it," Dawlish said, unwillingly accepting the evidence of disaster. The small brig-rigged ironclad had taken serious punishment, and not, he already suspected, from any enemy.

A lighter with a shearlegs was secured alongside and three score men were labouring in the driving rain to clear the wreckage. Others were replacing snapped stays to rebrace the foremast. Yet a wisp of funnel-smoke confirmed that the ship still lived.

"Lower the gig," Dawlish said, "I'm going across."

As he was rowed over he feared what he would find. He had counted on the *Alemdar's* single deck-mounted eight-inch and on her battery's four six-inch muzzle-loading rifles to complement the *Mesrutiyet's* heavier armament. Six months earlier, before the Eastern Squadron's other ironclads had been withdrawn to support the blockades of Odessa and the Crimea, the *Alemdar* had done well in the attack on the port of Sokhumi which had resulted in its brief occupation by an Ottoman force. But now, as the ironclad loomed closer, her damage looked even worse and despite the rain Dawlish caught the unmistakable stench of burned flesh.

The *Alemdar's* Hassan Kaptan, with his upturned moustache and his superbly tailored uniform, might have been jaunty, dapper and vain at a normal time. Now grime and sweat, slumped shoulders and black-ringed eyes told of exhaustion and disappointment. He welcomed Dawlish wearily – a coded telegram from Nusret at Trabzon had warned him to expect the *Burak Reis* – and then pointed to the debris above the battery.

"A burst gun," he said, "Yesterday. At sea." His English was halting but clear. He was another Ottoman officer who had been to Britain at some stage to take delivery of a warship.

"Exercises?" Dawlish asked. Nusret's threats had indeed worked – the *Alemdar* had been brought to readiness for sea within the week, though the cost had been high.

"Exercises. The sixth shot." Then Hassan added unnecessarily: "A weak barrel."

"Casualties?"

He looked puzzled.

"Dead? Injured?"

"Twenty-one dead. Eight burned, badly. Ins'Allah, they will not live. It would be better for them."

Dawlish recoiled inwardly at the image. "Bring me below," he said. "I must see."

The battery was smaller, lower and more congested than the *Mesrutiyet's*. The smell of extinguished fire and charred flesh was overwhelming. Dawlish choked back nausea. Much of the white-painted interior was blistered by flame and the deck was ankle-deep in ashy sludge. The failed six-inch cannon's ruptured barrel had torn itself from its mounting and had lashed across the ship to impact against its fellow on the port side. It lay jammed across the other weapon and Dawlish turned his gaze quickly from mangled human fragments and torn clothing smeared and draped beneath. He looked upwards – the initial force of the detonation and impact of the barrel had been vertical, which explained the buckled deck and external damage.

"There were other explosions?"

"One. Powder charges."

102

That eruption had blasted part of the mounting against the frame of the gunport, dislodging armour that had been designed to withstand impacts from without, not within, and had ignited hammocks and mess tables stacked nearby. It must have been like Hell in here. The only mercy was that the trapdoors to the magazines had been closed.

"You got the fire under control, Hassan Kaptan?"

"With God's help. And the steam-pump was working. We flooded the battery."

Hassan had got the stricken ship back to port, and already had repairs underway. Not a great victory, but at least a greater loss avoided and it showed competence and indomitability. Hassan's inaction during Haluk's domination of Trabzon had shown him to be self-servingly cautious but he could hardly be blamed for a casting fault by a British cannon-foundry years before. The two remaining battery weapons, at the mountings aft, port and starboard, were scorched but otherwise undamaged. And there was one other weapon, capable of bearing on either beam from its pivot mounting abaft the funnel.

"The eight-inch? The gun on deck?" Dawlish asked. "Is it serviceable?"

Hassan nodded. "Yesterday we fired it – before the accident – three times."

It was some consolation, yet the *Alemdar* was still handicapped badly and left without any weapon that could bear ahead. It would be days, maybe longer, before she was ready for sea again, longer still before the crew had been exercised to a level they could be trusted in action. The cannon-burst, and the loss of comrades, would have had a shattering effect on morale that only relentless exercising could expunge.

Dawlish's mind raced. Without the *Alemdar's* support, he could not immediately follow up the devastation at Poti with blockading action further north, even when the *Mesrutiyet* arrived. Intercepting every Russian brig and schooner slipping down the coast will be impossible with the ships available. And yet the Russian commanders facing winter snows in the mountains to the southeast must even now be learning of the threat to their supply lines, fearing that it would grow. Their fears must be stoked.

Maintain momentum, a small internal voice told him. Strike hard again, that voice said – and it might have been the voice of Topcliffe, or the voice of Hobart, ruthless men who knew that offense, even from weakness, was almost invariably the best option. Strike where

103

surprise will be absolute and risk least, that voice urged, seek out a point of vulnerability and strike savagely there. The Russian thrusts towards Kars and Erzurum can best be menaced hundreds of miles to their rear. Archduke Michael must be made to face a winter in which his infantry would freeze in summer uniforms and broken boots and starve on reduced rations. Just find the point to deprive him most mercilessly of food, clothing and munitions.

His mind searching for possibilities, Dawlish left the *Alemdar's* battery's foul interior and its stench of death, thankful even for the icy blast that greeted him on deck. "I need a chart, Hassan Kaptan," he said. "A very detailed chart."

*

Dawlish warmed himself before an inadequate stove as the telegraph chattered in the background. Two trusted clerks were laboriously decoding the material already received and he resisted the temptation to ask Onursal to provide a word-by-word translation. Better to wait for complete, coherent messages. From this office in the Town Governor's headquarters he could see across the wind-lashed harbour towards the raging waves of the open sea. A day later and the *Burak Reis's* exploit at Poti would have been impossible. He had been lucky there and it would be unwise to count on such favourable weather again.

"From Nusret Pasha in Trabzon, Kumandanim." Onursal approached with a hand-written sheet. "His congratulations and thanks to Nicholas Kaptan." Dawlish's message had contained a brief account of the attack on Poti. "There's no news from Kars – the cables are cut. The Russians must have surrounded it. Erzurum is threatened too. But Plevna is still holding out."

In Istanbul, in London, in St. Petersburg, in half a dozen other European capitals, grave men would be pondering that same news. While Plevna's starving but resolute defenders in their miles of trenches and earthworks still defied Alexander II and his army it was impossible for the Russian colossus to surge southwards towards their goals of Istanbul, the Bosporus and the Dardanelles. While the fortresses of Kars and Erzurum still stood firm Archduke Michael's forces could not thrust into Turkey's Anatolian heartland. Russia's domination of the Eastern Mediterranean still lay outside its grasp – but only just.

104

But a Turkish rout, a Russian breakthrough on either front, would signal more than disaster for the Ottoman Empire. Those grave men in European chancelleries and palaces would know that a general European war could well result and would already be positioning their countries for it. Dawlish could imagine Topcliffe poring over a map in Downing Street with Lord Beaconsfield, and the wily old Prime Minister calculating when the moment would come when intervention against Russia would be unavoidable to preserve Britain's lifeline to India. Ambitious men in Vienna would be eying Turkey's remaining European provinces, perhaps already secretly mobilising the forces that could move quickly into Bosnia and Herzegovina and claim them for the Austro-Hungarian Empire. In Paris, opportunistic politicians still smarting from humiliation by Prussia seven years before would be considering whether some scrap of French advantage could be won by intervention on one side or the other – and only cynical self-interest, not principle, would determine which. And in Berlin, most imponderable of all, the ruthless Iron Chancellor who had forged a half-dozen German kingdoms into an arrogant and powerful empire would be deciding how best to exploit the situation to expand its burgeoning power yet further.

Hobart would have relayed news of the attack on Poti to London by now. Topcliffe would have recognised its significance, would perhaps have felt reassured by it that he had chosen wisely in sending Dawlish eastwards. He might even have mentioned his name to Beaconsfield as an officer who might achieve high rank were he to survive. But Admiral Sir Richard Topcliffe would not be satisfied – he never was. He would see Poti as a start only, one that needed to be followed up quickly by yet greater devastation. He had put Dawlish in a position to blunt the Russian's offensive on the Anatolian front, had given him the opportunity to earn further advancement. He would expect nothing less than success. Dawlish knew that if he was not to stagnate in his present rank forever - and to be a Commander in the Royal Navy at thirty-two was an achievement to be envied, but a half-pay Commander of sixty was to be pitied – then he must wreak more havoc.

"Yes, Kumandanim. Plevna is still holding out." Onursal, apprehensive of Dawlish's abstraction, was repeating the news.

"Any news of the *Mesrutiyet?*" Dawlish shook himself from thoughts of European chancelleries.

"Still at Trabzon. Her bunkers are empty. The furnaces are drawn."

It will take two days to reheat them properly and to raise steam, Dawlish thought.

"Any news of the colliers from Zonguldak?" he said. Hobart had assured him in Istanbul that the coal mines there were working night and day to maximise output. But the weakness was transportation from there. "They should have been here by now."

"They're delayed." Onursal nodded towards the window. "It's November, Kumandanim. The gales delay them. Two are off Trabzon, but can't enter safely. Another put in to Samsun with damage. A fourth left Zonguldak two days ago."

Dawlish hid his disappointment. "Then note this for the reply, Onursal Mülazim. At least a thousand tons to be delivered here once the *Mesrutiyet* is coaled."

Batumi would provide a closer base to the Russians for the operations he must now undertake. Its land defences were formidable enough to withstand any forces the Russians could afford to divert from their main axis of advance further inland. But the shortage of skilled seamen would be harder to satisfy than that of fuel. The disaster on the *Alemdar* had wiped out many of her most critical complement.

"Add to the reply that we'll need gunners. Thirty at least, more if possible. All that can be spared from the Trabzon batteries." They might not be seamen, but if they understood artillery they could, and must, adapt quickly.

"But there are gunners here, Kumandanim," Onursal reminded him.

Dawlish shook his head. "After Poti the Russians should be thinking of taking our base here. The landward defences will need every last gunner if they attack."

"From Trabzon then, Kumandanim. It is noted."

"Good men, not drunks or cripples or incompetents," Dawlish added. If the Ottoman forces resembled the British little else could be expected from a forced levy on an unwilling commander. "State that Zyndram Birinci Yüzbashi is to see personally to their selection"

It was one more burden to lay upon the Pole, but his shoulders were broad enough.

11

The next days at Batumi were an agony of frustration and labour. The sustained poor weather slowed work on the *Alemdar* and the coal shortage put paid to any idea of a further foray with the *Burak Reis*. To Dawlish's relief, Hassan Kaptan accepted his authority easily, grateful for the energy with which he flung himself into supporting efforts to clear the ironclad's wrecked battery and re-secure its loosened armour.

With infinite difficulty in the battery's confined space, a spider's web of blocks and tackles, aided by several jacks, allowed the wreckage of the burst six-inch, and of the twin it had crippled, to be lifted clear through the access hatches in the deck above. Two modern four-inch Armstrongs mounted ashore in a Haxo casemate offered promise as replacements. The *Alemdar's* chief engineer and his assistants looked less than hopeful when Dawlish explained his sketches for improvised mountings. The gunnery officer had died in the explosion and was badly missed. Overall responsibility for shifting the shore-mounted Armstrongs to the ironclad would have to fall to Onursal. It would be brutally hard, heavily reliant on the ships' crews to lift the cannon from the land emplacements and drag them on improvised sledges to the harbour over muddy tracks and rain-washed cobbles. The men would resent it at first, and some would shirk, but Onursal's transformation of the *Burak Reis* from a floating slum into a lithe killer had assured Dawlish that he was the man who could get the best from them.

The work was slow – human muscle could only accomplish so much, and numbing cold and wet did not help. While it progressed Dawlish concentrated on his search for his point to strike, examining charts and maps in detail and quizzing anybody the governor could identify – merchants and traders and fishermen – with detailed knowledge of the Russian coast and its harbours. Sochi and Tuapse were substantial ports, but heavily defended with masonry batteries, and Novorossiysk, the largest harbour, was massively fortified. Assaulting any of them would be suicidal, even for the *Mesrutiyet*. He sought further and on the second night, late, crouched over a coastal chart on the wardroom table with Hassan and Onursal, he found what might be what he wanted. And not one point of attack either, but two. But the information on the chart was meagre and it was necessary to send Onursal across the harbour to seek more detailed land-maps at the governor's office. The wait felt interminable until he returned two hours later, cold but triumphant.

"It's even better than we thought, Kumandanim." He smoothed a Russian map and stabbed at a point where several contour lines piled close together. "Look here, Nicholas Kaptan! It's a gorge – and it's deep."

Dawlish saw immediately that it must be his first objective, for it was probably the last the Russians would expect. "Getting to it won't be easy," he said, fighting to restrain his excitement. "But if we do ... And yes, by God! It must be possible." It would be, once the *Mesrutiyet* arrived with the means of reaching there. "They'll feel the loss immediately and it will take weeks to repair!"

And there was a second target, more daunting still, yet vulnerable if surprise could be ensured - and if the *Alemdar* was ready. Planning for that attack would need yet more information – on water depths, on access channels – and every scrap of insight that could be wrung from charts or eyewitnesses.

Dawlish was eager now to be in action. It irked him that the *Mesrutiyet* was still in Trabzon, though later telegrams advised that the storm-battered colliers had at last entered port there. Two grimy days of coaling her would follow, and another of careful stoking that would not overstress the boilers' firetubes, before she could put to sea. The days of brutal work shifting the guns to the *Alemdar* continued meanwhile at Batumi, hampered by rain, sleet and wind that lessened only gradually. The sun only appeared on November 5th, when the first Armstrong four-inch arrived at the quayside, men and oxen straining on the traces of the sledge that carried it.

"It was well done, Onursal Mülazım," Dawlish said, "You and your men can all be proud."

"Our forefathers dragged galleys overland to the Golden Horn to let the conqueror Mehmet capture Istanbul." Onursal looked relieved for the first time since the work had started. "We could not fail their memory."

The barge-mounted shearlegs waited at the quay to load the barrel and its mounting separately on to a waiting lighter for transport to the ironclad. The exhausted shore-party that had somehow pushed, dragged and cajoled the piece over a mile of uneven ground and city streets broke into a ragged cheer as the tackles were rigged. There was further backbreaking labour ahead to hoist it to the *Alemdar's* deck above the battery and to lower it into place, and then the process must be repeated for the second weapon, but the triumph of arrival thus far seemed to have breathed new enthusiasm into the men. Work was blunting the memory of that disaster in the battery.

Dawlish was feeling pleased until he saw Hassan hurrying towards him along the quay, his face ashen, a paper grasped in his hand. Dawlish steered him away from the men nearby, unwilling that bad news should be overheard.

"There's been a battle, a big battle, at Dexe Boyun." Hassan's expression told that it had not been a victory.

"Where?" The name meant nothing to Dawlish.

"Near Erzurum – very heavy losses. The army commander, Mukhtar Pasha, is falling back on the fortress."

There was more. Kars, the other stronghold, was surrounded and under bombardment. If these last bastions fell there would be nothing between the enemy and Central Anatolia. Exhausted by months of combat, and starved of supplies that had been diverted to support the desperate resistance in the Balkans, the Ottoman eastern front was at the point of collapse. Only in their rear, their far-rear, were Archduke Michael's victory-flushed forces vulnerable.

But there was a second telegram, and its news was better. The *Mesrutiyet* had left Trabzon, in company with a collier laden with eight hundred tons of coal.

The Archduke, Dawlish thought grimly, would not have it all his own way for long.

*

The *Mesrutiyet* entered Batumi in the drizzle-darkened gloom of late afternoon. As she made fast to the mooring buoy Dawlish saw with satisfaction that steam launches Numbers Seven and Nine were stacked aft. Several of the ironclad's own larger boats has been left behind to make space for them, yet even so the after-ship was cluttered enough to impede fire directly astern. Clearance for action would have to be ruthless – not good for morale, for no seamen liked to see his last means of rescue abandoned to drift astern – but there was no help for it. The launches' promise outweighed their disadvantages.

Dawlish hurried on board to be met by Zyndram. A quick inspection impressed. The exacting standards that Dawlish had demanded had not slipped and it was clear that the crew were taking pride in increased efficiency. Despite his dandyish exterior the Pole was proving a very efficient officer. The *Mesrutiyet* had been in good hands, and could be entrusted to them again.

The artillerymen which the *Mesrutiyet* had carried here from the Trabzon batteries, two officers and thirty enlisted men, were already being transferred to the *Alemdar*.

"They're good," Zyndram said, "But they're soldiers, and garrison troops at that, not seamen. Half were sick all the way here and the remainder were terrified with every roll we made. Let them ashore and half will disappear."

"Training, discipline and yet more training," Dawlish said. "There's no other way." Britain's naval hegemony had been built for centuries on recruits and pressed men, frightened and unwilling, who had been tempered to invincibility by relentless application of that principle. But Hassan Kaptan had only days, not months, to work the miracle on his patched-up ironclad.

The collier that had plodded in the *Mesrutiyet's* wake moored alongside her. The filthy, backbreaking misery of coaling would be brief for once. The passage from Trabzon had consumed little fuel, but given the ironclad's limited bunkerage – little over five hundred tons, sufficient for a thousand miles of economical steaming – Dawlish was taking no chances. And he wanted to be underway by midnight.

They adjourned to the captain's saloon on *Mesrutiyet*, now Dawlish's again. Coffee was brought and both men lit cigars.

"Any message from Nusret Pasha?"

"Only that he wishes you luck."

Nusret could have said no more, Dawlish thought, for the plans he had refined in the past days had been approved already by an exchange of coded telegrams. With rout threatening Erzurum and Kars, Nusret was wedded to holding Trabzon and Batumi while Dawlish ravaged the enemy's coastal supply lines. The slaughter at Dexe Boyun had wiped away the last hopes of victory on this front, but Nusret was banking on a stalemate brought about by lack of supplies and the imminent and savage Anatolian winter.

"And…" Zyndram looked uncomfortable. "Some news too, maybe very bad. Certainly for Nusret Pasha. Maybe for you also, Nicholas Kaptan, for Hobart Pasha. For me too perhaps."

"I don't understand."

"It's Haluk Pasha," Zyndram said. "The Sultan freed him when he reached Istanbul."

"Why?" Dawlish was shocked.

110

Zyndram shrugged. "Perhaps because His Majesty hesitates to offend the Istanbul medresses. The medresses received Selahattin and his Bashi Bazooks like heroes when they arrived there. Now they've been sent to Bulgaria."

"To murder and to violate? Those blackguards won't have gone there to fight!" Dawlish felt disgusted now at his own partial retribution against Selahattin that night in Giresun. He should have killed that monster then. He guessed that Nusret was probably feeling the same about Haluk. Selahattin was vicious, but petty in the larger scheme of things. Haluk was a greater menace. Everyone recognised the Sultan as weak and if Haluk was close to him he would again be in a position to undermine all Nusret's endeavours. Then Dawlish stopped himself thinking further. He had known that the Ottoman Empire was rotten with palace politics when he accepted this assignment and he could not change it. But he still despised intrigue and intended to stand aloof from it. He was a naval officer, proud to serve and pledged to honour and to loyalty, whether for Queen or for Sultan.

"Forget them," Dawlish said. "Forget Haluk and Selahattin and their whole damn crew. Our enemy is closer."

"Yes, Nicholas Kaptan." Zyndram, obviously conscious of a mild reproof, began to sip his coffee, then stopped, reached inside his tunic. "My apologies – I almost forgot. Two letters for you, forwarded from Istanbul. Personal letters, I think." He reached them across. "Shall I leave you to read them alone?"

Dawlish shook his head. "Stay, Zyndram. It won't take a moment, and we've more to discuss." He was glad of the company, if only briefly, for command was lonely. The handwritten address on the uppermost letter showed him that it was from his father, and so too was probably the other. They would not detain him long. He felt little affection and some distaste for the Shrewsbury solicitor who had at last remarried only two months before, his bride a wool merchant's stout daughter half his age.

There was little in the letter to surprise him. The Scottish honeymoon had been deliriously happy – the adverb was underlined three times – and a small surprise might well be on the way. Dawlish had been groomsman at the wedding and had hoped that it might at last bring an end to the liaisons with barmaids and market-women that had been the stuff of town gossip for years. As children he and his brother and sister had been embarrassed and repulsed by their father's ill-disguised fumblings with the housemaids. Their nurse's efforts to shield them failed to save them from servants' sly references to possible half-brothers and half-sisters in the town. Had it been otherwise he might not have been so eager to have escaped to the Navy at twelve, and might not have so idolised the mother whose face he could not remember but whose love he thought he could still feel. There had been so little other love in his life ...

He dismissed the memories and looked at the other letter. The address, care of Hobart Pasha, was in an unknown hand. The envelope contained a single sheet, the script rounded and generous, a transcription that began "Much have I travelled in the realms of gold." He recognised Keats, "On First Looking into Chapman's Homer". There was only the poem, no other message, nothing else but the initials F.M. – Florence Morton – and yet enough to make her come alive.

Suddenly he felt his hand shaking and was surprised by the emotion that pulsed through him. He had tried to forget her but she had stirred feelings in him which he had resigned himself never to feel again. And now, unexpectedly, this.

Zyndram must have noticed his disquiet. "Are you all right, Nicholas Kaptan? Is it perhaps bad news?"

"No," Dawlish said, "not bad news," though he was not sure even of that.

He read the poem twice, three times, and he was again on the poop of that packet-steamer, and the plains of Troy were slipping past, and he remembered, painfully and longingly, being happier with her than he had realised at the time. And he understood with sudden, terrible clarity why she had sent it to him. She knew his life was in danger, that he might indeed die, yet wanted him to know how much their brief time together had meant to her. Even though she too knew that nothing could come of it...

It must have taken all her valour, all her strength, to overcome social convention and write those words for him. He knew there could be nothing mercenary in her motivation, nothing of a poor woman, almost a servant, trying to snare a richer man – not that he was worth much, for the profits of the few small Shropshire farms he had inherited from his uncle, and which an agent managed for him, brought him little more than the cost of his uniforms. A few minutes with her had been enough to convince him that such mercenary thoughts would be alien to her. It was obvious that she had realised that he had been attracted to her, that she felt as powerfully towards him, and that she had the courage – courage greater than his own – to admit the fact. He could not ignore this attraction, was even unsure if he wanted to, and yet he did not know how he could deal with it should he survive what lay ahead.

His hand was still trembling as he folded the paper and put it away. He noticed that Zyndram was looking away diplomatically. He was glad now that he had something else to speak of, an idea that had struck him in recent days and which might help morale by appealing to the pride that was so strong a Turkish quality.

"The steam launches need names, not numbers," he said. "Men love them. British seamen call themselves by their ships' names, Terrors and Conquerors and Mastiffs and Rattlesnakes. They rally to them in action. Can you think of better names than Seven and Nine?"

Zyndram thought for a moment. "*Seyfi* would be good. It means swordfish."

"Excellent! Appropriate too for the spar torpedo. And the other?"

"Maybe *Muzaffer* – triumphant?"

"It might be tempting fate! No – something else?"

"Why not *Ejder* – dragon? And you are right, Nicholas Kaptan, the men will like it."

The men did, drawn up under oilskins on the dark rain-swept quarterdeck to hear Dawlish speak and Zyndram translate and to see Mehmet Birinci Yüzbashi, whose drunkenness had demoted him from command of the *Burak Reis* to responsibility for two small craft, remove covers from newly painted names on the launches' bows. His hands no longer shook and he no longer smelled of brandy. He led the crews' cheers afterwards and Dawlish wondered if they would have been so enthusiastic had they known what he had planned for them.

Departure was an hour away when the men were dismissed. There was time for last instructions at a conference in the *Mesrutiyet's* wardroom attended by Zyndram, Hassan and Onursal. Weather permitting, Onursal in the *Burak Reis* would cruise off Poti, capturing or sinking any Russian ships still slipping along the Georgian coast. The earlier raid had proved him and his crew to be well up to the task. She would join the *Alemdar* when she was ready for Hassan to bring her north to rendezvous with the *Mesrutiyet*. Dawlish's last inspection of the half-repaired *Alemdar* had been cheering. The dislodged armour had been adequately if not perfectly restored, the battery cleared of wreckage, the undamaged weapons test-fired satisfactorily with blanks.

113

The first Armstrong had been dropped safely into the battery, the second would follow closely. Provided Hassan could drill the newly arrived gunners from Trabzon into passable efficiency the *Alemdar* might yet prove invaluable.

But Hassan Kaptan must manage on his own for now. Dawlish and the *Mesrutiyet* had business further up the coast.

*

Dawlish snatched ten minutes for himself before the *Mesrutiyet* cast off. Had he more time to consider he might not have done what he did – scribble a few brief lines to Miss Morton. Beyond formal thanks for her note they were but a bald statement that he was in good health and busily engaged. He hoped she was well and that life in Istanbul agreed with her. He signed by his initials only. As he handed the envelope to a steward for delivery onshore for forwarding to Istanbul he told himself it was an act of courtesy, nothing more. Nor must it be.

And yet, and yet ...

12

The *Mesrutiyet* slipped from Batumi and into the darkness scarcely eight hours after she had entered. She headed due west for the open sea, her ram ploughing under as she drove forward at half speed. Within her rust-streaked black hull and white upperworks some two hundred and eighty men watched, laboured, slept, talked or simply thought fearfully of the uncertainty ahead. Now, perhaps more than the enemy, these men were Dawlish's greatest concern. Language was a greater barrier than religion, and yet he sensed that an officer who counted the mode of address "My Sons" as no mere formula, even though he spoke through an interpreter, would have their loyalty unto death. Like their British counterparts, their best could only be earned by the correct mix of firmness and justice and care.

He moved across the *Mesrutiyet's* rain-washed decks and through her iron passages, going from damp chill to steaming heat to numbing cold again, ascending and descending, checking for weakness and omission, praising smartness and initiative. He accepted the inevitable chai, scalding and bladder-straining, in the boiler room and in the galley, and the equally inevitable bitter coffee and sweet lokum in the wardroom. He commended cleanliness in the heads and order in the

114

magazines, and tapped gauges and felt the temperature of bearings. He brushed aside the engineer's protests that the bunkers were too filthy for him to enter and praised the coal-blackened trimmers there for their backbreaking labour even though he knew he would have to change his uniform afterwards. As he moved through the ship – his ship – he felt a glow of elation. This was the moment of command, of total responsibility, which he had dreamed of since boyhood and the satisfaction it gave him blotted out apprehension about what lay ahead.

The huge armoured battery was festooned with slung hammocks, and mess tables and benches lined the bulkheads. Between them the twelve-inch cannon beloved of Selim the gunnery officer were gleaming and spotless. It was cold there, miserably cold, for there could be no stoves in a space with access, albeit closed at present, to the munitions stored three decks below. Despite the men's layers of clothing many coughed and sniffled.

The marines' accommodation was in one corner of the battery and Dawlish felt their welcome even as they were roused to attention on his appearance. The desperate minutes they had shared as the *Irene* had borne down on this very ship had forged an unforgettable bond. Bülent, the marine chavush had re-joined them. After his cool performance in capturing the tug and brig at Poti Dawlish wanted Bülent with him in the coming action. The marines had been cleaning their weapons, including the fifteen cavalry Winchesters Dawlish had requisitioned for them in addition to the one he had secured for himself. He reached for the nearest, and silently, without looking at it, stripped it quickly – a drill he had practised in private until he could do it in darkness – and then, just as faultlessly, reassembled it and handed it back to its amazed owner. As he turned away he heard what sounded like muttered approval and admiration, and was glad of it. In the coming raid he needed these men to trust him as much as he would rely on them.

Yet language would remain a potentially impenetrable barrier between him and his men. Zyndram had suggested a young mehendis, Nedim, as translator. "He's from Rhodes," he said. "His family have a few caiques, they're small ship-owners. They all speak good English – they need to for business. He's the first in the family to gain a commission. They're proud of him."

Dawlish had Nedim come to his cabin and explained there what he expected of him. Nedim was seventeen, slight but wiry, eager to please.

"Are you nervous, Nedim Mehendis?" He hoped not to sound intimidating, remembering how as a midshipman he had been daunted by interviews with his captain.

"A little, Kumandanim." Nedim paused. "I've never been in combat before."

Dawlish was suddenly reminded of himself before his first action, a trembling thirteen-year old on the verge of nausea looking with terror across the mudflats towards a gun-bristling Chinese fort on the Pei-Ho river, dreading the order that would send him and those about him charging towards it, longing only to crouch forever in the flooded ditch he sheltered in. An ordinary seaman close by, a grizzled, middle-aged man from another ship than Dawlish's, had recognised his terror but with rough kindness had not spoken of it. "You'll be fine, lad," he'd said, ignoring the gap that yawned between even the youngest midshipman and the oldest lower-deck veteran. He had stayed with Dawlish as they floundered across the mud, urging him forward and dragging him free when he was bogged down. Something of the man's calm determination to advance regardless of the hail of gunfire had communicated itself. He'd fallen close to the fort's wall, instantly dead from a ball through the chest, and when the assault's failure had ended in retreat his body had remained as a trophy for the defenders. Dawlish had never known his name, though he had afterwards buried what was left of his head when he found it, decayed and hideous, impaled on a stake, when the fort was finally taken a year later. But Dawlish had never forgotten that anonymous seaman nor the lesson that fear could be conquered by trust and example.

"And you're afraid of being afraid, Nedim?"

"Evet. Yes, Kumandanim. I fear..." He sought for a word, then found it. "Dishonour."

"Then you're an honourable man, Nedim Mehendis. You fear what we all fear." Dawlish laid an arm on his shoulder and led him to the door. "If it's needed, you'll find you have the necessary courage. You would not have chosen to be an officer had you not got it already. Nor would I be relying on you tonight. Just stay close to me. You'll be fine."

Nedim flushed. "Teshekkür ederim, Kumandanim," he said, "Thank you."

Mehmet, the *Burak Reis's* former commander, was waiting in oilskins by the steam launches on the quarterdeck, as pathetically eager for approval as before. And even with him shared experience had

116

created a bond, for with Dawlish he had come through the terror of the trial of the spar torpedo at Trabzon. Mehmet indicated with pride the jury-rigged measures for hoisting the craft outboard and the improvised and heavily lagged piping he had arranged to run from the boiler room to offtake points close by. Flexible hoses completed the connection, so boiling water could be fed to the launches to minimise the time needed to raise steam.

"Have the Nordenveldts been fitted?" Dawlish asked and Nedim translated.

The machine guns had been fitted and tested. Each craft carried four thousand rounds.

"My compliments then to Mehmet Birinci Yüzbashi," Dawlish said. "I need him to come to my quarters. I want to show him Archduke Michael's jugular."

For though the ironclad mounted four massive twelve-inch ship-smashers it was with Mehmet's two frail launches that Dawlish would inflict injury on the enemy. Daring had paid off twice already, at Trabzon itself and at Poti. As he turned to go below Dawlish hoped he was not tempting fate by hoping for a third indulgence.

*

The following midday saw the *Mesrutiyet* steaming slowly north-westwards against a brisk breeze, parallel to the coast and eighty miles from it, sufficiently far offshore to make contact with any vessel capable of outrunning her unlikely. Thus far the horizon had been empty.

Dawlish had come to the bridge to observe the noon fixes. They were fruitless, for the sky was uniformly leaden. Dead reckoning must continue to suffice. In another hour it would be time to turn due north. Landfall should be just before the early winter dusk, with just enough light remaining to find the chosen spot before darkness obscured the vessel from observers onshore. Though normal duties and watches still prevailed an atmosphere of anticipation was palpable. The story of the triumph at Poti had gone about the *Mesrutiyet* like wildfire and similar action was widely expected.

"I wish I had been there." Zyndram's voice betrayed almost sensual regret as he shared coffee and cheroots with Dawlish in the cold lee of the wheelhouse.

117

"Your chance will come soon enough. God knows it's butcher's work." Little skill had been needed at that blazing harbour.

"May I ask you a question? With all respect, Nicholas Kaptan?"

"Ask me."

"You picked up Russians from the water at Poti. Why?"

"Not Russians – seamen, like you and me. I once survived as much myself. I couldn't abandon them." Dawlish found Zyndram's attitude incomprehensible – any British officer, would have saved them, any British seaman either. "They were no longer enemies. They were dying of cold. Many already had."

"I'd have left them," Zyndram said with sudden vehemence. "Every last one of them." He paused, then said: "I hate them."

There was a brief uneasy silence, Dawlish embarrassed by his lieutenant's passion, as if he had stumbled on some private secret, Zyndram aware that he might have betrayed too much.

"Because they're the enemy, or because they're Russian?" Dawlish asked at last.

"They enslaved my country." Zyndram's loathing was palpable for all his quietness. "I've never seen it. Can you understand that, Nicholas Kaptan? Perhaps I never will see it. Poland rose against them nearly fifty years ago and was crushed. My grandfather fled at the end of it, with his wife and children. My grandmother miscarried in the back of a cart and bled to death at the roadside."

"He came to Turkey? Why?"

"Because he was welcomed, and hundreds more like him. They believed the Sultan would always welcome any eternal enemy of Moscow. And he did. He gave them Polonezkoy to settle."

"Polonezkoy?" Dawlish vaguely remembered hearing the name before.

"On the Bosporus, north of the city. You would be an honoured guest there when this is over. It's little Poland, with our own schools and churches and language. And it's free."

"Your grandfather never regretted it?"

"No, nor my father either, not even when he lost an arm for the Sultan in the Crimea." His eyes filled with tears. "Adam Zyndram, Miralay of the Ottoman Dragoons. He never gave up hope of our liberation, not to his dying day, not even when the Czar crucified Poland again in '63 and we welcomed another generation of exiles in Polonezkoy."

118

He looked Dawlish full in the face, his voice full of terrible sincerity. "I was a boy then, but I'll never forget it. They came poor and ragged and famished, with nothing but their courage. Nowhere else on earth welcomed them or wanted them. But the Sultan offered them a uniform and a chance to serve him against Russia when the time came. The Mahommedan Sultan, the Unspeakable Turk your Mr. Gladstone condemns so righteously, gave us what no Christian monarch did, freedom and dignity and a place to call ours until Poland's own day dawns."

"And until then you'll hate Russians – any Russians?"

"Have you never hated a man, Nicholas Kaptan?"

"Several," Dawlish said softly. "Two most of all." One he had killed, indeed murdered, by any legal standard, and without regret, though he must keep telling himself that nothing had ever happened one night, not long since, on the Victoria Embankment. But the other...

"What came of it?" Zyndram said.

"It's best not talked of," Dawlish said. For that other man had bested and humiliated him in a past he wanted so much to forget that he had all but blotted it from his memory. And the woman he had once loved, the girl who had once been like a sister to him and later was so much more, had preferred that other man, a more powerful, richer, older man, to him. He had hazarded everything for her, his life, his career, his honour, and still she had rejected him, not with regret or even pity at the end, but with amusement at his presumption. A decade had passed, years in which he had resolved never again to risk such injury, such humiliation, never to lose his heart to a woman. Until now... His hand moved unconsciously to feel the oilcloth packet under his shirt that contained his resignation letter and Miss Morton's transcription of the Keats poem. It was all he had of her ...

They stood in silence, both conscious that perhaps too much had been confided that was perhaps better left unsaid. They smoked on quietly, then walked to the bridge wing and cast the glowing stubs into the wash alongside.

"Almost time to alter course, Zyndram Birinci Yüzbashi," Dawlish's voice was coldly formal.

Dusk – and action – was four hours away.

*

The sky was clearing in the west, the cloud breaking, and the sun falling like a scarlet ball. The wind was dying, the sea with it, when dead reckoning brought the *Mesrutiyet* to a point on the Russian coast between Tuapse and Lazarevskoye. Of more value now than maps and charts, if the sought-for estuary was to be found before darkness, was the memory of a seaman who had plied this littoral in his civilian days as deckhand on a small trading vessel. Each peak and gully and headland on the rugged shoreline was familiar to him and at his bidding the ironclad swung to port and crawled north-westwards, three miles from land. There was little sign of habitation – the ground fell too steeply to the sea for that – and only the odd pinpoint of light against the darkening mass indicated some isolated hut that gave little threat of a raised alarm. The ironclad showed no illumination and as the sun died only the dim orange glow above her funnel betrayed her presence.

Aft, both launches had been hoisted outboard. Their boilers had been charged with scalding water from the *Mesrutiyet's* boilers and intense fires glowed in their tiny furnaces. Their crews were aboard, and their complements of marines also. Their Nordenveldts were loaded and their most lethal cargoes, deadly for friend and enemy alike, were stowed in their bows. Mehmet, the officer responsible for them, was still on the bridge, intent on his telescope. Dawlish and Zyndram stood by him, also searching for the narrow gash where a cliff-flanked river met the sea.

"That must be it, Nicholas Kaptan."

They had almost lost it in the dusk, another jagged inlet, remarkable only for its width. Beyond the low line of foam where it met the sea's greater expanse the river showed as a dark placid surface perhaps sixty yards wide. The steep, gully-seamed slopes to either side rose towards an uneven ridge and other, higher, hills lay behind, a mile further inland.

"The railway can't be seen from here," Zyndram said. He had studied the maps intently, inadequate though their details were. They showed no more than the river's winding course, the landscape's contours, the black snake of the railway. "It's there, in the valley beyond, parallel to the coast."

There too would be the bridge, invulnerable to sea bombardment, the structure that carried the single track high across the river's chasm. If it was like other Russian railways it would be jerry-built and uneven, good only for speeds that would be unacceptably low in Western Europe. But it was a lifeline nonetheless, a link which carried men and

120

equipment south-eastwards from Central Russia for loading on coasters at the port of Sochi, where it terminated. Heavier freight was still being shipped directly from the large harbour at Novorossisysk, and from Gelendzhik, but the weather-independent rail route shortened the sea passage significantly for lighter supplies and facilitated urgent troop reinforcement.

It was dark now, and the moon was out, broken cloud drifting across it. Dawlish had a few last instructions for Zyndram and then went aft to the launches. The ironclad hove to, her ram towards the light breeze. Mehmet had already boarded the newly named *Seyfi*, the Swordfish.

Outreached hands hauled Dawlish into the second launch, the *Ejder*, the Dragon, which swayed suspended over the water to starboard. Nedim was already aboard, eager to conceal his trepidation, and Bülent Chavush, hardened and confident. Dawlish crowded with them and seven marines in the tiny cockpit aft. They left little space for Yussef Onbashi, an engineer's mate, to tend the furnace and engine, or for the helmsman standing by the miniature wheel. They were luckier however than the marine Nordenveldt gunner and his loader, and the two other marines and the four seamen who would huddle with them in the open space forward, where spray would drench them on the run inshore. A winch creaked and the launch dropped, an opened throttle urging her engine into life just before she touched the waves. Released, she chugged away from the ship's side, her motion lively, and headed shorewards. *Seyfi*, similarly dropped on the port side, came curving round the ironclad's stern and followed in her wake.

Steering was by hand-held compass, for the river mouth was indistinguishable against the dark mass of land ahead and Dawlish and Nedim were crosschecking each other. The *Seyfi* was a half-glimpsed presence following astern. The *Mesrutiyet* had already turned westwards and was lost in the night. The low waves that had imparted the ironclad only the slightest roll tossed the smaller craft unmercifully and showered the occupants as they broke against their bows.

The approach took thirty minutes. There was silence but for the rhythmic panting of the engines and the brief corrections of the navigators. All were cold and damp, for with action in prospect no oilskins were worn. Dawlish was no less chilled than the marines endlessly fingering their weapons, or the seamen glumly contemplating the long poles mounted in rails on either side, hoping they would not have to be run out, nor the explosive charges at their tips activated. He

121

hoped as much himself. The spar torpedo was a crude and unreliable weapon and he had no wish to repeat his single experience of exploding one, against that rock near Trabzon. If the bridge would be unguarded he was resolved to employ a safer method of demolition.

The gorge was now clearly visible. *Ejder* nosed forward cautiously between the high, fissured walls, keeping to the centre, a seaman in the bows sounding for bottom with a pole and not finding it. Her sister followed a hundred yards astern. Even after the recent rains the current was sluggish here. Ahead, the deeply shaded cleft curved gently, restricting the forward view to some two hundred yards.

Marines on either side scanned the cliff rims above for any sign of movement. Forward, seamen and the Nordenveldt crew searched the shadows ahead. Dawlish felt a mild claustrophobia and a concern that an observer above could not miss the smoke and funnel glow. Worse still, an enemy could pour down a merciless fire on the slowly moving launches without fear of retaliation.

The river narrowed at the curve, the current quickened. The helmsman nudged over into deeper water close to the opposite shore and increased revolutions slightly. After two hundred yards the stream twisted again. The banks were lower here, bluffs rather than cliffs, forty, fifty feet high.

An unseen sheep bleated. There came silence again, enhanced rather than broken by the low panting of the engines, by the lap and gurgle of water alongside. There was a heightened tension, a single, unspoken thought shared by all – where there were sheep there would be a shepherd. The hills along the coast had dropped astern and the higher range was perhaps a half-mile ahead. Human presence must be inevitable in this sheltered valley, though the skimpy Russian maps had shown no details of it. The river twisted and narrowed, the current more rapid here and the banks still high. With revolutions increased again, *Ejder* pulled across to the outside of the bend and swept around.

There were lights ahead, three, four hundred yards, a few on each bank.

A whispered command brought the launch to a standstill, engine throttled back to breast the current. The shutter on a shaded red lamp rose and fell to signal astern to *Seyfi* to follow suit.

A scattering of houses, low and single-storied, clustered above the bluffs. A few were lower, nestling in clefts. A few points of light, five, no more, flickered weakly. It was a sleeping village, strung out on both banks, poor and thatch-roofed, smoke drifting from a score of chimneys in the damp, dead, chill air.

Dawlish reached for his telescope. A decision could not be delayed, but every detail counted in arriving at it.

The dividing chasm was perhaps forty yards wide. A jagged mass of boulders at it centre split it in two roughly equal channels. The current there was fast enough for riffles of white water to show in the moonlight. From this half-submerged foundation in midstream a vertical pillar rose level with the banks on either side, thirty or forty feet above the level of the river beneath. It formed the central support of a flat wooden bridge that linked both sides of the hamlet.

It was not the railway bridge – that must lie further upstream – but the launches must pass beneath it, not just now, with stealth still an ally, but afterwards, when the destruction they hoped to wreak would have woken every living thing for miles around.

Dawlish knew there could be only one decision. He took it.

Ejder nudged into the current at walking pace and her consort followed.

13

The bridge was close – a hundred yards – and there was debris piled in the northerly of the two channels beneath it, tree trunks and branches jammed against boulders, with water racing steeply through the clutter. The southerly channel looked relatively clear, though there too the surface foamed white. Rising from the rocks in midstream, the column supporting the bridge's centre was now revealed as a rough lattice of timber balks. The narrow wooden spans to either side were wide enough to carry a single cart and flanked by spindly handrails. There was no sign of life, not on the bridge, not at the few slumbering hovels visible from below.

The current was stronger now. "Increase revolutions," Dawlish whispered. Nedim relayed the order, a slight quaver in his voice. The seaman sounding by pole in the bows had not found bottom yet as *Ejder* continued steaming slowly upstream, enclosed by the forty-foot bluffs. In that cleft – the lips of which the Marines' Winchesters might reach, but which the Nordenveldt's limited elevation range would never allow it to rake – the engine's panting seemed like the thunderous beating of some giant heart that must surely wake every living being within miles. A hundred yards astern, the second launch was a dark mass against the moonlit centre of the river where the shadows did not extend.

"Signal *Seyfi* to heave to," Dawlish said quietly. He would have to trust to Mehmet's judgement to make his run upriver at his own discretion.

Nedim flicked the red lamp's shutter four times – the agreed signal. *Seyfi* lost way and moved into the shade.

It was fifty yards to the bridge now, the launch lurching with the eddies and rocking slightly. There was still no sign of life and the dark windows and few guttering lights of the closest houses seemed close enough to touch...

Suddenly there was movement ahead and above. A figure emerged from the shadows, heading slowly and wearily towards the centre of the bridge. His plod conveyed reluctant fulfilment of unwelcome duty and his glance was cast neither right not left but down to the planks beneath his feet. He was bundled in a long greatcoat, its hood shielding his face, a rifle slung casually on his shoulder.

Every eye on the launch was riveted on the sentry. Bülent Chavush's raised arm directed the carbines of his two best shots silently towards him. He glanced towards Dawlish, mutely seeking permission to fire and not receiving it.

The launch beat forward slowly, swinging towards the narrow southerly channel where the waters rushed unimpeded. High above, the Russian paused. He turned slowly, blowing on his fingers, and moved towards the rail. Only then did he seem to hear something. He raised his face and looked into the cleft below. He shouted – it might have been a challenge – and struggled to lift his rifle.

Dawlish yelled "Atesh!" and both marines fired, the crash echoing and re-echoing from the enclosing cliffs. Splinters flew from the handrail above and the sentry began to run towards the southern bank. The marines ejected, reloaded, fired again. Their victim stumbled and fell. Crying out, a dreadful moaning punctuated by howls, he began to drag himself along the planked roadway.

"Increase revolutions!" The need for stealth was past and speed must bring them through. Throttle open, engine beating at maximum, *Ejder* plunged into the swirling eddies beneath the bridge. Every carbine was raised – Dawlish himself was carrying one in addition to his revolver and cutlass – and eyes flitted from one building to the next. Lights were showing and doors opening and dim figures were visible, curious, confused by the shots.

124

Another soldier emerged on the bridge and the sight of the slumped body caused him to dash forward. Looking down, he glimpsed the boat below. He turned and ran back, shouting loudly. Dawlish realised that there must be a small garrison billeted here, perhaps troops assigned to guard the railway bridge upstream.

The launch swayed in the seething channel, ploughing forward at twice her previous speed. The span was almost directly overhead. The rush of water was furious – the obstruction on the other side of the bridge support must be funnelling most of the flow into this racing twenty-yard gap. The tiny wheel span through the helmsman's hands as he reacted to the buffeting, holding the bows directly into the current.

Boots drummed on the planking above, shouts rang out and suddenly there were also figures scrambling down the steep banks towards the few still-dark houses that nestled halfway down the bluff face. A rifle barked from the shadows to starboard, then another and another. Russian voices yelled what by their brevity could only be commands. More boots pounded on the bridge as men were drawn into line and strung along its length. Despite the chill few wore greatcoats and flapping white blouses and bare legs told that many had been roused from sleep.

Under Bülent Chavush's bellowed instructions the marines blasted a volley upwards, driving back the knots of Russians who were leaning over and aiming down. Brass cartridges bounced on the decks as the Winchesters were reloaded. Bülent roared again – Hold Fire!

Rifles crackled from the banks, from the houses built into the bluffs. A marine standing next to Dawlish fell, his head ripped open, instantly dead. Firing erupted astern also as the second launch, the *Seyfi*, moved forward to support her sister. Her marines were blazing up at the bridge but her Nordenveldt, the weapon that would have swept it clean, was silent, incapable of elevating sufficiently.

A dozen or more rifles crashed down a ragged fusillade as *Ejder's* bows emerged under the upstream side of the bridge. Heavy slugs hurled a seaman overboard, killed a marine in the act of firing back and tore down through the shoulder of another so that he collapsed beneath the feet of his fellows. But the Russian rifles were single-shot Berdans, and it would be seconds yet before fresh cartridges had slid into their smoking maws. In that brief respite Bülent Chavush's iron discipline ensured his men were despatching two volleys in quick succession with their Winchester repeaters. Dawlish was firing too, and Nedim also, nervousness forgotten, their aims as wild as the others',

125

content that the hail screaming upwards was beating chips from the bridge edge and forcing the troops back from it.

The bridge was slipping astern – and still more Russians streamed on to it, extending in a ragged smoke-enveloped line from which spurts of flame darted. The marines were concentrated in *Ejder's* stern now, lashing successive salvos aft to a rhythm chanted by Bülent as he fired and loaded and fired again himself. Another marine was down, his chest a bloody crater. The carbine magazines were almost empty now and Nedim was reaching into an open ammunition box, thrusting cartridges to eager hands around him. Mehmet's *Seyfi* was still downstream of the bridge, wreathed in the smoke of the carbine fire it poured upwards.

The channel was broadening, the current slackening and the banks were slipping past faster now. Dawlish glanced forward to see a curve – salvation – ahead. He heard a scream at his side and felt something clawing at him as it fell. He turned to see the helmsman slipping down, surprise and entreaty on his face at the instant that life left it. The wheel spun free but even as Dawlish reached for it he knew he was too late.

The bows swung wildly across to starboard. With a shuddering impact that knocked most of its occupants from their feet, the launch crunched over a half-submerged rock-fall at the cliff foot. It heeled slightly as the full force of the current hit it on the port flank and then seemed to settle. Dawlish had grounded small craft often enough to feel that it was firmly lodged.

"Astern! Full Revolutions!" he shouted. Yussef, tending the engine, threw the valve lever. The small engine thrashed in reverse but the launch did not shift. Another volley, better controlled, less ragged, crashed from the bridge. Slugs thumped into the hull, splintered the coaming and perforated the funnel. A seaman toppled overboard and disappeared downstream, thrashing and shouting.

There was nothing for it but to get the men into the water at the bows and heave her off – and that meant giving the lead.

"Stay here!" Dawlish shouted to Yussef. "The rest of you! Jackets and jerseys off, then follow me!"

Nedim's translation was unnecessary – example and action were enough. Dawlish scrambled forward past the boiler and towards the bow. Nedim followed closely and Bülent hustled the marines after them. Rifle fire rippled from the bridge, throwing up spurts alongside or slamming into the hull. At this range – some eighty yards – only the

126

deep shadow in which the vessel had grounded was saving her from more accurate raking.

"Drop your weapons!" Dawlish tore off his outer clothing – soaked garments could kill as surely as lead – and dropped them with his carbine in the forward cockpit before stepping on to the bow. The swirling water beneath was dark and though the depth could be no more than thirty inches, the launch's draught, he recoiled for an instant from plunging in. But his men were crowding behind and there was no option but to bend down, turn, grasp the edge and drop.

He cried out as the cold lanced up to his waist. He lost his grip and stumbled forward, soaking his arms and chest. He groped towards the stem and others splashed down beside him, eight or nine of them, some howling as the chill bit.

"Here, lads! To me!"

The stones underfoot were slimy and men lost their balance and dragged others down as they fell, but somehow they rose again and managed to converge on the tapered bow. Bülent was bellowing encouragement, his own shoulder rammed against the stem, and Dawlish was beside him, shoving in an agony of cold and screaming muscles, his water-filled boots slipping as they sought purchase.

"Push, lads! That's it! All together!"

There was no sense of the hull budging, however much they strained. Bülent dived under to heave beneath the keel but he emerged a long twenty seconds later, coughing and choking, his attempt futile. And still rifle slugs bit into the hull or pinged metallically off the funnel. Somewhere to Dawlish's left a man cried out and convulsed a flurry of bloody water, then drifted away, ignored by his straining comrades.

This is failure, a hard internal voice told Dawlish, and death is upon you in this freezing stream – yet still he heaved and shouted encouragement.

Suddenly a jerk and a grating rumble. The hull slid back a foot before grinding again to an abrupt halt. Dawlish fell forward, his face going briefly under, others falling around him. Spluttering, he somehow regained his balance.

"It moved, lads!" He yelled, "It'll move again!"

"Ins'Allah! Ins'Allah!"

They threw themselves forward again, numbed hands straining on the timbers, hope rising. And yes! There was another movement, slight, but steady.

127

"Again, lads! Heave!"

At that moment, even as some cheered, there was a sharp crack from the bridge. Almost simultaneously a fountain of spray rose to their right and an instant late a dull explosion raised another, more convulsed plume. Dawlish cried out as pain coursed through him, as if some massive, rapid blow had been delivered to his groin and stomach. His legs failed him and he went under. The others were down around him, half-stunned by the shockwave that had hammered through the water from the shell-burst just upstream.

They have artillery!

The realisation was terrifying as he fought to find a footing. Choking, scrabbling ineffectively for grip on the slime underfoot, avoiding a dozen flailing limbs and grasping hands about him, he somehow surfaced. He reached for the launch's stem and steadied himself on it, coughing, nauseous from the ache in his midriff. Others struggled to him – Bülent, indestructible and resolute, Nedim, bleeding from the mouth and nose, five others, all stunned and spluttering.

"Again, lads! Heave there!"

They threw themselves at the hull again, but weakly. Yet every eye was drawn to the bridge, Dawlish's also.

And hope died.

Half-way across the southerly span was the unmistakable outline of a light field piece, a mountain gun perhaps, a two or three-pounder. The handrail before it had been smashed down to provide a clear line of fire. Several figures clustered round it, heaving on spoked wheels to aim it for the next shot. Discharge could only be seconds away.

But a direct hit was not needed, Dawlish knew with terrible clarity. The shockwave of another explosion in the water would beat the life from the men in it.

The gunners stepped back behind their weapon, ready to fire. To either side of them there must be some thirty soldiers, their rifles barking through a cloud of rolling smoke that half-obscured them. Suddenly Dawlish realised that none was firing upriver towards the stranded launch – their backs were turned to it. They were crouched at the far edge of the bridge, facing downstream, blasting almost vertically downwards.

Dawlish dropped his glance to see the *Seyfi* cleaving up the narrow channel. The Winchesters of her marines, those still alive and unwounded, were pouring fire at the Russians above. Foam surged

128

around her and something long and thin extended ahead beyond her port bow, a dark mass at its tip.

"He's run the spar out!" Dawlish felt hope suddenly blazing anew within him like an ember exposed to a gale. Mehmet had extended one of his spar torpedoes and was driving towards the central bridge-support.

The Russian gunner was stooped, his fist extended to jerk the firing lanyard, when *Seyfi's* charge – thirty-two pounds of tin-encased wet guncotton – came skidding across the bridge pier's rocky base. It impacted against the wooden lattice and jammed there, the spar behind it splintering as it bowed beneath the launch's momentum.

In that instant, as Dawlish and those with him watched numb from upstream, and as the doomed Russians above despatched their last volleys, Mehmet, the erstwhile sot, threw the switch. An electrical current sped down the cable strapped to the breaking spar, detonating the charge.

The flash was blinding, a white-hearted orange flower that disintegrated the lowermost section of the bridge pillar into a thousand flying splinters that scythed down a half-dozen of *Seyfi's* occupants and scoured her bows with flame. Yet somehow she still survived, still answered her helm. She turned, scraping against the opposite shore, then tore free with the current and rushed downstream. Above her the upper half of the lattice pier seemed to hang suspended for a moment, though deprived of its support, then dropped vertically, tearing down with it the bridge spans to either side. The Russian mountain gun blasted uselessly as it skidded down the toppling incline, ploughing through the clusters of struggling men who grabbed frantically for any hold as the planking beneath them collapsed. Beams, bracing, decking and railings plunged into the chasm below, rupturing and tearing, all semblance of structure lost, screaming men tumbling among them to be crushed on the mound of wreckage rising beneath.

A cheer rose from the cold and bedraggled group clustered by *Ejder's* bows. Dawlish yelled with them, his howl not just of triumph but also of realisation that he would live – somehow. Nothing seemed impossible at that moment.

"We'll do it now, lads! We'll free her!" he shouted, "One more heave!"

The others seemed to share his renewed energy and flung themselves at the bow. Bülent went under again, somehow grasping the keel and heaving up as the others shoved.

And it shifted.

This time the launch kept moving, floating free, pulled into open water by the still-beating screw. Yussef, still crouched by his engine, eased it into slow ahead. The vessel nudged forward again and held stationary against the current.

Bülent and Dawlish were the last to board, standing chest deep, backs against the side, cupping their hands like steps to propel the exhausted survivors – Nedim, four marines and a single seaman – up into the launch. At last they too were dragged aboard, shuddering with chill.

"Upriver!" Dawlish gasped, gesturing forward. *Ejder* nudged ahead into the current.

He glanced astern. A tangle of debris blocked the gorge there like a giant smouldering bonfire, a fog of dust and smoke enveloping it. Where rifle-fire had crashed so recently a silence now reigned that was only accentuated by the moans of injured survivors and the desperate calls of would-be rescuers on the banks.

Dawlish's brain raced as it analysed the altered situation. The river was blocked and the *Ejder* was on a one-way journey upstream. Return to the coast would have to be on foot. He could only hope that the *Seyfi*, however much damaged by her own murderous weapon, would somehow limp seawards to rendezvous with the *Mesrutiyet*. Unless the news of the *Ejder's* isolation upriver reached the ironclad his group's chances of being picked up were negligible.

But the true objective of the mission still lay ahead. The priority must be to restore purpose to the pitiful remnant left to him.

The cold had been numbing in the water. Here in the air it was agony. Dawlish himself was shivering uncontrollably, the touch of his sodden clothing a torment, the water sloshing in his boots a misery. The others –only Yussef was dry – were huddled by the warmth of the tiny boiler, trembling hands extended to the glow disclosed by the open furnace doors. He would let them enjoy it a fraction longer.

"Assist me, Nedim." He forced himself forward, found his discarded weapons and clothing and somehow buckled on the belt with hands that screamed for respite. Then he and the midshipman picked up the carbines and lugged them aft.

They had rounded the bend now, and the current was sluggish in the wide channel. Another bend lay ahead, deeply shadowed by bluffs.

"Tell him to hold her stationary," he said to Nedim, gesturing to Yussef. He had to repeat himself twice, for his chill made him stutter.

130

A few minutes warming, however meagre, would be necessary if these men were to handle weapons again. He stripped off his shirt and vest and wrung a stream from them. Nedim helped him to pull off his boots, drain them and somehow jam them on again. He pulled on his jersey and jacket and their dry touch was a pleasure beyond comprehension. The others followed his example. He passed round his hip flask of brandy. Muslims or not, only one refused a mouthful and he himself drained the scant remainder. Little as it was, the spirit and the pitiful warmth from the boiler stayed their shivering.

"Get the bodies overboard." It might sound callous, but the activity would restore circulation and clear the decks of their dispiriting burden. Bülent seemed to understand the intent instantly and hurried the others to lug the corpses over the side – living comrades only minutes since and now soiled and crumpled in death. One man still lived in the forward cockpit, smothering in blood, his lung laid open by a plunging shot. There was little to do for him but lay him down gently and hope for speedy release.

Dawlish could sense fear among the chilled, exhausted men who had already given more than could be reasonably expected of them. And fear could all too easily degenerate into despair, despair that could turn into paralysis. Only confident leadership could combat those enemies. That – and action. But for action he needed a plan. He rapidly weighed alternatives, balancing the still not-inconsiderable resources at his disposal against whatever might be awaiting upstream. He knew that he had lost his greatest asset, surprise. If the railway bridge ahead had a guard, then the noise of the battle, and the cataclysm, downstream would have roused it. A direct assault from the river must be ruled out.

As the last body dropped overboard he had decided his new plan.

*

The launch prowled upstream and moored in the shadows of the northern bank just short of the next bend. The low bluffs here were seamed with flood-cut gullies, and it was through one of these that Dawlish threaded his way inland with Nedim alone. Bülent would have provided more reassuring support for this reconnaissance, but he spoke no English. In the worst event Nedim could carry Dawlish's last instructions back and the marine chavush could be relied upon to do his damnedest to execute them.

131

They stumbled painfully as they moved over the small boulders strewing the ravine's dark bed. They toiled on for five, seven minutes, movement easing their numbness. The cleft was shallower now, its sloped walls dotted with brush. They climbed to the lip and crouched there, raising their heads carefully. The ground ahead was broken, open patches of frost-scorched grass grey in the moonlight and interspersed with patches of leafless bushes. All was deserted. The river was somewhere to their right, hidden below its steep banks. The railway could not be more than a mile beyond, but a low ridge ahead blocked any view of it. From behind the faint sounds of shouting carried on the still cold air and a red glow and a column of rolling smoke told of the debris piled in the gorge by the *Seyfi's* attack having taken light. The village could not be seen from here but there was every hope of enough chaos there to keep its stricken garrison occupied.

They flitted from the gully's cover towards the first clump of brush, skirted it, paused. The next dash would take them to the ridge's crest and the intervening ground was bare.

"Keep low," Dawlish whispered to Nedim. The open space intimidated him. "Drop before the crest. We'll crawl to it."

They moved forward at a fast walk, hearts thumping, cold forgotten. They crouched ever lower as they neared the ridge, then edged forward, first on hands and knees, then on bellies, and found what they sought.

The railway lay before them, a dark streak raised only slightly above the broad, open ground beyond. Regularly spaced poles alongside carried telegraph wires. It was scarcely two hundred yards distant and beyond it the ground sloped steeply upwards again to another ridge, jagged and broken, its slopes scrub-clad. But to the right, towards the river, the ground fell away and the embankment rose higher above it to keep the track level. It curved gently away from there, its destination hidden by a rocky spur jutting from the ridge. There must lie the bridge they had come to destroy.

They dropped back, moved rightwards below the crest, checking cautiously if the bridge was in view, continuing further when it was not. The undulation had all but faded and only individual rocks provided a modicum of cover. The sensation of exposure in the icy moonlight was unnerving. Dawlish forced himself to breathe slowly and still his thumping heart. They covered some three hundred yards laterally and crawled into the lee of a boulder. Dawlish pulled his field-glasses from his jacket and wormed forward into the open.

132

There was the bridge, the vital link in the land route that led from Russian supply depots in the north to the forces now advancing so remorselessly into Eastern Anatolia. He had found Archduke Michael's jugular, and he was going to sever it.

14

The railway bridge was a wooden truss that crossed the river in a single hundred-foot span. Its base carried the track and the uprights and diagonals of the sides rose above it. The masonry foundation upon which it rested on the opposite shore was visible, a dressed-stone buttress built into the gently sloping bluff, but that on the closer bank was blocked from Dawlish's view. There was a hut on the nearer approach, perched on a wide wooden platform built against the earthen embankment.

Dawlish studied the hut. It looked unoccupied. Smoke spilled lazily from its single chimney but the door was closed and the two small windows were dark. He knew the bridge must have a guard since the garrison at the isolated village downstream could have no other purpose but to house the unit that protected it and patrolled the railway. The hut might provide temporary warmth to sentries between bouts of duty. But the noise of the battle and of the explosion scarcely a half-hour since must have been heard. In the absence of any information the guard commander, a sergeant perhaps, must have deployed his men in anticipation of an attack.

Closer towards the bridge a dark bulge showed against the embankment's side, its details indistinct in the shadows. A sudden movement by its top – a man's head and shoulders briefly showing, as quickly withdrawn – gave purpose to its shape and revealed it as a breastwork of earth and stone. It might have been six or eight yards long and the darker gashes in its sides must be loopholes. There were men inside it – but how many? The stonework of the truss's support commenced only yards beyond. That was the point of the bridge's vulnerability but while that small redoubt was manned there could be little hope of approaching it. He swept his glasses along the truss towards the opposite bank and there found a duplicate earthwork. There was movement among its shadows also, indistinct forms raised above its parapet and watching downriver.

Worried now, he swept his glasses back along the railway line on the near side, past the breastwork, past the smoking hut, two, three

133

hundred yards further back to the point where the embankment's deepening commenced. A dark hummock resolved itself as another, a third, low earthwork. The lack of movement there gave no reassurance, for he knew it must be manned like the others.

Dawlish realised that these defences, three substantial earthworks sheltering an unknown number of men, were stronger than he had anticipated. Even had both launches reached this far unobserved the odds would have been formidable. Now, with the defenders alerted and with his own force decimated, they might be impossible.

Then, as so often in his life, pride asserted itself more strongly than fear. He had faced odds as daunting before now, yet had somehow prevailed. Even now the initiative lay with him while the Russians skulked fearfully behind their breastworks. They could be no better than second-line reserves to be assigned to such a duty and they would be confused and frightened by the tumult downstream. The advantage would be with the attacker.

There had to be a way...

Dawlish focussed on the bridge. He saw that the banks were sloping so that the level railway embankments on either side rose clearly above them. The river's sluggish course was straight for two hundred yards downstream until lost in a bend. He raised the glasses again, scanned the calm black waters, slowly, estimating distances and angles and trajectories. At last he was satisfied, not completely, for the risks would still be near-suicidal, but he could think of nothing better.

He wriggled back behind the rock. "To the launch, Nedim!" he whispered. "Keep low!"

As they hurried back he mentally queried every detail of his plan again, for failure would mean certain death and success might cost scarcely less. They did not rise to their feet until the ridge's cover was well assured. The muffled sound of shouting still carried from the direction of the collapsed bridge downstream where the flames had died but a pall of smoke still hung. They passed the scrub and found the ravine they had emerged from. Within minutes they were back by the riverside and answering Bülent's challenge.

The veteran chavush had used his time well to fulfil Dawlish's instructions. One of the marines had earlier experience of the Nordenveldt. He had been given charge of it and was instructing the surviving seaman how to act as his loader. Two men had been posted as lookouts on the banks above. The others had removed the explosive canisters from the spar-heads and had freed the rubber-sheathed

134

copper wiring that connected the detonators to the electric battery and firing mechanism in the stern cockpit.

Nedim translated Bülent's report. "See, Kumandanim," he said with a hint of pride, "all ready to be carried where you wish." He motioned to two knapsacks into which the explosive heads and batteries had been packed and to the coil of wire that could be easily slung over a shoulder. "I spliced the two sections into one. It's insulated with strips of Yussef's shirt." He nodded towards Yussef, who grinned. "It was the only dry one."

"Winchesters?"

"All checked. And plenty ammunition. Each man has forty rounds in bandoliers."

"Cutlasses also. Who's the best shot?"

"Sedat Onbashi can take down a hawk at two hundred yards."

Dawlish inwardly thanked the fate that had spared this man. He would need him to take down more than hawks this night.

"The man on the Nordenveldt?"

"Abdurrahman? He knows the weapon, but he's out of practice. Good to three hundred yards. Not more."

It would have to do. His objective would be terror, not accuracy.

"The wounded man?"

"Dead." A gesture confirmed that he had been helped to a merciful end.

Dawlish understood, and was grateful.

"Gather the men then, Bülent Chavush. The bridge is ahead. We're going to destroy it and each man's role will be critical."

"Immediately, Kumandanim!" Bülent was as calm as if he had been ordered to gather a detail to clean the heads.

Yet for all the preparations the force available seemed pitifully small for the task ahead. With Yussef left to tend the engine, and the gunner and his loader to man the Nordenveldt, Dawlish's attacking force would consist of Bülent, Nedim, Sedat the sharpshooter, and two other marines, Yashar and Davut. Nedim was unproven in combat but was critical as interpreter and strong enough to carry an explosive knapsack and the cable. Yashar would carry the remaining guncotton. Bülent had already shown that he was worth two men.

They crouched in the cockpit, Nedim translating as Dawlish explained the plan, using lumps of coal to represent ridges, a cutlass the railway line. As he spoke he was conscious of precious time bleeding, time in which order might be reasserted downriver and reinforcements

135

despatched towards the railway. Yet the briefing could not be rushed. Each man's understanding was essential and with clarity would come confidence. When he finished one question, the most important, remained unasked even though it hovered among them like a palpable presence. Dawlish provided the answer himself.

"We're a long way from the *Mesrutiyet* and our enemies surround us. But our comrades won't have forgotten us. Mehmet Birinci Yüzbashi will bring them word of our situation. They'll be searching for us along the coast. That's where Bülent Chavush and I will be leading you once the bridge is blown. With God's help we will come there."

There was a murmured chorus of "Ins'Allah". With it the die was cast.

*

Dawlish led the assault force inland along the now-familiar ravine. It was almost one o'clock and awareness that only six hours of darkness remained oppressed him. He forced the prospect of a daylight retreat from his mind. Failure to achieve surprise in the action ahead would make such concern irrelevant. Critical now was the need to skirt far to the left of the defensive redoubt furthest from the bridge before crossing the railway. He had allowed an hour for this approach and hoped desperately that the launch could also remain undetected through this time.

They reached the ridge further to the left than before. It was higher here, the railway below it closer. The ground the track followed was so level that there was no embankment. Dawlish gestured to Sedat and Nedim to join him. They crouched behind a thin screen of boulders as Sedat received his last instructions.

"You see that thicket of scrub?" It lay to their right, starting halfway up the rocky slope leading down from the ridge and extending to close to the track itself.

"Evet, Kumandanim."

"It's hiding the Russian post from our view – the one I told you of, the earthwork redoubt furthest from the bridge."

Sedat nodded. He was small and wiry, with high-cheekbones and deeply sunk black eyes. Dawlish suddenly recalled him at the storming of the *Mesrutiyet*, shinning up the ironclad's side, agile as a monkey. He had shown no fear then, but he had been surrounded by comrades,

136

buoyed up by their excitement. Now the courage demanded would be of a lonelier, more patient kind.

"Stay under cover and get as close to the redoubt as you can. Stay on this side of the railway – don't cross it. Then wait."

"Evet, Kumandanim."

"Don't open fire until you see movement – you understand? Then rapid fire. With your Winchester you'll be like ten men."

The hard smile that spread across the onbashi's face told Dawlish that Sedat was one of those rare men who enjoyed killing. Low-quality garrison troops armed with single-shot Berdan or Krnk rifles would be no match for this cruel marksman hidden in the darkness if they sallied forth to support their comrades under attack at the bridge. The most difficult moment would be deciding when to withdraw. The only man to operate alone, Sedat would have to make his own decision.

The onbashi went gliding noiselessly towards the scrub, his cat-like movements losing him among the shadows. The next ten minutes were interminable, but they brought no alarm and Dawlish decided that the marksman must now be in position. He signalled to his remaining men, dispersed among the cover behind him, and they moved to the left, hidden from the railway by the ridge's crest.

They crossed the line where a curve hid it from the unseen redoubt. The ground was open and as Dawlish scuttled across, crouching, he saw that the sleepers were roughly hewn and that the rails undulated slightly. There was every sign of a rushed job, of progress accelerated and corners cut to get this strategic artery running. It was a good sign – it gave hope that the bridge might be equally ramshackle and more vulnerable to demolition than he might otherwise have hoped.

The small force joined him, one by one, in the cover of the low brush on the slopes of the opposite ridge. Now came the hardest part of the approach, moving along the ridge's lower slopes, parallel to the railway, carefully, silently, padding through the shadows, scurrying between rocks and scrub patches. Five minutes brought the first redoubt into sight. Dawlish saw with relief that scattered bushes and boulders extended to within a hundred yards of it. Sedat would be ensconced there somewhere, sheltered by some slight hollow, protected by some rock, obscured by some shadow. The earthwork's occupants, oblivious of his presence, would be nervous and confused. The earlier explosion at the lower bridge would have riveted their

137

attention on that side. They would have little concern for the slope behind them along which five men now moved stealthily.

Progress was slow and Dawlish fretted over the chance of some officer downriver keeping his head amidst the chaos and despatching reinforcements towards the railway. The *Ejder* was secured in deep shadows but must still be visible to anyone venturing close along the bank. Every minute's delay strengthened the possibility of discovery, and yet he was loath to push the pace further. Each stone dislodged by a boot, each carbine scraping against a rock, even his own by-now laboured breathing, seemed loud enough to rouse the deepest sleeper.

The railway below them was curving towards the river now, the embankment rising above the surrounding ground. The bridge came into sight, its lattice truss outlined against the silvery grassland beyond, the river a black chasm beneath. The trackside hut was still dark.

They moved closer and assembled behind a cluster of rocks. Dawlish pulled out his field-glasses. The redoubt close to the bridge was two hundred yards from them, and he was sufficiently high to have some view down into it. Built against the embankment, its parapets were level with the rail bed and it formed rectangles perhaps eight yards long and three deep on either side of the track. Even as Dawlish watched a man emerged from the position on the far side – there seemed to be steps there – and on to the track. He paused and looked round, then fixed his gaze on the now-faint smoke column downriver. A light flared briefly as he lit a cigarette. He looked down into the fortification on the near side and spoke. Three heads and shoulders appeared in response. After a brief exchange he sauntered towards the bridge. He disappeared among the truss's wooden diagonals, heading for the redoubt on the opposite side. The defenders settled down behind their loopholed rampart again.

Dawlish felt a surge of hope. Whatever concerns the attack downriver had caused earlier, the caution of the guard upstream was slipping, whether from bravado or stupidity. He could not have hoped for better.

One by one he let his force study the scene below through the glasses. One last feline approach was needed and each man must understand the ground and his own role. Nedim's whispered translations left no doubt of what was expected. Their tension was palpable now and yet Dawlish knew it must be nothing compared with the agony of waiting that their companions in the launch were enduring, or Sedat in his solitary vigil.

There was a muttered exchange between the marines just before Dawlish ordered the final movement. Bülent whispered to Nedim, his face grave, his glance fixed steadily on Dawlish. The mehendis interpreted.

"The men say you are a true Turk, Kumandanim. They are proud to follow you," Nedim said. "And so too am I."

It was a good note on which to face death.

15

They advanced with agonising slowness, crouching at first, later crawling. Dawlish was nearest the river, Nedim ten yards to his right, Yashar, beyond him, all moving diagonally towards the corner between the redoubt's shorter wall and the embankment. Forty yards further right Bülent and the other marine, Davut, were creeping towards the corner on the other side.

They had still not been detected. They were now close enough to discern the rifle-ports in the redoubt's sloped wall – three in the long face, one in each side – and to hear the occasional short phrase uttered by a bored lookout within. Shreds of cloud still passed slowly across the moon, throwing a steel-grey gloom across the still landscape.

Eighty yards remained. Kneeling behind a bush, Dawlish gestured towards Nedim, prone behind a boulder – time to dump the explosives temporarily for greater agility. The youth wriggled free of the knapsack's straps, then signalled for similar action to Yashar, further across in the shadow of a small fold. Bülent and Davut were invisible to the right.

They crept forward again, still undetected by the complacent guards. They might have come close enough to have touched the walls had a figure not emerged from the bridge. Dawlish, glancing to his left, saw him – the man who had sauntered so nonchalantly across to the redoubt on the far side a quarter-hour before. He was no less relaxed, was again smoking.

Yashar had left the shadows and was crawling forward. Dawlish's hissed warning came too late. The movement was attracting the smoker's attention. He froze for a moment. Then his arm rose to point and he began to shout.

Dawlish flung himself to his feet, throwing the Winchester to his shoulder. The man at the bridge seemed to fill his sights and he fired, ejected, fired again. With the second crash he was aware of his victim

139

going down and of a rush to his right as his companions stormed forward. He sprinted after them. Nedim and Yashar were already making for the short wall with its single rifle-port.

Further over, Bülent and Davut were pounding across. A tongue of flame flashed from one of the long-side ports, a panicked sentry blazing uselessly at some shadow in front and missing the threat on the flanks. A head bobbed above the parapet and a rifle was thrown across and its owner seemed to search for a target. Bülent fired on the run – inaccurately but enough to panic the Russian to drop down from sight.

There was shouting now, and more random fire, this time from the nearer rifle port, sharp pinpoints of orange flashing through the smoke rolling around the earthen wall. Dawlish was grateful for the clamour – the noise of rifle shots was the signal for the *Ejder* to slip her moorings and come chugging upriver, her Nordenveldt manned.

Yashar reached the redoubt. He crouched along the long wall until beneath a rifle-port, paused to satisfy himself that it was not manned, then raised himself and fired blindly inside, once, twice, three times, working the Winchester's ejection and loading loop with machinelike rapidity. On the far side Bülent was pouring fire towards the short-side loophole as he dashed forward and his companion was scrambling halfway up the embankment to take down any reinforcements crossing from the position on the far side of the tracks.

A rifle muzzle emerged from the nearest port as Dawlish approached but Nedim was beneath it and grabbing for it, and thrusting it skywards. It crashed out, its bullet lost in the darkness above. Dawlish thrust his own weapon into the hole and fired. A scream rewarded him and he fired again, even as Yashar blasted in again from his right and Bülent added his fire through the loophole on the far side.

A ripple of fire echoed from downriver, from beyond the embankment, a burst of five shots, a pause, another five, another pause, then five more. *Ejder* had moved forward into midstream and the gunner, Abdurrahman – good to three hundred yards – was hurling heavy .45 inch Nordenveldt rounds at the redoubt on the opposite side of the bridge. Whether he injured the occupants or not was immaterial. The barrage was intended to keep them behind cover and deter them from reinforcing their comrades under attack by Dawlish's group.

Dawlish sensed movement above, figures rising above the embankment, silhouetted darkly against the lighter sky behind, the occupants of the earthwork directly across the tracks. He fired at the

140

nearest but Bülent and Davut were already shifting their fire to them, dropping them mercilessly, then scrambling up on the embankment to lash fire down into the redoubt itself. Dawlish himself dashed up – Nedim was ahead of him and Yashar close behind – and emptied his weapon into the closer position, half-blinded and half-choked by the swirling gun smoke, conscious of something screaming past his face as howls of agony rose from the shambles pit beneath.

Suddenly it was over.

The launch's Nordenveldt was still hammering the position beyond the bridge, not continuously, but spaced bursts that simultaneously cowered its defenders into abject inertia and conserved ammunition. Only dead and dying occupied the redoubts where Dawlish and his exhausted, trembling men, marvelled at their own success.

"Reload!" Dawlish had no idea how often he had fired but knew that his carbine's twelve-round tubular magazine must be close to empty – the others' no less so. "Bülent – secure that hut! Nedim! Take Yashar and fetch the charges!"

Between the Nordenveldt's staccato ripples came the reports of single, deliberate shots from the north. Sedat Onbashi, that cold killer of hawks, had the distant trackside redoubt under fire from his concealed position. Its occupants might have attempted to move towards the bridge to reinforce their fellows there but Sedat's deliberate marksmanship could be relied on to keep them behind their ramparts.

One last clearance was needed now. Bülent and his faithful Davut approached the hut cautiously, flattened themselves by either side of the door. The chavush blasted at the catch, kicked the door open and Davut entered, firing rapidly. He emerged an instant later, shaking his head. No occupants. Now both men aimed upwards to shatter the telegraph wires' white ceramic insulators. A few shots brought down the cables and several powerful cutlass chops severed them. Then they crouched in the lee of the hut, alert for hostile movement while Dawlish moved towards the bridge.

He slithered back down the embankment – he wanted it between him and the sporadically chattering Nordenveldt – and moved towards the stone buttress. Its surface was sloped at about forty-five degrees. He moved forward until the wooden bridge truss was above him and the river below. He peered carefully around and there, a hundred and fifty yards distant, held stationary against the sluggish current by slow

141

revolutions, was the *Ejder*, black against the moonlit waters. A flicker of orange flame spat from her upperworks, and then another as Abdurrahman rocked his firing lever forward and hosed a volley towards the farside redoubt.

Nedim and Yashar appeared with their explosives and cable. Dawlish gestured to them to stay in the cover of the buttress. He scrambled up and found it topped by a platform of smooth stone, with a space of perhaps eighteen inches between it and the underside of the truss. A cylindrical roller, some fifteen feet long, supported the structure and showed that this end of the bridge was free to move under thermal expansion and that the structure must be fixed on the opposite side. Dawlish crawled to the end of the roller and found there was another on its inner side. The two cylinders, of cast iron, were some two feet apart. The channel thus formed would be ideal for the charges. There would be leakage at the ends and he had neither the time nor the materials to tamp these, but the heavy metal rollers and the stone beneath would serve to direct most of the explosive force upwards.

"Nedim! The charges!"

The two tin drums were passed up. Each carried twin detonators from which two insulated wires ran before terminating in bare copper ends.

"Follow me, Nedim! Bring the cable!"

He crawled into the space between the rollers, pushing the charges awkwardly before him. Nedim wriggled behind him, dragging the ends of the cable stripped from *Ejder's* torpedo spars. Dawlish twisted the ends to the wires protruding from the detonators embedded in the guncotton.

They extricated themselves unhandily, and slithered down the buttress to where Yashar was waiting with the batteries. Dawlish checked the splice Bülent had made between the two cables, then carefully replaced the insulation improvised from Yussef's shirt. It was still dry. It would serve.

"Go back," Dawlish said. "Join Bülent. Move at least a hundred yards up the track. Find cover."

Fear filled him. Even with the cables from both spars spliced together the line was too short for comfort and when paid out barely extended beyond the point where the stone buttress merged with the earthen embankment. Crouched there, he would be shielded from the direct blast of the explosion, but nothing could protect him from falling debris.

He fitted a battery into the exploder mechanism. It carried a brass screw-clamp on each terminal. He looped first one bare wire-end under a clamp and tightened it, then the second. It only remained to push in the plunger and send an electrical impulse down the cable to the detonators. He paused, conscious that the next two-inch movement might end his life.

The Nordenveldt barked into life again, five rounds. As it fell silent he drove the plunger down.

• Dawlish's eyes were closed tight, yet even so the flash that jetted out horizontally from the channel between the rollers seared them with brilliant light. Only later did others tell him how the entire bridge-end bucked upwards as flame and smoke burst beneath it, tearing away the track bed's cross members and whipping the rails like tortured, writhing serpents. The truss lifted three feet or more, rested for an instant on its cushion of expanding fire, then crashed back down on the stone buttress. A shiver rippled along the structure's length as timbers splintered under the impact. The lower longitudinal member on the upstream side was the first to fail, splitting at half-span with a crack like an artillery shot.

• Something thumped into the ground close to Dawlish and he opened his eyes to see the bridge twisting sideways, spilling sundered planking into the water beneath. Then the top member of the upstream truss failed with an even louder report and an instant later the entire structure was folding in the middle and plunging downwards in a maelstrom of foam and debris.

• The jugular had been severed.

• Dazed, yet triumphant, Dawlish staggered to his feet and stumbled back along the embankment. Scattered fragments of timber littered his path and he knew he was lucky to have survived their lethal rain. One idea dominated his mind now – survival. The coast was eight, maybe ten miles away, a range of jagged hills lay between and he was without a map. Daylight was three hours away and as the euphoria of success faded cold and exhaustion would begin to tell on his men. Scattered as they now were, they must be gathered – and convinced that escape and rescue was not just possible but a certainty.

• Nedim and Yashar came hurrying towards him, their faces elated.

- "You did it, Kumandanim!" the mehendis yelled, forgetting rank enough to hug Dawlish to him and kiss his cheek, "As you said, Kumandanim, as you promised!" Behind him Yashar was grinning and nodding wildly.

- "Back to the hut!" Dawlish found that his hands were shaking.

- A short ripple of fire from the river told of the launch still giving cover. Another volley or two and it should be slipping downstream. As it fell silent, four individual shots, spaced and deliberate, from up the track confirmed that Sedat was still keeping the redoubt there under fire. He would have to disengage soon – his orders were to do so within five minutes of the explosion at the bridge – and commence his retreat. He could only hope that the position's defenders would be too demoralised to follow.

At the hut. Dawlish brushed aside Bülent's greeting.

"Ready to move? Have you found anything useful?"

"Food, Kumandanim. Black bread, some dried beef."

"We'll take as much as we can."

"It's in those three knapsacks we found. And a canteen of water for each of us. And there's clothing, Kumandanim."

There were hooded woollen greatcoats for three men, three pairs of leather gloves and a dozen blankets, lousy and foetid with sweat, but potential lifesavers in the cold ahead.

"To be carried – not worn," Dawlish said. "We need to keep mobile. Divide them – here, let me carry my share."

They checked ammunition – nobody had more than twenty rounds – and recharged magazines.

The launch opened fire on the far-bank's redoubt for the last time as they left the hut at a fast walk, their objective the low ridge from which Dawlish and Nedim had first spied the bridge. From their right came a last crackle of rapid fire, as Sedat emptied a magazine towards the redoubt he had so successfully terrorised into inactivity. A long silence followed, punctuated only by isolated rifle shots as dispirited defenders fired at shadows and as Sedat commenced his stealthy withdrawal.

They gained the ridge. Dawlish looked back. The moon was unveiled and its pale light showed the river as an uninterrupted, unspanned, silver ribbon. Only a dark mass of debris piled against the opposite side showed that the bridge had ever existed. There was no

144

sign of the launch downstream. It had already retreated and its three-man crew must be preparing to abandon it.

They headed towards the ravine through which their initial landing had been made, moving quickly across the gentle scrub-dotted slope. A low challenge came from brush to the right, Turkish, not Russian. Bülent answered and Sedat emerged from the shadows.

"Has he been followed?"

A brief consultation. "He doesn't think so," Nedim said. "They made one attempt to head for the bridge when our attack started. He brought two down. The rest retreated and didn't leave their position afterwards. He kept them under fire to the last."

For all the haste of his withdrawal Sedat looked pale and was shivering badly. While the others had marched and charged he had lain in wet garments, slowly chilling, ignoring all discomfort in his single-minded stalker's determination.

"Give him a greatcoat," Dawlish said.

Gunfire suddenly rippled from the direction of the river, the unmistakable sound of the Nordenveldt again loosening a five-round volley, pausing, then another.

"To the ravine! Move fast!" The crew should have already abandoned their craft and be waiting for them at the end of the gully. That they were still with the launch, and in action, boded ill.

More shooting sounded from the river – rifles as well as Nordenveldt. As they reached the head of the gully the Nordenveldt fell silent with a stutter but a ragged crackle of rifle-fire still continued. Dawlish halted his group, unwilling to head down the ravine. Soon after there was a noise of stumbling, hurrying footsteps coming towards them.

Yussef blundered into view, laden with two Winchesters and festooned with bandoliers. The sole surviving sailor, the Nordenveldt's conscripted loader, followed, similarly laden. Abdurrahman, the gunner, brought up the rear. Even in the moonlight his face showed black, begrimed with the smoke of a half-hour's sporadic raking of the Russian redoubt. All three were uninjured.

"What were they shooting at?" The necessity of translation through Nedim occasioned Dawlish agonies of delay.

"Cavalry on the far side. Moving up towards the railway bridge. The crew was about to abandon the launch when they spotted the horsemen."

"And they opened fire?"

145

"They surprised the troopers – scattered them, maybe killed some. But some came down the bluffs to fire back."

The unseen cavalrymen were still firing, uselessly, blazing at imagined movements among the shadows or at the abandoned launch. With both bridges down they had no hope of pursuit. Yet their very presence indicated that somebody back at the village had regained control. And there could be no guarantee that all the Russian forces were isolated on the opposite bank.

"Has Yussef attended to the boiler?"

He had. He grinned as he confirmed that the relief valve had been screwed down, the grate opened for maximum draught and coal thrown in the furnace. A satisfying explosion was brewing to confuse the Russians further. The *Ejder*, the dragon, would die by her own fire.

Five minutes rest before leaving. They each gnawed a mouthful of bread and washed it down with water. There was a quick redistribution of loads. All now carried a greatcoat, or a blanket or two, rolled sausage-like and carried diagonally across their torsos. Only Sedat, miserably cold and trembling, wore his coat.

Dawlish and Nedim still had their hand-held compasses to rely upon for direction, but Dawlish inwardly cursed his oversight in leaving the Russian map, inadequate as it was, on board the ironclad. He knew only that between this point and the sea lay the range of hills through which the river had cut its gorge. The gradient towards the coast on the far side was steep – even precipitous in places - as they had seen from seaward, but he could remember little of how the contours had been on this landward side. The steeper the route they would follow, the slower would be their progress, but the more difficult also any pursuit. The greatest concern would be to emerge at cliffs too high to allow descent to the shoreline. That would necessitate painful movement along the ridge, parallel to the coast, until an easier route down was found. Dawlish's final decision was to head directly westwards. The river's axis from here was roughly northeast to southwest. The coast was roughly at right angles to this and a westerly retreat would not only maximise distance from the garrisons of the destroyed bridges but also avoid the cliffs by the river's mouth.

The initial march covered open grassland, broken by patches of thorny scrub. The saw-tooth crest of the coastal hills lay like a dark rampart ahead. They moved in open file, Dawlish setting the pace, a moderate but steady one that he hoped could be sustained, with short rests, until daybreak.

146

Behind them the ragged Russian fusillade faltered and died. The dull explosion of the launch's boiler some ten minutes after they set out evoked a new blaze of futile shooting, but soon that too ended. The silence left Dawlish with the nagging thought that some Czarist officer must even now be working out how to shift his forces across the river – by some ford much further upstream perhaps, or by improvised rafts – if there were not already troops on this side. Careers would have been wrecked by the night's debacle and only by swift elimination of the attackers could bureaucratic vengeance be deflected.

A roadway, a rough, winding track, lay across their route, extending leftwards towards the village. They flitted across singly towards the slope beyond, the first sustained gradient of the coastal range. The cold-seared grassland was giving away here to clumps of rougher vegetation in the fissures of broken ground. Patches of scrub still provided cover and as they toiled higher the boulders increased in size, offering in concealment what they took away in ease of progress.

And they were cold.

Only Yussef, who had tended the engine, had been spared soaking when the launch had grounded and the meagre opportunity to warm and dry around the boiler had given more the illusion than the reality of comfort. Jackets and jerseys had remained dry, and most had taken off wet shirts and stuffed them behind their belts, but their trousers and boots remained saturated. The suppressed excitement of the approach to the railway and the attack that followed had diverted minds from discomfort. Now however, plodding towards an uncertain future, the grim agony of freezing limbs and chafing skin could not be denied. Dawlish allowed them to muffle themselves now. The greatcoats went to those who needed them most – Yashar and the seaman-loader were showing signs of chilling as serious as Sedat's – and the others had to make do with swathing themselves in the looted blankets.

Dawlish tried to ignore the cold and the lice he felt burrowing into him from the foul-smelling blanket. He guessed that each man was trying to do the same but he knew nonetheless that this marrow-chilling agony was accelerating fatigue and sapping morale. It was this, as much as potential Russian pursuit, which they were racing against. He glanced eastwards. A soft pink glow ran in a narrow streak along the horizon. Full daylight was less than an hour away.

It would be time for a rest soon. A low ridge ahead, an undulation against the hillside's larger gradient, offered the promise of a resting place invisible from the track that was now a mile behind and below. Beyond lay the climb to the crest and already Dawlish was picking out a route that would carry them towards a gap lower than the flanking summits. It would be a hard climb. Better to rest before it.

"Kumandanim! Look!" Nedim was hissing urgently.

Dawlish turned. The mehendis was crouched behind a rock and pointing downwards towards the moonlit roadway. Dawlish followed his finger. He heard a drumming sound.

He had his glasses out now and was focussing. A troop of cavalry was cantering down the track, heading towards the village, not from it. Their pace was steady – whoever commanded them had the sense not to exhaust them on what might have been a long ride. There were twenty-five horsemen, probably Cossacks judging by their tough-looking, shaggy horses, and they carried lances. They must be from some garrison further north, heading to investigate the explosions along the river. The fact that their commander had the initiative to do so was worrying. Once briefed he was likely to come searching for the attackers.

Further down the slope the other fugitives had crouched under cover. Oblivious of their presence, the riders continued down the track. As they disappeared round a bend Dawlish feared he had not seen the last of them.

Rest was now out of the question. It was essential to gain the crest before daylight, to put the screen of the hills between them and those merciless lances. They pushed upwards over ever more broken and ever steeper ground. Vegetation was scant and only boulders offered cover, but over long sections Dawlish knew they must be standing out like cockroaches on a suddenly illuminated floor. There was no option but to scramble onwards, boots slipping in scree, bloodied fingers grasping for a purchase, sometimes falling, sometimes slipping back, yet always somehow advancing towards the cover offered by the next fissure or boulder.

By now they were throwing their shadows against the reddened ground before them. The sun had risen like a scarlet sphere above the distant ridge to the east. Daylight, that remorseless foe, was upon them.

The crest was still two hundred yards distant – ten, fifteen minutes toiling climb, part of it exposed. Dawlish considered briefly going to ground in a deep cleft here but then dismissed the idea. Once ensconced there they could not move before nightfall if there was enemy presence in the valley below. He resisted the urge to use his glasses to look for movement. Sunlight flashing on the lenses would mean instant betrayal and those Cossacks must have reached the village by now and might already have started their search. With the naked eye he could see nothing threatening yet. He decided to keep moving.

A cold breeze spilled down from the crest, deepening their chill on their last climb. The sky ahead was grey, heavy cloud moving inwards from the sea, pregnant with the threat of snow.

Sedat was coughing and flagging, and Bülent was half-dragging him. The others were also moving more slowly, panting in rasping breaths, heaving themselves upwards on numbed limbs, using their carbines as supports. Dawlish felt every muscle screaming as he found the will to fight the pebbles sliding underfoot and to keep climbing. The others too were somehow keeping pace, driven by the thought of those vengeful lances somewhere behind.

They reached the summit at last. It was not, as it had seemed from below, a sharp knife-edge but a rough plateau a quarter-mile wide and littered with boulders. Dawlish, gaining it first, paused for breath in the lee of a rock. The wind was stronger here, whistling cruelly. Further westwards, towards the sea, the sky was almost black. The others joined him one by one, their exhaustion all too apparent, their misery pitiful to see as the full lash of the breeze caught them.

Dawlish left them cowering behind rocks and went forward with Bülent to discover shelter. They found it in a long cleft close to the far side of the plateau, a deep gully, its sides eight or ten feet deep, its orientation such as to deflect the wind above its bed. Equally important, it offered a clear view across the rock-strewn summit. It afforded minimal comfort but nothing better could be hoped for. Bülent returned to fetch the others. Dawlish pressed on, eager for sight of the sea.

It lay a mile beyond, grey and white-flecked, snow flurries drifting across it in dark columns, visibility fading to misty nothingness scarcely three miles from the coastline.

And it was empty.

16

Dawlish felt despair howl within him as he scanned the empty sea. On the weary trudge he had resisted imagining the *Mesrutiyet* hovering patiently close inshore, ready to scoop him and his men to her iron bosom. Yet that image had lurked comfortingly in his mind and had

149

given energy to his faltering steps. Now that hope was near-extinguished he had to face the possibility that the *Seyfi*, weakened by the explosion of her own torpedo, had perhaps foundered as she had clawed seawards again. If so then Zyndram could well be concentrating the ironclad's search along an incorrect stretch of coast.

Through his glasses he scanned the terrain between him and the shore. To his left he could see the start of the cliffs that led towards the river mouth. Straight ahead however the slopes were gentle, open and rock-strewn close to the summit but grass-clad and scrub-dotted closer to a long stretch of beach on which low surf broke. There was no sign of life. It was cold, perhaps below freezing, and the wind carried a few flakes of snow.

He returned to the gully, striving to radiate optimism he did not feel. The men there were blowing on numbed fingers and rubbing calves. Bülent had posted Abdurrahman as lookout at the ravine's lip. The chavush hurried towards him with Nedim.

"*Mesrutiyet*, Kumandanim? Has it come?" Nedim had all the eagerness of the youth he still was.

"Not yet, but it will. Depend upon it." He saw the boy struggling to hide his disappointment and added: "It will be searching for us. We'll need to post a watch."

Nedim translated and Bülent's neutral expression told that he was not deceived. He could be relied upon to keep that knowledge to himself.

Warmth was the immediate priority. There was kindling aplenty, thorn clumps nestling in crannies. Had the wind been lower Dawlish would have hesitated to risk a fire – the smell of wood smoke could carry over a mile in still air. With the wind rising however, and the threat of snow to sap will and strength further, the chance was justified. Two men were set to gathering faggots and Bülent's flint and steel soon raised a small, almost-smokeless blaze. They had nothing in which to heat water or soften the dried beef they carried but even so the small ration that Dawlish allowed them proved welcome as they warmed themselves around the embers.

The watch was set – one distant sentry at the inland side of the plateau, looking into the valley beyond for signs of pursuit, one at the ravine, also tending the fire and ready to waken the sleepers, and one looking out to sea for the *Mesrutiyet*. They would be relieved after two hours. Abdurrahman and Nedim were first for the valley and ravine watches. Dawlish himself took that to seaward. When he left, those yet spared duty were already slumped in uncomfortable sleep near the fire. Yashar and the seaman were seriously chilled and Sedat burned with fever. Getting them down to the shore promised to be a nightmare and every hour of sleep they could snatch must improve their chances.

Dawlish bundled a second blanket around himself and found a shallow dip behind a cluster of boulders. It saved him from the direct blast of the wind, but not from the wet snow it carried in ever-increasing quantities, blocking for long minutes all sight of the sea below. Increasingly numb, almost incapable of adjusting his field-glasses with hands that had lost all feeling, he settled down to endure.

Cold was the enemy now, insidious, bone-deadening, sleep-inducing cold. To keep awake was vital and Dawlish challenged his brain with options for escape should they indeed prove to have been stranded. A north-westerly retreat along the coast, with the possibility of commandeering a boat at some small harbour, seemed the only prospect, but an unreal one, given the weather, the state of his men and the lack of supplies. Yet the alternative of surrender appealed even less. He doubted if those grim Cossacks understood the concept of quarter.

Drowsy now, and the image of Florence Morton came unbidden, her bony face transformed to beauty by her smile. He longed to look into her great brown eyes and tell her that …

Suddenly, somewhere in the far distance, he heard a scream. It was lost just as quickly in the wind's moaning but it roused him from thoughts of Florence and returned him to his bleary-eyed search of the grey sea. Numb as he was, the burrowing and itching of the lice that had but recently invaded his clothing was a degrading and persistent torment.

At last a blanket-swathed Bülent came to relieve him. He passed the glasses to the chavush, gave him his gloves also – inadequate as they were, he knew he would miss them – and plodded back towards the ravine. Stepping below the rim, out of the wind, gave instant comfort. He stretched his trembling hands towards the low fire, stood with his feet almost in it.

Abdurrahman, replaced by Davut, had returned from the valley watch. Nedim translated his news.

"He saw the cavalry moving back up the road," he said, "Back the way they came."

"Where did they go?"

"He can't say. They passed from sight. But more troops came, by train, from the north."

151

That must have been the distant scream then, the locomotive's whistle. They might perhaps be reinforcements for the Caucasian Front.

"How many? Cavalry, infantry?"

"A lot – too far to see exactly, but infantry, yes, many infantry. They came off the train before the bridge and they're searching the valley."

"How long ago?"

"Five, ten minutes."

"Are they coming this way?"

Nedim questioned the marine, then shook his head. "No, he says. They're sweeping up the valley, parallel to the hills. Perhaps there's an easier way to the coast there. Maybe they think we took it."

So for now there was no benefit in any option but staying put. There was nothing to retreat towards and in a worst case they could defend this position to the last. Now, above all, rest was essential.

Dawlish warmed himself inadequately by the fire – Yussef had the watch here now, and had gathered more thorn – and then curled up uncomfortably in the hollow Bülent had earlier scooped for himself in the gully's wall. He slipped immediately into unconsciousness.

*

His body, cold and stiff, howled not to be roused as Dawlish realised that Yussef was shaking him and speaking incomprehensible words into his ear. Nedim was struggling to his feet behind, dazed and blinking. Years of rising to confront emergencies brought Dawlish to instant wakefulness.

"It's Bülent, Kumandanim," Nedim said, "He wants us immediately."

They heaved themselves from the gully and stumbled over snow-dusted ground towards the plateau edge, from where Bülent was waving them forward. The wind had fallen somewhat and the sky was largely clear.

"*Mesrutiyet!*" Nedim's cry was joyful.

She was moving parallel to the coast, three miles offshore, her buff funnel and white upperworks bright in the low sun. The low wave above her ram told that she was making less than five knots.

Bülent reached out the glasses. Dawlish fumbled with dead fingers and the ironclad sharpened into focus. The thought flashed through his mind that it would be warm there, with food and rest and clean bedding, and he longed desperately for the security of that great metal fortress. He swept the glasses towards the masts – lookouts were posted on them and figures were clustered on the bridge. A momentary flash of sunlight on a lens confirmed telescopes trained on this shore. He shifted his view aft. There was the *Seyfi*, hoisted back on her chocks. Mehmet had somehow brought his battered craft seawards for a safe rendezvous.

Dawlish's heart leapt. Zyndram had not abandoned him. He fought down the ludicrous urge to wave, knowing that something more obvious would be needed to mark their presence.

"Nedim, Bülent! Bring thorn, brush, anything! We need a fire! And wake the others!"

The possibility that the vessel might glide north-westwards without sighting them added to their haste. Chill and fatigue were forgotten as they dragged thorn clumps with bleeding hands towards the blaze that Bülent soon had going. Even Sedat, fever-racked though he was, struggled to it with an armful of kindling. Fanned by the breeze, piled against a natural hearth of rocks on the seaward slope, flames roared from the dry faggots.

Suddenly something was winking from the *Mesrutiyet*, the powerful glare of the fifteen-inch electric-arc searchlight abaft the bridge and across which a shutter was clattering open and closed.

"They've seen us!" Dawlish yelled. He fancied he saw a figure in the bridge wing waving slowly – Zyndram surely, as elated as himself. The ironclad was slowing now and there was a flurry of activity aft around the stacked boats.

"Nedim! Tell Bülent to gather the men. And have Davut fetched back here immediately!"

It was a mile, and downhill, to the beach – twenty minutes, with the pace set by the weakest. Yashar and the seaman could move themselves, though slowly, but Sedat's fever was by now bordering on delirium. His efforts to feed the fire had exhausted his last reserves and he now slumped against a rock, shaking uncontrollably. Two men were going to have to half-carry him. Yussef and Abdurrahman volunteered for the duty. Dawlish had the impression that after their performance with the launch both men felt capable of anything.

Two craft were moving away from the *Mesrutiyet* now, the *Seyfi* and a cutter, the latter under sail. The ironclad's bows were turned into the wind, her screws churning only enough to hold her stationary.

153

They set off downhill, Dawlish and Nedim in the lead, the invalids and helpers following, Bülent and Davut as rearguard. They slid and stumbled down the first half-mile of boulder-pocked scree, missing footings on deceptive, snow-masked inclines, but struggling cheerfully to their feet again, cold and exhaustion counting for less now that each step brought them closer to the boats nearing the beach ahead.

Now they were past the rocky upper levels and on the smoother grassy slopes. The going was easier and were it not for Sedat, they might have made a jog-trot. A fold in the ground had momentarily blotted the *Mesrutiyet's* boats from sight but they must surely have covered half the distance to the shore by now.

Nedim suddenly froze, his outstretched hand gesturing for a halt, then to his lips for silence.

Low, but undeniable, insistent and blood-stilling, the sound came from their right of unseen, drumming hooves. Motioning to the others to keep still, Dawlish moved at a running crouch towards the edge of the fold of ground which temporarily hid his group. He flung himself prone and edged forward, sick at the prospect he knew he must find.

There was open ground beyond, almost a mile of sloped, snow-streaked grassland. At its furthest extremity, where it merged into the scrub-clad rocks closer to the summit, a tight knot of horsemen was fanning out as they encountered open terrain. The gap in the crest behind them showed where they had crossed, dragging their squat horses with them, and the speed with which they were now moving left no doubt that they had spotted the fugitives.

Dawlish counted quickly – eighteen riders, already spread out in a ragged line, already swinging down their lances, already confident of committing slaughter. His mind raced: they had numbers and mobility and probably full bellies to boot – but he had Winchesters. If they remained bent on the objective of skewering that seemed to obsess every cavalryman, then there was a chance…

"Nedim! Everybody here! Fast!"

He placed them along the lip of the fold, and just below it – close together, for they must form a rough square quickly should the horsemen flow around their flanks. Bülent was invaluable, understanding immediately what was needed. He took position to the left of the line while Dawlish took the right, Nedim, as always, by his side. Even Sedat, half-blinded by fever, begged for a weapon and stood swaying in the centre.

154

"Tell them to hold fire until I order it! And aim for the horses!" Dawlish tried to keep his voice calm. The drumming was close now, very close, and a foot to the right of the wild eye of each shaggy horse a lance-point was hovering wickedly. "Each man to loosen his cutlass," he added. "If they've got to use them, go for the horses' legs, not the riders."

Dawlish felt for the oilcloth package in his inside pocket – his resignation letter, her poem. If he died on a lance there would be no diplomatic repercussions. And Miss Morton – Florence – would never know how her handwriting had been with him to the end. Or – he admitted it now – that he loved her.

He raised his head above the lip. The Cossacks were two hundred yards away, crouched forward across their mounts' necks, lances lowered, each man enveloped in a muddy-brown greatcoat crossed with black belting, their heads muffled in shaggy fur caps. The group split, obedient to the shouted commands of an officer in the centre, who alone carried a sabre upraised. The main body, ten men, still came thundering on directly but eight riders were peeling away to the right, down the slope, with the obvious intention of curving round and cutting off the retreat seawards.

Dawlish's group was still hidden from their attackers. Bülent's steady commands had ensured that each magazine was charged, that each breech contained a round, that any tendency to raise a head above the lip was quelled with a scathing reproof. Only Dawlish could see the thundering line of cavalry, half-frozen mud flying in clods from their hooves, steaming breath pulsing from dilated nostrils, eyes wild with excitement as spurs stroked flanks and the touch of reins on necks guided the half-crazed beasts towards their unseen quarry. He felt panic rising within him – the despairing terror that infantry have felt for millennia as horsemen have come storming towards them, massive and seemingly invincible – and somehow he summoned up the resolution that those same infantry have so often found to stand their ground.

They were close enough now to see the red and white badge on the leader's cap. The second group was a hundred yards to the left, skirting the hollow. Their turn inwards to storm on to the flank must be imminent. The main body of riders was eighty yards away now, their pounding deafening.

"Heads down still, lads," Dawlish shouted. "Wait for my word, then up and select your target. Rapid fire then! The horses, mind! The horses!"

155

Nedim was calling the translation in a loud voice, devoid of the quaver of doubt that it had carried only hours before. The night's slaughter had blooded him.

The ground was shaking as Dawlish heaved himself to his feet. "Up, lads!" he shouted and brought up his Winchester. The leading horseman was fifty yards away and filling his sights. He dropped his muzzle slightly, aiming for the beast's chest, then fired.

Gunfire blasted to his left and smoke swirled before him as he ejected, saw one horse tumbling, then another, cartwheeling heavily. He flicked his lever up, thrusting another round in the breech, and fired again towards the onrushing wall of men and animals. He ejected, loaded, fired again, and again, and again, one of nine men whose repeater carbines gave them the firepower of a half-company armed with single-shot rifles. Several horses were down and one was screaming as it tried to rise on a snapped foreleg. Hooves flailed in agony and bodies catapulted across broken necks and lances splintered. Unhorsed riders, dazed and winded, staggered to their feet, grasping for sabres or revolvers, and were smashed down mercilessly.

Dawlish felt a hand on his shoulder, pulling him to face right. It was Nedim, yelling something incomprehensible and pointing to two horsemen who had somehow surged to the right and were plunging into the dip and spurring at the defenders. Nedim fired twice at them, missing, and still they came on, lances arcing over towards him. Dawlish swung his carbine across, aiming now for the rider, not the horse. The Cossack's teeth were bared, savagely white against a black bearded face, a mask of fury and elation that changed instantly to mortal surprise as Dawlish's shot caught him full in the chest and hurled him from his saddle. The horse rushed past, the flying stirrups, empty now, hitting Dawlish painfully in the arm and deflecting his carbine as he threw it across towards the second rider.

Nedim died in that instant, transfixed by the lance that crashed through his chest. His scream, inhuman and unforgettable, was suddenly cut short as he crumpled. The rider was already past, expertly swivelling his arm to let his weapon rotate as he swept by, plucking it from the lifeless body.

Fury lent Dawlish accuracy. He lined his sights deliberately – time seemed to stand still – on the Cossack's back. It was arched rearwards and half-turned towards him. He fired and savage delight coursed through him as he saw scarlet erupt in through the muddy coat and the body pitch from the saddle. He turned to Nedim, but one glance told

156

him the boy was already gone. He returned to the lip and saw now that the remnant of the main charge – three riders – was in retreat, one slipping from the saddle while a companion riding alongside attempted to hold him there. A pile of dead and struggling horses and of fallen men marked the failure of the attack.

But now Bülent was facing the group around to confront a new danger. The second knot of horsemen had gained the hollow from the downhill-side. They had come over its edge as the battle had raged to the front and now were streaking towards the rapidly redeploying defenders. Dawlish hurried to join them – Bülent had ranged them compactly, in the semblance of a tiny square. There was no time to reload – most magazines must be emptied by now – and to his horror Dawlish realised he had no idea how many rounds he had fired. He checked that this holster flap was loose, the butt-lanyard secure. He alone had a revolver to fall back on.

"Atesh!"

The volley was ragged, though it brought down two horses and emptied the saddle of a third. The next volley was more meagre still. Hammers clicked on empty chambers and hands rushed to cutlasses. Two of the horsemen were among them, their mounts plunging and kicking as lances jabbed savagely. Abdurrahman was crouched down, hacking viciously, hamstringing a screaming horse and bringing it and its rider down. Single shots rang out – the remaining magazine rounds – and bloodied blades rose and fell in dull-sounding chops.

The last three Cossacks wheeled round the struggling knot. Two had the sense to cast their lances aside and draw pistols. The third spurred his beast towards Dawlish, the lance reaching for his midriff. He raised the Winchester. The rider was in sights and he would have been torn from the saddle if the carbine had not clicked uselessly. Dawlish had eyes now only for that gleaming spike rushing towards him. At the last moment he parried it with the carbine, throwing his full weight behind it. The lance-head glanced past and he flung the Winchester away and reached for his revolver. A scream behind told him that the Cossack had found another victim.

Something whistled close by his face. He looked up – one of the pistol-wielding horsemen had reined in and was aiming deliberately at him for a second shot. He threw himself down, fired blindly, knew he had missed, then saw the rider falling from his mount, his side bloody, struck down by Bülent, careful counter of shots. Bülent was leaping across him, throwing down his now-empty Winchester as he ran,

157

drawing his cutlass, and heading for the second pistoleer, three yards to the right of his fallen comrade. He had been shooting towards the meleé and too late he saw the chavush rushing forward, slashing across his horse's muzzle with a powerful backhanded stroke. The beast plunged, whinnying in pain, throwing the rider. Bülent hurled himself on him, cleaving his skull with a dreadful downward blow.

Dawlish gained his feet and saw that the last horseman, the lancer, was down and lifeless. His surviving men stood dazed amid the carnage, surprised that they still lived.

Time now to reckon the butcher's bill. A pistol-bullet had blasted away Yussef's face in the battle's last minutes. An engineer's mate, not a fighting man, he had nevertheless acquitted himself fearlessly. The seaman loader – Dawlish could not remember his name – had gone down to a lance thrust, fighting to the last despite the chill that had sapped his energy. Nedim, the youth who had performed like a veteran, and who had found the courage he needed, lay apart, already stiffening. Dawlish regretted him most of all. The caique-owning family on Rhodes had much to be proud of.

There was no time for mourning. The sooner that the sick and wounded were on board the *Mesrutiyet* the better. Davut, Bülent's faithful shadow, was bleeding badly from an arm ripped by a lance. Abdurrahman had got a tourniquet on it and with luck he would survive. Sedat, despite his fever, had fought with savagery but now he was on the point of collapse. Yashar was little better.

A horse was screaming, its bloodshot eyes straining in agony as it thrashed on broken limbs. Dawlish could not endure it and walked wearily towards it. He looked sadly into eyes that could never comprehend why they suffered, then sought the spot where imaginary lines between opposite ears and eyes might cross. He fired into it and the cries were stilled. It was the last shot of the action.

The landing party of seamen and marines found them on the battlefield, exhausted and dazed. Mehmet, still so eager to redeem the shame of his demotion from command of the *Burak Reis*, had insisted on leading them personally. Dawlish drew him to him and kissed him on the cheek.

They withdrew, carrying their dead for burial at sea, down to the beach where light surf broke under a leaden sky and beyond which the *Mesrutiyet* lay hove-to offshore, carrying the promise of further devastation to come.

17

Once the survivors' comfort had been assured and he was satisfied with Zyndram's brief report, Dawlish retreated to his own accommodation beneath the *Mesrutiyet's* quarterdeck. He would allow himself four hours to take the edge off his exhaustion, for he was on the point of collapse and was unwilling that anyone, even the Pole, should see it. He tore off his clothing, grateful to be liberated from the lice that had tormented him and told the steward to have it thrust in the furnaces. He wanted no reminder of the nightmare he had just survived. When the steward had brought warm water and stoked the stove he told him to leave him. He soaped and sponged himself, pulled on clean clothing and then lay down.

He slumbered fitfully. Twice he woke with a cry, and hoped the steward who would be hovering near had not heard it. The first time it was the memory of Nedim's scream on the lance-tip that panicked him into wakefulness and the second it was the recollection of the struggle to free the grounded launch while his men died around him in the bullet-lashed waters. He was trembling, cold despite the blissfully clean blankets he was swathed in. He struggled to his feet, fearful of a return of the malaria he had carried with him from the humid Ashanti forests of the Gold Coast three years before, and which had struck twice since. He always carried quinine and now he dosed himself heavily with it. He lay down again, staring into the darkness, forcing himself to rest even if he could not sleep, knowing that he must appear assured and confident when he emerged on deck.

But it was not the terrors of the last night that alone tormented him, nor apprehension at the yet more violent action that he had planned for the coming days. It was awareness that had he died on those Cossack lances he would have been somehow unfulfilled. His passing would have been honourable – for he had not flinched or panicked – and had word of it somehow reached London, as the copy of the resignation letter on his body might well have assured, Topcliffe could have closed his file with a favourable comment. And then the Admiral would have sought out some other ambitious young officer who would be ready to take on any task as long as it offered advancement. Dawlish knew that he would be remembered with little love. He doubted if there would be prolonged mourning in Shrewsbury. His father had seen little of him for two decades and now he had a young wife to console him. His sister Susan, married to a

159

drunken mill-owner and worn out by too many childbirths, would weep bitterly for him but all too soon there would be another difficult pregnancy to help her to forget him.

He rose, began to dress in his formal uniform, stiff with gold braid, suitable for the first sad duty that faced him. And as he did a doubt nagged him about the validity of the bargain he had made with himself a decade before, after... after he had made a fool of himself over that girl he had loved, after she had so painfully scorned him. He had resolved to find fulfilment in advancement and rank, in duty and achievement, in the command of ships and men, and to find it alone without a woman by his side, not another of spirit who might betray him, nor one dull and worthy who might smother his ambition with comfort. A year after his humiliation, service with a rocket-battery in Abyssinia had redeemed his career. He had gone on to build a reputation for technical aptitude, for understanding of electricity and torpedoes and steam machinery about which so many sail-obsessed officers feigned contempt. Service with a Naval Brigade on the Gold Coast had earned him the commendation of General Wolseley himself. He had volunteered for the East African Anti-Slavery Patrol, eager for the action it promised, and daring there had brought him to Topcliffe's notice, and to clandestine service, brutal but decisive. That had earned him promotion to Commander. With Topcliffe's hard-earned support yet higher command could be in his grasp and flag-rank at an early age was not inconceivable. But would that alone be enough to make his life worthwhile?

"The price seems very high," Florence Morton had said...

A small internal voice, one which he had heard before but had always stilled, reminded him now that the price was not paid by himself alone. Men had died because of his calculated risk-taking, had been sacrificed to advance his ambition. Captain Butakov was only one. Had that decent Russian civilian seaman been in peril on the sea in peacetime he would have faced any hazard to assist him. And Nedim's body was not alone as it lay, flag-shrouded, bloody, on the deck overhead. It was not just to preserve the Sultan's power that Nedim had died, nor even to secure Britain's route to India. In the raid on the railway Dawlish's own career had been at stake, and to further it he had not hesitated to lead simple men to almost certain death. As he would do again in the coming days...

And, as so often before, he stilled that small, disturbing voice.

160

He stared into the semi-darkness and heard the rush of water alongside the hull outside, the odd hollow reverberation of a wave breaking on the iron plating. He felt alone, wholly alone, and knew that he would be unmourned when his time came – and that could be in two or three days. Many would perhaps even rejoice in his passing, glad his ambition would no longer threaten their modest happiness – happiness such as he had denied himself, and yet which he had caught a glimpse of with Florence Morton. There could be happiness in exploring new places with her arm linked in his, in sharing her delight in discovery of books and learning, in drawing strength from her, from her courage and optimism and determination not to be shackled by her origins. And yet her origins, her life in service... it always came back to that.

He stopped himself, told himself that it was fatigue that was impairing his judgement and making him crave affection, just as when imminence of death on that hillside had made it seem so simple to love her. But that moment was past. He had prevailed against those Cossacks nonetheless, had survived his savaging of the Russian Army's supply lines and must have earned one more measure of approval from Topcliffe. And now he must consolidate that achievement with another, yet more deadly, stroke. By accepting the Sultan's commission he had pledged his honour that he would. He must not doubt himself, for self-doubt was as insidious an enemy, and perhaps an even more deadly one, as cold had been on the numbing retreat from the railway.

He would hold fast to the bleak bargain he had made with himself. In the life which that bargain demanded there could be no place for that brave, clever girl whose birth and background could only embarrass him. He would forget her. It would be better for her, and better for him.

He closed his tunic and moved to the door, buckling on his sword.

*

The burials were hard to endure, very hard, Nedim's worst of all. The gold braid on the uniforms of Dawlish and his officers seemed an inadequate tribute to the men who slipped one by one from beneath the ensign-draped stretchers into the foaming waters alongside. It chilled Dawlish to scan the faces of the men listening in respectful

161

silence to the imam's prayers and to wonder which next of them was already condemned to the same final plunge.

He went to the bridge afterwards. The coast lay forty miles away over an indistinct horizon. Darkness was falling and a twenty-knot wind was sending sleeting rain marching in grey columns across the foam-capped waves. The *Mesrutiyet* ploughed slowly into them, foredeck awash. Two cables to starboard a dark shape told of another ship keeping station, her poles bare, sparks spilling from her single funnel.

"The prize appears to be managing satisfactorily." Dawlish lowered the glass through which he had been observing the other vessel, a twelve-hundred ton merchantman.

"It's Fatih Mülazim's first command," Zyndram said. "He handled the boarding party well also."

Fatih was scarcely older than Nedim had been, another young officer keen to prove himself.

"You did well yourself." Dawlish said. "You thought and acted quickly." He had heard the bones of the story when he boarded.

"I can't take much credit." The Pole shrugged. "An hour after we had dropped the launches the lookout spotted her slipping along the coast with all lights doused. She was heading for Sokhumi – I doubt if any of them are risking Poti anymore. She didn't see us until our searchlight illuminated her. Fatih took the boarders across and there was no resistance."

"What ship?"

"The *Glukhar*, of Odessa. Sailing from Novorossiysk – food and winter clothing mainly."

"Her engine?"

"Five hundred horsepower, compound. Quite a new ship, reasonably maintained. So I followed your instructions and kept her in company."

Dawlish nodded. He had plans for the prize. Fatih would soon have another chance to prove himself.

"And the prize crew?"

"Fatih, an üschavush, two onbashis and ten men. The Russian engineer and stokers are still on board and the captain's confined to his cabin. The remainder are detained here."

"Information?"

There was plenty. In the first despondency of capture the *Glukhar's* company, from the captain down, was prodigal with details.

162

The raid on Poti had brought coastal movements to a near standstill, crowding the ports of Novorossiysk and Gelendzhik with shipping. Only fast steamers which could expect to reach the harbours nearer the front in a single night were attempting the run. No greater condemnation could exist of the Czar's tardiness in building a seagoing Black Sea Fleet in the six years since revised international accords had allowed him to do so. A fraction of the wealth squandered on Russia's circular Popovka ironclads could have purchased a half-dozen smaller craft suitable for convoy protection. Now, with the severed railway increasing the dependence on coastal transport, they would be missed.

Through the following day the *Mesrutiyet* and her prize steamed slowly back and forth within the rendezvous area. Dawlish made his rounds, praised and rebuked, drank chai, and witnessed a drill that showed that the guncrews had by now been raised to machine-like efficiency by their martinet leader, Selim Yüzbashi. Dawlish found that the survivors' stories of the bridge attack had flashed through the ship and he sensed new respect in the men's reaction to his presence.

No sail was sighted and the ironclad stayed deliberately far from shore. Dawlish had himself pulled over to the *Glukhar* – a drenching crossing, a hair-raising transfer and an even worse return. It was worth it for the information sullenly volunteered by the despondent Russian captain and for the detailed inshore and harbour charts the ship carried. Dawlish closeted himself to study them closely, translating their Cyrillic markings with the aid of a dictionary, scribbling ideas on a pad and covering the carpeted deck with crumpled balls of rejected notes. By nightfall he had a plan to share with Zyndram. Another four hours passed in probing it for weaknesses and modifying it to address them. When he slept it was with the knowledge that only absence of reinforcements stood in the way of the plan's realisation.

Those reinforcements arrived the following morning, November 10th The clouds had cleared and the wind was abating. The top masts of the now-repaired ironclad *Alemdar* stood out dark against the rising sun and as her hull also rose above the horizon the upperworks of the painfully plunging and rolling *Burak Reis* could be seen in her wake. A mile astern of the two warships a grimy collier plodded doggedly.

By midday conditions were adequate for the *Burak* to draw alongside the collier. They pitched and ground and rolled together, separated by rope fenders, as a hundred sacks of coal were slung across. When Onursal, now seasoned as the *Burak's* commander, made his way across to the *Mesrutiyet* for the conference Dawlish had called,

163

he left his bunkers replenished and a score of sacks stacked on deck. His pride was justifiable when he reported intercepting three coastal sailing vessels outside Sokhumi two days before – two sunk and the third sent under prize-manning to Trabzon.

The invited officers gathered round the cloth-covered wardroom table, unsure what to expect. Dawlish could sense their curiosity: Onursal and Fatih, outranked by the gunnery and navigation officers of the two ironclads and conscious of their junior status; Hassan, punctilious about receiving the respect his rank demanded and proud of the speed of his rehabilitation of the *Alemdar*; the *Mesrutiyet's* shaven-headed gunner Selim, obviously eager for an opportunity to bring his beloved guns into action; Zyndram, privy to what was to come, courtly as he saw them seated.

Chai was served in silver-mounted glasses by a steward who also brought mint lokum on a salver. Compliments and congratulations were exchanged, no less heartfelt, Dawlish realised, for a formality that seemed even more stilted when translated. God was thanked for the recent successes and for the safe return of Kumandanim. At last a raised eyebrow from Zyndram signalled Dawlish that the traditional courtesies had been fully observed, that the preliminaries could be ended. Dawlish moved to the tables.

"We have severed the enemy's communications by sea and by land, Gentlemen," he said. "Now their immobilised shipping crowds their ports. No finer target could be dreamed of."

He swept away the cloth to reveal a large-scale drawing of an oval anchorage, half-surrounded by mountains, and with a narrow opening seawards, that he and Zyndram had made in coloured inks the previous night. All heads craned towards it, recognition dawning instantly on several faces.

"Gelendzhik!" Hassan pronounced the name.

"Gelendzhik indeed, Hassan Kaptan! And I'd be hard pressed to name a finer natural harbour! If Novorossiysk didn't have easier access from the hinterland, then I've no doubt that Gelendzhik rather than Novorossiysk would be the main harbour of the Kuban wheat lands. But it's been neglected as Novorossiysk has grown. It's not even judged worthy of permanent coastal batteries, according to our intelligence. It has only gained importance as an anchorage recently as Archduke Michael's armies demanded support. And now it's packed with shipping – Fatih Mülazim, I believe you can confirm that?"

164

"Assuredly, Kumandanim! The officers of the *Glukhar* – our prize – indicate at least twenty ships anchored there, all held back after word was received of what happened at Poti."

"Onursal Mülazim? Any news from your prizes?"

"The same, Kumandanim. Maybe even thirty ships there."

"And Russian generals whose troops are freezing and short of food before Kars will be demanding that those ships risk sailing, regardless of what's waiting for them outside," Dawlish said. "Admirals commanding desks in St. Petersburg will be agreeing with them. I don't intend to hunt them on the open sea, gentlemen – we've neither the ships nor the time to run them down if they scatter. We're going to sink them in Gelendzhik itself before they can weigh anchor."

"Nicholas Kaptan!" Hassan's eyes were serious above his upturned moustache. "Is there information about the defences?"

There was, thanks to the fearful but cooperative captains and officers of the *Glukhar* and of the prizes that the *Burak* had taken. Dawlish's finger moved over the drawing. "Batteries – army weapons in earthworks – on the headlands here and here." It was easily said, but sailing even an armoured ship between artillery on either side of a harbour entrance was no small undertaking.

There was worse. "There are mines, electric mines, detonated from the shore." Dawlish motioned to a red-inked arc stretching between the headlands, concave inwards towards the landside. "We've reports from crews of three of the four prizes of seeing them being planted. There are no channel buoys and all ships entering and leaving are being piloted." He didn't say it, but these mines worried him more than the guns.

"With how many vessels will we enter the anchorage, Nichols Kaptan?"

"With all except our collier."

Then, picking up four coloured blocks from the table-corner, the *Mesrutiyet*, the *Alemdar*, the *Burak Reis* and the *Glukhar*, Dawlish began to demonstrate how.

165

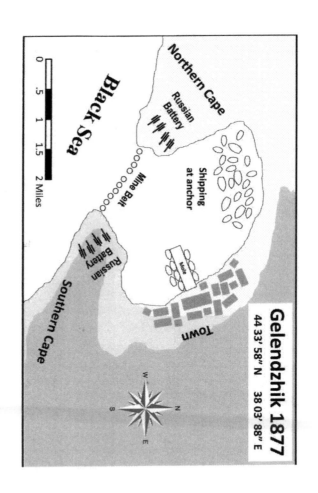

Gelendzhik 1877
44 33' 58" N   38 03' 88" E

18

The breeze was westerly, moderate but cold, piling clouds before it towards the rocky coast. The moon and stars were blotted out, making accurate position fixes impossible for the four ships steaming slowly northwards in line ahead towards Gelendzhik, the *Mesrutiyet* leading and only the dimmest of navigation lights visible to her consorts astern. They rolled gently in the four-foot waves coming in on their flanks. On each darkened ship the crew was at battle stations.

Dawlish held his watch to the *Mesrutiyet's* dim binnacle light. Five sixteen. By seven the mountains still invisible to starboard would be silhouetted by dawn and as the sky brightened his squadron would come sweeping shorewards from the still-dark sea. His rounds of the vessel were complete. Throughout the ship furniture and fittings had been broken down and stowed away, fire-mains were under pressure and watertight doors were clipped closed. The men had eaten at their stations. Far below the engines were panting smoothly. Inside the battery the twelve-inch cannons were charged and loaded, their crews standing to. It only remained to open the thick iron shutters blocking the ports and the great weapons could run out for action.

The *Alemdar* was an indistinct and blacker mass against darkness aft. Hassan had done well to get his ironclad to the rendezvous in time, and the gunnery exercise he had conducted while underway had gone well.

Shrouded by darkness, the *Glukhar*, the Russian prize, followed the *Alemdar.* Her new commander Fatih had been left with no doubts as to the dangers ahead and for once Dawlish did not find his response of "Ins'Allah" infuriating. A fatalistic outlook was perhaps desirable for any man faced with the task with which the young officer had been entrusted. Soon now Fatih would have the *Glukhar's* frightened Russian captain brought to the bridge, and would hold a revolver to his temple.

The *Burak Reis* was last in line, though invisible to Dawlish. Knowing Onursal well by now, he was confident he could rely on him to be battering ahead in his shallow-draught, uncomfortable yet deadly gunboat. Even-fatter prey than at Poti lay ahead for her deadly Krupp breech-loaders.

Dawlish paced from one bridge-wing to the other, conscious of the tenseness in the open-backed wheelhouse as he passed. He tried to force away the persistent memory of Miss Morton. He wondered how

167

she spent her days in Istanbul, an unwelcome guest of her mistress's brother Oswald. Lady Agatha, however well-meaning, would be absorbed in her own scholarly researches and innocently oblivious of any boorish slights he might inflict on the proud girl. She would be accompanying Lady Agatha to receptions at the Embassy and elsewhere, facing more nights of cold ostracism and stoic endurance as on that night at Hobart's soiree. There had been unconscious cruelty in Lady Agatha's decision to make a companion of her maid, however clever, and to expose her to a world that would never forget her origins, and to pleasures she could only share on sufferance. And if she were to marry above her station her life could only be worse, a succession of endless and petty humiliations. His decision to forget her was best for her, Dawlish told himself. He must not let sentiment move him again.

Dawn came slowly. The mountains were discernible now in faint outline, five miles off the starboard bow of the northerly-steaming warships, their forward slopes opaque masses.

"He recognises the peaks," Zyndram gestured to the seaman who had sailed this coast on a civilian trader. "He thinks we're about three miles southeast of Gelendzhik,"

"Maintain speed," Dawlish said, "Steam parallel to the coast."

As the ironclad swung to port, Dawlish knew that she and her consorts must be all but invisible from shore as they ploughed onwards at some eight knots.

There were lights ahead now, pinpricks at first, then clusters against the dark slopes. The diffused brightness in the eastern sky was growing steadily. Dawlish stood in the bridge wing, Zyndram by his side, both with telescopes.

"There, Nicholas Kaptan," the Pole said, "There's the entrance. You see the gap there? Lights to either side, weaker lights beyond?"

There was just enough light to make out the two headlands, the more northerly the lower, the opposite higher, topped by a lighthouse and blocking from view the greater part of the town that clustered on the south-easterly shores of the oval bay. The Russian batteries would be guarding the mile gap between those headlands, creating a gauntlet that now must be run. There was still no sign that the defenders had spotted the ships approaching from the dark sea.

"Battle formation," Dawlish said. "Initiate the signals, Zyndram."

Now the sequence of movements commenced that had been so exhaustively rehearsed with wooden blocks in the saloon. Triggered by the lanterns hoisted to the *Mesrutiyet's* signal yard and relayed by the *Alemdar*, the Russian prize, the *Glukhar*, pulled from her position in line, increased revolutions and came steaming ahead to take station two cables ahead of the leading ironclad. As she ploughed past Dawlish could just discern Fatih by the wheel, the wretched Russian captain pinioned by a seaman at his side. The young officer's pistol was raised and the prisoner was being left in no doubt that he was required to pilot the vessel into the harbour. Upon his memory, and the strength of his desire to save his own skin, would depend the squadron's ability to navigate safely through the mine-belt.

The *Burak Reis* was also racing ahead, passing the *Alemdar*, and reducing revolutions again so as to match speed with the *Mesrutiyet* as she drew level with her, fifty yards to port. The heavier batteries, Dawlish reasoned, would be on the higher, southerly, headland and the ironclad's interposed bulk would offer some protection to the gunboat.

The gun-port shutters opened with metallic clangs. The muzzle-loading rifles on both ironclads ran out. The instructions to the gunners were unambiguous – engage shore artillery as it identified itself. The harbour entrance was a mile ahead and there was light enough to discern individual buildings. The northerly part of the great oval bay was coming into view and so too were the masts of shipping anchored there, barely distinct against the dark hills behind. The cold winter brightness was growing by the minute. Detection must be imminent.

A rocket suddenly rose from the southerly headland and exploded in incandescent white. Somewhere there a lookout had spotted the nearing warships and, though the battle-ensigns whipping aloft – white crescent and star on a blood-red background – were still invisible, had deduced that they must be Turkish.

Three minutes passed before the first flame lanced out from the headland. The weapon's deep report reached the approaching ships instants before a white plume rose harmlessly to starboard of the *Glukhar*. A second stab of orange, and a third, and a fourth, followed, all from the same hummock now becoming identifiable as an earthwork high on the southerly cape. They were twenty-four pounders or heavier, siege artillery, Dawlish surmised, hastily diverted to coast-defence. Their carriages would be ill suited to the rapid realignment needed for engaging moving targets. The next shots were as harmless as the first, but the range was shortening and the gunners must be correcting frantically.

169

A seaman listening by the voice pipe passed a message to Zyndram. "Selim Yüzbashi's compliments," he told Dawlish. "He believes he can reach it with the starboard forward twelve-inch."

"Remind him that he has full discretion, port or starboard."

Underfoot Dawlish felt the rumble of the twelve-inch's rollers being hauled about on their iron track. It was full daylight now, easing aiming for friend and foe alike. Two flashes to port, followed by two more in ragged succession, the reports sharp cracks, indicated a lighter battery opening from the northern side of the entrance – nine-pounder field guns like those at Poti. Their shells plunged close to the *Glukhar*, which was now commencing a turn to starboard to run straight towards the middle of the entrance. On the *Burak Reis*, advancing steadily in the *Mesrutiyet's* lee, masking her port cannon, the forward Krupp six-inch was slewing towards the new threat.

The heavy weapons in the southerly earthwork opened again. Their aim and ranging was better now, but the *Glukhar's* turn brought her a hundred yards inside the cascading fountains that they threw up.

The *Mesrutiyet's* starboard twelve-inch roared, its billowing smoke obliterating all view until the vessel's forward movement shook it free. It fired on close to maximum elevation as the ironclad's roll reached its peak, hurling its seven hundred and seven-pound explosive projectile into the hillside eighty yards short of the earthwork. It erupted in a volcano of flame and flying soil, hiding the Russian battery behind a wall of cascading debris. Inside the *Mesrutiyet's* armoured box Selim's toiling gunners sponged and reloaded with the precision and speed to which he had trained them so relentlessly.

Over to port the *Burak Reis's* forward Krupp barked sharply towards the northerly nine-pounders. Dawlish spared it no thought – direct hits were less important than distracting the enemy aim. The *Mesrutiyet* was swinging to starboard now, following in the *Glukhar's* wake, and his gaze was riveted on the merchantman which must now be only yards from the worst threat of all. She was close to the centre of the entrance, and turning slightly to starboard, then straightening out again. Fatih's terror must be no less than that of the Russian captain acting as unwilling pilot as she ploughed towards the invisible mine-belt. He had revealed under questioning that the cleared channel was a hundred yards wide but no buoys marked it. Somewhere onshore, probably high on the headland near the earthwork, Russian officers would be observing the *Glukhar's* progress and plotting it on a chart. A hand would be poised above a battery of switches, ready to send an electric current down a cable to explode whichever unseen mine the vessel blundered closest to.

One of the Russian siege-weapons fired again, her target now the *Mesrutiyet*, for the *Glukhar* had passed beyond the battery's arc of fire. The shell screamed overhead – the aim was good, even if the ranging was poor – and plunged a hundred yards beyond. But the starboard forward twelve-inch had been run out again and it fired on the uproll, its shell tearing once more into the hillside short of the redoubt but rippling a tremor through it to distract the gunners and blind them by a hail of falling soil. Another report announced the *Alemdar's* first salvo. She opened with the single four-inch in her battery that could yet be brought to bear, one of those hauled so laboriously from the Batumi defences. Its shot fell short of the earthwork but it added to the veil of dust and smoke obscuring the aim of the Russian gunners. The *Burak's* six-inch was now in almost continuous action, laying down an effective barrage on the northerly battery, slowing its rate of fire and disrupting its effectiveness. As the Russians fired from both north and south white plumes rose around the advancing ships, some close enough to drench them in spray.

With a dull roar the sea rose like a glassy mountain beneath the *Glukhar*. A feathery geyser burst from it and rose past her starboard bow. A convulsion ran through the ship and her foremast whipped. Almost instantly her fo'castle plunged and disappeared, water rolling aft to break against the raised deckhouse.

"A mine!" Zyndram called, "She's hit a mine!"

Dawlish's mind raced – the *Glukhar*, the sacrificial offering, had served her purpose and a keen-eyed Russian observer had detonated the mine closest to her as she strayed blindly to the side of the clear channel. But to which side? Did safety lie to port or starboard? The chances were equal, and he had to decide immediately if the *Mesrutiyet*, following a cable and a half astern, was not to share the *Glukhar's* fate.

"Pass to port," he said quietly. It was a guess but he tried to sound confident.

Zyndram rapped out the command. The wheel spun through the helmsman's hands. A long blast on the steam whistle alerted the *Burak Reis* as the ironclad's ram slewed across and she followed suit. The *Glukhar* was sinking now, her stern lifting, her churning screw visible, her surviving crew jumping into the boat they had dropped. She was turning slightly, her stern swinging to port as it the wind caught it.

171

Suddenly the sea erupted beneath her again and another fountain went climbing past her canted funnel – another remotely detonated mine.

Dawlish saw her back breaking, her stern crashing down in maelstrom of spray and foam, but it was not that which filled him with horror but the realisation that this explosion had been to port, not starboard. He had made the wrong guess and the *Mesrutiyet* was ploughing straight for the same cluster of mines that had destroyed the Russian prize. Her wreckage was a cable ahead, the hull already submerged, waters foaming around her settling upperworks.

Desperate, bracing himself for the explosion that might convulse the ironclad within seconds, Dawlish cried out "Pass to starboard!" but Zyndram was ahead of him, throwing himself on the wheel and spinning it over. For long seconds the *Mesrutiyet* seemed fixed in her course as she bore down on the shattered merchantman, but then, slowly, agonisingly, she lurched to starboard. Spars and floating debris from the wreck scraped along her port side as she moved into the open water beyond.

There was no explosion. The mine belt had been passed and Gelendzhik lay at Dawlish's mercy.

19

The *Mesrutiyet* forged onwards, the great open expanse of the bay before her, secure from the arc of fire of the land batteries. The *Burak Reis* was stationary close to the tips of *Glukhar's* sloping masts – still visible, for she seemed to have grounded – and picking up survivors. The *Burak's* after weapon was barking defiance towards the field guns to the north.

On the southern headland the Russian battery blasted out again, the *Alemdar* now its sole target. The shells fell closely but uselessly and the ironclad replied with the turntable-mounted eight-inch rifle amidships, which could now be swung round to bear. Her shells flung up gouts of soil on the hillside short of their target as she too passed beyond the battery's arc. She churned safely past the *Glukhar's* grave and the *Burak* followed after.

Dawlish felt a flush of triumph. He had three undamaged warships inside the Russian anchorage. The ships it sheltered, and the town, were at his mercy. The bay was an almost perfect oval, three miles long, half that wide, its long axis lying southeast to northwest, athwart the path of the advancing warships. The land was lower to port, but ahead

172

and to starboard rose steep hills. In the half-mile of level ground between them and the water lay a straggling town, its buildings concentrated to the southeast, behind the headland carrying the heavy battery. There the bay was beach-rimmed and a single mole jutted out, shipping moored along its sides, several double against each other, eight or ten in total, and two cranes and mounds of crates and sacks. A locomotive was scurrying townwards along a track laid on the pier. The stone building beyond must be the railway station, with trucks in a yard behind it. Wooden warehouses, many unpainted and obviously hastily erected, stretched between it and the beach.

More shipping, two dozen vessels perhaps, large and small, lay anchored in the centre of the bay. Most seemed heavily laden. The yards of the sailing craft were bare and the meagre smoke drifting from the steamers' funnels told of only harbour-pressure, all confined here in passive fear of the wrath that had now found them. Already boats were dropping from them and were pulling in panic for shore.

It was Poti, but on a larger scale.

The *Burak Reis* steamed slowly towards the cluster of shipping in the middle of the anchorage. She turned so that they lay on her port flank, exposed to both her vicious Krupps. They opened on the nearest vessel, a small steamer, tearing into her waterline at point-blank range as the gunboat moved calmly past, then swung across to bear on the next target as their first victim began to heel. The slaughter had begun.

The *Alemdar* was already in action. Held stationary on her engines, she was firing on the open rear of the battery on the southerly headland. The four heavy Russian pieces inside the earthwork were clearly visible, naked now to attack from a direction never anticipated. The ironclad's gunners were firing uphill with weapons of different calibres, making sighting difficult, but their projectiles were falling only fifty or eighty yards short of the now-exposed artillery. Dawlish saw with satisfaction that another few salvos should see the aim corrected and the threat posed by the battery to his ships' withdrawal eliminated.

It was now the *Mesrutiyet's* turn to devastate.

She lay broadside on to the end of the mole, her engines alternately eased into ahead and astern to hold her virtually stationary. Both twelve-inch weapons to starboard were run out and trained on the beam. The jetty's hammer-headed end was three hundred yards distant. Behind it, as along a narrow roadway, the last of the crews of the ships moored alongside were fleeing for safety. Secured to the pier, and to each other, the ships were defenceless.

173

The reports of the *Mesrutiyet's* guns were ear-shattering. Dawlish saw the twin flashes of impact, one in a vessel at the end of the mole, the other in one halfway along it. Fragments of wood and metal arced skywards and a mast flailed, then staggered over. The first flames licked hungrily amid rising smoke.

Dawlish glanced toward the centre of the harbour. Two vessels, a steamer and a topsail schooner, were burning fiercely. A brig was heeling over, her stern awash. A patch of flotsam and bobbing black dots showed where another vessel had already gone down. A score of other ships still awaited their fate and the *Burak Reis* was circling them like wolf around a flock of sheep. At a cable range and in sheltered waters the Krupps' accuracy was absolute and a single shell into the flank was sufficient to rupture any hulls they ranged on.

The *Mesrutiyet's* twelve-inchers blasted again, their elevation raised slightly, so that their projectiles fell among the vessels closer to the town, tearing down yards and masts and ripping through decks and bulwarks before exploding. Sheets of fire erupted vertically as hatch covers yielded to infernos within the ships hit initially and as flames licked up tarred rigging, jumping to the vessels moored next to them. A crane on the mole toppled over and the stores piled by it were burning, oily black smoke billowing above.

Suddenly a loud explosion from the southern headland drew Dawlish's attention. One end of the earthwork there seemed bitten away and a flame-streaked column of dust and smoke rose from the crater. The *Alemdar* had bored a lucky shell into the magazine, effectively demolishing the battery. She was now free to join in the port's destruction.

A pall of smoke grew ever thicker over the anchorage and town as the carnage continued. On all three warships parched and sweat-sodden gun-crews laboured to make the harbour a hecatomb of blazing and sinking ships. The *Burak Reis* still circled, steering daintily between flotsam, burning wreckage and capsized hulls. A few boats threaded the maze of destruction, Russian crewmen too stubborn to have fled their vessels earlier, now dragging survivors from the debris-laden waters.

Dawlish ordered the *Mesrutiyet* to come about – it was time to bring the port weapons into play. The ships along the mole were now engulfed in a single blazing shroud. The *Alemdar* had come in as close inshore as she dared – a leadsman was in action in her bows – and had also turned to employ her port battery, her target the cluster of wooden warehouses.

174

Dawlish gestured to Zyndram. "Tell Selim Yüzbashi to shift his aim to that grey building," he shouted, "the railway station and those yards beyond it." Zyndram moved to the voice-pipe to relay the order.

Once a few broadsides had rained destruction there it would be time to depart. The *Burak Reis* had fallen silent, for no targets remained for her Krupps, and the *Alemdar* had initiated a satisfying inferno among the warehouses. It was less than an hour since the shocked Russian gunners had sighted the squadron steaming out of the darkness. Dawlish surveyed the panorama of destruction and misery. Russian troops would freeze in Anatolia this coming winter because of this morning's work. Nusret and Hobart would rejoice for it and in London Topcliffe would smile and reflect that he had chosen well.

The *Mesrutiyet's* port weapons opened on the railway station, hurling up shattered wagons and gouging craters amidst the rails and points. The ironclad fired again, one projectile hitting the station building squarely this time and tumbling a full third of it into rubble while the other added to the destruction of the marshalling yard.

"Cease firing, Zyndram Yüzbashi." Dawlish lowered his telescope. "Signal general withdrawal."

A word from Zyndram sent the yeomen to bend on and hoist the necessary flags. The order was pre-decided: *Mesrutiyet* leading, *Alemdar* to follow, *Burak Reis* in the rear. With the projecting topmasts of the sunken *Glukhar* as guide to the cleared channel the passage through the mine-belt should be without significant hazard.

"My father and my grandfather should have seen this day, Nicholas Kaptan," Zyndram said. "To have seen the Russians so humiliated, to have …"

But Dawlish did not hear him. His gaze was riveted seawards, towards the harbour entrance – and what he saw there shocked him.

A single slim buff funnel was slipping into sight past the northerly headland, approaching from the direction of Novorossiysk. It vomited black smoke and surmounted a short, low hull that was almost awash. Above its deck rose a meagre black-painted superstructure and the unmistakable shape of an armoured breastwork, the barbette, over which two massive cannon projected menacingly. It advanced slowly into the gap between the headlands, and as it did it turned. The single funnel split and showed itself as two individual units placed athwartships. High above, on the signal mast, the ensign of St. Andrew – a blue X against a white background – whipped in the breeze. As the vessel turned its hull grew neither longer nor shorter. Dawlish knew

175

then what he confronted, what now blocked retreat through the harbour entrance.

The three circular ironclads Russia had built to protect the Dnieper Estuary and the Straits of Kerch were little more than floating batteries, slow and poorly manoeuvrable despite their six screws. Experiments that were unlikely to be repeated, the *Popov, Novgorod* and *Kazan* had evoked mirth and sarcasm from officers of other navies. But somehow a Russian captain had navigated one of them – which of them could not be known – this far. She had arrived too late, if only by hours, to serve as Gelendzhik's guardship, but not too late to block the entrance with her two twelve-inch rifles. Supported on hydraulic rams, these weapons could drop for loading below the rim of the nine-inch thick circular barbette that protected them, heave upwards above it to fire, then drop down again for reloading. An iron tortoise, with armoured decks sloping down to the curve of her hundred foot diameter hull, running no risk from the moored mines her confederates onshore could detonate at will, her presence at the harbour mouth had transformed the bay from a slaughterhouse to a trap. Only by sinking her could Dawlish extricate his ships.

The real Battle of Gelendzhik must now commence.

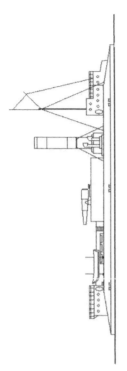

Popovka class Circular Ironclad: *Kazan*
Imperial Russian Navy

Builder: Nikolayev Shipyard
Launched: March 1873
Sisters: *Vice-Admiral Popov, Novgorod*
Displacement: 2500 tons
Diameter: 101 feet

Machinery: 6 Engines, 6 shafts & screws
          3360 Horsepower
Speed: 6.5 Knots (Maximum)
Armament: 2 X 12" Muzzle-loading rifles
          on disappearing mounting
Armour: 9" Belt, 9" Barbette

20

Dawlish could sense the shock around him on the bridge, all eyes locked on the squat hull blocking escape. Only resolute leadership could prevent that dazed astonishment blossoming into panic and faulty decisions.

"Instruct Selim to load with Palliser, Zyndram," Dawlish snapped. "Quarter revolutions. Place the ship in the centre of the anchorage." The Palliser shot was solid, capable of punching though several inches of armour. His brain was churning options and he had only minutes to conceive a plan. He had three ships… three ships differing in speed, armament and protection. Three ships, three targets for one enemy ship. But there was the mine-belt …

Sound and gunsmoke thundered from the Popovka. Two white geysers rose two hundred yards wide of the *Mesrutiyet* and three hundred over. The aim might be poor but it was clear that the Russian commander had chosen the largest enemy as his initial target.

"Both port weapons can bear when run out, Kumandanim." Zyndram was at Dawlish's side.

"Hold fire until ordered." The range was upwards of a mile, a hit unlikely.

Dawlish raised his telescope. The Russian sharpened into focus, an armoured raft, almost awash. Her guns had dropped behind their iron bastion on their hydraulic scissors-mountings for reloading. The circular hull must be difficult to hold stationary. The captain would have his hands full juggling those six screws and in the harbour entrance the ship was exposed to the full effect of the waves running in from the Black Sea astern.

Only the *Mesrutiyet* could afford to close. *Alemdar* and *Burak Reis* could only provide diversions. The *Mesrutiyet* alone had the armour to withstand the Popovka's twelve-inch ship-smashers. Her weapons alone matched the Russian's. And she had her ram…

Dawlish lowered his glass, conscious that the enemy was hypnotising him as a snake might fascinate its prey. The Popovka's guns were again heaving up above the barbette's lip, then blasting. The shells dropped and tumbled in running cascades of spray a hundred yards ahead of the *Mesrutiyet's* bows. They were wasted shot, but the barrels would be heating now, and the next trajectories would be more predictable as the gun-crews settled into the familiar routine of firing

178

and reloading. On the tiny bridge the Russian commander would also be weighing his options. Three vessels, three targets…

"Signal *Alemdar* to engage!" Dawlish ordered. As if anticipating the order the smaller ironclad's battery thundered towards the harbour mouth, raising a harmless curtain of spray ahead of the Popovka. "*Burak Reis* to engage – rapid fire."

"And the *Mesrutiyet*, Nicholas Kaptan?"

"Steer towards the enemy."

A string of signal flags rose overhead. *Alemdar* acknowledged. Her bows swung over and she began steaming slowly across the main axis of the oval bay some seven-hundred yards from the enemy, her port flank exposed. Her leadsman was still posted and she was preparing to turn close to the northern shore to bring her starboard battery weapons into action.

The *Burak Reis* surged forward only seconds after confirming Dawlish's order and her Krupp six-inch sent a shell to plummet harmlessly beyond the Russian. The gunboat had the range to hit the Popovka, and though her shells would never penetrate the armoured barbette they could lash splinters across decks and upperworks.

The Russian had shifted fire towards the *Alemdar*, now the nearer menace. The shells' track was close and the trajectory low. Two racing plumes of foam tore past the *Alemdar's* bows as her turntable-mounted eight-inch spoke defiance in reply. Its solid shot struck the Popovka at the curved, armour-encased deck edge and it shattered, throwing fragments harmlessly into the sea.

Gunfire crashed – the *Alemdar's* last port broadside before she would have to turn, the sharper report of the *Burak's* Krupp bowchaser, the deeper thunder of the Popovka's still inaccurate but potentially deadly twelve-inchers. The Russian had hardly shifted position since arriving, as if anchored halfway between the flanking headlands. The jutting masts of the sunken *Glukhar*, two hundred yards short of her, showed that she was staying just on the seaward side of the mine-belt. Suddenly there was a flash upon her deck itself.

"The *Burak's* hit her!" Zyndram exclaimed.

Dawlish had seen the orange ball exploding to one side of the armoured citadel, ripping planking off the metal deck and shattering a chock-mounted boat into fragments. But the main weapons were lowered behind their armour for reloading, and their crews must be unharmed. An instant later both muzzles heaved into sight again and the circular vessel rotated ponderously, seeking the *Alemdar*. The

179

ironclad had reached the end of her transit of the bay and was now turning to run back south-eastwards. The target she presented was difficult and the Russian fired too soon. Her shells fell short.

The *Burak Reis* was now steering parallel to the harbour entrance. Both Krupps were in action, maintaining a rapidity of fire impossible except with breechloaders. One shell struck a low deckhouse between the Popovka's armoured wall and the deck edge. It penetrated before exploding, convulsing the structure outwards as flame lanced from within.

The *Mesrutiyet* steamed towards the harbour entrance. The *Alemdar* was bearing down from starboard, her course perpendicular to her larger consort. She was firing again, her shells straddling the Russian, none hitting. The *Mesrutiyet* turned to port and was now running ahead of the *Alemdar*, across the harbour and towards the southern headland. The mine-belt lay to starboard.

"Commence firing," Dawlish's message passed from Zyndram to the seaman standing by the voice pipes and down to the battery.

The Russian's guns fired an instant before the *Mesrutiyet's* gunners jerked their firing lanyards. The Popovka's twin muzzles vomited solid shot towards the *Alemdar*, their aim accurate – or lucky. A vicious metallic clang announced one massive projectile's oblique impact against the *Alemdar's* seven-inch armoured belt. It gouged a channel, yet did not penetrate, and tumbled harmlessly away. It was the second shot that unleashed havoc, tearing through the unarmoured bulwarks abaft the central battery and smashing into the base of the mainmast. Shorn of its support, yet held for an instant by the standing rigging, the mast dropped vertically, wavered and then arced forward. Stays parted and whipped and yards tore free as it dropped. It crashed down on the eight-inch's mounting and crew and pounded down on the funnel, knocking it aside. The maintop, shearing down along the side of the foremast, brought the forward yards plunging down as well. Black smoke and sparks billowed around the heap of shattered wood and tangled cordage. The *Alemdar* shuddered and lurched off course.

The *Mesrutiyet's* broadside was wide but the *Burak's* Krupps scored another hit on the Popovka's deck, scything away another ventilator and demolishing the remaining boat. The Russian cannon had emerged again after reloading and the vessel seemed to pivot on some invisible axis.

"She's turning on screws," Dawlish breathed, impressed by the coolness of the Russian captain who must be juggling his six propellers ahead and astern to rotate his freakish vessel. It was lining up on the stricken *Alemdar*, on the deck of which smoke and flames were rising from the mound of wreckage amidships. Figures moved over it frantically and somebody had got a water-hose playing.

The *Burak Reis* ploughed past the burning ironclad at maximum revolutions, pumping shells towards the Popovka. Yet still the armoured raft sat there unmoved, shrugging off the four and six-inch explosive shells the gunboat was now landing with increasing frequency.

The *Alemdar*, blazing now, was losing way. Onursal – cool and daring, with the makings of an Admiral, if he survived – had not just placed the *Burak* as a decoy between the stricken ironclad and her Russian tormentor, but had now brought her into a tight circle there. Onursal's gunners – and they must be beyond exhaustion now, and their weapons red hot – continued to combine rapidity and accuracy. But they might score a hundred hits on the massively armoured deck and barbette and still they would do no more than give slight pause to the Russians gunners sheltered by that great curved metal rampart. The *Burak* could only distract – some other vessel must administer the deathblow.

And that vessel could only be the *Mesrutiyet*.

The action, Dawlish knew, must be immediate, while it was still unexpected, now, when the *Mesrutiyet* was ploughing south-eastwards across the bay and leaving the slanted topmasts of the sunken *Glukhar* to starboard, when her twelve-inch cannon were loading, when the crews were still on the safe side of total exhaustion. He hesitated for five, six seconds and then committed himself.

"Order Selim to cease firing!"

Zyndram looked at him incredulously, then translated the order down the speaking tube.

"Signal to *Burak Reis*: Take *Alemdar* in tow and follow *Mesrutiyet*."

"Follow where, Nicholas Kaptan? Surely…"

Dawlish cut him short. "Order the signal! And order Selim Yüzbashi to train both forward battery cannon dead ahead. Palliser shot, minimum elevation, to fire on my command only – or yours if I'm dead!"

"Immediately, Kumandanim!"

"Recheck closure of all watertight doors! Alert the engine room to stand by for instructions!"

181

Signal flags whipped up the mast, Zyndram's barked orders were relayed down the speaking tubes, messengers scurried from the bridge. The *Mesrutiyet* was still driving across the harbour mouth, parallel to the unseen girdle of mines.

"Selim confirms. He awaits your order, yours alone." Zyndram was looking towards the Popovka, uncertain, waiting for its next broadside.

"And *Burak Reis?*"

"She acknowledges." The gunboat's bows were already swinging towards the *Alemdar.*

"You have voice contact with Mahmut Mülazim?"

"He's at the engine-room voice pipe." The engineer and his crew had been isolated in the steamy hell below since the action started, ignorant of actual events above, yet feeling the firing that had reverberated through the hull.

"I'll speak, Zyndram, you translate. We can't afford ambiguity. You relay to Selim as well."

The southern headland loomed close. In under two minutes it would be essential to commence the turn to bring the *Mesrutiyet* back towards the centre of the bay's mouth. A thunderclap rolled from astern – the Popovka firing again, raising two useless waterspouts in the *Mesrutiyet's* wake.

Dawlish grasped the two voice pipes Zyndram indicated. "Selim Yüzbashi! Mahmut Mülazim!" he shouted.

"Evet, Kumandanim!" A voice loud, staunch and proud, from the battery underfoot.

"Evet, Kumandanim!" A weaker voice from remote in the bowels of the ironclad, almost drowned by the hammering of machinery.

"In thirty seconds I'm ordering maximum revolutions – all you can give, Mahmut Mülazim."

Zyndram translated, listened, nodded vigorously. "Mahmut says Evet, Yes."

"One minute afterwards I will order a turn of twenty four points to port." Dawlish looked into Zyndram's eyes and saw recognition dawning. The turn would sweep the ironclad through three quarters of a circle, heading back initially into the harbour, building up speed on the turn, and ending by heading straight for the open sea. "Zyndram Birinci Yüzbashi will personally steer this vessel to port of the *Glukhar's* wreck and carry us through the mine-belt."

182

Zyndram paled but his eyes were hard with determination. "Rely upon me, Nicholas Kaptan."

"We'll steer straight for the Russian at ramming speed. We're going to impale the Popovka." It was the tactic he had despised, as dangerous to attacker as to victim, the ultimate tactic of desperation – but the tactic for which the *Mesrutiyet* had been designed.

"On the approach Selim Yüzbashi will personally supervise the aiming of the forward guns but he will fire only on my command – or Zyndram Birinci Yüzbashi's."

Dawlish could hear the voices sounding up the pipes even before Zyndram translated – Evet, Evet, they would obey to the letter and to the death, Ins'Allah.

"And now – maximum revolutions!"

Down in the engine room valves were opened to full throttle. Superheated steam screamed through them, flailing pistons accelerated, sweating men shovelled yet more coal into the insatiable furnaces and the *Mesrutiyet's* screws bit. The die was cast.

21

As the *Mesrutiyet* surged forward the knot of officers and seaman in the wheelhouse parted to let Zyndram accept the wheel from the quartermaster.

"Turn twenty-four points," Dawlish said.

"Turning twenty-four points." Zyndram confirmed and spun the wheel.

The *Mesrutiyet* arced back into the bay in the initiation of its three-quarter circle turn, gaining speed, her bow wave climbing over her long ram and breaking on the fo'castle. She swung away from the headland where the mine-control post must be observing her manoeuvre with surprise and towards the devastation at the mole, where half-sunken ships still blazed.

The Pole's face was a mask of concentration. The wheel was slipping ceaselessly through his hands, making minute corrections to the radius of the *Mesrutiyet's* continuing turn, his glance flitting between the *Mesrutiyet's* creaming bow-wave and the jutting mastheads that marked the *Glukhar's* grave, now over to port.

The *Alemdar* and the *Burak Reis* lay four hundred yards dead ahead, both stationary, the gunboat alongside the smouldering ironclad. Remotely, as in a dream, Dawlish was conscious of scrambling figures

183

there, of flames doused on the *Alemdar's* deck, of a cable being dragged across, of a ragged cheer echoing across the waters as the *Mesrutiyet's* intent was discerned. She sped past them, shuddering as the beating screws still accelerated her in the turn, her bows now swinging towards the bay's northern shore.

Dawlish's eyes were locked on the Popovka. She had been silent since the *Mesrutiyet's* turn away but it was now obvious that her commander had overcome whatever surprise the manoeuvre had occasioned. The circular vessel was rotating slowly, as if on a fixed axis, to align the twin weapons jutting over their curved bastion on the approaching menace.

The *Mesrutiyet's* three-quarter turn was complete and Zyndram was straightening her course. The expanse of open sea directly ahead was broken only by the Popovka's squat mass and by the sunken *Glukhar's* wave-lapped masts, towards which the *Mesrutiyet's* bows were aimed. Every eye on the bridge was riveted on the waters flanking those masts, searching desperately for some indication of the mines that strained unseen on mooring cables beneath. All had witnessed the disembowelling of the Russian prize and each imagined his own vessel similarly eviscerated, and himself with her.

Beads of sweat stood on Zyndram's face as he eased the helm over, ever so slightly, nudging the bows to port of the *Glukhar's* wreckage. He was in a universe of his own, one of total concentration, the ship an extension of his being. Dawlish stepped back from his side and reached for the battery voice pipe.

"Selim Yüzbashi?"

"Evet, Kumandanim! Guns ready to fire!" Selim's tone resolute and proud.

"Wait for my order!"

"Assuredly, Kumandanim!"

A roar to port announced an unseen Russian hand in an observation post on the headland pushing a remote detonator. A mine was exploding, and a hammer-blow reverberated through the entire ship. Fifty yards to port the waters heaved up, a mound, then a hillock, its grey surface unbroken. Then it convulsed and a plume of raging white foam burst through, climbing, pluming, feathering. It hung for a moment like some ice-encased tree before collapsing. The *Mesrutiyet* shuddered as the shockwave battered her, but she held course. Another massive thud hit her and a second waterspout rose to starboard, followed almost simultaneously by yet a further detonation to port.

Caught between the impacts, the ironclad jerked and lurched and rolled, seams straining, screws momentarily exposed as she rode through the maelstrom.

Then, suddenly, the *Mesrutiyet* was through the mine-belt, she and her crew shaken, incredulous and intact.

The Popovka was four hundred yards ahead, two points off the starboard bow. Zyndram spun the helm, hauling the ironclad about. Rumbling in the octagonal battery underfoot told of the two forward twelve-inchers being dragged around on their bearing tracks, correcting an aim that was now all but point-blank. The muzzles protruding from the ports were aligned fore and aft, ready to blast on either side of the slab-sided funnel and the mast. It was a gun-bearing never adopted in exercises, for the weapons' fiery breath would scour all before it from the deck ahead.

The range continued to close. Dawlish could now look down on the Popovka. He saw its sloped decks awash, and the wrecked deckhouse, the shattered remnants of the boats, the blue cross of St. Andrew still whipping bravely. But, most of all, his gaze was drawn to the blast-marked iron breastwork over which the Russian's twelve-inch muzzles gaped like dark, open mouths.

"Ramming! Brace yourself!" Zyndram yelled twice, in English, in Turkish.

The *Mesrutiyet's* ram was lost beneath an incoming wave, water surging over it and on to the fo'castle. Then it was rising again, the pointed horn lifting. The moment was upon them.

"Atesh!" Dawlish shouted down the voice pipe. Selim's voice echoed back at him as he relayed the command to the gunners. "Atesh!"

The bows lifted further and then the gunners, judging the instant, jerked their lanyards. Flame and smoke belched from the muzzles, hurling two quarter-ton hardened steel shots, towards the half-submerged enemy raft.

The Popovka fired simultaneously, smashing almost identical missiles towards the *Mesrutiyet*. Nobody on board her, half-stunned by her own salvo, wholly blinded momentarily by the swirling smoke, saw the Russian's discharge but they felt the impact of her shots. One struck with a clang against the forward face of the battery to one side of the funnel. It punched through partly, so that its pointed nose protruded two inches into the space beyond but the eight-inch armour held it, though it dished inwards for three feet around. The second shot

185

struck the massive frame of the starboard gun port. It shattered, spraying fragments through the portal to scythe down the crew that had already started sponging the twelve-incher's reeking barrel.

Dawlish, staggering like the others in the wheelhouse from the shock that had risen through the deck, uncertain of the damage sustained, strained to see through the clearing murk. The Russian was eighty yards ahead, enveloped in black smoke vomiting from the jagged stump of a funnel mangled instants before by the *Mesrutiyet's* shot. A long gash ploughed across the breastwork's curved surface confirmed that nine inches of armour had withstood and deflected the second shot and preserved the crew and weapons behind. The twin twelve-inch mounting had sunk back into the barbette and its crew had not given up the fight. Dawlish, looking down, saw the toiling, smoke-blackened figures clustered around the squat black barrels, an officer urging them on, deliberately ignoring the doom bearing down upon them.

The *Mesrutiyet's* bow, lifting on a wave, displayed her ram. It rose clear, water streaming from the terrible point, then plunged again, white foam submerging it. At the moment of impact it was deep beneath the Popovka's protective belt, thrusting and gouging into the rounded plates that merged sides to bottom, ripping through iron, shearing rivets and rending supporting frames. A shudder ran visibly across the circular deck, a rippling buckle that heaved up plating, snapped stays and brought the remaining funnel crashing over in a volcano of smoke and scorching soot. Metal screamed as the ram still tore and mangled and as the *Mesrutiyet* still drove ahead, dragging the impaled Russian with her.

The shock still flung Dawlish to his knees. He struggled up – others were dazed about him – but Zyndram still had the helm and was spinning it over to break the *Mesrutiyet* free.

"She's finished," he cried, eyes savage with elation. "She's finished, the Russian bitch!"

Juddering and grinding, both hulls remained locked, the Popovka tilting as the ram rose with an oncoming wave, water rushing up over her half-submerged deck and breaking against the barbette. Confused men dragged themselves from hatches.

Now the tortured Popovka half-dropped, half-tore off the ram. Scoured to gleaming, naked metal as it ruptured its way through the flank, the point flashed clear for an instant, then plunged under as the *Mesrutiyet* forged ahead. There was a brief glimpse of interior beams and

186

framing and plating bent and shredded like paper. Then water rushed into the void and the circular deck dipped, heeling the entire vessel. The *Mesrutiyet* heaved past, spinning the sinking Russian as flank ground on wounded flank.

A cheer, involuntary, animal in its triumph and relief, rose from the *Mesrutiyet's* bridge and decks. Dawlish found himself joining in before he checked himself, and Zyndram was yelling with triumph at his side. The cheer rose higher, the lookouts aloft joining in, and it sounded even from the battery where the stricken crew of the starboard forward mounting were still crawling in their blood and calling for assistance while Selim's iron discipline kept their fellows standing to their weapons. A signalman was yelling down the engine-room voice pipe and through it also a distant howl of rejoicing echoed back.

"She's sinking, Nicholas Kaptan," Zyndram said, "She's going down!"

Half the Russian's deck had disappeared and waves lapped against the barbette. Steam mingled with billowing smoke as water cascaded into the funnel. A great half-circle was rising, black metal streaked with torn planking, hatches gaping, fragments and wreckage and struggling bodies sliding down it as the incline grew. Higher still it reared, and two, then three, four-bladed bronze propellers emerged, one still rotating sluggishly.

Pity, horror and delight conflicted within Dawlish as he watched. The reddish-tinged bottom plates, streaked with slime, were visible now, and then the rudder and three more screws, all still. Men were flinging themselves into the sea, striking out for whatever flotsam offered support, some dragging comrades, others intent only on their own survival. A stay snapped and the thin signal mast collapsed, sweeping the St. Andrew's ensign down in an unconscious gesture of reluctant submission. The lip of the barbette was inches above the surface and the black twelve-inchers were lurching in their mounting and the last survivors – magazine crew perhaps – were struggling up from the spaces below.

The end was dreadful in its suddenness.

Waters boiled across the barbette's top and raced into the open cylinder beyond and surged through unseen passages and hatches at its base. The rearing half-circle jerked higher, shuddered, then snapped to the vertical, loose wreckage and grasping bodies dropping from it like an avalanche. It stood like a defaced tombstone for an instant, then

187

dropped vertically. Great bubbles burst from the seething disk of heaving water where it disappeared. Only the black dots that were the survivors and the litter of shattered wood that had been its boats and decking remained.

The cheering died, cut off by a spontaneous realisation of shared humanity. And with it, Dawlish knew, would come exhaustion and lassitude. It was time now to reassert control.

"Call the men to order, Zyndram!" His tone was sharp even if his knees now trembled. "And quarter revolutions if you please!"

Speed reduced now, the ironclad circled slowly outside the harbour mouth, well clear of the mine-belt. Inside the bay the *Burak Reis* crawled slowly towards the gap marked by the masts of the sunken Russian prize, the *Alemdar* wallowing under tow in her wake. The fires were out on the small ironclad and once at sea the *Mesrutiyet* could assume the tow.

Astern of the toiling gunboat and her charge Gelendzhik burned. Ash-laden smoke dimmed the sky and glowing hulks slipped under, their passing marked by brief flurries of steam. Others drifted towards the shallows, beached themselves, and burned quietly to their waterlines. The jetty, what was left of it, was a pyre of blazing shipping and supplies and on the shore the warehouses were wrapped in a shroud of flame.

"It was a triumph, Nichols Kaptan!" Zyndram's eyes were gleaming as he joined him on the bridge. "You plan was ..."

"It's what I'm paid to do," Dawlish cut him short. The elation he had felt was already gone.

There was a butcher's bill to be reckoned in the *Mesrutiyet's* battery and beyond the bobbing heads of the Popovka's men struggling and dying in the harbour mouth, the *Alemdar* would have her own register of misery. As the battered flotilla turned for Batumi later that day hastily shrouded bodies would be dropping overboard to chanted prayers. Archduke Michael's supply base had been destroyed, but the price had been high.

A long, weary day lay ahead – the passing of the *Alemdar's* tow to the *Mesrutiyet*, rendezvous with the collier, recovery of ships' boats, emergency repairs and topping of bunkers while the weather was still moderate, and afterwards the start of the long slow haul back to Batumi. The thought of it alone fatigued Dawlish, just as awareness of death and loss now oppressed him. But others, hundreds on this ship alone, would be feeling the same this moment. Now, more than ever, they would be looking to him for leadership and example. The worn-out gun crews in the battery, the exhausted trimmers in the grimy recesses of the bunkers, the sweat-soaked stokers in the boiler and engine rooms, the wounded and dying in the sick bay – there must be a word of thanks and encouragement for them all.

But first for Zyndram. Dawlish turned, reached for the Polish officer's hand.

"My congratulations. No man could have handled this ship better. Your father and your grandfather would have been proud."

He left the bridge, embarrassed by the Pole's stammered thanks. The sky to the west and north held every promise of deteriorating weather and Batumi was a long way distant, a very long way, far across an inhospitable sea.

The endless, weary day had just commenced.

22

It had all been too late.

Regret and disappointment welled through Dawlish as he reread Nusret's terse telegram yet again, as if desperate longing could somehow change what was already history. The severed railway, the devastated harbour, the sunken shipping – it had all been too late to make a difference to the defenders of the fortress at Kars. Standing in the Governor's office at Batumi, cold and exhausted, still soaked with the spray that had broken endlessly across the *Mesrutiyet's* bridge, he hoped the tears prickling behind his eyes were unnoticed. The battered squadron had limped into port an hour before and he had rushed here directly to report his triumph by telegraph to Nusret.

For this.

"Four days ago?" Zyndram said, incredulous that the battles, the losses and the agony had been in vain.

Dawlish nodded, not trusting himself to speak. So much endeavour, so much courage, so much sacrifice. All too late.

While his squadron was devastating Gelendzhik and fighting its way past the Popovka, Archduke Michael's forces had been massing for the final assault on Kars. While the *Alemdar's* cable was parting on the first night of its tow by the *Mesrutiyet*, while seas were rising and as the injured ironclad was drifting helplessly in the darkness, Russian troops had been storming the bastions of the fortress. The Czar's banners were now fluttering on the ramparts of Turkey's most

189

powerful frontier fortification. Now only Erzurum lay between the Russians and the Anatolian heartland.

"If only..." Zyndram's voice trailed off, realising the futility of those two saddest of all words.

"I know. It's hard to endure." Dawlish said, conscious that too-close contemplation of "ifs" would only lead to self-pity and despair. "But we must still go on." For that was the only response to defeat. To refuse to accept it, to seek some weakness in the enemy at his hour of triumph, to look to the next battle, however feeble the resources available. He had not come this far to be beaten. He had left behind the doubt that had assailed him in the darkness of his quarters a few days since.

Zyndram's voice had the slightest of quavers. "Poles know that men's worth is proven more in defeat than in victory," he said. "I'm a Pole – and a Turk too."

Dawlish remembered that the men he had led to destroy the railway bridge an aeon since had told him he also was a Turk. All that had happened since had proved it something to be proud of.

"We didn't save Kars," Zyndram said. "But we've made sure that the Russian swine freeze and starve this winter outside Erzurum. It wasn't all in vain." There was bitter triumph in his voice.

"We've got to keep telling ourselves that," Dawlish said.

"Why does Nusret Pasha want us at Trabzon?" Zyndram was obviously bemused by the telegram's order for the *Mesrutiyet's* withdrawal. It was also emphatic that Dawlish should accompany her.

"I don't know."

It made no sense to Dawlish either. The *Mesrutiyet* was close to action-readiness. But it would take two, maybe three weeks, before the *Alemdar* could be ready for sea again, and the season's merciless storms would limit the *Burak Reis's* usefulness. The *Mesrutiyet* was the only combat-capable Ottoman ship in the Eastern Black Sea, and she was to be withdrawn.

"Perhaps there will be reinforcements from Istanbul?" Hassan asked. The *Alemdar's* captain was near collapse. He had not left the crippled ironclad's bridge during the gruelling tow.

"I doubt it." Dawlish shook his head. Hobart had made it plain that the main fleet would remain concentrated in the west. If Plevna collapsed, and the Balkan front with it, the navy's guns would represent Istanbul's last defence.

"What can I achieve here if the *Mesrutiyet* is gone?" Hassan's voice had a tinge of despair. Already crippled at Gelendzhik, his ship had taken further battering from angry seas as it had wallowed and strained in the *Mesrutiyet's* wake, breaking its tow twice. It had suffered thirty-one dead, another forty odd wounded and its most powerful weapon, its eight-inch, had been wrecked.

"Rest your men for one day, then get ready for sea as soon as possible," Dawlish said. It sounded brutally simplistic and harsh. Yet any other course would foster uncertainty and despair among the crew. "You've won a victory, Hassan Kaptan. Remember that, tell your men. The Russians know it too – they won't venture down this coast soon. Get to sea, show yourself off Poti, off Sokhumi, even off Gelendzhik, and I guarantee no Russian supply ship will risk getting past you."

It would be two days, maybe three, before the *Mesrutiyet* could depart. The weather had taken its toll on her also, and her tow of the *Alemdar* had punished her engines. At least she showed no ill effects from the ramming – Samuda's yard had built her massively well for the purpose and not a single frame forward was buckled nor a plate sprung. But the crew was exhausted and though the casualties in the battery had been mercifully low there were still wounded to be moved ashore and arrangements to be made for them, and for the larger number of injured from the *Alemdar*. There would be repairs and replenishment and coaling and cleaning of weapons and a thousand and one chores, starting with drying sodden clothing and provision of the first hot meals for days. But Zyndram could be relied on to look after all that. Dawlish himself could concentrate on giving Hassan and Onursal the encouragement they and their crews needed to get their vessels back on station.

"There's work ahead, Gentlemen!" he spoke with forced joviality that his chilled and sleep-hungry body did not feel. "But first there must be coffee! Some of that thick black coffee would do me no end of good – that and a cigar! What do you say, Hassan Kaptan? Onursal Mülazim – you agree?"

Ten minutes respite, no more, he promised himself, hoping he would not doze off, though unspoken fears about why Nusret needed him at Trabzon would probably prevent it. Outside the wind howled and the sleet lashed and the grey sea heaved and foamed. It was November 15th and winter – the greatest killer of all – had arrived in force.

191

*

The *Mesrutiyet* steamed gratefully into Trabzon four days later. Rough seas and a westerly gale had extended the passage and tried engines and crew still further. Trabzon's harbour was empty but for a few coastal traders and a single steamer. There was no sign of the bustle that Dawlish had hoped for, no signs of troop reinforcements being fed in from Istanbul to counter the Russian threat to Erzurum, the last Turkish bastion in the east.

The first snow had fallen, a light dusting, but the dismal grey skies promised more. If it was cold here, Dawlish thought, it would be like some Norse hell inland on the mountain tracks where exhausted and hungry Ottoman troops were freezing and dying as they fell back from the defeat at Kars. He nestled deeper into his fur-lined jerkin, pulled his kalpak lower over his ears and drew his oilskin coat closer against the spray breaking over the gig carrying him to the quayside. He felt ill. It was perhaps only a cold, brought on by days of exposure on deck, but he feared it might trigger a bout of malaria. He promised himself a strong dose of quinine before he retired.

An escort waited above the quay's steps, a half-dozen Circassian cavalrymen whose wolfish smiles of welcome told that they remembered him from that night in Giresun. He only realised the full depth of his weariness when he hoisted himself painfully on to the horse they had brought for him. As they clattered along the icy cobbles he noticed that all rode with sabres drawn and looked about constantly. Dockworkers and passers-by scurried from their path. A muezzin called for prayers from a nearby minaret. Others followed, their voices weary, like wailing dirges for a dying city.

They passed into the town and commenced the sloping climb towards the citadel. Townspeople shrank into doorways as they passed and their glances betrayed fear that had been absent when they had acclaimed Nusret less than a month before. Guards stood at street corners, alert and suspicious. In one narrow stall-lined street a green-turbaned youth stood in the escort's path and spat before taking to his heels. He disappeared among the cowering throng to either side as a horseman spurred at him, sabre raised. Another street revealed three shops gutted by fire. The houses beyond it were shuttered, though eyes flickering at peepholes confirmed the presence of terrified occupants. Market stalls that had previously been laden with produce were now bare and deserted. Further on a small burnt-out Greek church still smouldered and a corporal's guard with fixed bayonets patrolled before it. Dawlish looked enquiringly towards the escort commander.

"Hiristiyani," he said, shrugging, as if venting resentment for defeat on the Christian community was regrettable but inevitable.

The calls for prayer had ended. The city seemed more silent than Dawlish remembered it before – and more crowded. Every mosque courtyard, every archway, seemed to contain its own knot of misery, entire families of refugees huddled beneath blankets, desperately warming themselves and attempting to cook over meagre fires. Rag-swaddled children slumped in makeshift shelters or begged hopelessly while wan mothers tried to suckle infants already close to death. Bewildered fathers, peasants uprooted from their distant plots, strangers to the town, wandered hopelessly in search of food or sanctuary. Some were surrounded by the detritus of the pathetic belongings they had carried in their flight before the invader. Others shivered in total destitution. Their despair was palpable.

Circassians guarded the citadel at double strength. Dawlish dismounted in the courtyard and was led towards Nusret's quarters. A cavalry yüzbashi whom he recognised rose as he entered the anteroom and advanced, unsmiling, gesturing peremptorily towards his holster. As he did the two troopers standing by the door leading to the sanctum beyond crossed their drawn sabres.

Dawlish flushed with anger.

"Damn you!" he said, simultaneously knowing he should not lose his temper, and yet determined for once to indulge it. "I'm tired, wet and cold – and I have been for the last week – and if I'm damned it I'm handing you, or anybody, my pistol." The Circassian stepped back. He might not understand English but he recognised outrage. "If I can't be trusted then Nusret Pasha is welcome to my resignation here and now!"

"It won't be necessary, Nicholas Kaptan," a weary voice said in almost accentless English. Nusret had flung the door open. "My apologies. Developments here make our men understandably overzealous." Yet there was little sense of understanding in the rebuke he snarled in Turkish towards the yüzbashi before drawing Dawlish with him, arm across his shoulders.

The overheated chamber was heavy with tobacco smoke and strewn with maps and files. Nusret's semi-military uniform was rumpled. He had pulled off his boots and the bottoms of his breeches flapped about his calves. His face was stubbly and behind the

193

spectacles he never wore in public, and had not bothered to remove, his red-rimmed eyes suggested days of inadequate sleep. He smelled of brandy. Dawlish recognised that Nusret was glad to see him, not only for his success, but as a link to a world he had glimpsed and admired and felt comfortable in. Yet more, that Nusret saw him as someone whom he could trust, as he could trust no Ottoman, and be open with, because he would never be a threat.

"Somebody tried to kill me," he said, no longer the triumphant, confident Nusret Dawlish had last seen, but somehow sadder, more conscious of his mortality. "Three days ago, after midday prayers. Outside the Hatuniye mosque. He had a knife – a student, a softa from the medresse, not twenty years old."

"Taken alive?"

"Cut down before he reached me."

"Was he acting alone?"

"I doubt it. Since Kars fell the medresses preach that it's God's judgement for ousting his servant Haluk. They know what I stand for, and they hate me for it."

He guided Dawlish to a rug-covered settee, gestured to a tray with glasses and brandy. Dawlish shook his head.

"I missed you, Nicholas Kaptan," Nusret said when they settled. He extended a gold cigarette case, then selected one himself also, lighting it from the glowing butt that had not left his lips. "I missed your English rationality, your organisation, your discipline."

"I think I was better employed at sea." Dawlish said. "We've damaged the Russian supply lines with a vengeance, it will be weeks before…"

"Yes, Yes, it was well done, damned well done. Hobart's friend chose you well." Nusret's voice betrayed sadness bordering on despair. "But it don't signify anymore, Nicholas Kaptan, it just don't signify."

"Kars? It's one battle lost, not the war!" Dawlish felt Nusret's low spirits challenging him to optimism. "But surely you still hold Erzurum? The Russians are short of supplies – we made damned sure of that. They can't move on Erzurum yet in this season! And Batumi – there are fifteen thousand Ottoman troops there behind masonry fortifications! And here, Trabzon! Reinforcements can be poured in here by sea and the enemy isn't in any state to intercept them! A thrust inland from Batumi could cut off the entire Russian army at Kars! And you hold the port here, and the *Mesrutiyet*! And Hassan will be at sea with the *Alemdar* within the fortnight and terrorising the coast again! You can…"

"Look there." Nusret waved tiredly towards the maps covering the desk and floor. Red, blue and green-ink arrows were slashed in bold sweeps across them. "Grand strategy, grand designs, grand opportunities! But I've neither the men nor the resources to realise them."

He pulled Dawlish to his feet, propelled him to the window. Far below the few vessels strung along the mole emphasised the greater emptiness of the harbour. "Look there – do you see ships? Reinforcements? Munitions? Horses? Food?"

"But surely they must be underway? Istanbul must be…"

"…reserving every bullet, every man, for its own defence." Nusret completed the sentence. "Plevna is still holding, just. But Osman Pasha can't work any more miracles there. His army is wholly cut off, starving. Nobody is moving to relieve it. And when it falls …" He held up his palms in despair. "Kars, Erzurum, Batumi, even Trabzon, they don't count anymore. When Plevna falls the Russians will be thrusting for Istanbul and we haven't the forces to stop them. And if Istanbul falls the Sultan falls and with him the empire and the *Mesrutiyet* – no Nicholas Kaptan, not your ship, but the Constitution she's called after. And without that, Turkey, what will be left of it after the Czar seizes Istanbul and the Straits, will be plunged back into corruption and squalor and lethargy and backwardness for another generation." He spoke now with the weary passion of a man who foresaw the worst, but little way of avoiding it.

"It won't happen, Nusret Pasha," Dawlish said. "Britain won't allow it." But in his heart he knew that though British intervention might save some rump of the Ottoman Empire it would not necessarily save Nusret. Scapegoats would still be needed.

"I must get back to Istanbul." Nusret, absorbed in his own vision of failure, had not heard Dawlish's interjection. "Haluk has his ear now, he's poisoning him against the Constitution, he's arguing that it's the source of our misfortune. And he's weak, he always was, even as a boy. He's listening to Haluk and he fears the Istanbul medresses…"

"Who? Who is he? Who's weak?" Dawlish was confused.

"The Sultan, Abdul-Hamid, my half-brother," Nusret's voice was weary. "He heard Haluk's excuses when he arrived in Istanbul, and he freed him because it would be popular with the medresses he fears so much. And now he's giving him a command in Bulgaria – Bashi

195

Bazooks, Selahattin's among them – and no matter how it turns out Haluk will be hailed as a hero..."

"...who defended Istanbul in its hour of peril, while you commanded a secondary front." It was Dawlish's turn to complete the sentence. He could see it clearly – Haluk, the cadaverous, bearded traitor, whose seizure of Trabzon had precipitated disaster in the East, transformed into a warrior of the faith who had held fast to the old traditions while modern ways had brought the empire to the brink of ruin. It was the strategy of a ruthless ambition for which Nusret and the Constitution were hindrances and the real target the Sultanate itself.

"I must go there," Nusret said, "I must be there, to defend the city myself, to stop Haluk dominating Abdul-Hamid. Because without me, Nicholas Kaptan, there will be no Constitution, no reform, no modernisation, no education, no sanitation. We'll be a laughing stock among nations, again the Sick Man of Europe, the..."

"And you want me to get you there, Nusret Pasha, and the *Mesrutiyet* to back you," Dawlish cut him off. His heart was sinking. The strikes at Poti and the railway and Gelendzhik were all for nothing. The sacrifices of the nameless marines dying as they pushed *Ejder* from the shallows, and of Nedim transfixed on the Cossack lance, had been futile.

"It's not just me who wants you back in Istanbul, Nicholas Kaptan." Nusret's voice was soft but firm. "Hobart Pasha, even Sir Henry Layard, Britain's ambassador. They want it too. They know that we can survive losing lose half Anatolia, but never Istanbul."

The telegraph had been busy, Dawlish thought grimly. The lines extended all the way to London. If Hobart and Sir Henry wished it then so did Topcliffe – and if Topcliffe did, then so surely did Lord Beaconsfield in Downing Street. All of them believed in Nusret and must know that he was still the Ottoman Empire's best hope, maybe its only one.

As I do too, Dawlish thought, remembering Zyndram's words. Men's worth was proven more in defeat than in victory. Nusret might be at the limits of exhaustion and surviving on little more than brandy and cigarettes, but he was defiant and unvanquished still. He was perhaps more impressive now than when he had strode unarmed into the fray on the *Mesrutiyet's* afterdeck and won the crew to him. A vision, however ill-defined, for what the Ottoman Empire might be, a dream of something other than brute tyranny and religious fanaticism and paralysing tradition, was driving Nusret more than any personal ambition. Dawlish realised now that he felt more than just formal loyalty to this man. His own acceptance of an Ottoman commission had been a necessary price for Topcliffe's continued patronage in the Royal Navy, but that bargain seemed tawdry now. Whether in rout or in triumph Nusret was worth standing by for himself alone.

"The *Mesrutiyet* needs two days in port," Dawlish said. Suddenly he wanted to sleep very badly indeed. "We can sail then for Istanbul."

The mention of the city reminded him that there had been one more disappointment. Despite his resolve to forget Miss Morton he was saddened that there was no letter for him, not even another transcription from Keats. He felt all the more foolish for having half-hoped for one.

If only... The saddest of all words.

23

Dawlish looked shorewards from the bridge as the *Mesrutiyet* left Trabzon. It was snowing again and the city with its refugees was already shrouded in white. The frigid blanket might dampen for a while the anger that coursed through the streets when it became known that Nusret was leaving. The signs had been small and isolated at first: two isolated sentries beaten to death; a Greek café ransacked; an Armenian priest hanged. Still the refugees had poured in, each with his own story of privation and rapine, each feeding the conviction that Nusret was abandoning them to the Russians. Yesterday a softa-instigated mob had exploded simultaneously from a dozen mosques after midday prayers, gathering more followers with each Christian church and business torched, ransacking food-stores after guards had been put to flight – or had joined the rioters.

Before departure Dawlish had exchanged his last telegraphed messages with Hassan at Batumi. That was where he wanted to be himself, he thought bitterly. He should be hastening the *Alemdar's* repairs, plotting further harassment of the north-eastern littoral, turning the *Mesrutiyet's* ram towards Novorossiysk, not westwards to where the issue would be decided by land, not by sea. He did not know what would be expected of him, or of the ironclad, once Istanbul was reached. He doubted if Nusret yet knew how to act when he got there, only that he wanted the *Mesrutiyet's* crew and guns with him.

The *Mesrutiyet* ploughed westwards, rolling heavily as she took the sea on her beam, her decks awash. Trabzon was lost to sight, still a

197

fortress, well garrisoned and still secure behind its defences, but seething with resentment at its desertion. Beyond the ice-capped mountains to its south supply-starved remnants of Turkish armies were fleeing towards Erzurum, waiting hopelessly for Archduke Michael's final thrust. It would be long in coming – the recent savaging of the Russian supply lines would assure that, and Dawlish took bleak pride in that knowledge – but the outcome was no longer in doubt. Even though Plevna was still somehow holding out, the Ottoman Empire had all but lost the war.

Dawlish turned towards the angry sea ahead. There was a task to be done, whatever it was. That must still be his concern. And yet – he was reluctant to admit it, even to himself – he longed to be in Istanbul. Florence Morton was there and he hungered to see her despite all his resolutions to forget her. The idea was preposterous, even inappropriate, but it would not go away. They had conversed only twice, for less than two hours, and yet her memory haunted him. He had read and reread that poem she had copied for him – feeling foolish, even guilty, as he did – as if the sight of her handwriting could somehow bring her closer. And repeatedly he had pushed her image from him, as he now did again.

His uncle had also loved such a woman, a dignified, graceful woman, and yet fear of ostracism had prevented him ever acknowledging her to the world as more than his housekeeper, even though that world was no more than a provincial French spa. Miss Morton deserved more and he hoped that the few formal lines he had so unwisely sent had not awoken impossible hopes in her. It was not just better to forget her, it was essential for her happiness.

Nusret was in the wheelhouse with Zyndram, feigning interest in the navigation and struggling to disguise his increasing seasickness.

"I'm going below for an informal inspection," Dawlish said, looking him straight with one eyebrow raised. "You might wish to accompany me, Nusret Pasha?"

"A capital idea. Capital." Nusret recognised the opportunity for retreat to the quarters Dawlish had relinquished to him. He was a pitiful figure as he descended, diminished by the failure of his dreams and the furtiveness of his departure from the city that had hailed him as a deliverer.

This was the weather that tested ship and crew as much as combat did for it brought the prospect of endless, cold, exhausting, sodden labour just to keep the vessel functioning. It was now, Dawlish knew, that he himself must be most seen to be concerned with every detail of efficiency, ready to praise as well as censure, to be careful of the crew's wellbeing, careless of his own. As he moved through the ship, often ankle deep in the frigid water that sloshed through its passages, he found much to please him. For all the discomfort, and the prospect of more ahead, there was an air of work being done purposefully, whether it was the fight to pump out incoming water, or to secure loose fittings, or to prepare food or to keep the furnaces fed and the engines turning. Victory at Gelendzhik had been dearly purchased but it had brought the crew a sense of indomitability as well as pride.

The wind rose through the afternoon, piling up steep waves that rolled the ironclad unmercifully. Dawlish ordered a course alteration, north-westwards, to put ample sea room between the straining vessel and the savage lee shore to the south. By darkness a full gale was blowing. There was no option but to steam slowly onwards, decks awash, pitching and cork-screwing like a half-sunken barrel, breasting the full fury of the storm.

It continued unabated through the night, the next day, the following night. Far off the coast, the course could be safely westwards again. Watches were changed, brief uncomfortable sleep was snatched, men sloshed through passageways knee-deep in surging water, pumps sighed and pulsed, stokers fought to keep their footing as they fed insatiable furnaces, deckhands secured by lifelines braved wave-washed upperworks to secure loose fittings. Hot food and drink became objects of longing. Dawlish stood watches alternately with Zyndram, ignored the headache and the fever that added misery to exhaustion – for he was but one of dozens who coughed and sneezed and ached – and concentrated his whole being on the care of the vessel and her crew. Yet somehow, for all the discomfort, he felt contentment return, for this was his ship, his first major command. For this he had submitted to discipline, hardship and danger since childhood and even now, for all the wet, cold misery of the moment, there was satisfaction in it.

Dawn came again, disclosing an unchanged vista of heaving grey streaked with foam and of driving spray stripped from the wave crests. Dawlish was fighting sleep as the sky lightened in the southeast and his body ached for the slumber that his relief by Zyndram would bring.

The oilskin-clad figure who struggled to the bridge was not the Pole however, but rather the engineer, Mahmut. Still red-faced and sweat-drenched from the steaming atmosphere of his domain, he was

199

shivering violently as the topsides cold bit into him. Before he spoke Dawlish knew that only a problem of the utmost seriousness would have brought him here.

The main bearing of the starboard shaft was running hot and remedial efforts had failed. There was no alternative to shutting down the engine to avoid seizure. Repairs were impossible in these conditions. The ironclad clawed slowly westwards in the continuing storm, its remaining engine straining, hoses playing on the port shaft's bearings lest they too fail and leave the vessel helpless before the tempest.

A day of punishment followed, but the night brought abatement and the next day only a fresh breeze. Though Nusret fretted for pushing on Dawlish was adamant that the shelter of a port was essential for repairs. He was not going to risk either ship or crew in the next spell of bad weather that the season made almost inevitable between here and Istanbul. He was damned if he was continuing without the second engine serviceable. Nusret, faint and gaunt from days of nausea, yielded reluctantly.

The presence of rudimentary maintenance facilities at the port of Sinope, half-way between Trabzon and Istanbul, decided the destination. *Mesrutiyet* arrived a day later and moored within the mole on the eastern side of the peninsula on which the town stood. Zyndram went ashore to secure the Governor's co-operation, the total dedication of the small dockyard's resources and the provision of garrison troops to seal off the port area.

The already exhausted engine-room crew set about the repair. Wooden blocks were wedged beneath the shaft to support it and the work of opening and demounting the bearing commenced. It took nineteen hours, working in shifts because of the confined space. Dawlish followed progress closely, worried as to what would be revealed. It proved worse than he feared.

"Badly damaged, Kumandanim." Mahmut Mülazim's words were unnecessary. The curved bronze surface was galled and scored. It must have been minutes away from welding itself to the shaft when the engine had been closed down.

"Can you repair it?" Dawlish knew roughly what was required, but it was daunting. His interest in technical matters had amused many of his colleagues in the past – few officers ever ventured into a boiler room and many refused to associate socially with commissioned engineers. Now he was glad of his eccentricity.

200

"Difficult, Kumandanim. A great task. It would be best left to experts."

"Are the experts here?"

"In Istanbul, Kumandanim, maybe in Izmit. They can do only simple work here."

Dawlish was less certain. He had already inspected the dockyard workshop, had found a half-dozen lathes of varying sizes, a heavy-duty vertical drill, a single miller and a slotter, all in poor condition and supervised by a foul-mouthed Scot who had somehow established himself here. He had been drunk at eleven in the morning when Dawlish met him. His stock in trade was the maintenance and minor modification of the engines of small steamers.

"If the expert were here, could the bearing be refaced?"

Mahmut looked at the deep grooves torn in the bronze and paused. He was afraid of the responsibility of decision, Dawlish realised. In this ramshackle despotism, where blame and retribution were arbitrary, even competent men hesitated to commit themselves.

"Could you build up the surface?" Dawlish prodded him, his voice quiet. "I've seen it done –perhaps I could assist?"

Mahmut nodded slowly. "There is a small furnace in the workshop," he said. "It might perhaps be done, Ins'Allah, if Kumandanim could give his advice. And the biggest lathe might turn it."

It could, Dawlish knew. He had measured the throw and there would be a half-inch to spare. If Fuad Bey – otherwise Fred McConachie of Dumbarton – could be kept off the brandy long enough to keep his hand steady then the inner surface could be skimmed back to smoothness and the correct tolerance. Mounting the massive bearing on the faceplate was going to be a nightmare and a boring bar of the right length would be essential and... He stopped himself.

"Send word to have the furnace fired, Mahmut Mülazim. We're going to do it."

As he pulled himself up the ladder from the dark, cold metallic space he realised that the world he had grown up in, the world of masts and yards and miles of rigging and acres of canvas, had not prepared him for this. This world of machines was his future – if he lived.

201

24

Nusret visited the Sinope Governor's office daily and sat with his codebook, personally deciphering the messages chattering to him over the telegraph there. Dawlish accompanied him when he could spare the time, glad of the distraction from the grimy workshop. It seemed to make no difference where Nusret found himself – within hours of arrival he had taken control of a telegraph and was in contact with his small army of sympathisers and supporters, paid and unpaid, high and low, open and covert, Muslim, Christian and Jewish, officials and merchants and police and military, spread across half an empire. He kept few papers – a stove to consume his decodings as soon as he had perused them was his other essential item of equipment. "This is my archive," he told had Dawlish, tapping his head. That it was an effective one was proved by the assurance with which he updated his notes on the sheaf of maps which littered his saloon on the *Mesrutiyet* when he returned there. It was foul and untidy there now, sprinkled with tobacco ash, reeking with smoke and strewn with empty brandy bottles and dirty plates, for he trusted no steward to pass the marine guards that stood outside it day and night.

Marines, thirty of them, provided Nusret's escort now and he moved nowhere without them clearing the streets before him first. Bülent Chavush commanded the close bodyguard – ten men who included the uninjured survivors of the bridge attack. They emptied even the Seyit Bilal mosque when Nusret went to pray there and Sedat Onbashi, the marksman, still pale, still recovering from the pneumonia that had nearly taken him, was posted in the minaret to cover his arrival and his leaving.

The situation before Erzurum was serious, but each day brought confirmation that in Bulgaria it was desperate.

"Plevna can't hold much longer!" Nusret balled a paper and flung it angrily into the flames. "Yet Suleiman Pasha could still relieve them! He should be impaled for this!"

He caught Dawlish's look of disapproval and laughed.

"My apologies, Nicholas Kaptan! In our new enlightened, constitutional Ottoman rebirth shooting would be sufficient! But I'd gladly pull the trigger myself."

Dawlish understood. Other than treachery there was nothing to explain Suleiman Pasha's inactivity or why the army he kept in idleness within the Quadrilateral, the complex of fortresses to the northeast of Plevna, had not fallen on the flank of the besieging Russians.

"Haluk?" Dawlish said. "You think Suleiman is his man?"

"I know it," Nusret said. "They're deliberately creating a disaster together. They want the Russians before Istanbul, so they can be seen as the saviours! Haluk as Sultan and Suleiman as Vizier – that's their aim!"

It was the fourth day since arrival in Sinope, the last of November. Each morning had brought the same news, of ever-greater Russian forces massing about the dwindling garrison dying in the trenches around an unremarkable town south of the Danube. Outnumbered, pounded by artillery –

a spy's report mentioned five hundred guns – famished by hunger, decimated by disease, tortured by frostbite, starved of supplies, Osman Pasha's small army of heroes had stood firm within Plevna's improvised defences for almost five months and had repulsed massive assaults. Now they were at the end of their resources. If Suleiman did not move to its relief, if Plevna fell, then only winter itself could prevent the Czar's victorious army sweeping southwards across the Balkan Mountains towards Thrace and Istanbul itself.

And in London, Dawlish surmised, Topcliffe might already have convinced Prime Minister Lord Beaconsfield that the time had come to bring the Mediterranean Fleet to readiness. The telegraph cables would be hot between the Admiralty and Malta. A succession of massive ironclads would be following each other through dry-dock for urgent overhaul. Non-essential stores would be getting landed. Shells and bagged charges would be replenishing magazines and leave would be cancelled. Half-pay officers would be filling Admiralty ante-rooms and clamouring for appointments. For if readiness passed into actual mobilisation, then the war that Britain would fight would be the Royal Navy's war. Alone of the European powers Britain had no conscription, no massive reserves of trained soldiery to hurl directly into battle on land, only a small if superbly professional army suited to colonial service and ill-prepared for rapid expansion. It was the guns of the Royal Navy alone that could save Istanbul if the Russians got that far. But it would be better, far better if the risk of a general European war was to be averted, if the Turks could still somehow bleed the Russians to exhaustion before the Mediterranean Fleet was ordered east. And Dawlish knew that Topcliffe and Beaconsfield, equals in

203

guile, calculation and daring, would be expecting him to play his part in that bleeding.

Haluk, whose very existence seemed to absorb Nusret's every waking hour, had established himself with his Bashi Bazooks in southern Bulgaria, near Plovdiv. There had been further massacres of Christians there.

"The atrocities are as bad as last year," Nusret said bitterly. "The softas love it. They see Haluk and Selahattin as warriors of the faith."

"Selahattin's involved?" Dawlish could not forget that brute's malignancy.

"Haluk's using him to clear out Christian villages. He claims they're spying for the Russians. But for every village wasted and every woman raped there are another dozen Bulgarians heading to join the Russian forces."

"I should have killed him that night in Giresun," Dawlish said. Each death, each violation, stood as an accusation against himself.

Nusret laughed. "You're becoming a true Turk, Nicholas Kaptan," he said. "You won't be over-merciful again."

"These massacres are grist to Gladstone's mill," Dawlish said. Even before he had left London the opposition leader already had widespread support for his denunciations of Britain's sympathetic stance towards the Unspeakable Turk. It was public knowledge that several in Lord Beaconsfield's cabinet felt just as strongly. Every new atrocity would increase the difficulty of justifying British support when it was most needed.

It was time for Dawlish to return to the quayside workshop. The casting of the bronze had gone well and now a new layer, rough and furrowed, had been built up on the bearing's inner surface. Fred McConachie, inspired by the promise of two hundred gold sovereigns in cash on satisfactory completion, was now supervising mounting of the massive bearing on the lathe's faceplate. Only then could the slow, meticulous task of machining it smooth commence.

"I'll stop by the machine-shop myself, Nicholas Kaptan," Nusret said as they mounted. "I want to see the work's progress. Then I'll feel more confident that we'll soon be on our way again."

It was windless and chill beneath a cloudless blue sky. The cobbles were icy and the slope of the street steep. Only Nusret and Dawlish were on horseback and their beasts were nervous as their hooves skidded, gained purchase, slipped again. Pride kept both men from dismounting. They rounded a bend – houses to the right, their occupants driven inside by the escort, a drop towards the harbour on the other. The *Mesrutiyet* swung there. Men were on their knees on deck, holystoning despite the chill, others airing hammocks. Her buff funnel and white upperworks gleaming in the late morning sun, she looked efficient and potent for all the battering she had taken. The sight gave Dawlish a thrill of pride.

His horse plunged even as he heard the gunshot. Nusret's mount was rearing and whinnying beside him as it slipped on the ice and the marine alongside was falling beneath it, blood fountaining from his head. Another shot – and something screamed past Dawlish's own temple. Nusret was looking around in shocked surprise and Bülent was bellowing orders. Marines rushed towards the houses to the right. Sedat, the marksman, dropped to one knee and raised his carbine, sweeping it as his hunter's eyes sought a tell-tale wisp of gunsmoke from a window or rooftop.

"Hold on!" Dawlish yelled, grabbing the reins of Nusret's horse. He kicked his own mount into a slithering canter, dragging the other with him. They careered down the roadway, the marines from the escort slipping and stumbling as they followed. Shots rang out from behind, the rapid barking of a Winchester, single shots from some other weapon, a second Winchester joining in, then no more gunfire, just shouting. That too was lost behind as the street turned again, houses and shops again to either side. They had out-run their escort and townspeople were scrambling from the path of the two horsemen galloping towards and through them.

Nusret had taken the reins again. "Haluk! Haluk's work!" he yelled as they pounded on.

"To the ship?" Dawlish called.

"No! To the workshop! I won't be hunted! I won't let Haluk rule me!" Nusret's cry betrayed dogged fury.

The guard at the dockyard gates drew aside, surprised, as they cantered up. They were garrison troops, older men from the Redif, the Second Reserve, slovenly and overweight. Their officer came scuttling out, fastening his tunic, fumbling with his sword belt. Nusret shouted angrily and off-duty men were roused and sent to redouble the watches.

"Now to the workshop, Nicholas Kaptan," Nusret said, dismounting. His hands were shaking, his face pale but Dawlish saw in him what he had seen when they first took the *Mesrutiyet*: a resolute

205

man, though one not bred to action, conquering his fears and determined to act the part of leader.

"Bülent Chavush will find them if any man can," Dawlish said.

It was clear that Nusret did not wish to speak of it. "Leave it to him then," he said. "Haluk failed. Only that matters."

A dozen men escorted them to the draughty hall where the machine tools were housed and took position by the entrances. A boiler in the corner fed the steam engine that drove the overhead shafting from which the individual tools were driven. The hall was loud with the slapping of leather drive-belts. They warmed themselves gratefully by the boiler and sipped chai while Fred McConachie summarised progress. The bearing was securely bolted to the great circular faceplate by right-angle brackets and the turning had commenced.

"How long?" It was always Nusret's question, but now it had a new urgency.

"I'd be telling you a lie if I said shorter than two days," the Scot said. He might be talking to the Sultan's half-brother but his whole demeanour told of a man who would stand his ground. "I'll trust Murad – that's my foreman – with the rough turning. But when it comes to the fine work I'll have to do it meself and you'll mind that I've never done a job this big here before. If we were in Denny's in Dumbarton now, that would be a different matter. We'd have the tools. But we aren't, and we haven't got the best here either and we've got to take it easy and a man has to sleep between times if he's to keep his hand in."

"Show me," Nusret said.

For all the spinning of the shafting above, the lathe was geared down so that the *Mesrutiyet's* bearing block, its two halves now temporarily reassembled, was turning only three or four times a minute. Thin chips of bronze fell away from the cutting tool, exposing bright metal beneath the rough surface left by the casting process. With each revolution the foreman, Murad, advanced the tool a fraction and it was already obvious that this first rough skimming alone would take hours. Later, as the final bore was neared and the tolerance became critical, McConachie himself would be shaving away yet thinner slivers.

The process was hypnotic and Dawlish saw Nusret falling into a reverie as he watched the golden peelings fall away. And yet for all his display of unconcern his mind must be upon the recent assassination attempt, the second within a fortnight. Bülent and his men might find

206

the would-be killer, though it was doubtful if he would let himself be taken alive, but it hardly mattered. A thousand other fanatics would be ready to take his place. Nusret must realise that he could know no security until Haluk, who held out hope to such zealots, was eliminated. He himself might have a network of supporters who longed for a modern, secular, constitutional state but Haluk opposed it with a brotherhood no less organised and perhaps even more dedicated.

"That damned tool's blunting, Man! Can't you see that? Are you blind, Man?" McConachie pulled off his spectacles and thrust them at Murad. The foreman smiled, took them and peered at the bearing, then nodded. Dawlish was touched by the impression of a close partnership and a warm regard neither man would have confessed to.

McConachie reached for the lever that slipped the belt from the drive pulley to the idler. The lathe stopped and Murad began to unbolt the cutting tool. Nusret leaned forward to watch more closely.

Then the brick wall of the workshop blew inwards.

It bulged for an instant before disintegrating, hurling bricks and mortar dust and shards of glass from a high window across the floor. The roar of the explosion followed simultaneously, and the acrid smoke of the detonation seared behind, surging between the machine tools and storage racks and workbenches. Dawlish was lucky, and Nusret too, for their backs were to it and they were partly shielded by the bulk of a huge pillar drill that deflected the worst of the debris around them. McConachie took the full blast, thrown against the lathe bed and pounded to a bloody semblance of anything human by the bricks. Murad was flung towards the opposite wall to break his neck against a slotter.

Dawlish was choking and half-blinded by dust. He was somehow on hands and his knees and trying to rise. Nusret coughed beside him and was pulling him to his feet. Somebody, a machinist perhaps, was screaming and from the door came the sounds of panicked shouting. A groan overhead announced a short avalanche of tiles and splintered timber as part of the roof gave way. The air was thick with dust, visibility feet only.

"I'm not hurt, Nicholas Kaptan, I'm not hurt!" Nusret kept repeating. He gripped Dawlish's arm tightly.

Dawlish dragged his pistol from its holster, dazed, yet conscious that the worst might not be past. The breach in the wall was discernible only as a jagged-edged halo of light in the billowing haze. Outlined

207

against it, two blurred figures were moving in across the rubble, slowly, deliberately, obviously searching.

Nusret made to speak. Dawlish held a hand across his mouth, then picked up a brick. He heaved it far to his right, towards the far edge of the breach. It fell with a thud, and a low rumble followed as rubble dislodged. The figures ahead swung across to face the noise and almost instantly one fired, once, twice, three times, the unmistakable rapid barks of a Winchester.

Dawlish launched himself forward, boots scrabbling for grip on the debris, cocking his revolver as he ran. The nearer figure was five yards away and turning towards him. He was bringing his weapon up when Dawlish was close enough to see him through the dust. His ill-fitting uniform was a Redif's but the hard, lean features and the cruel young eyes were not those of a reservist. His movement was too late – Dawlish was already on him, shoving the muzzle against his abdomen as he fired. He felt his hand wet and hot with what he knew was spraying blood and he kicked the thrashing body away as he turned to deal with his second adversary.

It was unnecessary. Another figure was launching itself though the choking fog and scything at the other attacker with drawn sword. The man turned too late to meet Nusret's rush. He fired once, high and wide, before the blade chopped into his arm. He dropped the weapon with a scream and Nusret thrust into him, tore free and thrust again and again, continuing until Dawlish dragged him away. The face, contorted in a last rictus of agony, was of another young man.

Outside there had been firing also – they had heard it remotely, as if in another universe – but it was over when they emerged. A half-dozen genuine Redifs lay still, or moaned in pain, but there were two more in similar uniforms among them that would never now see twenty-five. One, crippled by a shattered leg, had put a Winchester muzzle in his mouth rather than be taken alive.

The guard commander approached, pale, terrified by the knowledge of what his negligence had allowed and blurting excuses.

"They were not my men," he stammered. "Not mine, Kumandanim." He sunk to his knees, weeping. "I don't know how they entered. It was impossible, impossible, Nusret Pasha, impossible I tell you. Have mercy…"

Nusret struck him across the face with the flat of his sword, streaking him with the blood of the assassin. Then he turned to

Dawlish. His anger seemed to have spent itself but there was a weary determination in his voice.

"Let's go back inside, Nicholas Kaptan," he said. "We must see if the bearing is damaged. You told me once you could operate a lathe. Now you'll prove it."

Aching, eyes smarting, with growing awareness of the myriad tiny skin abrasions scoured by particles of brick and mortar, they picked their way across the rubble and back into the clearing fog.

25

"You said they had Winchesters," Hobart was intrigued.

"Carbines," Dawlish said, "Cavalry issue. Yet none had been issued to the Sinope garrison."

"Serial numbers?"

"From a batch issued to the Fifth Macedonian Dragoons in February last year. What's left of that unit has been stuck in Plevna since July."

Dawlish had never been more impressed by Nusret's intelligence network. The information on the assassins' weapons had flashed in by telegraph within six hours of the attack. Yet it had helped little. The carbines had been misappropriated months ago, not an unusual event in an army in which corruption was rife.

"Any badges on the uniforms?"

"Removed. Nothing in the pockets either. They might have come from anywhere. But we're almost certain they didn't come from Sinope."

It had been hell there for two days, with terrified Redif reservists who had hoped to sit out the war in comfortable lethargy held to account for their every move for months past. Nusret's liberal principles had not prevented extreme measures in cases of uncertainty. Several dockyard guards whose veracity had been doubted would not walk for weeks on feet swollen to melon-size by the bastinado. But even then the trail was cold.

"It looks like Haluk's even better organised than we thought," Hobart said. "But then I think the Sultan knows that already. He's terrified, Dawlish, downright terrified. He's often not seen for days and it's said he sleeps in a different room each night – he chooses at the last minute."

The horde of Albanian troops guarding the Yildiz Palace confirmed that Abdul-Hamid feared closer enemies than the Russians. It was only months since his accession but he dreaded that his tenure of the throne might be scarcely longer than his predecessor's. Nusret had gone to see him immediately on arrival in Istanbul and even he had not escaped patting for concealed weapons before being admitted to his half-brother's presence.

Dawlish was standing by the window of the office Hobart maintained in the Yildiz, looking out over a rain-pocked Bosporus. To the right, beyond Galata, the *Mesrutiyet* lay moored in the Golden Horn, safely arrived last night after an unexpectedly easy passage from Sinope. The repaired bearing had performed faultlessly, rewarding Dawlish for the thirty continuous hours he had spent at the lathe, frozen by the wind blasting through the workshop's breached walls and personally feeding the cutting tool in microscopic increments to skim down the surface to a mirror-like finish.

He was painfully conscious that Miss Morton was not a mile from here, ensconced with Lady Agatha at Oswald's villa. She must have seen the *Mesrutiyet* arrive, have heard of the battle at Gelendzhik, know he had returned. He ached to see her but was resolved to forget her. The feelings that had seemed so simple on that icy hillside before the Cossacks attacked now confronted the hard threat of social exile were he to act on them. He might endure it, just, but for a woman the petty insults would be intolerable. That the decision to forget her was logical did not make it any easier.

Hobart had heard Dawlish's report in a silence punctuated with only the briefest of questions. At the end he shook his hand.

"I couldn't have hoped for more, Dawlish," he said. "The Grey Wolf returned with a bloody muzzle. Topcliffe was right to recommend you." Hobart paused. He looked at Dawlish as if wondering how he might react to what was coming. Then he said: "The only pity is that you'll have no more scope for such action at sea while you still wear the Sultan's uniform."

"Why, Sir?" Disappointment stabbed Dawlish. "The *Mesrutiyet's* ready for action and the crew's spoiling for it like fighting cocks. After Gelendzhik and the Popovka ..."

Hobart silenced him with a sad wave of the hand.

"We've done what we can at sea, Dawlish," he said. "But Suleiman and a dozen commanders like him have lost this war on land. Osman

210

Pasha is worth the whole lot put together but even he can't hold Plevna much longer."

"But even then, Sir, surely the Russians can't advance further in winter?" Plevna lay north of the Balkan mountain chain that lay west to east across Bulgaria. The winter was already proving to be savage and the passes would be snow-filled. "There must be still time to prepare, and while we control the sea …"

"It's too late, Dawlish." Hobart sounded gloomy. "We've intelligence that the Russians will continue attacking, winter or not. They've got the food, the clothing, the draught animals and the men. The Rumanians are with them already and Bulgarian Christians will flock to them every mile they advance. Their supply lines through Rumania are too damned far inland for you or me to threaten. Worst of all, they've got two army commanders of genius, Gourko and Skobelev, who won't rest until they're tethering their horses in the Süleymaniye Mosque."

"And the *Mesrutiyet*?"

"Will be disarmed."

The words struck Dawlish into horrified silence. He suddenly realised how much he loved the cranky, uncomfortable, tough vessel. In the few weeks she had been his he had somehow forged her and her crew into a weapon as deadly in his hand as a well-balanced cutlass. It might be a decade, even longer, before he could aspire to such a command in the Royal Navy. But it would not be the same.

"Not only the *Mesrutiyet*, Dawlish," Hobart said. "Half the fleet – the *Mahmudiye*, the *Asar-I-Tewfik*, the *Avnillah*, the *Orhaniye*, more besides, all to be disarmed. Their guns are needed ashore."

He moved to the huge map on the wall and directed Dawlish's gaze to the landward approaches to Istanbul and the twenty-five mile arc of entrenchments and redoubts that were already being thrown up by a host of conscripted labourers. One end was anchored on the Black Sea coast and the other on the Sea of Marmara.

"The lines of Büyük Tchemedji!" Hobart's finger traced their course. "They've got a precedent, a damn successful one. Wellington built the Lines of Torres Vedras to save Lisbon and withdrew behind them. The French battered into them and couldn't take them. They starved outside them through a winter and had to retreat. We've got to hope for the same." He turned away. "We can just hope they'll buy us time for Britain to send a fleet."

211

Dawlish hardly heard him. He felt frustration, despair. I did not put on the Sultan's uniform for this, he wanted to shout. To fight a ship and to stand on my own bridge, and to feel the engines throbbing beneath my feet and spray cold on my face – Yes! But not for this!

"So I'm to land my guns? And my crew also?" Dawlish felt sick with apprehension.

"As a naval brigade, Dawlish. Land them, entrench them and fight with them. Like our friend Sir Richard did in '57."

As a captain, admired and feared, Topcliffe had waited for no orders before marching his ship's company on his own initiative across mutiny-torn India towards Lucknow, manhandling two 68-pounders across every obstacle and blasting a path for the Army in the final, bloody reckoning with the sepoy mutineers. His guns had been huge weapons in their time, but dwarves compared with the *Mesrutiyet's* twelve-inch, twenty-five ton monsters. Even getting them ashore, much less inland, would be a nightmare.

"Where are the guns needed, Sir?" Dawlish knew that he must accept the inevitable. He held the Sultan's commission, had pledged his service.

"Here." Hobart's finger stabbed at an insignificant town at the head of a small inlet of the Marmara, twenty miles west of Istanbul. "At Catalca. They're already building earthworks there. You can get close enough with the *Mesrutiyet* herself, but there's no wharf or jetty. You'll need a lighter, a large one, to land the guns and oxen to pull them when you get ashore."

Already Dawlish guessed that securing oxen – any animals – would not be easy. The two-mile journey to the Yildiz had given him a taste of the chaos that was descending on Istanbul as Muslim refugees crowded in from Bulgaria, terrified of the Russians and desperate for food and shelter. Already there was every sign of administration collapsing, of already-inefficient ministries failing under unprecedented demands and of the rich and influential crowding with their valuables on to boats that would take them to the greater safety of the Asiatic shore.

"Nothing tries men more than times like this, Dawlish." Hobart's sombre tone was all the more disturbing for its contrast with his usual ebullience. "I saw it in the Southern Confederacy near its end, the timeservers and opportunists scurrying for cover, but the bravest still standing resolute when honourable defeat, and maybe death, were the best they could hope for." He paused, then looked Dawlish in the eyes.

"I'm glad you're with me," he said. "Damned glad." His forced a smile. "But things are never so bad that we can't enjoy a good cigar," he said. He opened a box and reached it across.

They talked for another hour and, as Dawlish learned more, the problems ahead seemed ever more daunting. He would have the support of an army engineer, Adnan Binbashi – "He sounds like a good fellow – spent a year at Woolwich Arsenal and learned his trade from the Royal Engineers," Hobart said – and a company of Turkish sappers. For the rest he would be dependent on his *Mesrutiyet* crew. On them, at least, he knew he could rely.

*

Dawlish found himself back unexpectedly in the Yildiz Palace the following morning, drawn from a conference with dockyard authorities, during which the impossibility of providing shearleg lifting tackles for removing the *Mesrutiyet's* cannon was explained to him with endless courtesy. Through the window he could see two barge-mounted shearlegs lying idle among a shoal of shallow-draught lighters that were apparently equally unavailable. He was happy to leave Zyndram to complete the negotiation. "We'll have them in an hour, Nicholas Kaptan," the Pole assured him. "Negotiations always start like this here. It just takes patience."

The summons was delivered to the dockyard by an immaculately tailored and perfumed cavalry miralay. Dawlish opened an exquisite vellum envelope to disclose a thick pasteboard card covered in golden Arabic script. He looked at it, bewildered.

"It's a summons from His Majesty." The officer's English was faultless, his eyes dead. "He will see you immediately."

"Then I must change." The working rig Dawlish was wearing was shabby and salt-stained.

"When the Sultan says immediately, that's what he means, Nicholas Kaptan."

A cavalry escort waited outside, their horses glistening from fine grooming. There was a spare mount for Dawlish, a grey stallion, a four or five-year old he guessed, an Arab, sixteen hands, strong, lithe and handsome. As he swung himself into the saddle he knew that he had never mounted a finer beast.

Dawlish was relieved of his sword and pistol at the Yildiz guardhouse. There was no apology.

213

"Remove your outer clothing and boots, Nicholas Kaptan," the miralay said.

The implication was insulting and could not be let pass.

"A British officer would be trusted to approach his sovereign bearing the arms of his profession," Dawlish was unable to suppress a quaver of anger.

"But you're an Ottoman officer now, Nicholas Kaptan. So take off your tunic and boots."

He submitted with bad grace, made even worse when the miralay ran hands over him. A penknife was removed from his pocket, his wallet opened and examined. Even his letter of resignation was unfolded and read, Miss Morton's poem perused with a sneer. All would be returned when he left, but he would enter the Sultan's presence with empty pockets.

"You can dress now, Nicholas Kaptan. We can proceed."

There was no single palace, rather a haphazard sprinkling of smaller half-built structures scattered across the landscaped hillside. They passed from one building to another, challenged at each doorway, waiting for minutes as the impatient miralay questioned minions and despatched messengers who returned breathlessly to direct them to yet another shabby pavilion. Somewhere in the background an animal was roaring, its calls answered by low growling. Dawlish had the impression of being on a hunt for a quarry determined not to be found.

They had a long wait, sitting on the terrace of a miniature Swiss chalet on cast-iron chairs that would have been at home by an English lawn. Glasses of chai appeared. The miralay offered Dawlish a cigarette. The oppressive silence was broken only by the distant roars.

"I thought His Majesty said immediately?" Dawlish said.

"He's sometimes hard to find. He moves about frequently."

"That noise? That roaring?"

"The menagerie. Lions, leopards, tigers. His Majesty likes animals." He smiled. "Sometimes they are useful for drowning out certain human sounds."

"How should I approach him?"

"Respectfully but without ceremony. He doesn't like to be recognised, prefers being incognito. Address him like any Ottoman gentleman."

At last they were led to another pavilion, heavily guarded. A door opened into a dingy parlour packed with chipped gilt furniture. The

214

dusty smell gave the impression of a room long closed and opened only recently.

Hobart was there, and Nusret too, who advanced to meet them. "This gentleman, Abdul-Hamid Efendi," he said. "He wishes to thank you." He gestured towards a pale figure, still young, yet giving an impression of premature age, who sat smoking in an armchair in the far corner. Papers strewed the low table before him and he did not rise.

Dawlish bowed, then looked up to see two hooded eyes regarding him from above a wispy moustache. The face seemed infinitely melancholy and weary, the body thin and weak. A threadbare frock coat was buttoned to his throat and a faded fez, too large, rested on his ears. He conveyed neither Nusret's intelligence nor Haluk's cruelty. He might have been an impoverished clerk in some obscure ministry.

Nusret spoke rapidly in Turkish and the pale figure answered in a monotone, his eyes flickering restlessly around the room, never meeting anybody's. Nusret translated.

"Abdul-Hamid Efendi says that he has heard that the Sultan is pleased with your efforts."

"Please assure Abdul-Hamid Efendi that it was no more than my duty." Dawlish bowed again.

"Abdul-Hamid Efendi says that the Sultan would like you to have something."

He beckoned, a small, hesitant wave, as if he feared proximity. Dawlish approached slowly. Abdul-Hamid tapped ash from his cigarette into a cheap tin tray, then reached for a small leather-covered box on the table beside it. He muttered something as he thrust it forward. Dawlish took it, bowed and retreated.

"Abdul-Hamid Efendi wants you to open it, Nicholas Kaptan," Nusret said.

Dawlish pressed the catch and the lid flipped open. The brilliance within seemed immediately out of place in the decrepit surroundings, the dust and mustiness. Resting on a bed of white satin was a seven-pointed star of green enamel, a red circle at its centre bearing a gold crescent. A tiny diamond sparkled at each point and the topmost was linked by another golden crescent and star to a green and red ribbon from which it would hang when worn. It was a thing of breath-taking craftsmanship and beauty.

"The Nishani Osmani, the Order of Osman, First Class," Nusret said, lifting it from the box and pinning it to Dawlish's tunic.

215

"You're honoured, Dawlish," Hobart shook his hand. "It's restricted to fifty holders at any time."

Dawlish stammered thanks in imperfect Turkish. Abdul-Hamid murmured something. He seemed bored and impatient, like a man who wished to be somewhere else.

"Abdul-Hamid Efendi says he will pass on your thanks to the Sultan. And he hopes you will like Kivilcim."

"Kivilcim?"

"The horse that carried you here, Nicholas Kaptan. His name is Kivilcim. It means "Spark". He's yours. From the Sultan's stable."

Dawlish was overcome. The short ride had confirmed that the stallion was a mount a sane man might well kill for. He resolved instantly that no matter what difficulties lay ahead he would keep and cherish the beast.

Abdul-Hamid spoke again, as indistinctly as before, gesturing to a map on the table, his eyes never meeting Dawlish's, or the others'.

"He says the Sultan expects much of you in your new task," Nusret translated. "He wants you to know that I will be in overall command of the defences of the city, the Büyük Tchemedji entrenchments, and when they're secure, of more fortifications west of them in Thrace. He knows you will continue to serve the Sultan as well as you did before."

The nondescript clerk muttered again.

"Abdul-Hamid Efendi says the Sultan has many enemies." Nusret could not keep the satisfaction from his voice. "The Sultan relies on God's mercy, and on men like you, to protect him. And he trusts me to save the city and preserve the Empire and the Constitution."

And you've triumphed, Nusret Pasha, Dawlish thought, with this pathetic marionette in your power, while Haluk is exiled to futile persecution of helpless Bulgarian peasants and to command of a rag-tag mob of irregulars. Unless that sinister traitor's network of fanatical supporters could somehow strike more effectively than before then Nusret, the enthusiast for reform, sound finances and sanitation would be master of the Ottoman empire – whatever was left of it.

The interview was at an end. They left the heir of Suleiman the Magnificent, and the ruler of thirty million souls, glumly lighting another cigarette off his last.

*

216

There was a small debt of honour to be paid that night.

After a short note to his father – as dutiful and as lacking in warmth as their communications had been for years – Dawlish wrote a longer to his sister Susan, as he had done as frequently as he could ever since he had first left home. He mentioned nothing of the action he had seen, lest it distress her, and he told only of the sights of Istanbul and reassured her that though his work was interesting it involved little danger. Her life was difficult enough already. Her husband Adolphus, a Preston mill-owner, had seemed a reasonable catch when she had met him on an Isle-of-Man holiday twelve years before but she had learned too late of his fondness for drink. Now she was old before her time, a bloated old woman at thirty-five with swollen hands and face and a blotched complexion whose next confinement might well kill her. Was this what marriage meant? Dawlish suspected that his own mother's life had been little better. It troubled that he could not visualise her face. The single photograph ever made of her was stiff and posed, conveying nothing of the warmth and kindness that he so vaguely remembered, of his hazy memory of her reading to him, of her saying the Lord's Prayer with him as she put him to bed.

But his letter had another purpose, to ask Susan to forward Captain Butakov's wallet, which he would send with it, to his wife in Odessa. No prize court had yet been appointed to deal with disposal of Butakov's ship, the *Kataska*, nor any other prizes taken, and he feared that in this chaotic empire none ever would. If it did, he would be due a significant share of its value and he had resolved that the Captain's widow should have it. He could not bring himself to look at the creased sepia photograph the wallet contained but he folded into it ten ten-pound notes from the twenty he had brought from London. He paused, remembering the canvas-shrouded body on the *Burak Reis's* deck, then added the remaining notes. Susan should forward the package without details of a sender. He would have to trust to the efficiency of the Russian postal service.

Two hundred pounds. It didn't seem much for a life.

*

Dawlish rode out to Catalca the following day, leaving Zyndram in charge at the dockyard. A shearlegs had been secured, and three lighters, and a steam tug to manoeuvre them, but many other necessities were still outstanding, pulley-blocks, cordage, timbers,

217

windlasses, tallow, crowbars and dozens of other tools. Selim, the *Mesrutiyet's* gunner, was already relentlessly driving a team to remove the deck plating over the battery to allow his beloved cannon to be hoisted and swung outboard. Mehmet had been sent to search quarries in the area for broad-wheeled, heavy-capacity drays normally used for transporting stone blocks and for oxen and horses to supplement those already requisitioned by Nusret's hastily-constituted staff. Other officers, armed with search and seizure warrants, and accompanied by marines, were barging into warehouses to find boots and extra clothing hoarded by commissary officials in the expectation of private deals. Dawlish was determined that if his crew was going to campaign ashore in winter then it would do so warm-clothed and dry-shod. He was damned if he would let the greedy and corrupt rob the men who defended them even as the empire faced defeat.

A steady stream of refugees was flowing towards the city, plodding hopelessly through the sleet that had been falling for days, their scant possessions laden on donkeys or handcarts, their children, infirm and old piled on horse-drawn vehicles, all hungry, despairing, ragged and cold. Wherever shelter offered they crouched in miserable groups by smoking fires, knowing they must soon rise again and trudge onwards. They lined the road to either side in thin ribbons of want and exhaustion, spattered by the mud flung up by the hooves and wheels and tramping boots of the army units moving up the centre in the opposite direction.

"Bulgarian Muslims, all of them," Adnan Binbashi said. He was long and lean, thirty-five or six, and in addition to his secondment to the Royal Engineers in Woolwich he had, unusually, seen service with Turco-Egyptian forces in the Sudan. "None of them has been within fifty miles of a Russian yet. It is their own Christian neighbours they fear." He did not mask his contempt.

"They're still pitiful," Dawlish said. Back at Trabzon similar scenes had awakened his compassion and even today, for the first dozen miles, each shivering child or jaded mother had moved him. But now, overwhelmed by a thousand images of suffering, he saw only anonymous tribulation that he was powerless to assist and, despite himself, his mind was distancing itself from it.

"They were fierce and brave enough last year when they butchered Christians they'd lived next to all their lives," Adnan said. "It was they who gave the Russians the excuse to intervene and bring this disaster on us. But now that the tide is turning they fear that their own time will come. They know that whatever Christians they left alive will take vengeance when the Cossacks sweep through."

"But you're not a Christian yourself?" Dawlish asked, surprised by his vehemence.

Adnan shook his head. "I'm a Turk," he said. "That's all the Constitution asks us to be. Not Muslim nor Christian nor Jew. Just a Turk, and the rest should be private. It seems simple enough and yet it may be more than we can manage."

They moved off the main road a few miles further on and for the first time Kivilcim could have his head. He drummed down the track, nostrils dilated, muscles rippling beneath a flawless coat. As the escort dropped behind Dawlish knew that this was a gift better than a thousand Orders of Osman. The woe surrounding him fell momentarily away and he felt the same joy as when in youth he had flown across leafless Shropshire hedges on frosty mornings, hounds baying and horns sounding about him, racing his now long-dead brother for the lead. Feeling the beast beneath him share his pleasure, he could briefly ignore the feverish head-cold and cough that still plagued him and the rain-sodden grimness of the countryside about.

He cantered on, reining in finally in a squalid village beyond which, to the west, the ground rose towards rolling hills. A town nestled there, five, six miles distant, its minarets white against the dark of wooded slopes beyond.

"That's Catalca," Adnan said, joining him. "Where we'll mount the guns."

"Where's the sea?"

"There, to the left. The inlet ends about four miles from here."

"Take me there."

Even without the sleet shower that now descended, lashing their faces to rawness, the track leading to the narrow creek that stabbed inland from the Marmara would still have been little better than a quagmire. Landing the guns would not in itself be difficult – there was depth enough to bring the *Mesrutiyet* close inshore and, once the guns had been lifted out on to lighters, the lighters could be coaxed into the shallows. The problems would start thereafter.

"Can this track take the guns' weight?" Dawlish hoped his voice did not betray his dismay.

"With preparation, yes." Adnan said. "But it will take time – and much crushed stone. We can get plenty locally. Preparation is everything, Kumandanim."

219

"A sound policy." Dawlish suspected he was hearing a dictum drummed in at Woolwich. He noted too, with satisfaction, that the army engineer seemed to be stimulated rather than daunted by the challenge of landing, transporting and mounting the *Mesrutiyet's* massive cannon. Adnan was promising to be a good man to be by his side.

They rode on to Catalca. Beyond, dominating the ground that fell away ahead, rose a long earthen embankment. It glistened in the rain, its sides seamed with rivulets. Several hundred clay-streaked wretches toiled on its slopes, heightening it further with clumps of mud dumped from baskets they had filled by scooping out glutinous soil from a ditch ahead of it. A second wall, still low, was rising at an angle to the first, and the trace of a third was still only delineated by pegs and tapes.

The position was well chosen and with the *Mesrutiyet's* four twelve-inch cannon mounted here the southern extremity of the lines of Büyük Tchemedji would be firmly and impassably anchored.

"There's one advantage to these Bulgarian fugitives," Adnan said. "There's no shortage of labour. A bowl of soup buys them for a day and a loaf gets them for a week."

They were standing on top of the earthwork now, their boots sunk in uncompacted soil, and looking northwards at a jagged brown streak of embankments and trenches, broken at intervals with darker humps that indicated redoubts. It followed the contours of the gently heaving countryside until lost in the drifting sleet. It was speckled with a swarm of human ants, driven by hunger and fear and watched over by great-coated sentinels scarcely less wretched than themselves. It was a last ditch, the ultimate defence on which the armies still battling in Bulgaria must fall back if beaten. The effort being expended here, and the desperate decision to disarm the fleet's warships, confirmed that defeat was now all too probable.

They turned away, towards the inn taken over as local headquarters. There at least there would be warmth and shelter in which the maps could be spread. A long day stretched ahead, riding on the ground along those bold strokes on the map that had been so easily drawn in the Yildiz Palace. There were a half-dozen smaller redoubts to be visited between here and Dagyenice, the line's northerly anchor on the Black Sea, and each would require its complement of lower-calibre naval weapons to be drawn from other ships. Nusret had allocated Dawlish responsibility for all, and when they were in place, and the lines secured, it would be time to think of entrenchments further west, on river crossings that were still only names to him.

As he rode Dawlish forced himself to shrug off the gloom he felt descending on him. The weeks ahead would be of cold, damp and miserable exhaustion and frustration. Only dogged endurance would avail now.

The Russians might give some quarter, but the winter none.

26

Dawlish's resolution not to see Miss Morton weakened and failed. He knew now that only defeat could lie ahead, knew too that he might not survive it. He had faced the possibility of extinction before and had learned to deal with it by throwing himself into the work in hand. But he could not dismiss his awareness that in a month, maybe less, he might be just a name to be crossed off a list that would be filed and forgotten. What would it matter then whether he had seen her or not, whether he had one last image of her to carry with him into the unknown beyond? He would see her one last time and she would see him as he would wish to be remembered, as a proud captain on the deck of his own command, gold braid on his shoulders and the Nishani Osmani, First Class, sparkling on his chest.

Within days the *Mesrutiyet* would be an empty, echoing, toothless hulk, but for now, even though preparations for extracting her four twelve-inch rifles were far advanced, she was still a ship of war, and she was his. He might never command her like again and for one night only, the last on which she lay still potent in the Golden Horn, he was determined that he would enjoy his status. It was a small enough vanity.

Human flotsam in every stage of want might pack Istanbul's streets and courtyards but luxury was still obtainable, at a price. Zyndram's contacts secured not only the ingredients of a banquet but also the gold-edged cards that bore Dawlish's bilingual, bi-alphabetic invitation. Over two he paused, knowing they challenged both diplomatic and Ottoman protocol. The thought of the sleet-lashed landscape to the west decided him. He might be dead soon enough and established usage would matter little then.

A greatcoat-encased army band, its services secured by Zyndram, thumped and blared on the *Mesrutiyet's* quarterdeck as bobbing lights marked the progress of boats ferrying guests to it. The night was cold and clear, the profiles of the city's hills and domes and minarets dark against a starry sky. Dawlish paced, fighting chill rather than

221

impatience, as ten thousand captains like him, Roman and Byzantine and Varangian and Venetian and Turkish, had done before, men dedicated to defence or conquest of this pearl of cities.

"It's Hobart Pasha." Zyndram flipped his watch shut. "Dead on time. As expected."

The band crashed into a march and Bülent Chavush's marine guard snapped into a salute as the bearded admiral's red fez emerged at deck level. Resplendent in navy and gold, a gem-studded star sparkling on his left breast, the erstwhile blockade-runner's face broke into a grin as he shook Dawlish's hand.

"Smartly done, Dawlish," he said. "And time available, I'll warrant, for a quick tour of the ship before the rest arrive. I'll leave you here to freeze and my friend Zyndram will show me what's what with preparations for emasculating this poor beast."

A steam pinnace chugged purposefully towards the ironclad. In the half-darkness Dawlish strained to discern the figures standing in the after cockpit. His heart lifted as he saw they had come. He was instantly embarrassed by the absurd urge to impress that had prompted their invitation and by his delight that it had been accepted. The craft was lost to view as it drew alongside and dignity prevented him approaching the side to look down.

Lord Oswald's meaty face was as flushed and querulous as when Dawlish had first seen it appear above a deck-edge. He scowled at the band, threw a glance of contempt at the marines and gave Dawlish's hand the most perfunctory of shakes.

"A damned improper invitation, Dawlish," he said. "How did you ever expect the ambassador to dine aboard a foreign warship in time of hostilities? Sir Henry's been good enough to send his compliments as well as his excuses, but I've no doubt that only your ignorance of protocol has saved you from a formal complaint to your superior."

"I trust then you're not compromising yourself by coming here tonight?" Dawlish found it hard not to smile.

"I'm here in a private capacity, Dawlish. We need to get that straight. And if it were up to me I wouldn't be here at all. But Agatha was so damn persistent that it was easier to humour her. And by the way there was no need to extend the invitation to include that damned maid of hers."

Lady Agatha herself gained the deck at that moment, flushed by the effort, but beaming in delight as reflected lights flashed in her pince-nez. Her ample bulk was swathed in a cloak and Dawlish strongly suspected that Miss Morton, close behind, had rendered some assistance to her undignified ascent. A smile briefly lit Miss Morton's features as she glimpsed Dawlish and it pleased him.

Dawlish perceived a wave of amazement ripple across the deck as the ladies moved into the light. The band missed a beat and even among the marine guard heads turned involuntarily until Bülent's growled reproof called them to order. For perhaps the first time in history unveiled western women were treading the decks of an Ottoman warship as honoured guests and its commander was taking their hands and leading them forward to meet his officers. Zyndram was absent with Hobart – they alone would have shaken hands – but the other officers, no less shocked than their subordinates, could only hold a hand across their hearts and bow gravely, their expressions ranging from bewilderment to suppressed anger.

"I welcome you for the *Mesrutiyet's* gunners, Ma'am," Selim barked, bolder than the rest, proud of English learned in Armstrong workshops. The others seemed tongue-tied.

Miss Morton flushed slightly when Dawlish took her hand. No word passed between them beyond his formal welcome, her acknowledgement. Yet in her brief glance he sensed that she had longed for this moment as much as he had.

"You'll perhaps treat us to a tour of the ship, Commander!" Lady Agatha said

"On another occasion perhaps, Ma'am," he said. Ottoman precedents could be broken only so far and Dawlish gestured to a steward to conduct the ladies to the cabin assigned them as cloakroom.

At last, an hour late, his steam launch laden with heavily armed Albanians and escorted by another no less burdened, Nusret Pasha appeared. His features were drawn and Dawlish's report on the difficulties of arming the lines of Büyük Tchemedji had done little to comfort him. Yet his return to the *Mesrutiyet's* quarterdeck, where his courage had won over the crew on that day at Trabzon, seemed to give him a new zest.

"You promised me a surprise, Nicholas Kaptan," he said. "I know you too well to expect some gypsy dancer. I wait with trepidation!"

The warmth of the semi-circular saloon was welcome after the night's chill but the atmosphere was stiff and formal even though the Turks were draining brandy with the humourless intensity that always seemed to accompany their drinking. Hobart's easy bonhomie and Zyndram's frequent laughter seemed out of place. Oswald was eyeing one of the younger stewards with barely-disguised longing but his conversation with Nusret seemed morose.

Then the ladies entered. Lady Agatha's stout bulk strained at the purple silk that encased it but it was to the slim figure smiling behind her in white, her piled hair golden in the lamplight, that all eyes were drawn. Her dress might have been second-hand – Dawlish guessed that it was a cast off of her mistress's – but she held herself with almost regal poise and confidence. It was as if she had found some metier since he had last seen her, and had been excelling in it.

"My sister, Lady Agatha..." Oswald began, but Nusret was already striding towards them, impressed and beaming. He did not hesitate to take their hands – indeed he swept them in turn to his lips – and he was instantly again the exotic Ottoman prince who had so charmed the drawing rooms of Mayfair during his administrative apprenticeship in Whitehall.

Hobart was at Dawlish's side. "A damn fine girl that," he said quietly. His admiring glance was not directed towards Lady Agatha. "Not just looks, but spirit too! One in a million. Some young fellow's going to be damned lucky."

The words had hit Dawlish like a thunderbolt. Had concern for Miss Morton's happiness motivated his decision to forget her after this night, or was it sheer cowardice, greater fear for social ostracism than he had ever felt for enemy shot or steel? Might not continued service in the Ottoman Navy offer a chance for a life together here, where social conventions might be more easily challenged?

But Nusret was approaching, conducting the ladies to their places at table. "A brilliant idea, Nicholas Kaptan!" he whispered as he passed. "Proof to our officers that when our Constitution is fully established women no less than men will have their rights and their roles to play!"

Lady Agatha was flanked at table by the two pashas, Nusret and Hobart, while Miss Morton sat opposite, between Dawlish and Zyndram, with an increasingly ill-tempered Oswald to Dawlish's side resenting every attention paid to his sister's companion. To either side of the table's centre near silence reigned, the other officers inhibited equally by the presences of their commanders and of the foreign women.

Now that Florence Morton sat by him Dawlish found little to say. He sensed that she was equally uncomfortable. Neither alluded to the Keats poem, or to his reply, as if they had been familiarities too unwise to be mentioned and best forgotten. She too must think that it is

224

impossible, he thought, she must know that we can have no future. And this was not the place to broach his feelings, nor even to think of them. Half tongue-tied, he found himself listening to the discussion across the table.

"Your work excites much admiration, Lady Agatha," Nusret was saying. "It's an example to our Ottoman ladies."

She blushed with pleasure, candlelight reflected on her spectacles. "I could do no less when confronted with so much misery," she said. "When I looked across towards Scutari, and saw the mass of the Selimye Kislasi barracks, the memory of Miss Nightingale's labours there was like a reproach. I could not but emulate her in my small way. So I set aside the maps and charts of Piri Reis, fascinating as they were, for a happier day."

Florence – impossible now to think of her as Miss Morton – had been in conversation with Zyndram. Dawlish felt himself simultaneously pleased that his lieutenant should praise his recent exploits and leadership so enthusiastically and yet annoyed that Zyndram should have monopolised her so easily.

"What's this about Miss Nightingale, Miss Morton?" Dawlish asked, pleased that Lady Agatha had given him an opening. "I can't recall your namesake being a devotee of old maps."

"You haven't heard then, Commander?" But for the odd flat vowel she might have been a lady herself. "About our soup-kitchen for the refugees? Near the Spice Bazaar, by the Yeni Camii? We're feeding twelve hundred daily and giving beds to two hundred."

"You – and Lady Agatha?" With all the chaos in the city, Dawlish could not be but impressed.

She nodded, clearly more self-assured than on that morning off Troy. "For the last two weeks we've hardly left it. It's in an old warehouse. I'd seen it on my own explorations of the city – Agatha, Lady Agatha, is busy with her studies in the archives most days and I have time on my hands – and I'd seen the need. The misery of those people would melt any heart, Commander! When I suggested a soup kitchen Agatha supported it immediately. She forgot about her maps and took to pestering ministers and officials and merchants – and I don't know whoever not – for the money and food to get it started. She's a demon in her way, you know!"

Dawlish found himself smiling with her. "And you, Miss Morton, surely you weren't idle?"

225

"Me idle, Commander?" She laughed. "I was finding cauldrons and firewood and bowls and bedding and whatnot, like a proper workhouse matron indeed, and cleaning up the warehouse with lye and carbolic and elbow grease and putting the fear of the Lord in the dozen Bulgar girls I needed as helpers and who'd never heard of soap and water until I introduced them!"

"A damn stupid idea, Morton" Oswald growled. "You'll be lucky, both of you, if you don't catch typhus, or cholera, or worse. Those wretches are infected, every one of 'em."

Florence leaned forward to catch Oswald's eye, and Dawlish sensed her contempt. Her family might serve the Kegworths and she herself might be in paid employment, however it was disguised, but there was no mistaking her disdain.

"All the more reason then to help them, Lord Oswald," she said. "If men like Commander Dawlish and Mr. Zyndram can face an armed enemy so fearlessly then we poor weak women can at least succour the helpless." She emphasised the word "men" and it was clear that she did not apply it to her employer's brother.

"Bravo, Miss Morton!" Zyndram laughed, slapping the table with his palm.

"Damned easy philanthropy, Morton," Oswald spluttered, his face like a turkey cock's. "It's easy here in Istanbul with a warm bed and my hospitality to return to each night! You'll change your tune when Agatha drags you out to Thrace!"

"Thrace?" Dawlish said. The word chilled him. The province bordering Bulgaria was in chaos as refugees streamed through it, fearful of a Russian breakthrough.

"You've not heard of our new venture, Commander?" Lady Agatha's attention had been attracted by her brother's irritation. "We now have volunteers enough here in Istanbul to carry our work on without us! Miss Morton and I will be establishing another feeding kitchen on the main road these unfortunates follow on their flight."

"Near Istanbul?"

"No, Commander, near Edirne, at a caravanserai. In a town called Ljubimec. We leave in a few days. The caravanserai – romantic, don't you think? It reminds one of Omar Khayyam – is ideal for us I'm told. And when Nusret Pasha heard of it tonight he was so kind as to offer me a platoon – a platoon, that's the word, isn't it, Nusret Pasha? A platoon of Redif Infantry to protect it!"

226

Dawlish felt pity for her credulous enthusiasm – pity and alarm. Any Redif promised to be as useless as the ineffective reservists at Sinope whose slackness had almost cost Nusret and himself their lives. But to Lady Agatha they sounded like the Sultan's own bodyguard.

"You can't do this, Miss Morton," Dawlish said in an undertone after the conversation across the table moved on. The chaos he had seen on his brief reconnaissance westwards had shocked him. "Lord Oswald is correct. You'll be putting yourselves in mortal danger, Redif or no Redif. It's hell incarnate along that road. I've seen it, and it won't get any better."

"She wants to go," Florence said quietly. She looked across at Agatha with mixed care and admiration. "She's afraid of nothing, Commander."

"People only say that who can't imagine the worst." Dawlish shrank from suggesting the worst to her, but he had seen it often enough to fear and loathe it, in China, in Abyssinia and, most recently, in Giresun. He felt a fierce desire to protect her.

"Agatha will go anyway." Florence's voice dropped, "and where she goes, I go." She looked Dawlish full in the face. Her eyes, brown and beautiful, were grave. "I can imagine more than she can, Commander. I know more of life than any lady. People like me do. But I owe it to her, Commander. She lifted me up, made me almost a sister. I cannot, will not, fail her."

Dawlish looked away, humbled by her clear-sighted courage. He wanted to reach out to her, hold her, tell her how the single handwritten sheet she had sent him had sustained him and how he had remembered her even as the Cossacks had charged at him across that frozen hillside. But those were words he could not find, and must not use.

Instead he said "But still you should not go." He spoke very quietly, looking straight into her eyes. "I'm serious, Miss Morton. You must not go."

"You've no right to say that to me, Commander," she said, looking away.

"No," he said. "I have no right to say it." He too looked away, in mute misery.

The dinner was almost over and Nusret was rising to his feet, calling for a toast – to his brother, the Sultan. Faces flushed with drink answered the call, each, Dawlish reflected, worth ten of the pathetic

227

figure in the Yildiz Palace whom they served. Hobart rose in Nusret's wake, thundering first in Turkish and then in English.

"Nicolas Kaptan and the *Mesrutiyet*!" Hobart roared. "The man and the ship and the crew, the wolves that brought confusion to our enemies and wasted the Caucasian coast!"

Tears started to Dawlish's eyes as he felt the intensity of his officers' response. Now he must answer.

"Translate for me, Zyndram!" he hissed as he rose, holding up his glass. "Phrase by phrase, miss nothing."

Then he recalled the *Mesrutiyet's* crew, and the *Alemdar's* dead and injured, and the *Ejder's* seamen and marines who had died in the freezing waters upstream of that first bridge, and Yussef, and, bitterest to recall, Nedim, the boy who had supported him so resolutely only to die on a Cossack lance at the moment of deliverance.

"It's not over, Gentlemen!" he finished. "But the same spirit, the same courage, will carry us through! I give you the Ottoman Navy, the Ottoman Seaman and the Ottoman Marine!"

They were on their feet, cheering, and Nusret was thumping the table and the ladies were shouting "Bravo!" and Florence's look of unfeigned admiration was worth all that Dawlish had endured when an elegant figure was ushered in by a steward. Dawlish recognised the miralay who had conducted him to the Sultan. He scanned the throng for a moment, then saw Nusret and went straight to him.

The noise faltered, died. Nusret had paled, and was shaking his head slowly as the messenger's whispered tale continued. He had taken a telegram in his hand, a long one, and he scanned it again and again before he finally spoke. The words were no less devastating for being sooner or later inevitable.

"Plevna," Nusret said, and the word alone shocked them. "Osman Pasha tried to break out last night. He took the Russian front line, was repulsed at the second. He was wounded himself." He paused. "No man, no soldiers, could have done more. Osman Pasha surrendered this afternoon."

It was December 10th and a hitherto obscure Bulgarian town had entered history by holding up the might of the Czar's Army for five full months. And now 120,000 well-equipped and well-supplied Russian and Rumanian troops were free to flood southwards towards Istanbul.

Now, more than ever, the *Mesrutiyet's* guns would be needed in the Lines of Büyük Tchemedji.

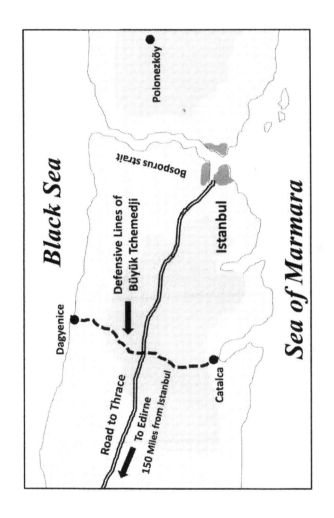

27

Dawlish celebrated his thirty-second birthday six days later with the rolling ashore at Catalca of the first of the *Mesrutiyet's* twelve-inch cannon. A lighter beached in the shallows by a tug brought it within twenty yards of dry land and a ramp of gravel and timber provided the path down which the quarry-wagon bearing the massive barrel was eased carefully.

"We're lucky." Adnan Binbashi, the army engineer, pointed to the frozen mud. The night had been frosty, providing solid footing for the eighteen straining oxen now inching the juggernaut forward.

"Lucky as long as the snow holds off." Dawlish drew his greatcoat closer, glancing up at the leaden sky. Neither it, nor the fur jerkin beneath, nor his thick whipcord riding breeches, could preserve him fully from the numbing cold.

A second wagon followed, laden with the cannon's mounting, and several smaller vehicles, loaded with shells and charges. Hundreds from Adnan's ragged workforce had slaved for days to prepare the six-mile track that now snaked from the inlet to the redoubt at Catalca, its course chosen to minimise inclines. Work was nearing completion at the far end, which the plodding oxen might reach by the end of following day. The fortification itself was as far from completion as the other defensive positions further north. Cold and exposure were claiming their first victims among the workers and their output was falling by the day.

Out in the inlet a barge-mounted shearlegs and steam winch were hoisting the second gun-barrel from the battery. Beyond the *Mesrutiyet* two other ironclads lay anchored, waiting their turn to have their weapons landed, lower-calibre cannon destined for the line's smaller redoubts.

The snow held off for another seven days. Seven days of backbreaking labour for man and beast, of icy winds and clear skies and sun that gave no warmth, of oxen collapsing and cut free from their traces to die by the roadside, of fresh beasts pushed beneath the yoke and themselves used up within hours in their turn. Seven days in which a hundred and fifty yards advance in an hour was considered exceptional and a hundred acceptable, and in which the gruelling crawl continued for twenty-four hours on end, and then another twenty-four, and afterwards the same again. Tired, cold men goaded the beasts and heaved on ropes to augment their efforts and shovelled crushed stone into ruts with bleeding hands, huddling for brief shelter and snatched sleep in hovels and sheepfolds along the way. Dawlish ensured that bread freshly baked on the ironclads reached them daily but warmth was more difficult to supply. Only the seamen and marines now labouring ashore were adequately clothed against the chill. Dawlish was in Kivilcim's saddle sixteen hours a day, ranging back and forth along the road, urging progress and pushing extra resources to any point where delay threatened.

The news from Bulgaria grew worse. Freed now from the siege of Plevna, Russian forces were pushing remorselessly southwards into the Balkan Mountains, crushing opposition wherever they encountered it. Soon, it seemed, they could be across, for though bitter last-stands by isolated Ottoman forces sought to buy time, the more general retreat they sacrificed themselves to protect degenerated all too often into disorganised rout. Prodigal of the lives of their peasant soldiers, and with commanders as inspired as the ruthless Gourko and the brilliant Skobelev, the Russians were already sensing that Istanbul was almost in their grasp. Within a month their surge might be washing up against the hurried earthworks thousands now slaved to complete.

The first of the *Mesrutiyet's* cannons was already bedded at Catalca and the barrel of the second was dropping on to its mounting there when the blizzard struck. Half-blinded by driving snow, Adnan and his sappers, supported by Selim and his crew, completed the operation before retreating to shelter. Movement along the road ended, white drifts built up around abandoned carts, oxen huddled miserably behind any outcrop, many dying there, and labourers and landed crews were withdrawn hastily into any shelter available to sit out the storm. Only the few still manning the now-weaponless ironclads to transfer the last of the stores were spared.

On the blizzard's second morning, with work at a standstill, Dawlish and Zyndram were huddled by a brazier in the cattle byre where they had slept, when two snow-dusted figures entered. Adnan and Selim loosened the shawls swathing their heads to reveal smiling faces.

"Merry Christmas, Gentlemen!" the *Mesrutiyet's* gunnery officer barked in English.

"God rest you, Merry Gentlemen," Adnan bowed gravely.

Dawlish rose, flushed with pleasure. He, like Zyndram, had forgotten the day. "I had not expected this," he said.

231

"Not from your Turkish brothers, Nicholas Kaptan?" Adnan said. "When I trained at Woolwich Arsenal your countrymen invited me to their homes to celebrate this day. Now here, under the Constitution, Christians and Muslims can celebrate like brothers also."

"At Armstrong's also, when I was there…" Selim was saying, for a brief moment no longer the martinet gunner feared by young Mehendis and lower deck alike.

Dawlish drew both men to him and kissed them on the cheeks, Turkish fashion. Zyndram did so too and said something in Polish that nobody understood but which pleased them nonetheless. Adnan gave Dawlish a small wooden box of lokum, and they shared it with the poor coffee that was all they had but which Dawlish fortified with a dash of brandy from his flask. He felt himself moved, all the more since for these few minutes both Turkish officers made no use of the formal modes of address they always seemed so addicted to. A few hundred miles to the west Selahattin's Bashi Bazook marauders might be marking this day with massacre but within this freezing hut there was hope of that better future under the Constitution which Nusret glimpsed and for which he had inspired others to follow him. Dawlish was glad to be one of them.

Soon it was time to break up, to venture out into the snow to inspect the situation, for the formalities of rank to be restored. As he moved from one wretched hovel to another, and wished that he had better rations to sustain both workers and draught animals. Dawlish thought of the caravanserai at Ljubimec. Lady Agatha and Miss Morton must be there by now and ensuring that at this Christmas there was room at that one inn at least for the endless stream of refugees from Bulgaria. Another memory of Miss Morton – of Florence – was stronger now than that of the morning off Troy. It was when she had told him in the *Mesrutiyet's* saloon that she understood and accepted the danger she was placing herself in. And that he had no right to tell her otherwise.

But he had hoped that Lady Agatha might listen to reason. It had been in hopes of dissuading her from the risks he feared that he had gone to the soup kitchen near the Spice Bazaar the first time his duties gave him a respite to do so. It had been two days after the dinner on the ironclad, just before he left Istanbul. It was Lady Agatha he wanted to speak to, he told himself, and he did not want to see Miss Morton. If she was present he would be formally polite to her, no more. Hobart's praise of her still echoed in his mind, reproached his courage,

232

challenged his decision to forget her. But it was easy for Hobart to ignore differences in rank, easy for the son of an earl whose place in society had been assured from birth, but otherwise for the son of an obscure solicitor for whom every advance was a struggle, and even harder for a woman who had started as a maid and might always be reminded of it. No Royal Naval officer, however senior, would shun a Hobart. A Dawlish and a Morton could expect no such indulgence. But though he had resolved to forget her, his heart had still sunk when he learned at the soup kitchen that she and Lady Agatha had already left for Thrace.

The huge warehouse, packed with misery and smelling of soup and carbolic and unwashed bodies, had been left to the supervision of two middle-aged Englishwomen with limited Turkish who had already lost control and were clearly on the verge of despair. He recognised one as the wife of a shipping agent whom he had met at Hobart's soirée, one of the women who had so markedly snubbed Miss Morton there. Now she was bewailing her absence. "I don't know why she had to leave," she said. "She's needed more here than wherever she's gone with her mistress. She was the only one these helpers here ever listened to. And she understood all about scrubbing and cooking and purchasing and mending. Women like her do. They're born to that sort of thing."

"Women like her, Ma'am?" Dawlish had flushed with anger. "I've seldom met Miss Morton's equal as a lady." He had turned and left, afraid lest he say more. Her life, he thought, must be full of such spiteful and petty slights. But now her safety –her very life – was a greater concern than social rejection. He was glad too that the work that now faced him, brutal as it must be, would be a distraction from the aching fear he felt for her safety.

The wind fell the day after Christmas, the snow ceased and a thaw set in that made every movement a drenching plod through slush and mud. Four massive quarry-drays normally used for transporting blocks of stone, each now carrying a gun-mounting or barrel, were strung out along the road, interspersed with a score of smaller vehicles carrying supplies and lighter weapons. They stuck fast, sinking in the frigid ooze, digging in ever deeper as exhausted men and jaded animals tugged and heaved to shift them. Windlasses and blocks were rigged to drag them free, inch by painful inch, across quagmires that swallowed crushed stone by the cartful. A small army of workers had been transferred from the redoubts to the roadway, and a nearby quarry was alive with refugee labour that broke stone day and night. Selim

233

Yüzbashi ruled there, driving the labourers as mercilessly as he drove his gun-crews and quickly developing an expertise in rock-blasting with gunpowder charges.

Death was a constant presence along the road – slow sense-dulling and flesh-numbing death that sapped hope and vitality until at last it seemed like luxury to crawl into some semblance of shelter and yield wearily. Dysentery struck, foul and degrading, weakening bodies already faint from cold and hunger. Chills and pneumonia claimed dozens more. They were thrust into shallow trenches, lightly covered and quickly forgotten as their places were filled by refugees conscripted from the endless stream that plodded along the main road further north. Dawlish was exhausted by a racking cough and frequently feverish, lousy since his first night ashore here, scarcely less mud-plastered than his splendid mount. He despised himself for the callousness growing within him as the weapons' slow crawl towards their redoubts dominated his waking moments. He felt the hollowness of his encouragement of men who had no choice, raged inwardly at his impotence to spare wretches whom a week's rest might have saved, fretted that his horse was better housed, and for good reason, than thousands of his workers and silently damned to hell Sultan Abdul-Hamid and Czar Alexander. But to Zyndram and Adnan and five thousand others he remained the unyielding commander who drove himself as mercilessly as themselves.

The night frosts returned, hardening the ground, cutting feet and hooves but giving purchase again, killing the sick and weak but hastening movement. The *Mesrutiyet's* remaining cannons creaked painfully into the Catalca redoubt, one at New Year – 1878, a date that offered only the prospect of defeat – and the last two days later. Barrels and mountings were reunited above thick mattresses of cross-laid timbers flanked by sloped earthen walls. Yet even then there was no respite. Attention shifted to the smaller redoubts strung out along the line to the north like beads on a necklace. Each mounted one or two guns, light by naval standards but ponderous giants ashore, each demanding its own small epic of exertion and sacrifice.

The weather held. By the end of the first week in January the key redoubts were gunned and the intermediate entrenchments far advanced.

"Impressive, Nichols Kaptan," Nusret Pasha said. "You've done as well ashore as afloat."

234

For all that they were on a bare hilltop south of Dagyenice, where the road from Edirne crossed the lines, and that his cavalry escort hovered on the slopes below, Nusret looked watchful, even hunted. On either side the defences stretched, a sinuous, contour-hugging barrier that stretched almost thirty miles from the Black Sea to the Marmara.

"The credit is Adnan Binbashi's," Dawlish said.

The engineer officer flushed with pride. He had personally sited each redoubt and traced the trenches that linked them with an unerring eye for terrain, capturing each small advantage that a fold of ground or a favourable slope might offer. It took little to see that an army established here with modern rifles, even a beaten army at the end of a long retreat, and supported by the artillery mounted at such cost in suffering, could inflict fearsome casualties on any attacker.

"The lines have only one disadvantage, Nicholas Kaptan." Nusret's tone was bitter.

"A disadvantage?"

"They're too close to Istanbul. If the Russians come this far we'll have already lost Bulgaria and Thrace." He sensed Dawlish's disquiet and added: "But we have no option. Above all the city must be saved."

"Will it come to that?" For three weeks now all Dawlish had heard had confirmed that the Russians had indeed unleashed the winter campaign that Hobart had predicted. Despite snow, ice and marrow-freezing cold they were battering their way southwards through the Balkan passes.

"They may already have taken Sofia," Nusret said. He had ridden out from Istanbul that morning and his news was fresh. "The last reports had General Gourko's army pushing towards it. And another under Radetzsky is moving south from the Shipka Pass." He paused, as if overawed by the import of his own words. "He has three separate columns, one of them under that devil Skobelev. And nothing, nobody, has checked them."

Dawlish understood why Adnan groaned. Once across the mountains the terrain would be more open, well suited to sweeping manoeuvres that could outflank fixed positions. Only rapid deployments of the still-formidable Turkish armies could counter the Russian thrusts, blocking advances and threatening flanks. Bonaparte or Jackson or Lee might have accomplished it but until now, other than the now-vanquished Osman at Plevna, no Ottoman commander had shown a spark of brilliance or initiative.

"And Suleiman Pasha?" Dawlish asked. "He is in command in Bulgaria, is he not? Surely he has whole armies that have not yet seen action?"

"Suleiman Pasha?" Nusret's lowered tone told Dawlish what was not for Adnan's ears. "Suleiman and my half-brother Haluk claim difficulty co-ordinating their forces. There will be resistance, fierce brief resistance, in many places but it will be a token only. They will retreat. Nothing is more sure. It's their plan."

Dawlish felt himself sickened by the naked cynicism of it. The disaster that Nusret had suspected was being planned was now coming to pass – the collapse that would carry the enemy to the gates of Istanbul, destroy Abdul-Hamid's prestige and precipitate his removal. The Sultanate would pass to whichever of his half-brothers could claim the greater share of glory in the final resistance before British intervention prevented ultimate humiliation and preserved a vestige of Ottoman power. Haluk and his henchman Suleiman Pasha would be the heroes of a fighting retreat – sacrificing thousands of doggedly heroic troops in the process – and Nusret would be master of the barrier that would finally stem the Russian tide. Two half-brothers would dispute the laurels and the third, that pathetic recluse in the Yildiz Palace, would beg the victor for comfortable exile rather than death by obscure accident.

Thousands still laboured on the earthworks, famished, shivering and, for the greater part, doomed. Each day the road from Edirne was denser still with fugitives struggling towards the bitter solace of the courtyards and archways of the imperial city. Even that was preferable to the vengeance that Cossack sabres and Bulgarian knives would wreak on the now-pathetic participants in the massacres that had shocked the world more than a year before. As Suleiman Pasha's army retreated, hell would follow. The soldier-to-soldier conflict in the Balkan Mountains further north, where men froze and died in futile efforts to delay the Russian advance, seemed somehow clean by comparison.

Lice were burrowing in Dawlish's clothing. For all his futile efforts at cleanliness he was unwashed, his fingernails black, his hair and beard unkempt. Yet it was none of these things that made him feel suddenly degraded, but rather the knowledge that he had found himself a player in a deadly game of intrigue, greed and treachery. But he had made his decision, given his word, pledged his loyalty. Now the game must be played out, whatever the outcome.

236

They turned their horses, heading back towards the escort. Nusret had mentioned new orders earlier. Now Dawlish would learn the details.

*

The following day, January 7th, Dawlish's Naval Brigade marched from Catalca. Seventy men, gunners, remained with Selim and Mehmet to man the twelve-inchers that now crouched potently in the earthwork's embrasures. Two hundred and ten men, the fittest of *Mesrutiyet's* company, sixty of them marines, followed Dawlish, Zyndram and Adnan northwards. Their ship, toothless now, had withdrawn to Istanbul. The last of the landed supplies trundled behind the marching column on requisitioned farm carts. Four sixteen-pounder cannon accompanied them, Army weapons that Hobart had prised from some reserve artillery park, and one of the *Mesrutiyet's* Nordenveldts mounted on a light field-gun carriage. The marines carried Winchesters, the seamen single-shot Martini-Peabodys. Zyndram had gone back to ransack the last stocks in Istanbul's military storehouses to provide them with stout boots, thick woollen uniforms and hooded greatcoats.

They began the long plod towards Edirne. There, along the river lines on either side of the splendid city on the border between Thrace and Bulgaria Nusret had ordered construction of new defences. With the Lines of Büyük Tchemedji now secure and slowly filling with garrison troops withdrawn from Western Anatolia he was now determined to establish another perimeter further forward. Far to the east the Russians might have taken Kars but there was now every indication that the devastation Dawlish had wreaked on their supply lines precluded any further offensive from there until spring. Erzurum would hold through the winter and Archduke Michael's forces would advance no further into Anatolia. Dawlish could pride himself on that. The greater threat was now from Bulgaria and it was towards its border with Thrace that the last reserves Nusret could scrape together were now being rushed.

The *Mesrutiyet* Brigade marched westwards. Days of thaw had left the road a winding ribbon of mud trodden to sludge by dragging feet and jaded hooves. To either side endless streams of refugees still toiled eastwards towards Istanbul.

Florence and Lady Agatha would have come up this road of misery too, Dawlish realised, on their way to the relief station they

237

would establish west of Edirne. He imagined them perched on a wagon of food and medicine, their useless escort of sullen Redif more reluctant each time to push them from the mud in which they would bog down every half-mile. He visualised Lady Agatha flushed with the naïve enthusiasm and blindness to danger that seemed to afflict so many of the most truly intelligent, and Florence, clear-sighted, pragmatic, under no illusion as to the risks but accepting them out of loyalty. But Dawlish wondered if even Florence could truly comprehend the horror threatening them, if she would know in time when to prevail upon Lady Agatha to retreat towards safety.

I swore I would never see her again, Dawlish told himself. But I had not expected this. It was not her happiness – or his – that concerned him now. It was her life.

A merciless wind from the west blew rain and sometimes sleet in the faces of the marching men, soaking their clothing and chilling them before they completed the day's first mile. By night they crowded into any shelter available, byres and sheepfolds and hovels already packed with wretches in the last stages of privation who crouched round smoking fires and tried vainly to dry sodden rags and warm numbed limbs. The strong, the healthy and the armed showed little compunction about evicting the weak, and Anatolians showed no sympathy for the Balkan refugees. Dawlish did not hesitate to use his riding whip to thrash a hulking army chavush who had driven a pregnant widow with four small children from the scant cover of a collapsed cowshed into a night of driving rain. The next day he sensed himself regarded with increased respect, not for his compassion but for his anger.

Obliged to appear always confident and cheerful to those he commanded, Dawlish silently fought the depression brought him by the misery about him. Why this is Hell, nor am I out of it, he told himself, remembering Marlowe, as he had done on that fateful day off Troy. He thought with hatred of the sleek, well-fed statesmen in chancelleries across Europe who must now be weighing the opportunities a total Turkish rout might bring. Soft, clean hands would be sweeping across maps to indicate advances and retreats or trace possible frontier adjustments. Polished and cautious phrases would be masking greed and calculation that reckoned little of the cold of a starving child, the despair of a bereaved mother, the exhaustion of a conscripted peasant. He recognised that he himself was caught up in that same web of cold manipulation, not as a passive victim, but as an active player. Topcliffe and Lord Beaconsfield would have been informed by Hobart that he was here, and would expect him to do all he could to bleed Russian strength before it could threaten Istanbul. Britain's Mediterranean Fleet was a card that the cunning old Prime Minister would play only when he was sure that the Czar was too weak to trump it. The game had seemed simple enough to Dawlish when he had accepted Topcliffe's proposal in London. He had foreseen action at sea and had accepted the risk to his life. He had not expected this Hell on land, nor that he himself would become a slave-driver in it.

But then, as so often before, he forced himself to silence his doubts and remember his bargain with himself to advance in rank, find satisfaction in achievement and command. And for that, his bargain with Topcliffe must be honoured to the end.

Half-way to Edirne Dawlish consigned the tramping column to Zyndram's command and rode ahead with Adnan. They left the road, paralleling it to the north on smaller, less frequented tracks. Both men were well mounted, Dawlish superbly, and their journey was like a brief holiday.

"The Tunca, Nicholas Kaptan!" Adnan reined in as they crested a ridge late in the day. The river lay two miles south-westwards, sinuous and rain swollen, blood-red as it reflected the sinking sun. Fifteen miles downstream it flowed into the larger Maritza at Edirne but it was not there they were headed.

"I can see a village." A ragged clump of buildings on the nearer bank sharpened into focus as Dawlish adjusted his glasses. "And a bridge – a trestle bridge." Maybe sixty yards long, two piers, the swirling waters almost level with the decking.

"That's Suakacaği. Where we build the redoubt."

The road that crossed the Tunca there was little more than a track but it could afford an escape path for a retreating army – or an outflanking route around Edirne for one advancing. It was here that the *Mesrutiyet* Brigade was headed, to fortify and hold. Already refugee labour had been diverted there from the city to the south to commence the work. Dawlish could foresee it already, a repeat of the muddy agony at Catalca: forced toil, hunger, cold and sickness. And in himself, outward callousness and inward revulsion.

He voiced the idea that had tormented him since his first sight of the refugee columns had given an inkling of the scale of the tragedy unfolding. "How far to Ljubimec?"

"Florence is there!" a small voice shouted inside his head.

239

"Ljubimec?" Adnan seemed surprised he knew the name. "About thirty miles west of here."

It was on the main road from Central Bulgaria to Edirne, Dawlish knew, the route the principal Russian thrust towards Istanbul must surely follow. There was little to stop them now – the latest reports he had heard confirmed Sofia's fall and indicated unstoppable advances. Desperate rearguard actions might yield local checks but the Russian colossus was brushing them aside and lurching inexorably southwards. Lady Agatha's soup kitchen lay directly in its path.

"There's a track from here to Ljubimec?"

Adnan nodded. "The same track that crosses the Tunca at Suakacaği."

Florence Morton, no less than Lady Agatha, was potentially exposed to outrages as unspeakable as on that night in Giresun. Even as Dawlish's mind recoiled from the thought a resolution formed within it.

A party of Adnan's sappers had preceded them to Suakacaği and an obviously competent üschavush had pegged the outlines of the new earthwork, slightly upstream of the wooden bridge. A dozen substantial stone-built village houses were incorporated in its faces, their two-foot thick walls capable of withstanding light artillery. Four hundred conscripted refugees had been herded north from Edirne and were already at work, delving earth and stones from nearby fields and staggering towards the worksite with laden baskets. Most of the local population had fled eastwards already and the most substantial house, a merchant's, had been requisitioned for Dawlish and his officers.

A thin stream of fugitives plodded across the bridge, day and night, Muslim Bulgarians fleeing from the anticipated fury of their Christian countrymen. Dawlish directed the sapper üschavush to select the younger and stronger ones, despite the wailing of their families, and set them to work on the defences. Many were townsfolk – shopkeepers, petty officials, craftsmen – and unused to heavy labour. Even though he knew that many had at best stood passively by while their Christian neighbours had been murdered and raped eighteen months before, Dawlish found himself filled with a pity for them that he could not afford to show.

As the redoubt walls rose workers began to die as miserably as they had done at Catalca. Eight or ten were being buried daily when Zyndram led the footsore naval brigade into Suakacaği two days later.

It gladdened Dawlish's sad heart to see them arrive.

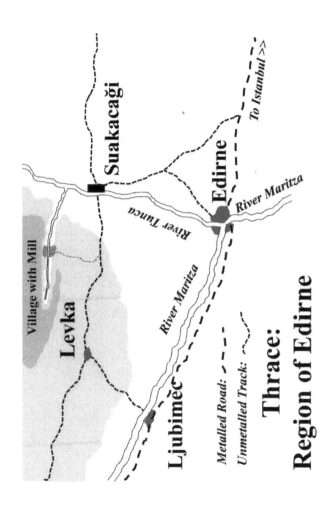

Thrace: Region of Edirne

Suakacaği

Edirne

To Istanbul >>

River Maritza

River Tunca

Village with Mill

Levka

River Maritza

Ljubimec

Metalled Road:

Unmetalled Track:

The cannon were already mounted at Suakacaği to dominate the bridge and the open ground beyond when Nusret Pasha arrived at the head of two exhausted squadrons of regular Circassian cavalry. He almost collapsed from the saddle and accompanied Dawlish stiffly to his quarters. His eyes were red-rimmed and he smelled of brandy.

"It's total rout now," he said.

His voice gave a hint of the despair Dawlish had first heard in it when they left Trabzon, defeated. His hand trembled, spilling ash from his cigarette, and he gratefully drained the coffee Dawlish poured him. They were alone before a map tacked on the wall. Pencilled marks recorded what disjointed information Dawlish had received as to movements and reverses. Zyndram, unasked, but always sensitive to Dawlish's language handicap, had inked in the town names for him in English. By now he was well familiar with them, and with one name above all – Ljubimec. The two ladies might be gone from there by now, but he suspected that Lady Agatha might be reluctant to abandon her charges, and be too confident of the immunity that her mission of mercy might afford her. The idea of the women's exposure tortured Dawlish.

"I understand that Suleiman's army is holding firmly around Plovdiv." he said. He had heard of Ottoman counterattacks, several temporarily successful, around the Bulgarian city to the west.

"Holding, but cut off nonetheless." Nusret shook his head. "Outflanked to the east by Radetzsky's forces." His cigarette traced the Russian thrust. "They're heading for Edirne. They'll be here in a week, maybe sooner. They're allowing Gourko's forces – which are pushing here, and here and here, from Sofia – to destroy Suleiman."

"Can't Suleiman break out eastwards? If Radetzsky is moving that fast, surely his forces are over-extended?"

"Suleiman strike into Radetzsky's flank? He could and he should – but he won't! He'll withdraw directly southwards, to the Aegean. He's already requesting shipping to evacuate his forces by sea."

"You're sure?" Dawlish could scarcely credit the boldness of the treachery implied. It would leave only scattered forces to contest the Russian advance on Edirne and on towards Istanbul.

"Sure, Nicholas Kaptan? Of course I'm sure. My informant is on Suleiman's staff and I had his coded message last night before the line was cut. Withdrawal south, that's Suleiman's plan, and Haluk's too, damn him – to yield up Bulgaria and sacrifice Thrace!"

"Where's Haluk? With Suleiman?"

Nusret laughed bitterly. "God only knows. Impaled on a Cossack lance I hope! The last report had him here" – he stabbed the map with savage glee – "at Gulubovo, straight in the path of Skobelev's column. He was virtually cut off and trying to reach Suleiman."

"Can Edirne hold?" Dawlish asked.

Nusret threw himself on the divan, fumbled for another cigarette, lit it off the last. "You have brandy here, Nicholas Kaptan? Good!" He tossed it back, then refilled the glass. "Edirne? Edirne can't be held – nor this place here either. They're important now only as river crossings. We need to hold them only long enough to get across as many as possible of the units retreating this way. We must get them to the Büyük Tchemedji Lines! We've scraped Anatolia for reserves, and put the lame and the sick and the old into the trenches, and still it isn't enough! We need every man retreating before Radetzsky and Skobelev to supplement them and once they're across the river the bridges can be blown! That's why you're here, Nicholas Kaptan."

So the full weight of the Russian onslaught would come this way, Dawlish realised, ignoring Suleiman's retreating forces, thrusting for Istanbul, Constantinople, the Second Rome, Russia's goal for centuries. But before the blow fell here it would fall at Ljubimec – where Florence was – as the Czar's forces smashed through it towards Edirne.

Dawlish realised that he must act now or face regret for the rest of his life.

"Do you intend to stay here long, Nusret Pasha?" he asked.

"Tonight, only. I wanted to be assured that the crossing here was secure." He reached out and took Dawlish's hand. His eyes were glistening. "I need not have worried, my good friend Nicholas. You've never failed me and you won't now. I wish I could be so certain at Edirne. I ride there tomorrow."

"I need a favour, Nusret Pasha." It was perhaps the most important to his happiness he had ever asked. He would act anyway, even if Nusret refused. But it would be better to have his approval.

Nusret nodded sleepily. "Ask, Nicholas Kaptan."

"You remember Lady Agatha? Lord Kegworth's daughter?" Dawlish paused for emphasis. "Lord Kegworth – the friend of the Prime Minister, Lord Beaconsfield?"

243

The name was enough to stir Nusret from his torpor. He would need British sympathy in the form of the Royal Navy's cannon if the Russians arrived before Istanbul. His consent was immediate. Dawlish gained what he needed – twenty Circassian horsemen, ready to depart for Ljubimec at first light – and permission to transfer command of the Suakacaği garrison to Zyndram for a single day.

He expected to be back by nightfall and to have the two ladies with him. They could be on the road back to Istanbul and safety next morning. He would never see Florence again after that, but he would have given her life. That would have to satisfy him until the end of his days.

*

The bridge was slippery with frost and the eastern sky was brightening as the small cavalcade clattered across. Dawlish took Adnan with him, not just as interpreter but because experience had proved the engineer-officer to be tough, competent and resourceful. The escort was commanded by a leathery cavalry chavush named Alper who placed two pairs of scouts well ahead.

It would be mid-morning by the time they reached Ljubimec and Dawlish anticipated an argument before Lady Agatha would consent to leave. The winter day was short, and heavy grey clouds promised snow, and it would be a race to return to his garrison before dark. His heart was beating fast at the thought of seeing Florence but he was steeling himself to be coldly formal when he did.

They encountered refugees, sometimes in knots, sometimes strung out, but always unvarying in their despair, their exhaustion and their grim determination to press on. Few had draught animals – those who had gone before had scoured the countryside of whatever beasts the armies had not requisitioned – and most were in the last stages of destitution.

"What's he concerned about, Adnan Yüzbashi?" Dawlish asked as he watched Alper interrogating the leader of a small group they had stopped. He looked obviously worried by whatever the jaded refugee was telling him and he gestured to the north as he barked questions. The others, two men, four women and half dozen children looked on with dead, hopeless eyes. They were filthy, swathed in rags and their mostly bare feet were bleeding from the frost-hardened ground. A little girl looked up, her hair matted, her face pallid beneath the grime, her

244

thin body shivering uncontrollably. Dawlish felt ashamed of his own warmth and full stomach. He reached into his saddle-bag and handed down the rough bread and soft white cheese he had brought for himself. The mother moved first, tearing the food from him, ripping it in pieces and sharing it among the children before the other adults could react.

"I asked what is he saying, Adnan Yüzbashi!" Dawlish repeated, covering his distress with gruffness.

"They've seen Russians – two days ago, twenty-five, thirty miles north of here. They shot several people, set fire to the village, then withdrew."

Alper Chavush was right to be concerned then. Previous fugitives encountered had been flying from fear of an as-yet-unseen enemy, but these refugees had experienced the reality. The attack they spoke of bore all the characteristics of a reconnaissance by a cavalry screen in advance, perhaps far in advance, of a stronger force. It was the first confirmation of Russian presence so far south.

"Did these people come through Ljubimec?"

They had not, they had come due south and so could give no confirmation of the presence of the Englishwomen. They might have left already, this might be a wild goose chase, but Dawlish knew he could only press forward.

They rode on, more alert now, glancing ever rightwards for the sight of Cossack pennants bobbing over a crest. Further on, in a deserted village, they found evidence that it was not only Russians who burned and killed. The mosque was intact, and perhaps half the houses, though their doors and shutters had been torn away and used as firewood by passing fugitives, but the remaining dwellings had been gutted by fire, and the small Orthodox church also, and whitened skulls and protruding bones lay scattered among the ashes. Here, where Christian and Muslim had lived intermingled, hatred had erupted long months before and neighbour had slaughtered neighbour.

Snow began to fall around nine o'clock, large dry flakes drifting on a northerly breeze, quickly whitening the landscape. They were perhaps halfway to their destination but now the track ahead was obscured, slowing progress. The riders hunched within their greatcoats, pulled their hoods closer around their kalpaks and crouched lower across their mounts.

245

An hour passed. The snow was thicker now, the light dim grey, visibility a few hundred yards. Suddenly Alper's upraised hand halted the column.

"There, Nicholas Kaptan!" Adnan's pointing finger picked out one of the scouts cantering back. From the north came a crackle of rifle-fire. Dawlish pulled his hood back to hear better. In quick succession artillery – light, by its sharp bark – blasted twice, paused, sounded again.

The scout reined in, reported.

"He saw horsemen over there." Adnan pointed north-westwards. "Moving parallel to this track, turning north again. Then he lost sight of them."

"Did they spot him?"

"No. But he left his companion behind to observe."

"Nusret Pasha thought it would be a week before the Russians could reach here," Dawlish said, thinking aloud. Nusret, sweating and feverish, had repeated this conviction when he had seen him before leaving. Weakened by hard riding, exposure and constant fear of assassination, Nusret had been concerned enough by his own symptoms to agree to stay an extra day and night in Suakacaği. The *Mesrutiyet's* surgeon could do little more than order rest.

"They're here now," Adnan said, another distant artillery report confirming his words. He listened carefully. Another report, than another. "Russian, not Turkish," he said. "Light, four-pounders."

Rifle fire rose to a brief crescendo, then died. Once more came the characteristic bark of the Russian horse-artillery. No Turkish weapons replied.

"A light force?"

"Cavalry, probably dragoons. At least two galloper cannon, maybe more." Adnan said. "Possibly an advance column, to seize the Suakacaği crossing, to hold it until reinforcements arrive."

Dawlish felt disappointment well within him. He was perhaps twenty miles from the women he had come to save, but now there was a more immediate call on him as the most senior officer present. If there were substantial enemy forces close by then Nusret needed to know – fast. But more information was needed than could be deduced from the sound of gunfire.

"Tell Alper I want a rider sent back to Nusret Pasha immediately." He was already scribbling a message with numbed fingers. There was little enough to tell but better than nothing if what he now intended turned out badly.

"We're going to investigate," Dawlish said. He suddenly felt inadequate, a sailor on horseback, ignorant of the tactics needed to reconnoitre the situation stealthily and escape without detection or loss. "Tell Alper Chavush I need his advice."

The horses stamped impatiently and the riders beat caked snow from their coats as the hasty conference proceeded. The force was divided in two equal groups – Alper leading one, Dawlish the other, Adnan with him to translate. Alper's group headed directly north across the undulating open ground, two scouts well ahead. Dawlish's force trotted westwards up the track for a quarter mile, picked up the scout left behind there – he had seen nothing more since his companion had left him – and then also turned north. Through the swirling white to the right Alper's riders were only faintly discernible as dark indistinct shapes.

The sound of gunfire rose and fell, muffled as they passed through hollows, louder as they cautiously crossed each low crest, beckoned on by the scout confirming that the way ahead was clear. A track lay beyond diagonally across their path, curving northwards, disappearing over a rolling crest ahead. They crossed and stayed to the right of the track, avoiding its promise of firmer footing – the chance of an encounter on it was too great. The horses seemed to catch their riders' apprehension as they picked their steps slowly through the snow, sometimes floundering briefly in a gathering drift. The men rode with their Winchesters rested across the saddle, narrowed eyes scanning the swirling white for signs of movement.

A signal from the scout brought the small column to a halt. He was just below the low crest ahead, his waving arm counselling caution. Dawlish and Adnan left the others in the hollow below and rode to him. A quick exchange in hushed tones followed. A trooper was called forward to hold their horses. They slid from their saddles and advanced to the crest. The sound of rifle fire was louder now, the crack of the artillery more immediate. They dropped, edged forward on their stomachs.

The village lay some four-hundred yards beyond, in the shallow valley formed by the ridge they observed from and by another ridge, lower, a half-mile to the north. A ragged group of stone buildings huddled around a stone bridge that crossed a stream which ran down the valley, west to east, from the higher ground to the left. The track

247

they had crossed earlier ran down from their right towards the village. A single structure, larger than the rest, dominated the hamlet, probably a mill because of its position below the bridge. The shattered minaret of a small mosque jutted up like a jagged stump. A cluster of hovels lay north of the stream and several were burning. Figures flitted from cover to cover there, advancing towards the village. They were drawing a hot response from the occupants of the houses and mill.

"Look there! There's the artillery!" Adnan said.

Dawlish had seen it already, an orange flash through the drifting whiteness obscuring the opposite ridge, and then another to its right, and then the dual reports and the crash of the shells falling in the village. A roof collapsed in a cloud of dust. A brief rush from the northerly huts was repulsed in a storm of rifle fire.

"There's more artillery over there!"

Dawlish saw the fiery tongues lash out from the higher ground that closed the valley to the west. He strained his eyes and through the swirling snow could just discern the outlines of two weapons, sited to fire directly down the valley. Their target was a farmhouse some three hundred yards upstream of the village. They too were hotly defended against the dispersed group of Russian skirmishers – forty, fifty men at least – who were advancing hesitantly towards them along each side of the brook.

"Those guns are well sited," Adnan's tone conveyed grudging respect. "Nobody can withdraw from the village without coming under their fire. And if the Russians take that farm they'll have the village anyway. They'll be able to blast it from both sides."

Dawlish focussed his glasses with numbed fingers. Despite the murk there was no mistaking the gunners as Russian. Ignoring the cold, some had flung off their greatcoats for greater mobility and their green tunics stood out against the white. Beyond them horses were tethered, not only the artillery horses but also those of the dismounted dragoons advancing on the farm.

"But who's in there?" Dawlish was bemused. "No artillery of their own, but plenty of small arms. A damned strange unit."

"Should we withdraw now to warn Nusret Pasha?" Adnan asked.

It was the logical suggestion. Dawlish was about to agree when suddenly the memory of the skulls he had so recently seen among the ashes returned to him. The troops trapped in that village – men who had sworn the same allegiance he had – were doomed to a similar fate unless help arrived. There could be only one source of help.

248

"No, Adnan Yüzbashi," he said, half amazed at his own words. "We're going to save those people."

29

Alper's group arrived, fetched by a mounted messenger. A quick consultation decided tactics. Carbine magazines were checked, revolver chambers spun, sabres loosened in scabbards. Gloves were removed despite the cold, hoods thrown back, fur-swathed heads nodding in acknowledgement of orders passed in an undertone. The horses stamped and munched the handfuls of oats given to pacify them. Then they moved off westwards, hidden by the crest, still two columns, parallel, forty yards apart. Unseen beyond the ridge the Russian four-pounders still cracked and the rifle-fire in the valley rippled and died and then rippled again. The snow came in flurries, reducing visibility to fifty yards or less, clearing briefly, then thickening again.

The ridgeline curved north as it reached the head of the valley. The ground was rolling here, and broken. A fold provided a last shelter from view of the crews of the two artillery pieces directly to the north. The scout had halted just below the skyline and Dawlish joined him. His watering eyes narrowed to slits as he peered through the swirling white. The guns were three hundred yards distant. They were twenty yards apart and sited to fire due east down towards the farmhouse, from which rifle-fire still sounded. Two limbers were positioned behind the guns and their tethered horses were just visible beyond. The further weapon had just leaped back after firing and its crew was manhandling it forward again. Figures scampered back from the muzzle of the nearer gun – loading complete – and an instant later it too hurled another shell towards the farm's defenders.

Dawlish ordered the advance. The intervening ground seemed firm and the snow-cover was lightest at the crest, with streaks of shrivelled grass showing through. Surprise would be total. He raised his hand but suddenly the scout's hiss of "Dikkat!" – Look out! – spun him back. Ahead and to the left two tall dark shapes were advancing towards them through the drifting white, heads and shoulders rising above the crest. Dawlish recognised them as Russian horsemen, snow-dusted and crouched across their plodding mounts, sent to patrol the guns' southern flank.

Recognition was mutual. One of the Russians shouted, dragged his horse's head over and kicked it into a canter, heading back for the guns.

249

His companion paused and then he too wrenched his beast away to gallop northwards. He drew a pistol as he rode and fired it twice in the air as an alarm as the whirling snow enveloped him.

Dawlish's shouted order to charge was lost in the drumming of hooves as Adnan and Alper urged the Circassian troopers forward. They poured over the lip of the sheltering fold and on to the ridge crest, sabres drawn, bunched at first, jostling knee-to-knee, then fanning out into a ragged line. Alper was leading to the right, his men drumming behind, blades extended, faces snow-whipped, eyes locked on the retreating backs of the fleeing Cossacks and on the guns beyond. Dawlish and Adnan led on the left, their troopers following.

Dawlish felt fear leave him and a feeling of invincibility, no less dangerous, flood into its place. He left his sabre sheathed, for he did not trust himself with it on horseback, but he had drawn his Tranter revolver. Ahead, at the guns, he saw confusion. The fleeing horsemen were reining in there, gesticulating, and dazed gunners were turning uncertainly to peer through the snow towards the cantering line of horsemen. To the left, from among the tethered horses, men were running forward. He heard the sharp report of a carbine, then another.

The range was narrowing and yet time seemed to stand still. He glanced down into the valley. The skirmishers moving along the river towards the farmhouse were like black ants against the white snow. Smoke hung in a fog around the buildings – the sudden pause in the artillery fire that had tormented them was giving the defenders new vigour. Far beyond, at the village, the battle was raging as fiercely as ever.

The guns were a hundred yards away now.

Kivilcim, catching the madness from the horses that pounded on his heels, had his head down and vapour jetting from his flared nostrils. The nearer gun was being slewed around to face the wall of horseflesh bearing down on it but the crew of the other had abandoned such hopes. They crouched behind their gun and limber, blazing back with sidearms or grasping rammers and handspikes for a desperate defence.

A horse cartwheeled to Dawlish's right, screaming and thrashing in an agony of flailing limbs. Its rider crashed down ahead of it, instantly lifeless. Something was sweeping out of the snow to the left. For an instant Dawlish was aware of the two mounted Cossack scouts, who had somehow arced around behind the guns after raising the alarm and who now made their own lonely counterattack, futile but heroic. Adnan's revolver blasted twice, lifting one from the saddle, and the second found himself sandwiched between two Circassian troopers, one hacking wildly while the other went beneath his guard and skewered him through the chest.

Scarcely twenty yards separated Alper's riders from the four-pounder when it vomited towards them. A horse and rider exploded in a spray of blood but the others plunged into the acrid smoke, riding down the gunners who now abandoned their weapon – too late – and fled. Blades chopped and thrust mercilessly. The few who tried to make a stand by the limber – an officer with a revolver and two gunners who beat about them desperately with a ramrod and even a bucket – were despatched in a brief, quarterless orgy of slaughter.

Dawlish rode straight for the second gun. Pistols and carbines spat from the group clustered there, but a half-dozen other horsemen flanked him. The sight must have been terrifying, for the Russians' shooting was high and wild. He willed himself to hold his fire until he was closer. Adnan was shooting to his left and four other riders were spurring around on the flank to curve in behind the limber, cutting off retreat.

Then, suddenly, Dawlish was at the cannon, drawing his mount to a slithering halt, sweeping his Tranter around, blasting at a capless, shaven-headed gunner who rose with a carbine in his hand. His horse plunged, terrified by the noise and smoke and others were whinnying and rearing as their riders chopped and prodded. Somebody was under Kivilcim's hooves – he looked down, saw a wildly slashing blade, a desperate attempt at hamstringing. He jerked the beast back and fired downwards. The green-tuniced figure convulsed, fell, and then Dawlish lunged forward again into the press. A gunner had brought a horseman down with a swing of his rammer but the staff's momentum exposed his neck and shoulder and another trooper hacked down, biting deep. Blood spurted bright and the Russian fell with a scream. Dawlish emptied his chambers into the confusion of bodies, dropped the pistol to swing on its lanyard and reached for his sabre.

As he drew it he realised it was unnecessary. Three survivors were breaking from the cover of the limber to dash for their tethered horses. They blundered into the troopers who had ridden to their rear and who waited for this moment to butcher them. There were screams, then two tumbled bodies. The third man sprinted through the snow with blood running between the fingers he held to his face, but was ridden down and cloven to the jaw.

251

Dawlish found himself shaking, his brief sense of invulnerability suddenly shattered by the brief silence, the bloodstained snow, the ghastly remains strewn beneath the limber. He sensed the exhaustion, the flagging spirits, of the trembling men and blown horses that crowded around him. The next minute would be critical. He stood in his stirrups, saw Adnan and called to him.

"Man the guns! And Alper – forward with the carbines!"

Adnan bellowed the orders. Riders slid from their saddles and three men, one still dazed by the blow he had received from the rammer, were detailed to lead the horses back to the other tethered beasts. A half-dozen stayed with Dawlish, who was already poring over a four-pounder, a light bronze muzzleloader. Adnan and Alper disposed the remaining men in a single line to either side of the weapon, four yards between them. There was no cover, and so they knelt, reaching into pouches to pull out reserve ammunition for their Winchesters.

The snow had lightened. Down in the valley small arms barked around the farmhouse but the attack there had faltered. The Russian skirmishers who had been pressing forward boldly minutes before now paused in any cover they could find and were looking back in confusion towards the ridge from which the now-silent four-pounders had supported them.

"Hold fire, Adnan Binbashi!" With a dozen repeater carbines in line a murderously heavy fire could be produced – but only as long as the ammunition lasted, though there was little enough of that, forty rounds per man. And the range, three, four-hundred yards, was excessive for the visibility conditions.

Years of shore-landing exercises with the miniature field guns so many Royal Navy ships carried – welcome diversions from the monotony of peacetime cruising – now paid off for Dawlish. There were fewer than a dozen shells and bagged charges in the open limber. He hoped the other contained at least as much. He thrust one into a trooper's hands, satisfied himself that it was fused and oversaw the loading. The men were clumsy but eager - he could trust them with the later rounds. Then, inwardly cursing his inability to communicate articulately, he supervised bearing of the weapon, tugging alternately on the spoked wheels, squinting along the barrel sights towards the centre of the stalled scattering of Russian attackers, nudging the trail over the final degrees with a handspike.

"They're retreating, Nicholas Kaptan!" Adnan yelled.

Defenders' rifles crashed from the farmstead, driving the attackers into the shelter of a dip by the stream. Dawlish had his glasses out and discerned that the greatcoated Russian cluster was facing him. Two figures stood out from the others, one scanning the ridge through field glasses, the other gesticulating, both clearly arguing. Far beyond them, at the village, a separate battle still raged, marked by rifle fire and the steady slap of the other four-pounders on the northern ridge and the sharp detonations of their shells.

"The range, Adnan Binbashi! What's the range?"

He estimated three-fifty but the information was meaningless – there was no way of correlating it with elevation. Dawlish could only screw to depress the barrel from the previous elevation that had carried the shells to the farmhouse. Two full turns – he would have to correct further according to the fall of shot.

One last sight along the barrel and then he stood clear and jerked the lanyard. The gun bounced back and the crew rushed to run it forward again. Through the clearing smoke Dawlish saw a flash and a spurting fountain of earth and stones rise up between the Russians and the farmhouse. The elevation was still too high, though the bearing was perfect. But there was bewilderment among the Russians and as he watched they surged from cover, away from the farm, back towards the ridge.

"Hold your fire, Adnan Binbashi!"

Down in the valley some cool head had realised that, caught between two fires, there was no option but to recapture the artillery. A rush might carry it and already the force - fifty men spreading into an open line that offered a poor target – was heading for the slope, ignoring the ragged fire from the farm in their rear. Dawlish smiled grimly. The Russians had mistaken the threat. The Winchester repeating carbines, not the four-pounders, were the greater menace.

The gun was charged, loaded and primed. Dawlish wielded the handspike to aim, depressed the barrel yet more, stood aside and then jerked the lanyard. A pillar of mud and snow rose above a flash just beyond the furthest Russians. It claimed no casualties but men stumbled in panic away from the explosion, realisation dawning that the next shell might drop among them but unaware that their uphill flight was taking them towards the unseen Winchesters.

Adnan came to his feet, sabre raised, pistol in his other hand, glancing alternately at the advancing Russians – now two hundred yards below – and towards Dawlish, seeking approval to open fire,

253

receiving only a negative shake of the head. The three troopers who had tethered the horses were hurrying back to join the line. The four-pounder was loaded again and run forward. Dawlish depressed the barrel lower still. The dismounted Russian dragoons toiling up the slope were making heavy going. Their long greatcoats trailed in the snow and many had blankets slung diagonally across their chests. Two in the lead were waving swords to urge the remainder onwards. Their backs were now exposed to the steady ripple of rifle fire from the farmhouse and, though the distance from it was lengthening, one man pitched down.

The four-pounder's next round injured nobody in the nearing skirmish line but it panicked several men into a shambling run. The nearest was still well over a hundred yards from Adnan's kneeling troopers. He turned again towards Dawlish, was again ordered to hold fire.

Adnan's voice was a steady murmur as he instructed his small command to choose and sight their targets. He strode back and forth along the line, calm and erect, his expression deliberately scornful of the nearing attackers, giving a word of encouragement to one, correcting another's aim, as coolly as if he were on a firing range.

The Russians were a hundred yards away, and cheering – the gasping defiance of desperate men who knew they must regain the crest, the guns and their mounts if they were to survive. The slope was steep and they slithered and stumbled on the snow, yet still they came on, bunching closer as they saw the line of kneeling troopers and the artillery piece.

They must be calculating the odds, Dawlish thought, for they could see now that they outnumbered the Turks before them by more than two to one. But they would not have bargained for the Winchesters...

It was time. Dawlish yelled "Atesh!"

Adnan's sabre flashed down as he repeated the command. A dozen repeater carbines blasted down the slope, scything down half as many Russians. Right hands flicked the ejection and loading loops behind the trigger guards, casting out the hot, spent cartridges, feeding the next rounds into the breeches. The second volley crashed out, more ragged now, each man firing at his own pace at his chosen target, lashing the faltering Russians. Several were themselves dropping low and firing back but others rushed forward, shooting as they came, then reversing their bayonetless carbines to use like clubs. Thick grey smoke swathed the Circassians as they fired, ejected, fired again with a terrible cadence. Dawlish and his crew abandoned the four-pounder and rushed forward with their own weapons to add to the carnage.

The Russians broke. An officer came close enough to attempt to wrench a carbine from Alper's hand and to die as it blasted in his face. Another twenty lay scattered, dead or wounded, behind him. But the remainder turned and ran diagonally down the slope, tripping, stumbling and sliding in the snow. A merciless fire followed them, hurling more down until Adnan's shouts ended the fusillade. The fugitives headed for the northern slope, from the far eastern end of which the two other four-pounders were maintaining uninterrupted shelling of the village. One Circassian wounded, not seriously, had been the price of the repulse.

"What sort of troops down there?" Dawlish asked. He was surveying the farm in the valley through his glasses. Men were emerging from it, some firing wildly in the direction of the fleeing Russians. The sound of cheering carried through the snow-laden air. They surged about without any apparent sense of purpose, twenty or thirty men, some shooting in the air. For all that most were swathed in grey and brown cloaks their clothing was anything but uniform – great baggy pantaloons, sudden flashes of colour, ragged green turbans.

"Irregulars," Adnan said. "That's why they had no artillery."

"They'll do more good reinforcing the troops in the village," Dawlish said. Another sharp report from the northern ridge made him look up. The Russian guns there were still supporting the relentless advance on the mill and bridge. He could discern Russians pressing ever closer, slowed but not deterred by the fire that galled them.

"Those guns – how far?"

Adnan narrowed his eyes and concentrated. "Eight hundred yards."

Well within the range of the two four-pounders now standing idle – but range enough also for receiving fire in return. Dawlish knew that he did not possess the gun-laying expertise necessary to inconvenience, much less silence, those guns before the Russians, more familiar with their weapons, would be dropping shells around him. Those guns could not be his objective. His mind raced over the alternatives, all desperate. But Fortune had rewarded boldness so far and he resolved to test that fickle goddess one more time.

"Get the gun-horses harnessed," he said. "Guns and limbers. You can do it?"

"Yes. And the other animals?"

"Leave them tethered for now."

He outlined his plan quickly. Adnan looked uncertain, but he was not the man to dispute orders and he relayed them immediately.

Alper Chavush seemed everywhere as guns were linked to limbers and horses selected, teamed and harnessed. They stamped and whinnied, unnerved by unfamiliarity with their new masters. All the time Dawlish fretted to be gone, fearful of the moment when the distant Russian gunners might turn their weapons here. Down at the farm the exulting mob showed no sign of moving to the relief of the village.

"If those irregulars move along the stream – across there, on the far bank – they could threaten the enemy in those huts." He passed Adnan the glasses and motioned to the scattering of hovels north of the village from which the Russians advanced in cautious bounds.

"They won't move." Adnan's frown told what he thought of irregulars. "They won't stand fire. Not out in the open."

"The guns are ready to move?" Dawlish glanced back. "Good then! Send Alper Chavush down to the farm. Let him have four men, no more, his own choice, men he can trust. He's to get those irregulars moving towards the village. And to make as much noise as they can, shoot wildly, cheer, whatever. They must appear more numerous than they are."

Alper acknowledged his orders with a simple "Evet! Kumandanim!" He pulled himself into the saddle – he had found himself a Cossack horse better fed and larger than his own – and called for the men who would accompany him. They spurred down the slope towards the farm.

Dawlish gave one last glance towards the Russian guns still firing methodically from the ridge beyond. A sprinkling of black dots scurrying from cover to cover confirmed that the Russian attackers had pressed close to the bridge. The Russian commander had ignored the reverse on his flank and was concentrating all he had on his main objective, the village itself.

The order to advance. The mounted troopers, now mainly on Russian beasts, led the column. The gun-teams lurched behind, urged by the troopers who now rode the lead horses. A single man sat on each gun, hastily instructed on how to operate the wheel brakes, the only protection against the whole mass crashing into the pulling team on downward slopes. They headed south, following the partly snow-obscured spoor they had made on the approach, leaving behind the bloodstained white and the slumped corpses and tethered horses that neighed forlornly.

The going was slow – towing guns was an art not quickly mastered. One jack-knifed against its limber on a shallow descent and five minutes were lost in disentangling it and in calming the horses. The snow eased, then died. They turned eastwards and found the track leading to the village. A slight rise to either side defined the track's boundaries and beneath the snow the ground was firm. They surmounted the ridge. The track curved diagonally down and across the slope ahead. It was a quarter-mile to the village and Adnan spurred forward to alert the defenders that help was at hand. The guns swayed and yawed behind the horses, the brakemen on their bucking platforms jerking on their levers as the weapons threatened to outrun the teams ahead. There was no slackening of the firing from the village before them.

There might yet be time to turn the tide of battle …

30

The headlong descent ended safely as the teams swept around the last curve in a spray of thrown snow. It was two hundred yards to the village, close enough for the acrid smell of the burning houses there to sear the nostrils and to see Adnan's waving arm beckoning them forward. Dawlish gave Kivilcim his head. He could see horses tethered in the lee of the houses ahead, terrified, plunging beasts, driven frantic by the close explosions. Several figures clustered around Adnan. A narrow street ran through the village, a bend in it masking the bridge that must lie ahead. The mill, the improvised fortress that still blocked the Russian advance, rose to the right above the other houses. The rattle of rifle-fire rose and fell in waves, each denoting some short rush, some small repulse, some gain of yards. A loud crack sounded from the ridge that rose like a white wall beyond the village, then another, its reverberation lost in the detonations of the shells falling among the houses. A dusty plume erupted as a roof caved in.

Dawlish halted where Adnan sheltered behind a wall. The men surrounding him were no soldiers, more like theatrical caricatures of brigands in black-pantaloons, untanned leather boots, red sashes, and furred jackets. All were swathed in blankets and remnants of greatcoats and were festooned with bandoliers and swords in curved scabbards.

All wore green turbans – the sacred colour. Dawlish recognised instant hatred on their tanned and moustachioed faces as they saw him. They knew him for what he was – Hiristiyan, Christian – and they loathed him already.

"The Russians have almost reached the bridge," Adnan said. "They hold several huts on the far side. They're reinforcing them, maybe for a rush."

Another salvo fell. Another rattle of small arms followed, then died.

"How many here?"

"They started with about eighty. Twenty more over at the farm. The Russians surprised them yesterday, twenty miles to the north, and drove them here. They were too exhausted to keep retreating – they had to make a stand. They're low on ammunition."

The guns were approaching. Still no sign of movement from the farm, though Alper had been there for twenty minutes. Action would have to be fast if it was to be decisive.

"Go to the mill, Adnan Binbashi. Warn their commander that I'll be advancing the guns to the bridge. We'll give them the covering fire but they're going to have to make a sally and take those huts across the river. It may just panic the Russians into retreating. They'll assume heavier reinforcements are coming once our artillery opens fire."

"It's a slim chance." Adnan slipped from his saddle, handed his reins to an irregular. He drew his revolver and shrugged. "But it's their only hope."

"Get back here when you have agreement," Dawlish said. He was damned if he was moving forward without assurance of support. For him and his men at least escape was still a possibility.

"Evet, Kumandanim." Then, guided by the irregulars, Adnan disappeared at a running crouch up the street and into a side alley. The flash of another shell against the upper floor of the mill confirmed the urgency of his errand.

The guns and limbers had halted to one side of the track, sheltered by the bulk of the houses. Dawlish's commands in scanty Turkish brought instant compliance. The horses were hastily unharnessed, the limbers thrown open and the guns loaded and rammed. Thirteen men – plus himself – between two weapons. Six per gun – enough to run the light carriages forward, slew them round, fire, then race them back to cover for reloading.

Long minutes passed before Adnan returned. The guns and limbers were manhandled up the street to a point just short of the bend at which they were still invisible to the Russians. Dawlish edged forward to glance around the corner. The low-humped bridge was some fifty yards ahead, several houses flanking the street leading to it tumbled and burning. He jerked back as a shell exploded against a wall and showered stone chips like shrapnel. He peered out again. The huts beyond the bridge reached within some twenty yards of it – insubstantial structures, tradesmen's stalls, stabling, mud rather than stone walled, several thatch-roofed. That the enemy could have established themselves there was solely due to the defenders' lack of artillery. Russians flitted there from hovel to hovel, inconvenienced but not deterred by the spasmodic fire from the mill.

Adnan was flushed when he came pounding back. "The commander – you can't believe who..." he gasped.

Dawlish cut him short. "He's agreed to attack?"

"Yes. When you open fire. He's down to fifty men effective. He'll do it though. But ..."

"No buts!" Dawlish snapped. He motioned to the second four-pounder. "That gun – that's yours."

Another salvo fell among the houses, not twenty yards distant. One Russian elevation adjustment up on the ridge and the next shells could be dropping here. It was safer to act than to stay put. Dawlish quickly outlined what he needed. It was simply said but would be murderously dangerous in execution.

The men crouched by the carriage trails, three to a side, their eyes locked on Dawlish. He waited for the next Russian salvo – an eternity passed before two explosions in quick succession marked the fall of the shells close ahead – and then he yelled the command.

They snatched up the trails and raced forward ten yards up the street towards the bend. Wheels skidded as they dragged the weapons around the curve and into sight of the Russians beyond the bridge for the first time. Men threw their weight back to kill the forward momentum and then grasped the wheel spokes and spun them in opposite directions, rotating the guns to point up the street. Dawlish and Adnan crouched behind their respective weapons, sighting along the barrels – range point-blank and elevation minimal.

A line between Dawlish's fore and back sights shaved along the downstream side of the bridge and directly to a thatched shed. He yelled to his crew to stand clear and jerked the lanyard. The gun

259

jumped back as the muzzle belched flame. Adnan's weapon barked an instant later. Dawlish was already calling for withdrawal. His crew heaved up the trail and sprinted rearwards for the cover of the street-bend. Through the thinning smoke he had a glimpse of a great rent torn in the side of the shed and of Adnan's target, a smaller hut to the right, partly collapsed.

He dashed after his crew – they were already sponging. Strain told on their faces, but relief also. They had survived the tactic once and could do it again. Another bagged-charge and another round were rammed down the muzzle. Across the street Adnan's crew was similarly busy.

"Well done!" Dawlish yelled across. "Now more of the same!"

A Russian shell, its trajectory fractionally higher than before crashed down somewhere behind and to the left. Another followed. It was time to rush forward once more.

Again they raced down the street with the guns, skidded at the bend, heaved on the spokes. Both weapons fired together, punching their projectiles though the flimsy walls of hovels beyond the stream to explode in brilliant flashes somewhere beyond. A crowd of irregulars suddenly erupted from an alleyway leading from the mill. Several among them were firing revolvers in the air and yelling wildly. Many brandished swords, others bayonet-tipped rifles, as they rushed for the bridge, undeterred by the crackle of gunfire that greeted them. They streamed across the bridge, some falling, but the mass rolled onwards undeterred.

"We can't risk more fire!" Dawlish gasped to Adnan. Gunfire rattled from beyond the bridge. Suddenly shots also sounded from over to the left. "Tell the men to fetch their carbines."

The Russian artillery had fallen silent, the futility of continued shelling obvious as the battle raged hand to hand. Dawlish launched his force down the street, exhausted, but scenting victory. They headed for the bridge, fifteen men, their repeater Winchesters giving them the power of a hundred. Firing raged now among the huts where the conflict eddied, blood-crazed irregulars flushing out the Russians who clung so tenaciously to the hovels they defended.

"Look there, Nicholas Kaptan!" Adnan shouted as they pounded across the bridge. Another force, twenty men or more, closely bunched, was jogging forward from the left, a hundred yards distant. Alper, that tough Circassian chavush, was urging the erstwhile defenders of the farm forward. The irregulars who followed him were firing wildly and one had unwound his turban and was waving it from his rifle like a green banner of Jihad.

There was no call for tactics other than to throw the full force at the few huts the Russians still held. The Winchesters poured one deadly volley after another and the screaming irregulars pushed forward to exploit the paths blasted for them. The Russians were retreating now, falling back with a discipline that drew Dawlish's admiration, dragging their wounded with them, knowing too well the mutilation that would befall any left behind. A series of individual struggles erupted, one handful confronting another, short vicious encounters that flared and waned and then repeated themselves only yards further on. Time had no meaning. Dawlish felt his carbine grow hot in his hands, knew that he and his men were somehow still gaining ground, was aware remotely that he had personally killed once, perhaps twice, and knew only that they must keep pressing forward.

Then suddenly the Russians were gone, the living at least, streaming in disarray across the open ground north of the huts. Adnan's force caught them on the flank, lashing them with rifle fire, charging forward to hack the fallen, driving the remnant up the slope towards the Russian artillery on the ridge. The guns there were shifting their aim and the first shell to drop among the newly conquered huts killed three irregulars in their moment of cheering triumph.

Dawlish and Adnan urged their own men back across the bridge – three were dead, two wounded, neither seriously. They were carried across in a retreating mob of howling fanatics who flourished bloodstained swords and waved unfurled turbans. They regained the shelter of the village and glanced back at the ridge. The surviving Russians were clustering around the guns up on the crest. If they had any sense they would hold their position – reinforcements could not be far behind.

"Send half-a-dozen men there," Dawlish said to Adnan. He pointed up westwards to the ridge where they had first stormed the guns. "Let them collect the horses, bring them here."

Two men were pressing through the throng that milled around, cheering and shooting wildly in the air. Adnan touched Dawlish's arm.

"Nicholas Kaptan," he said quietly. "I tried to tell you who it was."

Dawlish did not know him at first, but as he neared, hand outstretched, he recognised the frail and bearded figure, long, cadaverous and sallow, whom he had first met, and vanquished, in the *Mesrutiyet's* saloon at Trabzon.

"Haluk Pasha!" Dawlish breathed, his stomach sick, his head reeling.

The face of the figure that followed Haluk a pace behind was a mask of malevolence. His eyes were of flint, his skin of leather and the left side of his head was disfigured where his ear had been brutally shorn away. Selahattin's glance towards Dawlish told that he had not forgotten him, nor how to hate.

Haluk smiled as he took Dawlish's hand, drew him towards him and kissed him on both cheeks.

"Teshekkür ederim, Nicholas Kaptan," he said, "Thank you. Teshekkür ederim."

31

They left the village burning behind them. The inhabitants had long fled but whatever few possessions they had abandoned were looted by Selahattin's Bashi Bazooks. They took a savage delight in torching what they could not take and their horses were festooned with plunder.

The column wound out of the valley, Haluk in the van with Dawlish, protected by the remaining Circassians, the captured four-pounders following, then Selahattin's rabble, some leading two or even three plunder-laden horses. It was snowing softly again and dusk would soon fall. Dawlish knew that they would be lucky to reach Suakacağı before midnight but it was how the meeting between the half-brothers would pass off that troubled him most. He had sent a galloper ahead with the news that Haluk was with him. How Nusret would react was a mystery.

Haluk rode by Dawlish's side, silent, obviously evaluating his options. He was clearly intelligent enough to know that he had escaped Russian vengeance by the narrowest of margins and that though the atrocities his irregulars had committed might endear him to the medresses they would have guaranteed him no quarter if captured. With mobile Russian columns racing for Edirne, and Ottoman forces collapsing in the chaos he had done so much to engineer, retreat on Suakacağı was his only hope of survival, for all that it was held by the half-brother whose death he had plotted for months. He had been fulsomely thankful to Dawlish and amid many references to Allah had assured him that his rescue had cancelled the wrong done him at Trabzon. Dawlish showed no less outward magnanimity and offered the protection of his escort in terms that could not be argued. His main

262

intent was to separate Haluk from Selahattin and his crew, and to keep Alper and trusted Circassian troopers between his own back and that malignant brute. There had been no kiss of peace from him, only a scowl that promised undying enmity.

Dawlish reined in at the crest and looked back. Only smoke rolling from the burning village told there had been a battle. Bitterness welled in him, for he had never regretted an action more. He had risked his life, lost men who in the single day he had known them had rendered him unswerving loyalty, checked an enemy advance, however briefly – and all to rescue two men he loathed. But the real price might be paid by the women he had set out to save - by the woman whose image haunted and confused him – and on whom duty now demanded he turn his back.

Darkness fell. The going was slow, the tracks obliterated by snow, the moon obscured by clouds. They were back on the main track to Suakacaği now, the glow of miserable refugee encampments marking their path. The only sounds were of harnesses creaking and of snow crunching beneath ironshod hooves and wheels. They paused five minutes in each hour, wretched breaks that eased aching muscles only enough to make resumption an agony.

At one stop Haluk spoke briefly to Dawlish while Adnan translated.

"How much are you paid, Nicholas Efendi?" Haluk asked.

Dawlish told him. Ottoman service was earning him double his Royal Navy pay, and on that he could hardly survive in dignity without his private income.

"Then I can't buy you," Haluk said, "Not a man who is satisfied with so little."

But I'd have done what I've done in the last three months for even less, Dawlish realised, for despite all the danger and loss he would never want any other life than this, if only… if only he could be sure he could see Florence to safety. As I could have done today had I not ridden unwittingly to the rescue of this treacherous intriguer and, worse still, of the murderer and violator Selahattin. The thought was bitter.

Towards ten o'clock hoofbeats sounded in the darkness ahead. The rider who answered the scouts' challenge threw open his furred jacket to reveal a naval uniform. Even on this freezing night Jerzy Zyndram managed to look elegantly groomed. Dawlish went forward to greet him.

"Can it be true, Nicholas Kaptan?" Zyndram asked. "At first we thought your messenger was crazy! Nusret Pasha would trust nobody but myself to confirm it. Is Haluk with you?"

"In the flesh," Dawlish said, "though I imagine he'd be happier fifty miles to the west with Suleiman."

"Nusret wonders why you didn't abandon him."

"I would have, had I known. What does Nusret intend to do with him?"

Zyndram laughed. "Treat him like a long-lost brother of course! Overwhelm him with fraternal kindness and send him back to Istanbul under escort."

Send him back a failure, Dawlish thought, while Nusret falls back to defend the Lines of Büyük Tchemedji, and earns glory as the saviour of Istanbul. And buys time until Lord Beaconsfield sends a Royal Navy squadron and dares the Russians to back away.

"I have a personal message for Haluk," Zyndram said. "That he'll be treated well, that he'll be allowed ten of his Bashi Bazooks to guard him in addition to our Circassian friends!"

"And the rest?"

"Will be disarmed, stripped of their booty and put to labour on the earthworks. Not gently either. But Haluk doesn't need to know that yet."

"And Selahattin?"

"Will be part of Haluk's escort."

Dawlish could not suppress a groan.

"What about the English ladies?" Zyndram said.

"We never reached Ljubimec." Dawlish could not hide disappointment in his tone.

"There's still a chance. Tomorrow, if the snow holds off." But the Pole did not sound hopeful. He reached out, touched Dawlish's arm. "Nicholas Kaptan," he said. "I speak as a friend." He paused, obviously uncomfortable. "You must let nothing stop you. That lady... Miss Morton." He stopped again, looked away. "You deserve her, Nicholas Kaptan."

He had thought he had concealed it so well.

"And she deserves you, Nicholas Kaptan."

"That's enough!" Dawlish's voice almost broke.

But the Pole persisted. "Yesterday, somebody got through from Ljubimec and had news. The ladies are still at the caravanserai there

264

with sick and wounded and women with child. Anybody who can walk has gone already. The ladies won't desert the remainder."

Dawlish, sick with apprehension, nodded. He knew that Lady Agatha's myopia was more than physical. He could imagine her attempting to remonstrate, with guileless, self-deluding self-confidence, with Cossack marauders and demanding they respect her small haven of mercy. He could visualise all too well how her protest would be received. And then... his mind recoiled.

"Forgive my presumption, Nicholas Kaptan," Zyndram said, "but you'll need to bring carts tomorrow for the weak, if the ladies are ever to leave, and men to protect those carts, and to fight all the way back if necessary. Not just for the ladies, but for your happiness, Nicholas Kaptan. You must understand that every man here will be proud to go with you. Myself most of all. Not just as our captain but as our brother. It will be the *Mesrutiyet's* last victory."

Dawlish looked away, moved by such loyalty. "You've got a message for Haluk Pasha, Zyndram," he said, forcing formality into his tone. "You'd better give it to him."

Recognition and hatred flushed Haluk's face when Zyndram rode up to him and bowed deferentially before relaying his message. Then Haluk was all forgiveness, as he had been with Dawlish.

"I bear no ill will for what you did at Trabzon, Jerzy Efendi," he told Zyndram. "It was God's will that I should leave there. You were but an instrument to send me to my work here." The news that he would be parted from his irregulars obviously stung. "God is merciful. I'm thankful that Selahattin will remain with me," he said. "He's a pious man, who does God's work."

The jaded column reached Suakacaği after midnight. Bülent's marines guarded the bridge and the carriage-mounted Nordenveldt had been sited to sweep the approach to it. Abdurrahman, the gunner who had acquitted himself so well on the railway attack, stood behind it. The double ranks of marines that blocked the bridge opened as the head of the column approached. Dawlish, Haluk and Adnan rode forward over the snow-covered planking, Bülent snapping into a parade-ground salute as they passed. Zyndram nudged his mount to one side, wheeled, halted beside the marines. The Circassians and the four-pounders followed Dawlish.

Haluk was almost on the opposite bank when the wheels of the second four-pounder crunched past the marines and it was only then that the full nature of his status dawned on him. A cry of command

265

caused him to look back. At a sign from Zyndram, Bülent Chavush was ordering his marines to level their carbines at Selahattin and the head of the ragged column of Bashi Bazooks. Simultaneously the Polish officer's cutlass flashed from its scabbard and pointed meaningfully towards the Nordenveldt.

Selahattin reined in, swearing. Only then did he recognise Zyndram as the man who had ground the plank against his neck in Giresun, Dawlish's accomplice in his mutilation. Screaming with rage, he reached for the revolver stuffed in his sash. Then he froze, a warning cry from Bülent alerting him, almost too late, to the Winchester aimed for his chest.

Zyndram's orders were unambiguous – none of the irregulars were to cross the river before morning. They could bivouac on this side as best they could. The grim ranks of marines, the Nordenveldt aimed into the surging, indignant knot of horsemen and the undisguised contempt of disciplined regulars for the riotous mob before them left no room for argument. Selahattin screamed abuse, reared his horse, spat and shook his fist, but his pistol stayed undrawn and in the end he had no option but to lead his followers back into the darkness to wait out the night.

Dawlish sensed Haluk stiffen with anger as he looked back and understood what had happened. Yet somehow he maintained his dignity, ignored the incident and walked his horse onwards. *Mesrutiyet* crewmen lined the street leading to Dawlish's quarters. Trussed in army greatcoats, Haluk did not recognise them for what they were, but they raised their rifles in salute as he passed.

Flaring torches illuminated the space before the merchant's house. The bulk of the Naval Brigade was drawn up there in a hollow square. Nusret Pasha waited at the doorway. His face glistened with fever but he was in full uniform and, despite the cold, his fur-trimmed cloak was thrown open to reveal the jewelled order sparkling on his breast. Dawlish and Haluk rode forward together to the foot of the steps before the house.

An eternity passed as the two half-brothers contemplated one another, neither showing a flicker of emotion, neither speaking. Then Nusret turned slightly, caught Dawlish's eye, and with an almost imperceptible tilt of the head told him to retreat. Dawlish edged his mount back a dozen steps. His right hand moved slowly to his holster flap, eased it open and grasped the butt. Eight hours' proximity to the man who had almost brought about Nusret's death, much less his own,

266

on the street and in the workshop at Sinope, had not lessened his distrust.

Haluk was the first to move, slipping stiffly from his saddle. As he did Nusret descended the steps and walked towards him. A momentary hesitation, then both men embraced, kissing each other on the cheeks. Dawlish was close enough to discern the cold anger in Nusret's eyes but Haluk's he could not see. The two men disappeared into the house together and the door closed behind them.

Dawlish turned away. He was tired, very tired, and for what remained of the night he must seek a bed in Zyndram's quarters. His own had been allocated to Haluk. Sleep beckoned. In the morning he must be on the road to Ljubimec again before the snow grew heavier still.

Before the Russians got there.

*

But there could be no departure for Ljubimec the next morning before Haluk was sent on his way to Istanbul. The two half-brothers slept late. The guard commander told Dawlish that they had remained two hours closeted together before retiring and had demolished a bottle and a half of brandy between them – Haluk's religious scruples did not apparently extend to alcohol, in private at least. Dawlish fretted at the delay, haunted by images of Cossacks storming into Ljubimec.

The rescue column was standing ready. "I need as many light carts as you can muster," Dawlish had told Zyndram in a businesslike tone, resolved that there should be no further reference to Florence. "Load all the food and blankets we can spare into them."

Zyndram had nodded, half-smiling and well pleased.

"I want Bülent Chavush and a dozen of his best men – include Sedat and Yashar too – to ride in them," Dawlish had continued. They had withstood Russian lances with him once before and he knew he could rely on them again. The retreat from Ljubimec would be slow, and the marines would have to march back on foot, but they would be invaluable.

"I'll be glad to come," Zyndram had said.

Dawlish had shaken his head. "You'll command here. I need a soldier with me so I'll take Adnan Binbashi." He could see that the Pole was disappointed. "The Russians will be here soon so you'll prepare the bridge for demolition. You'll need artillery charges on the

267

supporting piles. Adnan will leave instructions." He hoped he would not be on the wrong side of the river when the time came for detonation.

Adnan and the Circassian troopers, yesterday's survivors, were ready. So were the marines. Departure should not be delayed much longer. The sky westwards was snow-laden, promising another fall. Only Nusret's approval was now needed and for that they had to wait.

In windless but bitter cold Dawlish made a quick inspection of the defences, satisfied himself that Selahattin's rag-tag mob were still encamped a half-mile beyond the bridge on the far side and saw a thin ribbon of refugees permitted to cross. Among them was the group he had given food the previous morning. The little girl who had so moved him was no longer among them. There would be a scanty meal for them at the feeding centre he had organised on arrival here.

"What they're fleeing must be bad if they endure this," Zyndram said. "Most of them are too weak to reach the Büyük Tchemedji Lines, much less Istanbul."

Dawlish was summoned just after ten. Nusret and Haluk, bleary-eyed, sat by the remains of a breakfast that seemed to have consisted of brandy and cigarettes. There was no obvious air of hostility between them. Dawlish had the distinct impression of deals having been done, accommodations reached, perhaps even an empire divided.

"The Circassians are ready, Nicholas Kaptan?" Nusret asked. "The half-squadron I requested?"

"Waiting outside the town." To leave Haluk his dignity it had been directed that he would be escorted from Nusret's quarters by his own men.

"Then send a messenger for the Bashi Bazooks." Nusret spoke to Haluk, who scribbled on a paper and thrust it towards Dawlish. Nusret said "My brother wants Selahattin and a few others he names – but not more than ten in total."

An orderly was despatched. Nusret invited Dawlish to sit with him and Haluk. He listened to details of yesterday's action, translating as necessary when Haluk interjected compliments as to Dawlish's behaviour. But it was obvious that the matter did not interest Nusret greatly, though he welcomed Dawlish's presence. His business with his brother, whatever it had involved, was concluded, and now he wished him gone. There were long silences.

The messenger returned at last. Selahattin and his irregulars were now outside. Haluk rose and reached for Dawlish's hand. He sounded sincere as he drew Dawlish to him and kissed him.

"He thanks you again for saving his life," Nusret said. "He says that though you are an infidel he prays that you will see the true path in time."

Haluk moved before them to the door.

"I need your approval again to try to get to Ljubimec, Nusret Pasha," Dawlish grabbed his opportunity. "We never reached it yesterday. The ladies there…"

Nusret nodded approval, cutting him short. His mind seemed on his half-brother. "We talked of our boyhood also, Nicholas Kaptan." He sounded sad, regretful. "Of the days when we lived with our mothers in the seraglio, before we were circumcised. We didn't always hate each other. We were sometimes happy there."

Orderlies draped cloaks about the half-brothers' shoulders. Dawlish followed them out into the pale sunshine and paused at the top of the steps.

Zyndram had organised a marine guard, a dozen men, in the small square outside and it stood facing the house. He drew them into a salute as the princes appeared. Just beyond the lowest step a Circassian held Haluk's horse. The small escort of Bashi Bazooks stood to the left, muffled and exotic, all mounted. Selahattin had ridden closer and he had placed his mount just beyond Haluk's. On the edges of the square a scattering of onlookers had gathered, mostly refugees.

It was a tableau that Dawlish would never forget: the horsemen, the marines; a black-clad woman, hungry and wan, forgetting her misery for an instant to point out the wonder of two princes to a companion. The snow trodden and discoloured, breath drifting in the chill like steam, a horse stamping impatiently, a dirty child, barefoot, timidly looking up to a rider, begging with outstretched hand and scuttling from the swipe of his whip. The last farewell of the brothers. And then Haluk moving towards his waiting mount.

Selahattin nudged his horse closer and spoke to Haluk's Circassian groom. The man passed the reins to him so that both horses stood flank to flank, then bent, caught the stirrup and held it ready for Haluk's foot.

Haluk greeted Selahattin. The Kurd inclined his head, his thin lips drawing back in a smile. The reins were in his left hand – and his right was moving into his sash.

269

Dawlish saw, and understood, too late.

Haluk's left foot was in the stirrup, his left hand grasped the saddle and he heaved himself upwards. His face came level with Selahattin's as he rose.

Selahattin whipped his revolver free, jammed it into Haluk's torso and fired. Blood erupted from his back, a ghastly, spouting crater, scarlet against the dark blue of his tunic. He twisted as he toppled, his face contorted in surprise and betrayal and agony, and Selahattin fired again, hurling him down on top of the groom beneath. Then his revolver swept up, his arm straight, one eye closed as he squinted down the barrel and calmly drew back the hammer with his thumb. His target was Nusret, frozen in horror at the head of the steps.

The troop of Bashi Bazooks was exploding into action, casting aside cloaks, sweeping out the carbines they had concealed, blasting towards the stupefied marines who were too slowly reacting. The groom who struggled from beneath Haluk's lacerated trunk took a round full in the face and three or four of the marines were down already, hit before they could lower their weapons from the salute.

The black void that was the open muzzle of Selahattin's pistol filled Dawlish's vision. He tore his eyes from it, threw himself at Nusret, intent on pushing him down, knowing as he did that he was already too late.

Selahattin fired. Blood fountained from Nusret's right side, just above the hip. He spun as he fell, even as Dawlish carried him down. He screamed and Dawlish was aware that his own hands were already drenched with blood. There was a wound, a terrible one, in Nusret's back, where the round had exited to the left of the spine. Dawlish knew immediately that he could not live.

The square was a pandemonium of wheeling, stamping, rearing horses, of barking carbines, of shrieking women and scurrying children, of marines dying in shock where they stood, of their surviving fellows struggling to retaliate. Haluk's terrified horse pounded its master's lifeless body beneath its hooves and Selahattin fought to control his own mount. His revolver was raised again, sweeping to find its aim on Dawlish, who struggled to lay down the moaning Nusret as gently as he could. Selahattin fired, his round screaming close enough for Dawlish to feel its passage. Then he had to drag his horse's head around for he had sensed Zyndram rushing towards him, cutlass outstretched to gouge upwards. He fired towards the Pole but the beast beneath him was panicking and the shot flew wild.

270

With a final howl of anger, Selahattin wheeled his mount and spurred after his men, who were now clattering from the square and towards the bridge. One of them had been brought down by a marine who has survived the sudden hurricane of gunfire. Led by Zyndram the marines rushed after the disappearing riders. A rattle of shooting from riverwards told of them blasting their way past the confused opposition they encountered.

Nusret's eyes bulged in agony. His fists clenched and his breath was a succession of tormented gasps. Dawlish tried to settle him more comfortably, as if repose might give some ease. Nusret's back arched. He convulsed and the pain drew another terrible moan from him. There seemed to be more blood on the steps and Dawlish was aware of others crowding around.

"Kasim Efendi is coming." Adnan was by his side but his tone indicated little hope that the *Mesrutiyet's* surgeon could achieve anything.

Nusret was trying to speak. Dawlish found it hard to meet his eyes, afraid what the doomed man might find in his own. He lowered his ear toward him.

"Haluk... Haluk... is he dead?" Nusret's voice was a croak.

Dawlish looked down the steps. The bloody heap of rags trodden into the snow there bore no resemblance to the thin and sallow figure he had once vanquished, once saved. He caught Adnan's gaze as he looked away. Adnan shook his head slowly.

"He's dead, Nusret Pasha," Dawlish said. "Selahattin murdered him." He saw tears well in Nusret's eyes and was not sure they were due to pain alone. He looked away, cradled him gently to him, found himself praying to the God whose existence he so often doubted to let this wretched man's agony end as soon as possible.

The surgeon forced opium between Nusret's teeth. His body slackened after a while, and his features relaxed a little. But he screamed again, long and terribly, when they lifted him on to a blanket and moved him into the house and on to a couch. There was nothing to be done but administer more opium.

Zyndram rushed in, flushed with anger.

"They got away." His voice was close to breaking. "Across the bridge. They shot their way through, over to the far side, away down the track. The remainder were waiting there on each side of the road. They let Selahattin and his rabble through, then brought down a dozen of the Circassians who followed." Then Zyndram started to weep.

271

"Let them go," Dawlish said. In the wider chaos now descending there was no time for vengeance. He realised bitterly that he should have killed Selahattin, not just shamed him, that night in Giresun.

Nusret called for Dawlish. His breathing was quieter now but there was something terrible about its new calm. All the clichés about ebbing tides so often used to describe this moment seemed true. Dawlish kneeled to hear him. His voice was lower than a whisper and full of infinite regret. At first Dawlish could not comprehend and he sensed the dying man's frustration as he repeated each syllable with dreadful effort. But when he did understand the words, enlightenment was instant.

"Abdul-Hamid," Nusret croaked.

"Abdul-Hamid?"

"Not Haluk... Abdul-Hamid."

Nusret was trying to nod, but no further assurance was needed. That single name explained all. For both of the Sultan's half-brothers had been a threat to him, each with his own appeal to a major faction within the empire. Abdul-Hamid had assigned assassins to each of them. Nusret had survived his in Trabzon and Sinope. Haluk's had been by his side as he had rampaged around Bulgaria, and he had trusted unto death the killer who waited for the ideal moment to strike. It had not come, not until today, when two birds had fallen to his single stone.

"Lost, Nicholas, lost... the Constitution... reform... the empire..."

Each word an agony, of soul as much as of effort, a man crying out in despair because he was dying a failure. Nusret knew now that the future lay with that shabby recluse in the Yildiz Palace, no longer pathetic, who had plotted so coldly and so patiently and so well while his two half-brothers had careered about the empire, each pursuing his own futile vision of reform or reaction. Neither Nusret's network of telegraphs and constitutionalists and modernisers nor Haluk's of softas and medresses and fanatics had saved them from the cunning of the spider in the Yildiz. Both networks had most likely been penetrated long since and turned against them.

"Do you need anything, Nusret?" The question was futile but Dawlish hoped desperately to divert him from his sorrow. He was weeping himself.

"I'm thirsty, Nicholas."

They were the last words he spoke. Cradling him in his arms, Dawlish helped him sip some water, then felt another spasm shoot

272

through him as he laid him back. Nusret's eyes glazed slowly and his breathing weakened. Five minutes later it stopped.

And the Ottoman Empire entered a new dark age.

32

Dawlish's column crossed the bridge over the Tunca and moved westwards in early afternoon. Fresh snow had fallen, and more was threatening. Though the breeze was weak it cut keenly and promised greater misery when it would rise higher.

On the previous day Dawlish had set out in expectation of a fast return journey across largely deserted and uncontested countryside. Today he knew that Russian forces had once already penetrated almost this far and would inevitably do so again in growing numbers. Now he had taken more Circassian cavalry – fifty, with Alper Chavush and his men as the core – and Bülent's dozen Winchester-armed marines rode behind in five light carts. Yet even with this force he knew that his chances against any significant Cossack force would be negligible. The weather was worse than before and the only consolation was that it inconvenienced the enemy as much as his own men.

The enemy – the term's meaning had expanded to include Selahattin's Bashi Bazooks. They were out there ahead somewhere, looping west and south in all probability towards Edirne as their first step towards Istanbul, where Abdul-Hamid's protection and reward awaited them.

Selahattin! The man's existence was a bitter standing reproof to Dawlish, the suffering he spread everywhere a consequence of Dawlish's own insufficient retribution on the night of the riot in Giresun. The gloom that had descended on the Suakacaği garrison as the news of the double-assassination spread lay heavy on the plodding column. Dawlish fought it himself and tried to forget the scene as Nusret and Haluk had been consigned to hastily dug graves. Muslim custom had demanded they be buried within the day but little over an hour had passed between their last farewells at the merchant's house and the more final farewells in the village graveyard. As Hiristiyan, Feringji and yabanci – Christian, Frank and foreigner – Dawlish had stood with Zyndram just outside the porch of the small mosque as the prayers were called, barred from closer participation by a thousand years of distrust and hatred. At the graveside it had been easier and he had cast his own pebble on the mound that rose all too quickly to cover the cloak-swaddled bodies beneath. Only then did he realise just how much he had come to love Nusret, how much he had committed himself to Nusret's vision of a reformed, modern, liberalised Ottoman Empire. And now his officer's commission pledged his loyalty, however unwillingly, to the man who had ordered Nusret's death.

The cold was rendered worse by the knowledge that they could never reach Ljubimec in daylight. The march would continue as long as possible after darkness fell but a night in the open was unavoidable. They could only endure, shield faces against the knifing wind, beat away the snow that random flurries caked them with, hope that a horse would not go lame, long for the never-satisfactory respite of the next five-minute break. They passed the ruined village with the shattered church where the sight of skulls had disturbed Dawlish a day since, past the point where they had branched north yesterday to investigate the Russian threat. There was no sign of enemy movement and they continued westwards.

There was no sunset, just a fast waning from snow-blurred twilight into total darkness. They pushed forward another half-hour, picking their way carefully but blundering repeatedly off the track, endangering men and horses and carts alike. Alper nominated the spot for the bivouac – Dawlish noted with admiration that encampment in the open was accepted as an inevitable necessity with which these cavalrymen were well familiar. The carts were drawn into a defensive circle, scouts and sentries posted, horses tethered, food hastily consumed, weary bodies swathed in blankets and hooded heads laid on saddles. Dawlish insisted on the first turn of duty, leaving Adnan to sleep, and concentrated on keeping himself warm by movement.

The horses turned their tails to the drifting snow, dropped their heads and endured. White hummocks grew smoothly over the sleeping men. Sentries paced and stamped. Dawlish ensured that Kivilcim was adequately covered and wished he had oats left for him. The animal had proved a marvel of strength and endurance and he tried to forget to whom he owed the gift. He plodded about the perimeter, his mind oppressed with futility and loss. He was no stranger to death but Nusret's end troubled him in the same way as had that of his own elder brother, dead for years, yet still a presence. Like James, Nusret had courage and generosity of spirit that disarmed all unease at his weaknesses. But more, Nusret had had a vision that was greater than he might ever have been able to realise and which was, for all its ill-definition, noble and potentially epoch-changing. All was gone now,

274

tumbled into a pauper's grave, and Dawlish's loyalty was sworn to the malignant tyrant who destroyed him. Not for long, he promised himself – only until he could rescue Florence and Lady Agatha and their charges, and disencumber himself of his temporary allegiance as quickly as possible thereafter. He longed now for when he might tear up the letter of resignation that still nestled close to him and don the Queen-Empress's uniform again.

But then the sight of a man stirring uncomfortably beneath his blanket of snow moved him. It might have been Bülent, or Alper, or Adnan, men whom he had never seen until recently and who shared little with him in belief or culture, but whose fidelity was unquestioning, whose endurance was uncomplaining. It was to them he now owed allegiance and he knew that he could not bear to cast it aside until this war had ended – one way or the other. Until then, he was a Turk.

The night passed. Dawlish slept in his turn, slumber dulling him to the gnawing cold and chewing lice and the worries that tormented him about the women at Ljubimec. He was woken by Sedat, the marine marksman. He had somehow found enough twigs beneath the snow to start a small fire. He had brewed lukewarm chai and he offered it shyly to Dawlish. He sipped it, stiff, cold and hungry, his first thoughts of Florence. It cheered him that he would see her today, saddened him that he must resist the familiarity that rescue must bring. He would bring her life, even if he could not offer her love. Yet even that thought was painful, for that future life of hers might mean eventual marriage to some other, children with him perhaps, long years in which she might forget that morning off Troy and that one glorious evening in the *Mesrutiyet's* saloon, might even forget the man who now was coming to save her.

The column lurched onwards. The snow had ceased and the visibility had improved. Rolling countryside extended on either side with no sign of life. At Levka, a village deserted but for a few refugees, they crossed an ice-fringed stream by a humped bridge. Ten miles remained, initially across rising ground. The going was difficult, even for the riders, much less for the marines who had to get out of their carts to lighten them and to trudge forward on foot. By noon they had topped the low hills. The wind from the west cut crueller than ever, even though the snow was now little more than a dusting, but the frozen ground allowed faster movement.

275

The track forked. They took the leftward, south-westwards. There, in the distance, a long streak lay brown against the white. Dawlish scanned it though his glasses – trees along a river line, the Maritza, flowing roughly eastwards towards Edirne. Nestling on its banks, he could just discern Ljubimec, a cluster of buildings marked by a single minaret.

"Look, Nicholas Kaptan." Adnan pointed northwards. There, fifteen, twenty miles distant, smoke was smudging the horizon, rising from five different locations.

The Russian juggernaut was rolling forward, unchecked and unstoppable. Edirne was its immediate goal – and Ljubimec was directly in its path.

*

The scene at the bridge over the broad Martiza filled Dawlish with dread.

He had come cantering ahead of the column these last five miles, hooves drumming on frozen earth clear of snow, accompanied only by Adnan, Alper and a dozen troopers. His concern for Florence was unbearable now that he was so close. As they neared the river crossing – the town lay on the far bank, the southern – they encountered small groups of terrified fugitives, mostly townspeople. They had no idea where they were going, where they could find shelter. They only knew that the Russians would be here tomorrow, maybe even tonight. The rumble of artillery from the north confirmed their fears. None doubted the vengeance that would fall when the Russians arrived.

The river was high, eddying and sucking between the bridge's stone piers. Dawlish, expecting to be challenged, slowed to a walk as he approached and a trooper rode ahead to identify them to the sentries. There were none. The door of the stone guardhouse swung open, smoke still drifted from a stove within and a few papers littered the floor around an upset table. It had been deserted in a hurry. If such a significant strategic asset was devoid of protection, and not destroyed, then the situation must be desperate, the Ottoman collapse total.

They cantered across the bridge towards Ljubimec's first houses and found themselves in a broad street. The few people visible disappeared on being sighted. The houses were shuttered, shops boarded up and there was a sensation of being watched from within. An Orthodox church was untouched, but heavily barricaded and with sounds of movement inside. Beyond it a single house was gutted and still smouldering. Close by it others had crosses chalked on the doors. There must be Christians inside, hoping for deliverance, yet fearing indiscriminate rapine regardless of creed. A man darted furtively from an alley, a small box, looted perhaps, clutched in his arms. He almost blundered into Alper's horse and was too late to retreat. The chavush grabbed him and shouted questions. Frightened, the man's answers came in a flood. He gesticulated towards the next turn on the right. The caravanserai was that way.

A single shot rang out as they entered the next street, high, a warning from a single line of dismounted Ottoman troopers blocking passage. Shouted identifications allowed them to advance to a small square where a mixed force of artillery and Macedonian cavalry was preparing for departure. Both men and horses looked near collapse, hungry, cold and exhausted. A dozen carts were laden with wounded. Passing close Dawlish recognised the smell of gangrene. Adnan questioned a red-eyed binbashi who might not have slept for a week.

"They're the last unit here," he translated. "They're getting out now. He thinks there isn't another Ottoman unit between here and the Russians."

The binbashi was nodding glumly, adding details as Adnan spoke. Dawlish heard the words "chok, chok – many, many" and guessed what they must refer to.

"They've been retreating for ten days, in action all the time. Yesterday the Russians hit them badly. Only their guns saved them." He gestured towards the Krupp field guns, steel six-pounders, that teams of scrawny horses were being flogged into getting moving. The Ottoman weapons, Dawlish thought bitterly, were the best money squeezed from an oppressed populace could buy and the men might well be the toughest soldiers on earth. Only senior leadership was missing. And for lack of it, this misery, this chaos.

"Where are they headed?"

"Edirne. Most of the forces in this sector are there by now – but he doesn't think it will be defended."

It won't be, Dawlish thought, Nusret never got there to stiffen the defence, never will now. Which meant that the crossing Zyndram and the *Mesrutiyet's* brigade still held at Suakacaği would remain the single reliable route eastwards.

Dawlish turned to Adnan. "Send a trooper back to Suakacaği. Zyndram needs to know the situation, to be prepared."

277

"Evet, Kumandanim."

• They left the town, heading northwest, towards the nearing Russian threat. The road was strewn with the detritus left by the hobbling, trudging, limping remnants of an army in retreat. Discarded equipment, dead animals and broken-down vehicles littered the roadside. There were slumped bodies also, some lifeless, others simply incapable of further effort and waiting listlessly for death.

A mile further on Dawlish saw the caravanserai, a little off the road, a low, walled compound like a fort. It had a tower at each corner and a massive gatehouse, with a squat building set into the walls to its left. The gates were open and there was movement at the entrance. His heart leapt. He pressed Kivilcim's flanks and gave him his head. He slewed to a halt in the courtyard.

He knew it was Florence even though her back was turned and her figure enveloped in a hooded army greatcoat. Her language alone identified her, for she was forcing a large, protesting mule back between the shafts of a cart with oaths that could only have been learned in an English coach-house. The animal snapped with bared teeth but she ducked, surprised it with a punch of her fist and then forced it back the final steps. Under her instructions, in a fluent stream of Turkish, two black-swathed women lifted the shafts and began to harness the beast.

"Well done, Miss Morton." Dawlish found himself laughing.

She turned – she had not noticed his arrival. Beneath her open greatcoat she wore a soldier's tunic over her dark serge dress. She had pinned up her skirts to mid-calf, but they were still mud-spattered, and two enormous cavalry boots, several sizes too large, were visible below them. Grimy fingers protruded from her mittens, her face was dirt-streaked and her hair was matted. He guessed she was as lousy as he was himself. And she looked even more beautiful than he had remembered.

"I knew you'd come," she said, and there were suddenly tears in her great brown eyes. "Agatha knew it too. We both knew you'd come."

"I didn't promise," Dawlish said.

"I knew you'd come," she repeated, "no matter what."

Dawlish slipped from the saddle. He wanted to draw her to him, yet forced himself not to. He sensed a similar uncertainty in her. She brushed a tear away, embarrassed, smearing her face.

278

"More help is on the way, Miss Morton," he said. His heart was singing. She would live. Adnan and the others were reining in, dismounting, leading their horses to drink in the ice-scummed trough in the courtyard. "Not just these men," he told her. "More are coming, and carts for your sick."

"We need them badly, Commander." She gestured to the mule cart. "This is all we've got – and it took an hour's bargaining and the last of Agatha's money." Her voice was trembling with relief. Dawlish realised that she must have been living in terror.

"Lady Agatha, she's safe?"

She gestured towards the low building, the communal kitchen of the caravanserai, and led him to it though the yard. He had longed for this meeting and now he did not know what to say to her. Ragged children pointed at him and called their mothers from the small sheds nestling against the walls to come look at him. There seemed to be mainly women and children. He could sense their fear, their hunger, their cold.

They entered a large stone chamber, its walls lined with improvised beds, all occupied, a few by badly wounded men. There was a smell of sickness and human waste, overlaid with smoke and cooking. A boy had run ahead to alert Lady Agatha. Surrounded by several helpers, she stood by a steaming cauldron of watery soup, frantically wiping her misted spectacles on a filthy apron. Her garb was as bizarre as Florence's. She pushed the glasses back on her nose and her heavy sheep's face broke into a smile.

"I trust I find you well, Lady Agatha." Dawlish bowed.

"You must forgive my appearance, Commander," she said. "Had we known when you were coming we would have..." Her voice trailed off and he sensed that she was ashamed of her squalor. Her father owned a Piccadilly mansion where the Prime Minister and the Prince of Wales were frequent guests, but she looked like the landlady of a slum lodging-house.

"I never saw a peer's daughter better employed, Ma'am." Touched by her pride and courage, he meant it. "Nor any other lady either," he added, turning to Florence.

"I told Commander Dawlish we both knew he'd come" she said.

Lady Agatha was weeping, the unspoken fears of days past suddenly released. "I don't know what we'd have done if you hadn't," she said, "I really don't."

279

"What about the Redif?" he asked. "I understood you were to have a platoon to guard you."

"They cleared out three days ago," Florence said. "Not that it made any difference. They never did anything but eat and sleep and they'd have bothered the women too if I hadn't laid the law down early on."

"Miss Morton laid down more than the law." Lady Agatha said, brightening. "She laid down Mustafa Onbashi of the Redif as well!"

"With a broom handle!" Florence's eyes sparkled with triumph.

"You should have seen his black eye, Commander!" Lady Agatha dissolved into a fit of laughter, her large bosom heaving, and Florence joined her. The two women clutched each other, laughing helplessly, pausing to wipe their eyes and then starting again when Dawlish asked with mock gravity: "Was it the right or the left eye, Ladies?"

He suddenly felt unburdened, even boyish. He knew it was unjustified, with his only safe haven two days' march away, an unknown number of helpless fugitives to burden him and a merciless enemy only miles distant. Yet the laughter inspired him, despite its hint of hysterical relief.

The crash of gunfire echoed from the courtyard. Laughter froze on the women's faces, turned to instant fear. Dawlish pushed past them. "Close the doors, barricade them!" he shouted, dragging his revolver free.

He reached the door and one glance told him that the worst had happened.

33

Dawlish saw riders swirling around the horses tethered at the trough in the centre of the caravanserai courtyard, shooting from the saddle. Hell had arrived.

Adnan and the Circassian cavalrymen crouched behind the stamping hooves of their terrified beasts and fired back at their attackers. A shaggy horse tumbled, blood erupting from its head, catapulting its rider over its neck. He lurched to his feet before a bullet tore him down but as he flung his arms out in final surprise his furred jacket and baggy pantaloons and red sash revealed him for what he was – a Kurdish Bashi Bazook. The rider who followed jerked his mount's head around, but too late, and suddenly he too was piling over the stricken animal and going down amid flailing legs and frantic

280

whinnying. Adnan darted from the press by the trough and pushed his muzzle against the dazed horseman's skull before exploding it in a scarlet mist.

One of the Circassians was down, lifeless, and a second was slumped against the trough, his hands plucking weakly at his blood-soaked tunic. Another had climbed on the stone lip – Alper Chavush. Balancing precariously, somehow untouched by the bullets screaming around him, he held his Winchester to his shoulder and rotated his torso slightly as he followed a careering rider, leaning slightly forward into the recoil as he squeezed his trigger. Hurled from the saddle, one foot caught in the stirrup, his victim bounced across the cobbles as the horse hurtled onwards. Already Alper was swinging back to take aim on the next horseman.

Dawlish paused in the doorway. He sensed hesitation behind him. "Bar the door!" he yelled, glancing back to see reluctance on Florence's face as she closed it behind him. The melee eddied and surged before him – eight Bashi Bazooks on horseback, he counted, five down and Adnan and his group in their midst. He glanced towards the gate. It was open, foolishly, unforgivably open, and the bodies of two Circassian troopers lay there, hewn down as the attackers had surged through. There was a child there too, a broken heap ridden down in sheer malice and, oblivious of the mayhem around her, a woman was clutching it and screaming in misery.

Adnan was crouched behind the now-stilled horse of the rider he had slaughtered, using it like a rampart. Another horseman was coming straight for him, a curved sword raised for a downward slice – stupidly, for it was a stroke only a master cavalryman could manage, and he was an untrained irregular. Adnan swung his Winchester up slowly, waited until the horse's breath must have been hot upon him, and then fired. The Kurd spun from the saddle, and Adnan sidestepped the animal's frenzied charge, then yelled for another of his men to join him.

He's going to make his stand in the open, Dawlish realised as he crouched in the doorway, his mind racing over possibilities. Adnan was relying on the rapidity of the Winchesters to smash down the surviving riders.

Then the full significance of that open gate struck Dawlish. These savage marauders never hunted in packs as small as this. The rabble wheeling before him could only be the advance guard of a larger troop which might come through any moment. He guessed instantaneously who would be at their head.

Selahattin!

These could only be his men. After his escape from Suakacaği he had perhaps hesitated to head for Edirne, where Dawlish's vengeance might have reached him, and had instead fled westwards towards Suleiman Pasha's armies. But now the rapidity of the Russian advance had cut him off and he had no option but to turn anyway for Edirne – and the caravanserai would be directly in his path.

The gate had to be closed.

Another horse and rider were felled by gunfire. Orange tongues spat from the grey mist that billowed around the tethered horses. Adnan and his companion crouched behind a rampart of horseflesh, one firing rapidly, the other pushing rounds into his magazine, while the remaining riders flowed about them like a torrent round a boulder.

Dawlish hurled himself from the doorway and pounded along the wall. The gaping entrance was twenty yards distant but it seemed like a mile.

He reached the gateway. Its door was in two halves, both open. Iron-studded, they were massively built of seamed and knotted timber. It took his full, straining weight to get the right side swinging closed. It thudded to a stop beneath the archway above and he dropped the iron pin that would secure it to a hole in the stone beneath. The second door still yawned open. He rushed to it, looking fearfully outside as he did, and there, streaming down the road, still a half-mile distant, was a cloud of horsemen, moving fast from the north. Selahattin and his jackals were on their way.

Dawlish threw himself against the door, heaved with his full force. It rotated slowly, creaking. It ground against its fellow and now the six-inch square section beam that would close them both must be positioned to block them. It lay in the right-hand door, resting in iron rings, and must be pushed across to span the gap between left and right. He placed both hands against it and pushed, his boots slipping on the cobbles. It would not shift.

Gasping, he redoubled his effort and partly turned his face towards the courtyard. The movement saved his life.

The single surviving Bashi Bazook was cantering towards him, intent on escape from within, his horse's head down, eyes distended. The rider's emptied revolver swung wildly at the end of a rope lanyard and his curved sword was raised. A shot echoed from behind – the splendid Alper had survived on the trough's rim and was still firing – but the bullet missed its target by a fraction and slammed into the door by Dawlish's head. The rider's right arm was raised and his left guided his terrified mount directly at Dawlish.

Five yards – close enough to hear the horse's panting. Dawlish raised his revolver, knowing he must hit with his first shot. He had to get to the other side of the beast so that the rider would have to strike cross-body at him. His back to the door, he edged rapidly to his right, three paces. It was enough. His attacker – mahogany skin, dark eyes, a heavy black moustache and close grey stubble beneath a grubby green turban – jerked the beast's head around, seeking to pull it parallel to the gate so he could chop down on his right. It was too late. His momentum was lost and as he wheeled Dawlish's shot caught him in the side. He jerked, dropping his sword, but Dawlish fired again as the sweat-streaked horse shaved past, tumbling its lifeless rider.

Adnan and his men, eight in all, came pounding forward.

"The gate," Dawlish panted, "get it barred." He felt his knees trembling.

A dozen hands forced the wooden beam into place, sealing the doors.

"I'm sorry, Kumandanim," Adnan said. "We should have been on our guard…" The blood on the cobbles and the slumped bodies underlined the bitterness of his words. An injured horse was screaming and trying unsuccessfully to rise and the woman cradling the dead child was still howling in desolation. But there was no time for recriminations.

"Selahattin's out there," Dawlish said, "He'll be here in a minute." He saw horror on Adnan's face.

His brain was racing. The remainder of his own column could not be far away either. It was a matter of holding on – but for how long? Ten men, including himself, against that horde.

"Get Alper Chavush and four men up there," Dawlish gestured to the stone steps leading to the flat roof of the gatehouse. "Send one of them back first to bring them all the ammunition he can." The tethered horses stamping and whinnying by the trough carried the reserve supplies. The gatehouse roof was the highest point of the caravanserai and a deadly fire could be poured down to the front.

The Circassians ran to Adnan's shouted orders. "And myself, Nicholas Kaptan?"

"Over there! Take one man with you!" He pointed to the tower at the far left corner. It was lower than the gatehouse but commanded the walls meeting there. "And one man there," he gestured towards the

283

tower on the far right, "a good shot, mind you. He'll be on his own."
One trooper remained. "I want him to follow me," he said.

"Evet, Kumandanim." As Adnan turned to go the first shots crashed out from Alper's men above the gatehouse. The doors shook as they were pounded from without. Shooting sounded from there, and yelling and the noise of trampling hooves – Selahattin's horde were milling outside.

Dawlish ran towards the centre of the courtyard, the single Circassian following him. Kivilcim was quivering but he quietened when Dawlish approached, patted him and spoke softly. He pulled his Winchester from its bucket-holster, rummaged the saddlebags for ammunition and filled his pockets, the trooper doing likewise. He strove to recall if the building where the women sheltered had openings to the outside – if so it could be a weak point.

Florence unbarred the door when he hammered and shouted his identity. He pushed past her into the stone hall. Women and children cowered along the walls. Florence answered his question before he asked it: "We're trying to block the windows up there". She motioned towards two iron-grilled apertures, each a yard square, eight feet above floor level. The thickness of the wall provided a two-foot ledge inside each. The bars would prevent any entry but gunfire could be poured through them. A table had been dragged beneath one and Lady Agatha stood on it. Into the recess she was piling the stools and other furniture which other women were passing to her to block it.

"Thank God you're here, Commander!" she gasped as Dawlish mounted the table, pushed past her. The trooper joined him.

"There's a woman in the yard – get her in here!" Dawlish snapped. "A wounded trooper also. Bring him in if he's still breathing!"

Lady Agatha scrambled down clumsily, calling in Turkish to several of her helpers to follow.

Through the window Dawlish saw a swirling knot of horsemen firing wildly up towards the gatehouse. One jerked and fell as he watched but still the others blazed stupidly upwards. Selahattin was among them, holding his seat with difficulty on a plunging mount, waving a sword and screaming orders. In their fury none had yet noticed the barred windows.

Dawlish drew up his Winchester. Selahattin could be his now, he thought with cold fury. By his side the Circassian trooper was worming into the recess between the stacked furniture and the wall, sliding his carbine forward.

284

Then, suddenly, Selahattin surged from view, carried away by the press of riders, obscured from Dawlish's sight by the wall's edge. The Devil was still protecting his own. A rider jerked from his saddle, then another fell, smashed down by the ferocious volleys that Alper's men were pouring down from the gatehouse roof. Dawlish lined up his sights on a fur-capped irregular who was in the act of wheeling his mount, held his breath and squeezed gently. The round took the rider in the shoulder and he slumped across his horse's neck and lurched away.

The mob of horseman was shifting to the left, along the wall, away from the gatehouse, out of sight of the windows for now. Frustrated in his frontal attack, Selahattin was seeking another point of entry – and Dawlish knew he had to identify it quickly.

"Stay here!" he told the Circassian trooper, one man, a pitiful defence for these windows, but it was all he had. He dropped from the table and found Florence before him.

"I can use this, Commander," she said. "It's mine". She held out a small nickel-plated revolver. It moved him as the Chapman's Homer had done on that distant morning off Troy, an extravagance of proud poverty. "I had it in case ... in case ... you understand, Commander." She paused. "It would have been for Agatha first."

She was magnificent at this moment and he knew he loved her more than his own life itself. But all be could say was "You – and Lady Agatha – you could help that trooper defend these windows?"

Florence nodded. "I know how to fire this." She raised the pistol.

"No good. Too weak," Dawlish said. "You'll need better." He hastened towards the entrance. Lady Agatha was there, shepherding weeping, terrified women who had taken shelter in the sheds along the walls while the battle had raged in the courtyard.

"The wounded man?" he asked.

"Dead."

"Come with me!" The two ladies followed him outside.

The firing from the gatehouse roof was spasmodic. Two men remained there but Alper and two others were descending and sprinting towards the tower to the left – unmanned until now – and were climbing to take the horde outside under fire from that point. From the other two towers, one manned by Adnan and his companion and the other by a single trooper, Winchester fire now barked. Selahattin's riders were circling the caravanserai, searching for any weak point.

285

A Kurd's corpse provided a Colt. Dawlish used the man's own knife to cut his ammunition pouch free. He pushed rounds into the empty chambers. "This is how you load it, just like your own pistol," he said to Florence.

"I know." She tried to smile. "I've done it. I can shoot it. I can help you do it too, Agatha."

"I'm not afraid, Florence." Lady Agatha's voice was quavering.

"It's heavier than you're used to," Dawlish said. "Brace yourself for the recoil."

"I'll manage, Commander. We need that other one there for Agatha." Florence nodded towards another crumpled body. Her gaze did not flinch.

"Get the horses under cover – over there." Dawlish motioned towards the sheds. "Your mule also if you can. Then get back inside, barricade the door and the second window."

Dawlish left the nobleman's daughter rifling a corpse and the coachman's daughter calming and unhitching the horses. He ran for the tower from which the single cavalryman was firing down methodically. He scrambled up the steps, remembering that he had ten shots in his Winchester magazine before he must reload. Firing discipline would be essential.

The trooper was crouched below a low parapet, bobbing up to despatch a single round, then jerking below cover again. "Zor, Kumandanim," he said. Zor – that was the word for it – hard – but his glance told that he had not panicked. Dawlish did not know his name but he remembered him doing well in the fighting two days back.

The horsemen were clustered along the short wall between the towers now held by Alper's and Dawlish's tiny forces. The northern outskirts of Ljubimec were a mile distant and only from there could succour come.

Dawlish rose from cover, prompting a wild shot that screamed wide. There were over sixty riders down there, the same barbarians he had so unwittingly rescued from the Russians two days before. Bloodlust had blinded them to the fact that their assault on the caravanserai walls was futile.

But only futile as long as the defenders' ammunition lasted. And that could not be much longer.

The walls were low – fifteen feet – and riders were throwing themselves from their horses now and clustering at the foot while their companions maintained a fusillade against the defenders above. That only a handful of troopers was withstanding the attack was now pitifully obvious from the carefully rationed return-fire. A human pyramid was rising at the wall, half a dozen Bashi Bazooks at the base, hoisting others on their shoulders and they in turn dragging others up to surmount them. The towers were flush with the walls, and offered little enfilading capacity without exposure to a deadly fire from below, but even so the pyramid collapsed twice under the merciless volleys from Alper's group. The second time the cost was loss of one of his troopers. Dawlish exposed himself briefly but repeatedly, hoping each time to distinguish Selahattin in the tumult, always missing him, but content to smash another round into the heaving mass.

The first Kurd to gain the top of the wall held it for seconds only. Weapons converged on him from Dawlish's tower and from Alper's. He was plucked away but another scrambled behind, and another, some hurled down before they could orient themselves, but others reaching hands down to heave up others after them.

The Winchester volleys were dying and fingers searching in empty pouches found no further ammunition. Alper had called the men on the gatehouse to join him – their carbines were empty – and they were mounting his tower. Revolvers were out now and Alper was yelling to his men to hold their fire, to wait for the rush that must inevitably come along the wall. Dawlish and his companion hurled their last Winchester rounds, then, crouched behind their parapet, they too drew their pistols. Only Adnan and his trooper, across the courtyard, still had ammunition for their carbines but their attention was now distracted by movement adjacent to their tower.

Dawlish peered over the ledge. Twelve or fifteen irregulars were some twenty yards away on the top of the wall, shouting, gesticulating, dragging up companions, screwing up their own courage for the charge they must make. His Tranter's chambers were full – six rounds – and he loosened his sabre in its scabbard. If it came to that there could be only one end, a chopping, hacking, fracas that he could not survive. He wanted it only to be quick, without pain and mutilation. But as he glanced towards the squat building nestling in the opposite wall regret seared him. Florence was behind that barricaded door – doomed perhaps to an end worse than his – and she would never know that his feelings for her had reached a new intensity in the last half-hour.

The Bashi Bazooks launched their charge. They did not split to attack both flanking towers, for they had seen that Alper's was the more strongly defended, and their full force came surging along the top

287

of the wall towards Dawlish and his companion. It was little over a yard wide, making a front for one man, and they came on howling, swords upraised.

Dawlish and his trooper rose to their feet, lifting their pistols. Dawlish found himself as calm as on the range, steadying the barrel on his forearm, sighting on the red sash of leading attacker, squeezing, feeling the kick, smelling the gunsmoke and quelling a surge of delight as the Bashi Bazook convulsed and fell from the wall. The next man stumbled, fought to retain his balance, and crashed down outside. Dawlish's companion brought down the man who followed and at their rear Adnan's small garrison was pouring their last fire into the seething mass.

Dawlish fired again, missed, then again, found a mark, and again, this time missing, deafened by his own reports and those of the trooper by him. Yet still the irregulars pressed on, stepping across bodies slumped across their path, raised to a new level of fury now that vengeance was so near, losses so smarting.

He heard a gasp to his left. The trooper was toppling backwards, his hand arrested in the act of clapping it to his breast, dead before he fell into the courtyard. Dawlish fired again. The attackers were almost on him now. Then his hammer clicked on an empty chamber.

There was nothing now for Dawlish but to draw his sabre. The leading attacker was climbing across the parapet and simultaneously thrusting at him with his sword. It was clumsily done and he was facing a man who had enjoyed cutlass drill since boyhood. Dawlish stepped to one side, saw the man's crown exposed as his jab missed and his head dipped, then stamped forward as he had been trained to do so long since and swung his heavy weapon down in a chop that clove deep into his opponent's skull. The body collapsed across the parapet, an obstacle for those that followed. As the next irregular tried to pass Dawlish swung at him backhandedly, a terrible horizontal blow that bit between neck and shoulder. Blood gushed and the man stumbled and fell.

A pause. The attackers were unwilling to press forward to the towers along the deadly gauntlet of the wall-top and yet their group was growing as more scrambled up from below. No fire met them from the flanks, for Alper and his man also confronted them only with naked steel. Two Bashi Bazooks were dropping into the courtyard, swung down by their comrades. A burst of fire from Adnan's tower took one but now another was jumping down, and another.

Outflanked! The word screamed in Dawlish's brain. He gave one despairing glance towards the outskirts of Ljubimec. The road was empty. There was only one option.

"Fall back!" he yelled to Alper. He did not know the Turkish words but his bloodied sabre pointing towards the building where the women sheltered gave clarity enough. "Fall back!" he shouted to Adnan on his far tower, who alone, like the trooper with him, still appeared to have ammunition.

As Dawlish turned for the steps he heard shouting behind. The Kurds on the wall were in pursuit. He blundered downwards, breath heaving, heart pounding, knowing he was close to panic, fighting to restrain it.

At the foot of the steps a small, wiry irregular barred his path and raised a pistol. Dawlish's reaction was instinctive, his sabre slicing down and shearing through the outstretched wrist, dropping both hand and weapon to the ground. His momentum carried him past the man who was starting to scream as he comprehended his bloody stump. He raced diagonally across the courtyard, conscious to his left of two Circassians fighting their way through the knot that obstructed them at the base of their tower. Shots crackled from his right – Adnan and his man had descended and were blazing towards the growing number of Kurds crossing the wall.

Dawlish skirted the trough. Two troopers were ahead of him, one half-carrying, half-dragging the other, whose leg was a sodden mess of scarlet – both Alper's men, though there was no sign of the chavush himself.

He reached the door, pounded it with his sabre hilt, shouted Florence's name. The two troopers were with him and Adnan and his companion were a few paces behind, each dropped to one knee, steadily firing and ejecting and firing again, pouring their last rounds into the howling flood now pouring down the tower steps. The main gates were swinging open, for several attackers had reached them and had withdrawn the bolting beam. Within seconds Selahattin's full force would be inside.

It was Lady Agatha who opened the door, her face pale with suppressed terror. "You're safe, Commander!" she cried. "Thank God!"

He shoved the troopers past her, yelled to Adnan to join him. He and his trooper loosed one last volley before scurrying inside. Dawlish heaved the door closed. Agatha shot the bolts and the women began to pile the heavy benches behind it again that had prevented its faster opening.

The space was filled with drifting gunsmoke, the wails of frightened children, the sobs of women crouched along the wall, the sounds of despair. The trooper Dawlish had left there before still manned his window, his face powder-blackened but resolute, and Florence stood on a table by the second barricaded recess, revolver in hand. She glanced briefly towards Dawlish – and even at this extremity her bleak smile was beautiful – and turned again to scan the scene outside. Neither she nor the trooper were firing now. Selahattin's forces were now inside, not without.

The door shook under blows from outside. A splintered rip erupted – a bullet biting, but not penetrating – then another. Dawlish and the others hugged the wall to either side.

"How much ammunition have you?" he asked Adnan.

"Half a magazine." Six rounds.

The trooper had a few more, and another six in his pouch. The man by the window contributed another ten, still leaving him with five. Agatha's revolver, unfired, six rounds. Florence's Dawlish had not yet checked.

The door was being pounded, but it held. Soon Selahattin would be urging them to pile kindling there, as at that church in Giresun, and he would be savouring the vengeance to come.

This was how sieges had ended through history, Dawlish thought, desperate man and despairing woman and terrified children waiting in confinement for death, rape and mutilation, praying for deliverance that might never come. His spirit recoiled from the last, ghastly, brutal act of mercy he would have to perform for Agatha – and for Florence, whom he now knew he loved above his own life – and he knew that after it his own end by his own hand would be a mercy. Selahattin would be denied his triumph.

"Hold the door, Adnan Binbashi," he said. He felt respect and affection for this efficient, loyal man who had fought so faithfully by his side. For him, and for Alper, whose torn body must be draped across the tower outside and for the proud, simple, unflinching men who stood by him now. It was not bad company to die in.

He climbed up beside Florence at the window. There was blood on her coat and it smeared her face but he saw with relief that it was not hers. She was trembling, trying to suppress it. "I killed one," she said. "Like you said... it was heavier than I expected..." She began to

290

weep. "Down there," she said, pointing. He looked out. He could see boots, baggy trousers, a discarded sword. The head and shoulders were hidden by the ledge, too close against the wall to see. "He stood on his saddle, tried to pull himself up," she whispered. "His face was like .... like a devil. And then I..." She wept.

She must have pushed the pistol into his face, have been drenched herself as it exploded. But she still had not left her post, had waited for the attack to surge back this way.

"I'll take that," he said, taking the Colt from her. "Now go down. Wait with Lady Agatha. Keep the women as quiet as you can."

"Is there hope?" she said.

"Plenty," he lied. "The column will be here directly."

He wanted to embrace her, tell her he loved her, but there was no time. The door was splintering as more shots hammered into it. There was shouting outside, triumphant, savage, full of expectation of vengeance. Dawlish flattened himself at the wall by Adnan.

"We hold our fire until the last. Then it's every man for himself."

Adnan nodded, then drew Dawlish to him and kissed him on the cheek. Dawlish felt tears start to his eyes, then smelled burning. Smoke was wisping through the splintered door. The inevitable had commenced. A woman began to scream, and another joined her, despite Lady Agatha's attempts to calm them.

There was a terrible fascination in watching the dark patch spread on the door's inner surface as it charred, then glowed. Dawlish and the others shoved the remaining furniture behind it, piling benches and tables into a heap that might delay the attackers for precious minutes. The cauldrons were dragged over, their contents dashed over the furniture to soak it – worth another minute perhaps, for hope died hard.

The door was burning furiously now. Shots crashed through, blasting away chunks of flaming timber. The furniture behind was starting to blaze also, filling the room with throat-searing smoke. The shouts from outside were clearly audible and one of the troopers was hurling back his own abuse. He might as well – he had only that and his sabre to defend himself.

Dawlish glanced back towards the women, Lady Agatha with her back turned, comforting a weeping woman, Florence with two children pressed to her breast, her face buried in their hair.

Let them stay like that, he prayed, and they'll never know what I'm bringing to them.

291

The last of the blazing timbers collapsed and now only the heat of burning furniture barred access. Two screaming Bashi Bazooks hurled themselves forward, turbans wrapped around their arms, attempting to force a path. A trooper's sabre-thrust spitted the first and Adnan's downward chop collapsed the second into the fire. The sickening odour of scorching flesh wafted back. Gunfire crashed through the doorway, sending rounds screaming and ricocheting through the chamber. A woman spun, screaming, and another cowering by the wall jerked and died instantly.

It was time.

Five steps – the longest of his life – brought Dawlish behind Lady Agatha. He raised his pistol. She was speaking in a low voice, English words of which the woman she clasped could comprehend nothing but the kindness. She did not hear the click as he cocked the revolver. He raised it to the back of her neck and fought down the urge to vomit. Afterwards, and quickly, if she was not to know what was coming, it must be Florence.

Then Florence looked up. The face that he had found so beautiful when a smile had lightened it was infinitely sad now. He had never told her that he loved her, had never had the courage to cross the social chasm between them, but her large brown eyes told him that she knew it. In her slow nod he recognised that she understood what must now happen and that she was grateful for what would be his only act of love with her. Her face was as free of fear and as full of love as a woman's could be at such a moment. Do it, her glance said, but do it quickly.

He took up the first pressure on the trigger. The muzzle was an inch from Lady Agatha's neck.

Suddenly Adnan was knocking his arm aside and yelling like a lunatic 'Yok! Yok! No! No!' and the troopers by the door were cheering themselves hoarse and the gunfire was suddenly stilled. Rushing feet, clattering hooves, sounded from the courtyard.

"It's the column," Adnan shouted. "They're here."

Through the smoking doorway they could see the remnants of Selahattin's force fleeing towards the yawning gateway. Adnan was laughing hysterically and dragging Dawlish across the room and up on the table. From the barricaded window they saw the panicked mob of Bashi Bazooks streaming northward. Close to the walls Kurds on foot were still struggling to pull themselves into empty saddles. Others were wheeling their horses, pressing their flanks, urging them into flight. In the midst of them, Selahattin was standing in his stirrups, screaming

292

orders for retreat. Dawlish tore his eyes away for an instant from this monster he hated and saw the remainder of his own cavalry escort spurring from the fringes of Ljubimec, drawn by the gunfire.

Dawlish shouted for a carbine, but Selahattin was already putting spurs to his mount. He looked back to the caravanserai with eyes that were pits of hatred and spat before he careered away after his disappearing men. They were heading northwards and there was bitter satisfaction in knowing that there was no haven for them there as the Russians pressed ever closer. But Dawlish knew that he would begrudge any retribution in which he could not himself have a hand.

The doorway was clear, the barricade's burning embers pushed into the yard. The column's leading riders were drawing rein amid the bloodied corpses that littered the cobbles and the blackened scarecrows that staggered to meet them, gratefully gulping the cold air.

One danger had passed. Another, more vast, more implacable, more relentless, threatened – and safety was still two day's march distant. But even with that knowledge Dawlish's heart was singing.

Florence, magnificent, beautiful and indomitable, was alive and he had saved her.

34

Departure could not be deferred until morning. The Russians might be here at any time, pressing hard on the Ottoman troops retreating towards Edirne. The only hope of escape was in getting back across the Maritza, off that main axis of advance.

There were corpses, their own people, Alper among them, to be thrust into hastily scraped graves. Selahattin's scavengers could rot where they lay for all Dawlish cared. There were some fourteen cases that would need transport in the carts, six men among them, all civilian refugees but for the single surviving injured trooper. One man had been senile and bedridden long before the present disaster, and the others had been wounded either when looting or when resisting it. Dawlish knew that one would be dead within an hour of departure – his head was split, his brain exposed – but Lady Agatha wouldn't hear of leaving him. Two of the women had delivered in recent days, had haemorrhaged badly and were still bleeding. Dawlish noticed how both the ladies spoke frankly of subjects they would have blushed to mention at other times. Others women were suffering from the effects

293

of rape, wounds or fever. There were six babies and seventeen children too young to walk. The helpers added another nine women and girls.

They commenced loading the carts, three or four blanket-muffled patients in each, younger children packed between them. Dawlish and Florence had gravitated together, with the appearance of accident on either side, as the sick and wounded were carried out. She was more silent than before and he could guess that she, like him, was remembering – and would never forget – the moment when his pistol had been raised and their eyes had met in understanding and acceptance. Yet their exchanges were now businesslike and impersonal, awkwardness replacing earlier spontaneity, as if both were aware that a decision confronted them that would change their lives.

For one instant the thought struck him that he could indeed marry her, should ask her now, this instant, yet he just as quickly recoiled from it. Any life with him would be dogged with humiliations and slurs. The complications for his own career he could endure – it could be nothing compared to what he had come through in the last hours – but if he loved her he could not ask so much of her. To mask his agony he said "I must thank you for saving my horse."

"He's a beautiful animal, Commander," she said. In the first minutes the battle had raged she had somehow managed to get four terrified beasts into the sheds before retreating herself. Kivilcim had been the first. "Will you bring him home to England?"

"Yes," he said. "It must be possible. My father will be glad to care for him." The thought was suddenly comforting, the idea of setting Kivilcim at a fence on some frosty Shropshire morning as the hounds bayed and the other riders trailed far behind. Then, just as suddenly, he realised that any such pleasure would be empty if she were not somewhere near.

"It will be a cold night, Miss Morton" he said. "Are you sure you want to drive?"

"I'll be happier to be busy." She tried to smile. "Besides, I bought that wretched mule. I wouldn't wish him on anybody else." Two women lay in her cart, one tossing in a fevered coma, the other still and silent, staring blankly from eyes that must have witnessed, and endured, an infinity of degradation. The children around them looked shyly away when Dawlish smiled at them, but their hands always stole towards Florence, as if touching her could somehow reassure them.

"How long will it take, Commander?" Her voice was quiet, and he guessed that she realised the full gravity of their situation.

294

"It's about thirty miles." He saw that she was calculating times. "I fear there's snow for much of it. The carts will slow us."

"More than a day then." She had not grown up around stables for nothing. "Will we be in danger? From the Russians, I mean?"

He considered lying, then realised she would see through it. "Yes," he said. "It happened already, two days ago. A small group, but we beat them back." She had enough to cope with. She did not need to know that Nusret was dead. "We can beat them again if necessary," he added, "There's nothing to fear. You – and Lady Agatha, of course – you'll be our first concern."

She busied herself with the cart. He sensed that she found talk with him as awkward as he did with her. He ached to crush her against him and yet still he did not know what to say.

His mind raced. He had always scorned men – including his father – who had amused themselves with women whose lower station made marriage impossible. He would never be of their number. He could brave convention, make Florence his wife, but though the Royal Navy, that merciless taskmistress he loved and sometimes resented, might make no formal objection, many other officers and, worse still, other officers' wives, would never accept her. The same knowledge had made his well-meaning uncle shrink from marriage with the refined but low-born Frenchwoman he so clearly loved. But he might leave the Navy, return to Shrewsbury, article himself to his father and adapt to the life of a market-town solicitor. Or retire together to some Continental spa, as his uncle had done, and live off the income of his farms. There would be just enough for modest comfort. Yet even there, he knew, rumour would follow, condemning her to years of slights, of whispers and reminders that she had once been in service. If he truly loved her he must be silent. He turned away, wretched. It was time to saddle up again.

They retraced their route through Ljubimec, now empty of troops, the laden carts at the centre of the column, the marines and any women fit to walk flanking them, the cavalry equally divided between van and rear. There was life on the streets again, the start of chaos, figures moving furtively between buildings, flitting away at the sound of hooves. Several houses were burning fiercely and twice they heard isolated shots. The Russians were not here yet but looting had started. Fear-filled eyes followed them from behind closed shutters as they passed towards the Maritza bridge.

295

Darkness fell. The night was cold and dry, stars winking above in a clear sky. Dawlish drew rein in the centre of the bridge and let the column pass. There was silence but for the plodding hooves and feet, the creak of harness and the crying of an infant. Bülent Chavush saluted smartly as he passed and the mule Florence led was accepting begrudgingly that he had met his match. Lady Agatha went plodding gamely by, bowed like a beggar beneath her pack, children on either side holding her hands. The horsemen followed, leading mounts that had already been tired when they had crossed this bridge three hours earlier. All had an air of weary resignation, an acceptance that they must trudge through most of the night before rest could be risked. For to the northwest fires smoked on the horizon, the closest perhaps ten miles away.

Levka, the deserted village, would be the first halt. The road towards it was a climbing one, and snow still lay on it, and ice too – but the houses there were of stone and could offer both shelter and defence. Progress slowed as they ascended, the tired beasts slipping, exhausted men pulling them onwards. Several women and children, hungry and weak before they started, and worn out by their walk already, were placed on horseback. The carts slithered and men with rags tied across their boot-soles for greater purchase heaved on the spokes to propel them up the inclines. Cold and fatigue were biting and many shambled in a daze. At the rear Adnan somehow maintained progress, encouraging and haranguing. Dawlish ranged back and forth along the line, mostly on foot and leading Kivilcim, ready to drag himself into the saddle if necessary. His field glasses were constantly at his eyes, scanning the progress of those fires on the horizon, always fearing when for the first time an isolated conflagration closer by would signal the presence of a nearer enemy. But even Cossacks must rest, he told himself, for the pace of the Russian advance in recent weeks had been unprecedented in any winter campaign he had ever read of.

They gained Levka's shelter soon after midnight. Doors dragged from its empty houses provided firewood. It also added another nine to the column, the exhausted refugees encountered there earlier, stranded still by fatigue and infirmity. The already-laden carts would be burdened to their limit but Dawlish could not bring himself to leave them. Sentries were posted on two-hour watches, the horses stabled under cover and weary bodies slumped into all-too-brief sleep. Dawlish took the first watch, trudging around the picket lines in a near trance, his body screaming for rest. Shortly before Adnan relieved him he saw flames erupt to the southwest, a growing conflagration that cast a red glow skywards. The Russian vanguard had reached Ljubimec.

His own sleep was short and it was still dark as they prepared for departure. The dry, still cold persisted, old snow crunching underfoot. Breath hung like smoke on the chill air. Meagre meals were hurriedly warmed and eaten. Children cried and sick and wounded groaned as they were packed again into carts that would jolt them for hours to come. There was one corpse – the head-wound had finished its work – and no time to bury it even if the ground had not been frozen granite-hard. The sun rose blood-red and gave no warmth. The column got under way, weary already, cold, fear shared but unspoken.

The wheel ruts and hoof prints they had made a day since were solid now, cutting soles and hooves so that blood soon marked their progress. Except for the scouts the troopers were leading their horses, many of them carrying women or children. The pace was set by the carts and these were the special concern of Bülent, whose marines pushed them on the inclines and restrained them on the descents. All day the dark caterpillar toiled eastwards across the frozen landscape, the halts comfortless, each new start more miserable than the last, the miles still to go decreasing with agonising slowness.

A galloper summoned Dawlish to the head of the column in early afternoon. Adnan was there, earnestly interrogating a scout.

"He's seen movement there," he said. He gestured north-eastwards. Beyond the rolling hills, four, five miles distant, was the valley where they had rescued Haluk and Selahattin. A track led to it from the north – a track the enemy already knew of.

"Was he seen?" Dawlish felt foreboding. It had started like this two days back.

Adnan shook his head. "Two horsemen only, moving cautiously. They fell back. He thinks they were scouts also."

Which mean there must be a larger force, perhaps pushing down that same track the Russians had probed before. Dawlish glanced back. The column was strung out over a furlong – compact enough – but the terrain around was open. Unless the carts were abandoned it would be defenceless against any significant enemy unit, particularly if it had horse artillery. I'm a naval officer, a voice within him wanted to scream, I know how to fight ships, not manoeuvre men and horses on open snow-shrouded fields. But Adnan was looking expectantly towards him and inaction was not an option.

297

"Send out a screen. Fifteen troopers under a reliable man." He wished that Alper was alive, could not remember the name of his replacement. "Let them deploy along that ridge line." He pointed. Holding there would block any immediate thrust towards the road they marched on. "Let them dismount, stay below the crest."

"Evet, Kumandanim."

"They'll need to hold for an hour." That should give time – just – to reach that devastated village where he had seen the skulls. It had stone walls, burned-out houses, a place for a stand.

Troopers were selected, carbines pulled from holsters and magazines checked, sabres loosened in their sheaths. Uneasy glances and silent fear rippled down the column and "Ins'Allah" was repeated endlessly. Then the riders went struggling away from the track, hooves breaking through the frozen snow-crust, sometimes floundering in unsuspected drifts to belly height, leaving the column to press on with an extra haste that taxed exhausted bodies to new levels of misery.

They stumbled onwards, the weak mounted, the strong hauling on bridles and flogging rumps already raw. Dawlish rode back down the column urging speed he knew few could manage. Lady Agatha had taken charge of the mule-cart. "We're doing famously, Commander, famously!" she told him with unconvincing heartiness as he passed. Florence had somehow double-hitched two horses left riderless since the fight in the caravanserai to the most heavily laden cart. The smell of approaching death hung over its comatose occupants. She tried to look cheerful when she saw him but her face was gaunt with exhaustion.

"It must be close now, Commander," she said. "A few hours more?"

"A few," he said. Ten, twelve more, but he did not tell her that.

"We've managed this far," she said. "We'll manage to the end."

He had not meant to talk longer but her dismissal of her fatigue moved him. He slipped from his saddle and walked alongside. In this extremity he could compromise neither himself nor her by merely speaking.

"You'll be looking forward to returning to England after this, Miss Morton?"

"It will seem dull, Commander," she said. "But perhaps Agatha will want to stay longer in Istanbul with her brother. She thinks the war will end soon."

It was ending all around them, he thought, and perhaps the Ottoman Empire with it. The more important question was whether

298

any of them would survive it. But he could not bear to tell her that and instead he said "That will end my Ottoman service. I'll be returning to the Royal Navy."

"To command a ship, Commander. Another ironclad? A British one?" The idea seemed to please her. He realised that the dinner in the *Mesrutiyet's* saloon might have been the pinnacle of her existence, a glimpse into a world from which birth had excluded her.

"A moored ship, I fear," he said, "and I won't be commanding it either. I'll be an instructor, a schoolmaster, in Portsmouth, training other officers."

"You'll visit Agatha's father? He'll want to thank you for what you've done."

"I doubt it," he said. "I'll be too busy. It's a long way from Portsmouth to Northamptonshire." But the real reason he could not tell her was that he could not bear to encounter her in a subservient role again, not after he had known her heroism. Disturbed, he excused himself and remounted.

The pace was merciless now, the column driven from behind by the grim rearguard under Bülent. Dawlish rode with them, ears alert for gunfire, eyes scanning for Cossack lances surmounting the rolling crests to the north. A mile passed, breaths rasping, and then another, muscles aching, feet rising and falling mechanically, and yet another of shambling agony. No word was spoken but the column's tortured haste was marked by the crunch of frozen snow, the moaning of sick and wounded jolted beyond endurance in unsprung carts and the wailing of children who had forgotten any world but one of cold and hunger.

The half-gutted village where the skulls lay was in sight when Dawlish, looking rearward for the thousandth time, saw a single horseman spurring up the track in their wake. He was waving and even before he sharpened into focus in Dawlish's glasses there seemed to be something relaxed, almost joyful, in his gesture. By the time the rider reached him an alerted Adnan too had joined him from the head of the column.

Words poured from the trooper. Adnan's face lit up as he listened.

"The troops to the north aren't Russian," he said.

"An Ottoman force?"

"Cappodocian infantry. What's left of a battalion, and a handful of dragoons, They were mauled at Gulubovo a week ago. They've been retreating ever since."

299

They would have been heading due south, for Ljubimec and the other Martiza crossings. But the bridge at Suakacaği offered a closer hope of escape.

"How near are they?" Dawlish asked.

"Their scouts reached our screen. The main column is five miles to the north, and they reckon the enemy is as close again on their heels."

"In what force?"

"Cossacks. Three, four squadrons, with horse artillery. And a mob of Bulgarian Christians."

Cossacks, always Cossacks, implacable and relentless. But the Bulgarians would be the most to be feared, revenge-obsessed men who had survived the indiscriminate massacres that had precipitated this war and who had seen mothers and wives and daughters ravished and children slaughtered. The terror unleashed over them had kept them subdued until the Russian colossus rolled towards them. Now they had risen and only Muslim blood could slake their thirst for reprisal.

"Send this man back," Dawlish said. "Tell the troopers to hold their position until the Cappodocians get there, then guide them to Suakacaği. We'll keep the bridge there intact as long as we can."

But we'll have to get there ourselves first, he thought, and whatever the price in suffering or horseflesh there could be no let-up on the dozen miles still remaining. The sullenly defiant Cappodocians – indomitable fighters if they had lasted this far – might take the brunt of the enemy fury but there was always the chance of a Cossack troop outflanking them to the east and cutting the road to the river crossing.

The next hours were the worst. They had only a brief halts at the devastated village and it took blows and curses to get the exhausted column moving again. Three corpses were dumped from the over-laden carts and several exhausted animals were left to die, their uncomprehending eyes beseeching pity none could spare. The sun dropped and the temperature fell yet further and still the weary plod continued. Both Englishwomen now slumped on carts and Dawlish knew that if he himself was so close to stupor then they and fifty others must be in even worse extremities. Many of the horses were beyond riding and their troopers dragged them behind them, their own feet numb and lacerated in untanned leather boots never intended for marching. The column was straggling badly despite all efforts of Bülent and his marines to cajole the laggards forward.

Deliverance came in the form of a troop of Circassians sent by Zyndram. They brought a dozen unsaddled animals to relieve the wretched beasts that sagged beneath the cart shafts. Even Florence's dearly-bought mule earned remission. Women and children were shifted to the newcomers' mounts and even those still condemned to trudge on foot seemed heartened. The straggling column stumbled onwards over the last remaining miles. An hour after midnight it sighted the Tunca crossing at Suakacaği.

Zyndram emerged from the darkness as they reached the bridge, the relief and delight on his face tempered by concern.

"Edirne has fallen," he said after they had exchanged salutes and greetings.

"When?" The news chilled Dawlish. The Russians were a scant fifteen miles to the south.

"Yesterday. We only heard two hours ago. Our troops retreated through the city and then the governor, Eyub Pasha, yielded it without a fight."

"Why, in God's name?" Dawlish's anger rose. Straddling the Maritza, swollen there by its confluence with the Tunca, on which they now stood, a determined defence of Edirne's bridges could have withstood a larger force for days, maybe for a week.

Zyndram shrugged. "Too beautiful a town to be destroyed, Eyub said. He wanted to spare the Selimiye Mosque, and the Eskin Mosque and..."

"Nonsense!" Dawlish said. "He's a traitorous blackguard!" Because of him the main road to Istanbul was now open before the Russians. Only the Lines of Büyük Tchemedji lay between them and their centuries-held goal of the Bosporus.

"We'll be retreating also, Nicholas Kaptan?" Dawlish sensed the controlled fear in Zyndram's voice, the knowledge that unless the Suakacaği garrison withdrew eastwards soon, perhaps immediately, it ran the risk of being cut off. Even when it did it would have to race the Russians by a parallel track to reach the security of the defensive lines it had toiled earlier to construct.

"Not yet," Dawlish said, "not for a few hours yet." He knew the risk was a dreadful one but the column now filing past was at its last extremity and would need rest before it could be urged into movement again. Moreover, somewhere behind, plodding through the freezing darkness, was the remnant of the Cappodocian unit that had been retreating for a week and for which this bridge represented salvation. They wore the same uniform, Brother Turks. He could not abandon them, not yet.

Zyndram spurred forward as he saw the ladies approach, Lady Agatha driving a cart, Florence again leading hers with a determination that seemed only to have grown with her exhaustion. He slid from his mount, bowed deeply and kissed each grimy hand in turn.

"Your accommodation is prepared, Ladies," he told them. "Not palatial, but the best the *Mesrutiyet* Brigade can offer!" He looked admiringly at Florence, then flashed a meaningful glance to Dawlish.

"Congratulations, Nicholas Kaptan!" he said, smiling.

"But what about our charges, Jerzy Efendi? Is there accommodation for them?" Lady Agatha gestured to the comatose occupants of her cart, to the women and children swaying in half-sleep on the led-horses.

"For them also, Madame. And our surgeon's services, and food and warmth."

The seamen and marines guarding the bridge approach were drawn to a salute as Dawlish rode towards them. Zyndram called out as he drew near and suddenly the men were throwing back their hoods and tearing off their caps and cheering. Dawlish reined in and saw unfeigned welcome on their faces, heard the cry of "Kumandanim!" and knew the word never had deeper meaning. He pulled back on his reins, rearing Kivilcim and raising his own hand in salute. Then he walked his weary mount across the bridge's icy timbers, knowing that if those indomitable Cappodocians somewhere behind had not reached here by midday this structure would have to be blown to matchwood and that the next retreat must commence without them.

But midday was still hours away. There was time now to rest, and be thankful. Florence was safe. For now.

35

Dawlish had himself roused at seven. The room's warmth – he had yielded his own to the ladies – was a delight to be savoured, the smell of hot coffee a joy. But his dominant thought was that Florence lived. Then he recalled his resolution to avoid her. With it came sadness that he must feel for years, perhaps forever.

"The army column's in sight," Zyndram told him. "They're in a bad way."

The temperature outside had risen above freezing. A wet mist hung over the river and the ground beyond. Dawlish and Zyndram inspected the bridge. The stream was in spate and explosive charges

302

were packed round each pier, with double instantaneous fuses running back from each to the redoubt on the eastern shore.

They stood by Abdurrahman's Nordenveldt. Dawlish focussed his glasses on the figures emerging from the drifting fog. Two horsemen, one a Circassian trooper who had been detached yesterday, led limping mounts and behind them seven living scarecrows tottered forward on foot. Their hooded greatcoats were crisscrossed with blankets and shrouded with improvised cloaks. Their legs were wrapped with sacking. Their faces were blackened with the smoke of fires kindled from damp branches and their matted beards seemed to merge into their fur caps. They had cast away all but the smallest knapsacks and yet each still had his Martini-Peabody rifle, even if some used them as crutches.

One was an officer, Idris Mülazim of the Seventh Cappodocian Light Infantry, and proud of it. Blood had soaked and dried in the bandage wrapping his head and was crusted on his face. He was in better shape than most, he told them, and that was why he had been sent ahead, to appeal for horses. The remainder were still three miles behind. At least a dozen had been lost in the night to cold and exhaustion.

"The Russians? Are they still close?" Zyndram translated and was met with a grim laugh.

"He says they wouldn't be moving this fast if the Cossacks weren't on their tails. If there's anything worse than fatigue it's a lance in the kidneys. There's less than a mile between the tail of the column and the leading Russians."

Dawlish sent his own Circassian troopers clattering westwards across the bridge, five carts with them, their orders to scoop up the incapacitated, drive the remainder forward, and avoid action. Bülent's marines, supplemented by forty rifle-armed seamen, were positioned on the bridge's western side. On the eastern bank, in the earthwork that dominated the crossing, the four sixteen-pounders that had been dragged here with such effort, grinned evilly from their embrasures, loaded and ready.

More infantry hobbled in. One collapsed and died on the bridge but the others made it to the cauldrons of soup waiting on the eastern side. The mist was lightening, drifting patchily, so that the road was sometimes visible for a mile or more. The retreating troops were arriving in half-companies, with some semblance of organisation, but too debilitated even to smile or to acknowledge the cheer that greeted them as they shambled past the marines and on to the bridge.

Rifle fire sounded in the distance, muffled by the fog. Somewhere out there the Russians had made contact with the rearguard. The rattle rose to a crescendo, then subsided. A few isolated shots followed a little later, then another torrent of fire which also died.

The rifle-equipped seamen were disposed to the left of the bridge approach, the less numerous but repeater-armed marines to the right, both in the two-rank formation that Dawlish had practised for years on shore exercises. The carriage-mounted Nordenveldt lay between them. The men shuffled as their feet sunk into the ooze of an increasing thaw and strained their eyes for the enemy. Dawlish passed along their lines, giving a word of encouragement here, of praise there, touched as ever by the pleasure that lit stolid faces as he addressed them as Evlatlarim, My Sons.

Two carts emerged from the mist, vehicles sent earlier, laden now with wounded and sick. A half-company staggered behind, interspersed with the Circassians' horses, each led by his rider and laden with sometimes two slumped figures. More carts followed, each with its burden of suffering, men who yet somehow clung to life despite sabre-cuts and lance-thrusts and gunshot wounds and the freezing anguish of a week's retreat. Behind them in the fog gunfire rattled again, subsided, then flared before tailing into silence.

The sun was burning the mist away. It still ebbed and flowed in the stagnant air – and to the right, upriver, it was still dense – but the roadway was clear for half a mile. A final cluster of infantry, thirty or forty men, were hurrying down it in a shuffling jog-trot. Mounted men rode behind, wheeling their horses regularly to scan the fringes of the mist behind. Dawlish saw that they were his Circassian troopers, still fresh.

At that moment a dark mass erupted from the drifting mist on the track's left, the same sight that had chilled him on that desperate morning far across the Black Sea when the Cossacks had fanned out on a bleak mountainside. They were the same deadly marauders as then, hard, leathery men in muddy-brown greatcoats crossed with black belting, crouched over their horses' necks, lances lowered. A second troop was emerging from the mist further back, still at a brisk trot, and some fired from the saddle, then dropped their carbines into their bucket holsters and grasped their vertically-stacked lances, sweeping them down as they kicked their mounts into a canter. A Circassian

304

tumbled from his mount. The first two Russians to reach him gouged their lances into him before spurring onwards.

The last of the retreating derelicts began to run, their stumbling haste pitifully slow. The Circassian troopers behind them, some thirty, wheeled to face the threat. Responding to the shouts of their commander, they raised their Winchesters. The nearest Cossacks were fifty yards distant, slush and mud flying from the hooves of tired horses goaded to one last burst of speed. There was no single volley, just each Circassian slowing his mount and controlling it with his calves and firing and loading and firing again, three rounds in rapid succession rippling across the uneven line of riders. The muzzle flashes stabbing through the rolling wall of smoke shocked the charging Cossacks into a swerve to the left. As the third volley died the Circassians wheeled and dug their spurs and raced for the bridge.

The last of the Cappodocian infantry was being urged to cross the bridge and leave the fight to others. Zyndram yelled to the leading horsemen thundering towards him to follow them. Dawlish stood by Abdurrahman and his loader at the Nordenveldt, pointing to the target that was still masked by the troopers pounding up the track. Behind them the Cossacks were recovering from their check and were on the trot again, a more compact mass now than before as they clustered towards the roadway.

The Russians had not recognised the significance of the seamen and marines flanking the bridge approach. The riders they now chased with such abandon blocked their view of the bridge and the massive firepower that defended it – but within an instant that shield would be removed. This was going to be a massacre, Dawlish realised, and the knowledge both appalled and relieved him.

The Circassians drummed towards the narrow gauntlet between the seamen and the marines. A horse tripped, went down on broken forelegs, throwing its trooper. He struggled to his feet, then caught the stirrup leather of a comrade veering to his rescue and was dragged onward, feet trailing.

Zyndram was relaying Dawlish's orders in calm Turkish and the first ranks had dropped to one knee. Bülent Chavush was urging his men to choose their targets once they came in view and to fire rapidly. Sedat, the cold-eyed sharpshooter, and Yashar, who had stood by him when they had last faced Cossack lance-points together, stood shoulder to shoulder. The Nordenveldt was positioned to rake the track skew-wise a hundred yards distant, and Abdurrahman was squinting down

305

the sights above the centremost of its five parallel barrels, his hand hovering over the firing lever, his loader ready to drop fresh rounds into the feed-channels.

The leading horsemen pounded between the defenders and on to the bridge. The stream of troopers followed, unmasking the following Cossacks fully for the first time.

"Atesh!"

The seamen's Martini-Peabodys and the marines' Winchesters crashed out. The leading riders had seen them too late and were drawing rein when the full blast of fifty muzzles lashed into them. Men and horses smashed down, screaming and threshing and cartwheeling, an instant obstacle for those galloping behind.

"Atesh!"

Abdurraman's poised hand was released by Dawlish's cry. Fire rippled from the Nordenveldt's quintuple muzzles, scything down the horses and riders. Brass cartridges slid down the feeder channels, devoured by the smoking breeches as they flicked open, replacements fed in expertly by the loader.

"Atesh!"

The front rank of seamen were reloading their single-shot weapons and the second stepped between them, took aim and fired. Across the track the marines had ejected, reloaded and were firing again, Bülent steadily calling the rhythm.

It was the massacre that Dawlish had foreseen and, though it sickened him, he called no halt. A score of horses were down, some trying pitifully to struggle up again on broken limbs, others thrashing weakly, others crumpled in impossible poses. Men lay among them, or staggered hopelessly between, dazed and gory. Riders milled and twisted, desperately checking their rush, dragging heads around into retreat, but caught and scourged by the *Mesrutiyet* Brigade's storm of gunfire. An officer on a plunging mount waved his sabre and shouted orders to withdraw and then he too was down, plucked from his saddle by a master-shot from Sedat. The rearmost Cossacks had wheeled about and were spurting for the safety of the drifting mist to their rear.

"Time to retreat!" Dawlish called. "First the Nordenveldt, then the seamen! Marines to stand fast!" Once again Bülent would take the rearguard.

Abdurrahman, intoxicated with slaughter, had to be dragged from his weapon. A dozen sailors from the second rank heaved it from the ruts it had dug as it chattered, then ran back with it across the bridge as

306

their comrades from the first rank sent a final fusillade towards the escaping Cossacks. Then they too turned and ran for the crossing while the marines volleyed one last time.

Dawlish and Zyndram stood at the end of the bridge decking until the powder-blackened marines withdrew. As they passed Dawlish realised that, though he had commanded their equals, he would never command their betters.

"Wait on the other side for me, Zyndram," he said.

He turned to look westwards. The remnants of the repulsed Cossacks were hovering on the fringes of the fog and dim movements within it told of reinforcements arriving.

"Nicholas Kaptan! Hurry!" Zyndram's voice was insistent from the eastern shore.

Yet still Dawlish hesitated, wondering if any Ottoman officer would ever tread this ground again and if it was not lost irretrievably to the Empire. The Russians could see him clearly and an insane impulse of defiance impelled him to loiter, reach into his pocket, withdraw a cigar and light up. He drew the soothing smoke in and reflected that though he had little choice about donning the Sultan's uniform he had worn it honourably. Honourably – yes, and with pride too, pride that had nothing to do with that malign spider in the Yildiz but which was founded on his own bond with the magnificent fighting men who served Abdul-Hamid for so little gratitude. Yet every battle they had fought together, every hardship endured and every bitter loss accepted had done nothing to avert an outright collapse, had served by perverted logic to consolidate Abdul-Hamid's power.

Dawlish turned and walked slowly across the bridge in a silence broken only by the waters sluicing around the piers. He drew a last time on the glowing butt and tossed it into the surge below. Zyndram was waiting on the opposite bank. He had drawn up the marines in two ranks across the eastern approach and the Nordenveldt was aimed along the bridge axis.

"Join me, Zyndram," Dawlish said.

Together they mounted the steps on the earthwork's outer face and walked along the crest. The firing step was lined with the *Mesrutiyet's* seaman. The sixteen-pounders' crews stood expectantly by them. They were sighted and ranged on the open ground beyond the bridge that was already a killing ground littered with men and horses. Dawlish could feel their excitement. These men wanted the Russians to rush the bridge. He reached the point where Adnan stood by the termination of the instantaneous fuses leading from the explosives. He held a box of matches.

"Kumandanim wishes to ignite the charges?"

Dawlish shook his head. "Patience, Adnan Binbashi." There might yet be execution to be done, however distasteful. More Russian cavalry had arrived, the better part of two squadrons, and their lines were being dressed so that there was no doubt that action was imminent. To their rear other horsemen clustered and wheeled without semblance of order. Their clothing was varied, sheepskin jackets and undyed woollen cloaks and scraps of looted uniform – the Bulgarian Christian irregulars who rode with the Cossacks to seek revenge for oppression unspeakable.

Upstream of the bridge the fog still drifted off the river, obscuring the western bank. But it was towards there that Zyndram was suddenly pointing. Dawlish swung around and saw shadowy figures now emerging, now lost, in the swirling white. Horsemen were moving fast, parallel to the river, risking life and limb as they pounded over the uneven ground in visibility that could be yards only.

"They must be ours!" Zyndram said. "Thank God we waited!"

The edges of the mist were frayed and now horsemen flashed into view for an instant before losing themselves in obscurity again. Small horses, crouched men, ragged, no lances, no blades drawn, intent only on reaching the bridge. And somehow familiar...

The leaders tore through the last tendrils of white and into clear air. A dozen followed and then no more, sixteen furious riders rushing for the bridge, mud spraying from beating hooves, rumps whip-flayed, nostrils jetting steamy breath.

"It's Selahattin!" Adnan cried in the instant that Dawlish locked his glasses on the leading rider. There was delight in recognising terror on that leathery, moustachioed face, and even more in knowing that he had him at his mercy. But mercy was an emotion he did not feel.

"Orders to Bülent Chavush, to the Nordenveldt," he said to Zyndram. "Allow those men on to the bridge. Then kill them." Selahattin's crew had raped and looted across Anatolia and the Balkans. Now they would be given a taste of hope and have it dashed away at the last instant.

"Satan's children have their father's blessing," Adnan said, and so it was, for somehow, since being driven away from the caravanserai the scarecrow force of Bashi Bazooks had managed to cross the axis of the Russian advance, though at the cost of two thirds of their number.

Only absolute desperation could have driven them to risk this crossing where Selahattin had committed double murder. He had banked on the *Mesrutiyet* Brigade's earlier withdrawal and his gamble would cost him his life.

It was fifty yards to the bridge now and the horsemen's pace was unchecked. The Russians had seen them and the Cossacks would not be held on the leash much longer.

Oh Dear God, only let them reach the bridge! Dawlish found himself muttering aloud, his own thirst for vengeance insatiable. His glasses were locked on Selahattin and he willed him forward. Then, suddenly, the Kurd drew rein just short of the bridge, dragging his horse's head around, facing his men, urging them past. They lost momentum in the turn, then accelerated into the straight. The first of them drummed on to the bridge's planking. Selahattin's mount plunged and whinnied as he fought to wheel it about to follow the laggards.

These barbarians had crossed this trestle twice before, once welcomed reluctantly, then escaping in the wake of their bloody-handed chieftain, but now the solid wall of Bülent's massed marines sealed the exit before them. The foremost riders must have realised it, for some were shouting and gesticulating for their path to be cleared as the grim chavush yelled out "Atesh!"

The Nordenveldt rippled into vicious life, one volley, two, three in quick succession. A score of Winchesters blasted into an unmissable thirty-yard target. Horses stumbled and fell. One crashed through the flimsy guard-rail and into the river. Riders were snatched from their saddles or thrown forward on to a mound of kicking, struggling, screaming animals. A few dazed irregulars gained their feet and were torn down instantly. A half-dozen horsemen at the rear slewed to a halt. Behind them were the Russians, ahead was a rolling bank of gunsmoke from which tongues of flame spat mercilessly and to either side the icy waters of the Tunca sucked and eddied. They hesitated and knew despair, as Dawlish wanted them to know it, and then the Nordenveldt's merciless blast scythed them down also.

"Atesh kesmek!" Bülent knew what would now follow and that he must withdraw quickly. The firing died, the marines fell back and a dozen men grasped the smoking Nordenveldt's trail and dragged it away.

Dawlish tore his glance from the massacre on the bridge to the single horseman who now ranged back and forth in frenzy on the opposite bank. His turban had fallen away to reveal his shaven skull and the terrible scar that disfigured the left side of his head.

Selahattin looked towards the Russians and what he saw froze him. A group was separating itself from the massed ranks of horsemen and heading for him. They were not Cossacks. Their sheepskins and cloaks identified them as Bulgarians and the levelled lances and raised sabres and the cry of hatred that rose as of one voice from fifty throats told that they knew him for what he was. Bashi Bazooks had turned their homeland into a charnel house and the hour of reckoning was at hand.

Memories raced and flickered in Dawlish's mind: the butchery at Giresun, Nusret dying in his arms in despair and failure, the wanton attack on the caravanserai. He felt no pity, however dreadful he knew what would follow must be.

Selahattin hesitated. On one side the Bulgarians, on the other the bridge. Heaped as it was with his dead and dying henchmen he kicked his horse towards it.

"Light the fuses, Adnan Binbashi," Dawlish said.

The match scraped and flared. Sparks raced down the powder-packed tubes, across the ramparts, along the riverbank, out under the bridge decking to the charges lashed to the supporting piers.

Selahattin was yards from the bridge. Some hope must still have lived within that degraded mind that he could surmount the piled bodies blocking his path and negotiate some amnesty on the opposite bank. But now that last prospect was torn from him as flame and smoke erupted from beneath the bridge, first at the nearer pier, an instant later at the second. The decking bucked. Balks and timbers flew upwards and outwards. Its support sheared away at both ends, the central span collapsed, twisting and spilling bodies with it as it plunged. The outer sections disintegrated as they swung down from the supports on either bank and their timbers were torn away by the racing current.

Selahattin raised his arm to protect his face from the rolling cloud of smoke and debris. He wrenched his horse around – it was almost uncontrollable now – and was confronted by a semi-circle of riders a hundred yards distant. The explosion had checked their advance but now their lances were levelling again, their sabres rising. Selahattin spurred to his left but riders cantered forward to block him, to his right and he was foiled there too. He drew a revolver from his sash, emptied his chambers wildly – his plunging mount made aim impossible and the shots were inaudible over his attackers' howls of triumph as they thrust forward – and he flung it from him and reached for his sabre.

It was too late. The first Bulgarian was on him, lashing at him with the pole of his lance, not the point. Selahattin swung uselessly with his sabre but the wooden shaft caught him a blow on the side that nearly unhorsed him. Another rider came up. He too had reversed his lance and he struck Selahattin in the chest with the butt. He fell back in the saddle and the first horseman flailed at him again. This time he went down, dropping his blade. Other Bulgarians were crowding around, their cries paeans of vengeance as they slipped from their saddles and crowded round the figure trying desperately to struggle to his feet.

"Permission to open fire, Nicholas Kaptan?" Zyndram asked. The sixteen-pounders were ranged on the spot where the Bulgarians now milled.

Dawlish shook his head slowly. There would be time enough. Those enraged men had bought this moment dearly.

A piercing scream, prolonged, unforgettable, rose above the howls of anger. Then something was flung in the air above the surging knot of dismounted horsemen, a white body, naked, striped with blood, its broken limbs flailing. It dropped and the throng fell upon it again. Other riders were hastening up, throwing themselves from their saddles, scurrying eagerly forward to have some share in the ghastly ritual. Now the body was being hoisted on a dozen lances, a terrible gash hacked in its crotch, its face sliced away. Still somehow it lived, thrashing in unspeakable agony as sabres hacked at it. Men who had lost home and kindred in fire and terror wept and howled and rained blows on the hideous object until at last they turned away and let it fall lifeless into the mud.

The silence along the firing step was palpable, men hardened by battle shocked by a butchery none condemned. Dawlish felt himself shaking. He looked around, saw Adnan nodding silently, Zyndram also, both confirming the justice of mercy withheld, of some small part of the stain of atrocity wiped from Turkey's honour.

Vengeance had been absolute but now Dawlish must turn from it. Cold reason must prevail again. Six hundred souls, seamen, marines, refugees – and Florence – depended on him for salvation. Those implacable Russian and Bulgarian troops across the river were no threat for now but they would be searching for another crossing. He would not let them go unscathed.

311

"Order the artillery to take those horsemen, under fire. A dozen rounds will see them on their way."

Then it would be time to abandon this position, to start the trek eastwards. The Lines of Büyük Tchemedji were over a hundred miles away over difficult tracks, and the enemy was already racing there on a parallel road. It was starting to rain, a cold, wet drizzle that promised mud and slush and suffering.

The worst retreat of all, the last march of the *Mesrutiyet* Brigade, was about to begin.

36

"You're mad to go back," Hobart said. "There's a career for you here. Progression, riches."

Dawlish listened in silence. Far below the office in the Yildiz Palace eight massive ironclads of Britain's Mediterranean Fleet swung at anchor in the Bosporus. Their arrival was the guarantee that Britain would intervene to resist any further Russian advance. Lord Beaconsfield had not shrunk from the critical decision and he had carried his cabinet with him.

"I'm nearly fifty-six, God damn it!" Hobart was chewing his cigar in frustration. "I don't want to hold this position for ever, Dawlish! You're the man to succeed me and after what you did at Gelendzhik you could be a pasha tomorrow."

The appropriately named HMS *Sultan*, Admiral Hornby's flagship, lay off Seraglio Point, her massive cannon hidden behind their closed ports. She had ploughed up the Dardanelles and into the Marmara while Dawlish was still on the nightmare retreat that had finally brought his much-depleted column to the security of the Büyük Tchemedji defences. Seven ironclads had steamed in her wake, *Agincourt* and *Temeraire*, *Hotspur* and *Swiftsure* among them, proud names that emphasised Britain's determination that the Straits should not fall to Muscovite control, that Russia should not menace her communications with India. British troops had been landed in Turkey's possession of Cyprus, land power in reserve to back naval force should the Czar gamble further. And the Czar had backed down.

"The men love you and fear you, Dawlish," Hobart was saying. "They'll follow you to the gates of Hell. A crop of young officers look to you as a model and even Abdul-Hamid, damn his soul, knows he won't find better."

312

If I stayed, Dawlish told himself, I wouldn't just be Dawlish Pasha, with all that would imply in terms of wealth and prestige and the loyalty of men he admired. But more – Florence could be my wife, and her background would soon be forgotten, and we would be happy and …

He stopped himself.

Those black-hulled British ships must represent my future, he told himself, no less than they embody deliverance for the Ottoman Empire. The Russian advance had lapped against the fortifications built at such cost from Catalca to the Black Sea. Even after the losses on their lightning advance the Russians might have had the numbers to have punched through, but they were close to exhaustion themselves and St. Petersburg's coffers were emptied. Russia had taken Bulgaria and Thrace in a brilliant and unprecedented winter campaign, but her bolt was shot. War with Britain was unaffordable. An armistice had been signed on the last day of January. Russia had won the battles, but she had lost the war.

What those British ships stood for must now be his consolation, his consuming passion, his compensation for what he was turning his face from – from Florence.

"What's to stop you staying here, Dawlish?" Hobart flung his cigar into the fireplace in exasperation.

"Nusret."

That one name explained all. His friend, for so he remembered him, had been imperfect, but he had looked beyond his personal interest and had a vision that could have transformed the Ottoman Empire, ended the divisions, cured the abuses. Dawlish could never give his loyalty to the man who had encompassed Nusret's death.

"It's the way here, Dawlish. It always has been. It's still Byzantium," Hobart said. "We'll only change it slowly, ever so slowly."

There was no *Mesrutiyet* any more, not the thing itself, the constitutional government that Nusret had believed in so hopefully, so passionately, not even the ship named in its honour. Sultan Abdul-Hamid had suspended the infant parliament the previous day and a simultaneous decree had renamed the ironclad that had battered its way to victory *Hifz-ur Rahman*, Merciful Protector. For so perhaps did the malign spider lurking in this sprawling palace see himself. Dawlish was damned if he would serve him.

"Any news of the treaty negotiations, Sir?" Dawlish asked.

"Nothing, except that they're difficult," Hobart said. "The Czar will want his pound of flesh, even if he can't have the Straits."

313

For a fortnight now Ottoman delegates had been at the Russian Headquarters at Ayastafanos, desperately striving to retrieve something from the wreckage. Bulgaria was lost, that much was certain, and the question was now how much more would be lost with it. Not that Abdul-Hamid would care too much, Dawlish reflected bitterly, as long as he had absolute control of whatever remained.

"I can see there's no convincing you, Dawlish," Hobart said wearily. "You're a damn stubborn fellow but I'd be glad to have you with me if we have to fight those rascals again. It's got to come, you know. The Czar won't sleep soundly until he's heard mass sung in Aghia Sofia."

Which was where Dawlish was heading. He was spending his last days in this fabled city as a tourist while he convalesced from the privations that had brought him close to death during the withdrawal from the Tunca. Even now he was shaky on his feet.

"One last thing, Dawlish." Hobart reached into his desk and produced another small leather-covered box. "The Sultan wants you to have it."

Dawlish flicked it open with distaste. Another silver seven-pointed star, red enamel and gold at its centre, diamonds sparkling on the rays.

"The Mejidye Nishani," Hobart said. "The highest class." He sensed Dawlish's reluctance. "Better take it, no matter what you think of the man who gives it." He pointed to the three words it bore in Arabic script. "They mean Zeal, and Devotion, and Loyalty. Your men gave you those gifts, Dawlish, and you gave them to Nusret. Wear the medal in their memory."

As he slipped it in his pocket Dawlish felt tears start to his eyes. It was his debilitated condition that caused them, he told himself. He shook Hobart's hand and left.

Zyndram was waiting for him in the outer office and though he tried to make the meeting look casual it was obvious that he had been lying in ambush. The emaciation and illness of the retreat showed in his face no less than in Dawlish's own but he was once more immaculately uniformed and hinting of eau-de-cologne.

"Will you remain with us, Nicholas Kaptan?"

"I handed Hobart Pasha my resignation a half-hour ago," Dawlish said. His second letter of resignation in five months, though the first could now be torn up. "I start for England tomorrow." An exchange of telegrams with Topcliffe had confirmed that ten days from now he would present himself at HMS *Vernon* in Portsmouth, the new Deputy

314

to the Senior Instructor. A separate telegram from the Admiral consisted of two words only: Well Done.

"We hoped you'd stay, Nicholas Kaptan," Zyndram said. "We all did."

"And you, Zyndram? What now?"

"My home is here." His voice was sad. "In Polonezkoy. In the home the Sultan gave us. It's Polish soil and it'll serve us until our country is free."

"And until then you'll serve the Sultan?"

"Until the great day comes – and come it will. Someday. Poland will never die."

The carriage was waiting by the Yildiz gate, its coachman and postilion in traditional Turkish costume even if the doors carried the crest of Her Majesty's Government.

"You're late, Dawlish," Lord Oswald said as he stepped inside.

"You needn't take any notice of my brother, Commander," Lady Agatha said. "He's always been peevish, haven't you Oswald?"

To Dawlish's surprise Oswald laughed. It was impossible to like this pompous, bad-tempered man but his affection for his sister was his one redeeming feature. His relief at seeing her safe – he had ridden out to the Büyük Tchemedji defences to wait for her in an agony of worry – had been as unfeigned as the sincerity of his thanks to Dawlish.

The carriage lurched into motion, down the hill, heading for the Galata Bridge and across the Golden Horn. Beyond it, by the Spice Bazaar, Lady Agatha's soup kitchen still flourished. The city was more full than ever of famished refugees.

"You haven't seen Aghia Sofia before, Commander?" Florence's question drew a scowl from Oswald. Had she been left to the Bashi Bazooks it would not have worried him unduly. His benevolence began and ended with his sister.

"Only from a distance, Miss Morton, Dawlish said. "I understand it to be magnificent."

"Splendid, Commander. Quite splendid."

An outsider might have surmised that they had just met. Yet she had saved him on the final retreat to Istanbul, when the malaria he carried since the Ashanti Campaign had returned and he had tossed in delirium on the floor of the cart she drove. For mile after endless mile, in rain and sleet and through freezing nights, as the column dwindled and as the *Mesrutiyet* Brigade died by the wayside from exposure and hunger, she and Agatha had somehow kept him alive, forcing quinine between his gritted teeth, cooling his fever, warming him when cold shivers racked him, calming his raving, cleaning and changing him like an infant. A Cossack patrol had blundered into them once, though Dawlish remembered nothing of it, and its repulse had cost Bülent Chavush his life. Abdurrahman was dead too, of pneumonia, and Yashar also, and so many others whose names he was already forgetting, even if their faces would stay with him forever. Now Florence sat across from him in the carriage as they crossed the bridge amid the imprecations of the beggars who thronged it, beautiful and elegant for all that she wore Lady Agatha's re-tailored cast-offs. In an hour or so he would shake her hand formally, wish her a chilly farewell and never see her again. Regret gnawed inside him, as he knew it would for years to come, perhaps always. But he could see no other solution.

The Kegworths, brother and sister, proved a mine of information on Justinian's great domed creation and all that pertained to it. Lady Agatha claimed to have finished Gibbon before her tenth birthday and seemed to have remembered every word, while Oswald's Magdalen days had given him the opportunity for study of Procopius and a host of lesser Byzantine authors. Dawlish listened in a silence that was taken for admiration, interjecting only the odd observation. He sensed that Florence's unease was as great as his own.

"The Basilica Cistern is close, Dawlish," Oswald said as they left the Aghia Sofia. "You've heard of it? Good! You've seen it? No!"

"But you must, Commander Dawlish!" Agatha said. "It's superb! You can't leave without visiting it!"

A few minutes brought them to a bustling street with no sign of ancient remains. They stopped by what might have been a shop. Oswald's fluent Turkish gained admittance and procured candles from the caretakers who opened an iron grille leading to stone steps. They descended to find themselves in a vast cavern, its extent emphasised by the echo of their voices and the gloom beyond the weak light of their flames.

"Careful, Dawlish, don't fall in," Oswald said, catching his arm. They were on the edge of a jetty and a caretaker held his candle out to show two small rowing boats beneath. Black water stretched into the darkness, pierced by a forest of slim pillars that supported the multi-arched ceiling far above.

"Agatha will join me," Oswald said, helping her into the boat, obviously in no hurry to share Florence's company. The attendant took the oars and pushed off.

Dawlish assisted Florence into the second skiff. The touch of her hand thrilled him, even through her glove. The craft lurched as the second caretaker stepped in, throwing her against Dawlish. He caught her, held her as gingerly and chastely as he would a Ming vase, and helped her to sit. He sat on the thwart opposite her and the boat moved out.

The candles reflected in the water and cast great shadows on the arches high above as the boats passed between the columns.

"It's the city's reserve in time of siege." Lady Agatha called across the water. "It's as old as Aghia Sofia, Commander. Just think of that, Commander! Twelve centuries old and still of utility!"

"Remarkable, Lady Agatha," Dawlish said. "Most impressive."

"You are leaving tomorrow, Commander Dawlish." Florence's voice was almost inaudible.

"At noon, Miss Morton. By steamer to Athens."

"You'll be passing Troy again then." She was repressing a quaver in her voice.

"It takes its name from the Stoa Basilica, which was above." Oswald shouted. He might love his sister but he was not to be outdone by her in erudition.

"A basilica, you say?" Dawlish returned. But it was to Florence that he longed to speak.

"Long gone, I fear, Commander," Lady Agatha called through the darkness.

"You're taking up an appointment at Portsmouth? On a moored ship, you once told me." The low-spoken words were costing Florence a great effort.

"A ship that's going nowhere, Miss Morton. I'll have to seek quarters ashore."

The sound of water lapping, the silence painful.

"Look up, Commander. Do you see the Medusa head?" Oswald was standing up and holding his candle aloft to illuminate a snake-wreathed head on one of the columns. Quite bizarrely, it was on its side.

"I won't forget you, Commander, how you ..." Florence stopped herself, as if the words were agony.

317

At that moment he realised that if he did not speak now he would regret it for the rest of his life. No price could be too high, not promotion nor career, not ostracism nor exile. He raised the candle, heart thumping. "You've guessed, Miss Morton? How... how I feel?"

She looked him full in the face, even more magnificent in the candlelight than when he had come upon her at the caravanserai.

"Since we first spoke. Near Troy." It came in a rush, her voice just above a whisper. "You've known I felt the same."

"There's a second Medusa," Agatha called, "and that one's upside down! An error during reconstruction I'd say, Oswald, wouldn't you?"

Dawlish reached out in the darkness, felt for her hand and took it. He pulled the glove away and raised her unresisting fingers to his lips, heard her intake of breath.

"It won't be easy together... Florence." It was the first time he had addressed her by her name. "You know it won't be easy, don't you?"

"It wasn't easy on the road from Ljubimec," she said. "But we're here, Nicholas. Together."

The boat passed on through the echoing cavern, between the slim columns, across the still, dark waters, and into their future.

The End

318

A personal message from Antoine Vanner

I hope you've enjoyed *Britannia's Wolf* and that you'll also like later books in the series, *Britannia's Reach, Britannia's Shark and Britannia's Spartan.*

You probably know how important reviews are to the success of a book on Amazon or Kindle, especially for a writer publishing a series. If you've enjoyed this book then I'd be very grateful if you could post a review on **www.amazon.com** or **www.amazon.co.uk**.

Your comments do really matter and I read all reviews since readers' feedback encourages me to keep researching and writing about the life of Nicholas Dawlish.If you'd like to leave a review then all you have to do is go to the review section on the *Britannia's Wolf* Amazon page. Scroll down from the top and under the heading of 'Customer Reviews' you'll see a big button that says 'Write a customer review' – click that and you're ready to get into action. You don't need to write much – a sentence or two is enough, essentially what you'd tell a friend or family member about the book.

Thanks again for your support and don't forget that you can learn more about Nicholas Dawlish and his world on my website **www.dawlishchronicles.com**.

You might also 'like' the Facebook Page 'Dawlish Chronicles' or want to follow my weekly blog on **dawlishchronicles.blogspot.co.uk** in which I write short articles based on material found during my research but which is not necessarily used in the novels.

And finally – I can assure you that further Dawlish adventures are on the way. I hope you'll enjoy them, even though Dawlish himself might not!

Yours Faithfully: **Antoine Vanner**

A Note on Ottoman Ranks

The Ottoman Army and Navy went through major reforms in the middle of the nineteenth century. Success was variable but by the outbreak of the Russo-Turkish War in 1877 the overall organisations conformed to those of their Western European equivalents. The following were the nearest Western equivalents of Ottoman ranks.

Western Army	Ottoman Army	Western Navy	Ottoman Navy
Colonel	Miralay	Captain	Kaptan
Major	Binbashi	Lieutenant-Commander	Birinci Yüzbashi
Captain	Yüzbashi	Lieutenant	Yüzbashi
Lieutenant	Mülazim	Sub-Lieutenant	Mülazim
		Midshipman	Mehendis
Sergeant Major	Üschavush	Chief Petty Officer	Üschavush
Sergeant	Chavush	Petty Officer	Chavush
Corporal	Onbashi	Leading Seaman	Onbashi

The title "Pasha" was a non-specific one, implying high military or naval rank. Surnames were uncommon before the foundation of the Turkish Republic in 1923 and individuals were addressed by their given-name, followed by their title – "Efendi" in the case of civilians.

The Dawlish Chronicles
by Antoine Vanner

Britannia's Reach
(Dawlish Chronicles, Volume 2)
ISBN: 978-1492969389

It is November 1879 and on a broad river deep in the heart of South America, a flotilla of paddle steamers thrashes slowly upstream. It is laden with troops, horses and artillery, and intent on conquest and revenge. Ahead lies a commercial empire that was wrested from a British consortium in a bloody revolution. Now the investors are determined to recoup their losses and are funding a vicious war to do so. Nicholas Dawlish, is playing a leading role in the expedition. But as brutal land and river battles mark its progress upriver, and as both sides inflict and endure ever greater suffering, stalemate threatens. And Dawlish finds himself forced to make a terrible ethical choice if he is to return to Britain with some shreds of integrity remaining...

Britannia's Shark
(Dawlish Chronicles, Volume 3)
ISBN: 978-0992263690

1881 and the British Empire's power seems unchallengeable. But now a group of revolutionaries threaten that power's economic basis. Their weapon is the invention of a naïve genius, their sense of grievance is implacable and their leader is already proven in the crucible of war. Protected by powerful political and business interests, conventional British military and naval power cannot touch them. A daring act of piracy drags the ambitious British naval officer, Nicholas Dawlish, into this deadly maelstrom. For both him and his wife a nightmare lies ahead, amid the wealth and squalor of America's Gilded Age, and on a fever-ridden island ruled by savage tyranny...

Britannia's Spartan
(Dawlish Chronicles, Volume 4)
ISBN- 978-1943404049

1882 and Captain Nicholas Dawlish has just taken command of the Royal Navy's newest cruiser, HMS *Leonidas*. As she arrives in Hong Kong Dawlish has no forewarning of the nightmare of riot, treachery, massacre and battle ahead. Imperial China, weak and corrupt, is challenged by a rapidly modernising Japan, while Russia threatens both from the north. All need to control Korea, a kingdom reluctant to emerge from centuries of isolation. Dawlish finds himself a critical player in a complex political powder keg. He must take account of a weak Korean king and his shrewd queen, of murderous palace intrigue, of a powerbroker who seems more American than Chinese and of a Japanese naval captain whom he will come to despise and admire in equal measure. It's not going to be easy...

321

About Old Salt Press

Old Salt Press is an independent press catering to those who love books about ships and the sea. We are an association of writers working together to produce the very best of nautical and maritime fiction and non-fiction. We invite you to join us as we go down to the sea in books.

On the following pages are details of some recent offerings – and more are on the way.

Some recent offerings from the Old Salt Press

By Alaric Bond:

HMS Prometheus (The Fighting Sail Series Book 8)
ASIN: B018WDRQAS

Autumn 1803, and Britain remains under the threat of invasion. HMS Prometheus is needed to reinforce Nelson's squadron blockading the French off Toulon, but a major action has left her severely damaged and the British Fleet outnumbered. Prometheus must be brought back to fighting order without delay, and the work proves more than a simple refit.
Barbary pirates, shore batteries and the powerful French Navy are conventional foes, although the men of Prometheus encounter equally dangerous enemies within their own ranks.

By Linda Collison:

Water Ghosts
ISBN-10: 1943404003

"I see things other people don't see; I hear things other people don't hear." Fifteen-year-old James McCafferty is an unwilling sailor aboard a traditional Chinese Junk operated as adventure-therapy for troubled teens. Once at sea, James believes the ship is being taken over by the spirits of courtiers who fled the Imperial palace during the Ming Dynasty, more than 600 years earlier, and sailing to its doom. A psychological nautical adventure with strong historical and paranormal elements.

By V.E. Ulett:

Captain Blackwell's Prize
ISBN-10: 0988236060

A small, audacious British frigate does battle against a large but ungainly Spanish ship. British Captain James Blackwell intercepts the Spanish La Trinidad, outmanoeuvres and outguns the treasure ship and boards her. Fighting alongside the Spanish captain, sword in hand, is a beautiful woman. The battle is quickly over. The Spanish captain is killed in the fray and his ship damaged beyond repair. Its survivors and treasure are taken aboard the British ship, *Inconstant*...

By Joan Druett:

Eleanor's Odyssey: Journal of the Captain's Wife on the East Indiaman *Friendship* 1799-1801
ASIN: B00Q2E992S

"New Zealand-based novelist and maritime historian Joan Druett is one of this generation's finest sea writers ... This book is recommended for anyone who seeks adventure at sea."

Quarterdeck (Editor's choice)

By Rick Spilman

The Shantyman
ISBN-10: 0994115237

He can save the ship and the crew, but can he save himself?

In 1870, on the clipper ship *Alahmbra* in Sydney, the new crew comes aboard more or less sober, except for the last man, who is hoisted aboard in a cargo sling, paralytic drunk. The drunken sailor, Jack Barlow, will prove to be an able shantyman. On a ship with a dying captain and a murderous mate, Barlow will literally keep the crew pulling together. As he struggles with a tragic past, a troubled present and an uncertain future, Barlow will guide the *Alahmbra* through Southern Ocean ice and the horror of an Atlantic hurricane. Based on a true story, The Shantyman is a gripping tale of survival against all odds at sea and ashore, and the challenge of facing a past that can never be wholly left behind.